PRAISE FOR GLI

M000318354

"A master of plotting, [she] s̶u̶... innuendoes that keep readers guessing until the very end. Reminiscent of golden age mysteries, her latest will appeal to fans of classic mysteries."

Library Journal

"A finely drawn police procedural written in the style of Georgette Heyer, long considered queen of the British mystery genre. Appealing characters, creative plot and classic Agatha Christie style writing make [Menzies] a fierce contender for Heyer's reputation."

The Suspense Zone

"The investigation is fascinating to watch as the police follow the clues and eliminate suspects one by one.... An exciting baseball whodunit."

Midwest Book Reviews

"I had to stay up all night to finish it because I couldn't stand going to sleep not knowing [whodunit.]"

Armchair Interviews

"A book worth reading."

Hidden Staircase Mystery Books

"Baseball. There are few things that say lazy, hazy summer days than that sport. But this book is anything but lazy or hazy ... A Christie-style mystery, this one does a good job of it."

Mysterical - E

"I admit it. I didn't want to read this book. I'm not a sports fan. I am REALLY not a sports fan. The only sports I ever watch are the Olympics. So, when I picked up this book I didn't know what to expect. Well, I was delighted. It kept me hooked and reading until the very end. A wonderful mystery in the classic Agatha Christie style."

Linda Hall, award-winning author and Christie nominee

"The writing has humour, the story-telling is edged with compassion, and the characters are well drawn. The story is baseball, the language is the stress, ego and entertainment of professional sport and the result is an exciting stand-up triple."

The Hamilton Spectator

"The bases are loaded, it's the bottom of the ninth, who is on first, I don't know, keep reading to find out the answer in this nicely done "classical" mystery."

Book Bitch

"This would be a great book to introduce to a book club as its sports theme would be well received by men as well as women."

Tracey's Book Nook

"Wonderfully crafted ... one of the best mystery writers of our generation."

Radine Trees Nehring, author of the award-winning *Something to Die For* mystery series

"Believable characters, a plausible inside look at the world of professional sports—the players, management, media and the groupies—and dedicated, hard-working detectives.... Will keep you reading long past lights out!"

Carrie M. Wood

"I whole-heartedly recommend *Glitter of Diamonds*.... This author skillfully spins her yarn, drawing readers into the lives of her characters, until it is virtually impossible to put the book down.

Melody Metcalfe

"The suspense was terrific and this woman really knows baseball inside and out."

Tom Monie, mystery fan and former high school sports and Little League coach

GLITTER
OF
DIAMONDS

THE CASE OF THE
RECKLESS RADIO HOST

BOOKS & STORIES BY J. A. MENZIES

The Manziuk and Ryan Mysteries

Shaded Light: The Case of the Tactless Trophy Wife
Glitter of Diamonds: The Case of the Reckless Radio Host
The Case of the Homeless Pup: A Manziuk and Ryan Novella
Shadow of a Butterfly: The Case of the Harmless Old Woman

Short Stories

7 Mystery & Suspense Stories (including Paul Manziuk & Jacquie
Ryan in "The Case of the Sneezing Accountant")

The Misadventures of Stefan the Stableboy and Princess Persnickety

The Defenders of Practavia - middle grade epic fantasy

GLITTER
OF
DIAMONDS

THE CASE OF THE
RECKLESS RADIO HOST

A Paul Manziuk & Jacquie Ryan Mystery

J. A. Menzies

MurderWillOut Mysteries

Markham, Ontario

Glitter of Diamonds: The Case of the Reckless Radio Host

Copyright © N. J. Lindquist, 2007, 2016

ISBN: 978-1-927692-32-5

First published in hardcover and trade paperback in 2007 by MurderWill-Out Mysteries.

New cover design 2022 by N. J. Lindquist.
Cover image by woraphon.n@gmail.com in Deposit Photos.
Small microphone from Dreamstime.

This novel is a work of fiction. Names, characters, and events are the product of the author's imagination, and any resemblance to actual persons, living or dead, is purely coincidental. The city of Toronto, the Toronto police, the Toronto baseball team and its stadium, and surrounding media, and any other entities that may seem familiar are not intended to be accurate.

MurderWillOut Mysteries is an imprint of That's Life! Communications
Box 77001 Markham, ON L3P 0C8
Email: connect@thatslifecommunications.com
murderwillout.com

DEDICATION

Dedicated to the long-time radio voices
of the Toronto Blue Jays:
Tom Cheek, who died too soon in 2005.
Jerry Howarth, who continues to be among the very best.

Thanks for all the great hours I've spent listening to you, either
in the car, at the game, or while watching a muted TV. You
made me feel I was part of the team. It's been a blast!

P. S. Loving Mike Wilner now, too!

Major Players in Order of Appearance

Jacqueline Ryan: Cop who thinks a bullpen should be a place where you find bulls

Paul Manziuk: Tired cop who loves baseball but hates murder

Ricardo (Rico) Velasquez: Cuban pitcher whose success has gone to his head

Ginny Lovejoy: Sports columnist who owes her job to a colleague's hangover

Kyle Schmidt: Toronto sports columnist with a longing for a Booker prize

Alita Velasquez: Rico's wife, who is safely back in Cuba—or is she?

Lawrence Smith: The Toronto Matrix's most faithful fan

Stasey Simon: Outspoken sports talk show host with a huge following

Iain Foley: WIN 730's velvet-voiced *Prime Time Show* host

Eva MacPherson: Poor little rich girl who's thinks she'd be better off as Marilyn Monroe

Pat Davis: Agent who sees Rico as both gold mine and hornet's nest

Ted Benedetto: Producer of the *Stasey Simon Show* and scapegoat for any mistakes

Ferdinand Ortes: Baseball's #1 shortstop and Rico's best friend

Tony Kanberra: General manager who has a lot more to worry about than running a baseball team

Jonas Newland: Catcher and unofficial team leader for the Matrix

Blake Harrison: Matrix manager who seems to be sticking his head in the sand

Armando Santana: The pitcher who lost his starting job to Rico

Zandor: Mysterious Bond-like young man

Cary Grant: Mr. Brown's ever-present assistant

Mr. Brown: Invisible owner of the Toronto Matrix

WHAT'S IN A NAME?

Of course, everyone knows that the Toronto baseball team is called the Blue Jays. But writers have invented a few "new" names over the years—for example, Allison Gordon's Toronto Titans baseball team. So where did the Toronto Matrix come from? Simply this: I didn't want anyone to have the slightest reason for thinking I'm in any way, shape, or form referring to anyone from any of the Toronto teams or the actual sports media in this book. So the Toronto Matrix team is completely mine, as is its stadium, the incomparable Diamond Dome, and the personalities of the owners, staff, players, and surrounding media. All have sprung completely out of my head and bear absolutely no intentional resemblance to anyone or anything living or dead.

PROLOGUE

Better a diamond with a flaw than a pebble without.

—CONFUCIUS

I don't know why you want to do what you do," kimono-clad Noelle Ryan said as she joined her daughter at the kitchen table. "My little girl chasing after killers."

It was seven AM, and Jacqueline Ryan had already run for half an hour and lifted weights in her room before throwing on a navy pantsuit and white blouse, running a comb through her short, black hair, brushing blush and powder on her cinnamon face, and anchoring her gun firmly at the back of her slim waist.

"Somebody has to," Jacquie said. She'd been eating the breakfast her grandmother had prepared when her mother came in and settled at the other end of the table to drink her morning coffee and read the newspaper.

"Not my baby girl."

"You're the only one who sees me that way, Mom."

"What do the others see?" her mother asked petulantly. "A female Rambo? You don't look so tough to me."

"It's not about being tough, Mom. More about being smart."

Jacquie's aunt Vida entered the kitchen and leaned against the table next to Jacquie. "Well, you're smart enough, I'll give you that. But tell me, how many men are looking for a smart woman?"

Jacquie rolled her eyes. "You never know. Maybe I'm looking for a smart man."

Noelle snorted. "There's one of those whatchamacallit things. An ox or something."

"You mean oxymoron?" Jacquie asked.

"Yeah." Noelle nodded. "That's it. Something impossible. A smart man."

Vida laughed. "You got that right, Sister." To Jacquie, she said, "So, who are you going to arrest today?"

Jacquie grinned. "I'm not on a case right now."

Her mother shook her head. "So you sit around cleaning your gun and waiting for somebody to murder somebody else so you have a job? Bloodthirsty business."

Jacquie smiled between mouthfuls of toast. "It wouldn't bother me if I never had a murder to solve, Mom. But I know it won't happen."

"I know somebody has to do your job. Just hard to get used to the thought of my little girl putting her life at risk every day."

"Mom, it's safer on homicide than it is on traffic patrol!"

Stifling a yawn, Jacquie's cousin Precious shuffled into the kitchen in multicolored caftan, matching slippers, and a red turban. "You know, a few of us might be trying to sleep."

"Have your morning coffee," her mother said without a trace of sympathy. "Then you'll be in a better mood."

Vida sighed and picked up a cup. "Speaking of moods, I have to go to Mr. Ketchum's today."

Gram had been watching and listening. Now she said, "Why didn't you remind me? I'll whip him up a batch of my rock buns. That'll make him happy."

"You do that, Ma. It'll help for sure."

"How's he doing?" Jacquie asked as she ate the last of her yogurt and glanced at the time. So far, so good. She reached for her juice.

Vida paused with the coffeepot in her hand. "Not too bad. He's not in as much pain as before, and he's starting to get used to the walker, but that man is so negative, I think he spends every waking minute looking for new things to complain about, or new ways to complain about the old things."

"He knows when he has a sympathetic listener," Jacquie said.

"Huh!" Jacquie's mother grunted. "She's being paid to listen! You think she'd be there otherwise?"

Vida set down the coffee pot and put her hands on her hips. "Well, at least I have a job where I do something useful!"

"What's that supposed to mean?" Noelle leaned forward, her own hands on her hips.

"What time you have to be there?" Gram asked Vida.

Vida continued to glare at her sister. "Eleven o'clock."

"I'd better get busy then." Gram began pulling baking utensils out of the cupboard.

Jacquie also got up. "Got to run. See you all later."

Her mother leaned toward Jacquie and almost touched her cheek with her lips. "See you later, dear. Take care."

Jacquie gave her grandmother a quick hug, then grabbed her lunch bag and water bottles and headed for the hall closet, where she thrust her feet into comfortable black loafers and grabbed a shoulder organizer purse.

"Hey, you still haven't answered the question I asked last night," Aunt Vida called out. "Have you scoped out the other homicide cops yet, Jacquie? Are any of them single?"

"Bye now," Jacquie called as she let the door slam behind her.

In a few minutes, she was seated in her red Toyota, listening to the news as she pulled out of her parking space and headed for the police station.

Detective Inspector Paul Manziuk slammed the driver's door of his ancient van, punched the key in, and lurched out of his driveway.

Why did Mike have to pick this morning to start asking about a car again? No way did he need his own car! Not until he was at university, and even then—it was so hard to believe Mike was almost eighteen! Paul shook his head. Maybe what they said about the baby of the family being treated differently was true. Maybe Mike had been protected more than Conrad.

And of course, this morning was as good as any other morning in Mike's eyes. Better than most, in fact. His dad had finished a case. He was presumably in a good mood.

Well, he'd been in a reasonably good mood, right up until Mike hit him up for a car. Without thinking, he'd told Mike that a car was the furthest thing from his mind, and Mike had walked out of the room. Which meant, of course, that he was upset.

Loretta hadn't been worried. "He's just like you. Gets something on his mind and can't rest until he resolves it. Plus he thinks he's being perfectly reasonable, and he doesn't understand why you don't see it his way."

"I've got other things on my mind."

Loretta had tilted her head to one side. "But you always have other things on your mind."

Paul slammed on his brakes as a car swerved in front of him. The driver hadn't even looked before changing lanes! Probably a teenager. Ought to pull him over and give him a ticket!

He sighed. Why couldn't Mike keep using the bus? His mother used it. Of course, that was part of Mike's argument. If they got a second car, Mike and his mother could share it for this year, and then when Mike graduated high school, he'd keep the car and Loretta could decide if she liked the convenience enough to buy her own.

Paul made himself stop at a yellow light that was about to turn red. Had to set a good example. Way too many people running red lights these days. Everybody was impatient. Nobody's attention span was more than five minutes. Except Mike's. He never lost track of what he wanted.

The light turned green and Paul inched forward in the rush hour traffic. He found himself looking at the cars around him, noticing that most, if not all, were newer than his. That was the real problem. Mike had hit a sore point. Truth was, they needed to buy, not a second car, but a replacement for their ancient van.

Not that they needed another van. With Conrad at Oxford as a teaching assistant, and Lisa in college, it was just the three of them at home, and a small sedan would do.

Paul sighed. He should ask Loretta to look in *Consumer Reports* about which used cars were the best buys. Maybe Mike could help her.

The next few lights were all green. Finally someone had them working in sequence!

Should they let Mike have the wagon? No, it was too hard on gas, and Loretta would worry about it breaking down on him. Better to find a small used car that had all the safety features. That little Toyota of Constable Ryan's looked like it might suit Mike. In a less noticeable color, of course. And there was the room factor to consider, too. At nearly six and a half feet tall, Paul was well-aware that just any old car wouldn't do. Mike was six two and still growing.

Paul shook his head. The thought of having to buy, not one, but two cars, was too much. The three of them would have to talk it over and come up with a plan. A part-time job for Mike was a possibility, except Loretta wanted him to be able to enjoy being a kid for one last year before college loomed, and sports was a huge part of his life, especially Ultimate Frisbee, which seemed to have a tournament every weekend. Mike had good marks, too, and they didn't want to jeopardize that.

Speaking of sports, Paul suddenly realized he'd been so busy he'd barely had time to find out how the Matrix were doing. All he knew was that they'd won the last series, three games out of four, and that Rico'd been throwing more temper tantrums.

Was there any chance he could get to a game soon? Well, at least he'd try to get hold of the *Toronto Daily News* today so he could read Ginny Lovejoy's column. He enjoyed what she had to say—whenever he could find time to read it.

Loretta was right, as usual. He always had business on his mind. Paul sighed as he turned into the police station's parking lot and maneuvered the large van into the space reserved for him. They seemed to be narrowing all the parking spaces. Even when both cars were parked dead center in their spots, you barely had room to get out of your door. Be nice to have a smaller car.

Paul took the elevator to the third floor and walked through the large open area of small cubicles and desks with attendant computers, heading for the offices for senior staff along the far wall. Glancing neither right nor left, he went directly to his office, tossed his straw hat on the wooden stand put there for it, and glanced at his watch. Eight o'clock. Good. Another busy day.

PART I

Diamonds are a girl's best friend.

—From *Gentlemen Prefer Blondes*, 1953.
Words by JULES STYNES and music by Leo Robin
Written for the 1949 Broadway musical
Gentlemen Prefer Blondes, sung by Carol Channing,
and later used in the movie of the same name,
sung by Marilyn Monroe and Jane Russell.

ONE

Pitcher Rico Velasquez stormed into the Diamond Dome's home team's lounge, picked up one of the baseballs waiting to be autographed, and threw a 90-mile-an-hour fastball into the middle of the television screen.

Three of his teammates had been playing cards and watching the July holiday afternoon baseball game on the television monitor. As the screen shattered, they jumped to their feet and, to a man, scurried into the adjacent locker room. At six foot three, with 220 pounds of well-coordinated muscle and bone, Rico wasn't someone you confronted without a good deal of thought.

As the rest of the team began coming in after the game's end, Rico yelled in Spanish, "They're useless! I want some muscle behind me. We need some trades!" Spotting a bat lying on a chair, he picked it up. Shouting "I want to win!" he shattered one of the plaster walls with the wooden bat. Then he laughed and dropped the bat, his anger appeased by the gaping hole.

Rico's teammates kept their distance.

Ginny Lovejoy and Kyle Schmidt, along with other members of the sports media who trailed the players into the locker room, made copious notes.

Sitting on a rough bench that was bolted to the floor beside the cabin of a fishing boat working its way to Florida, Alita Velasquez took a much-folded piece of paper from her pocket and read it for the twentieth time. In Spanish, it said:

Lita

I pitched again today, and I was amazing. My manager and my team were as happy as little kids with candy. I'm not just a baseball player; I'm a hero. I'm 8 and 3 with an ERA of only 1.96. The rest of the team is pretty good, too, except for a few players who should be replaced instead of kept only because of sentiment. The fans love me. The other players on my team, except for a few who are jealous, love me too. Even the opposition players admire me. We have a very good chance to win the pennant and then the World Series.

There's some money in the bank account for you to use for the next few months. My agent knows how to do that. See that my parents get half.

It's too bad you have to be stuck in Cuba, but really, it's for the best. Toronto's a big city and would seem very strange to you. And you'd be alone most of the time. Later we'll work out some way for you to come to Canada and we can begin a family. Think what my sons will be able to do! I didn't even own a decent glove until I was 14—and that was a cast-off. My sons will have everything they could wish for, all of it new.

Your husband,

Rico Velasquez

Alita refolded the letter and put it back into the deep pocket of her skirt. She shut her eyes and hugged herself. Was she doing the right thing, or was she the fool her father had called her the night before she married Rico?

A wave hit the boat and her stomach lurched. Pulling herself to her feet, she staggered to the railing. Why, on top of everything else, did she have to be one of those unfortunate people who become seasick the moment they go on water?

"God, why do you allow this?" she muttered in Spanish.

Late Tuesday morning, baseball fan Lawrence Smith sat in his kitchen eating a ham sandwich while reading the sports section of the *Toronto Register*.

"Why does he have to say things like that?" Lawrence complained aloud. He knew Kyle Schmidt was only doing his job as the sports reporter for the *Register*, but why did he always seem so negative? And was it really necessary to use thousand-dollar words like *crepuscular*?

Pushing his plate aside, Lawrence read the offending paragraphs out loud, carefully pronouncing each word, doing his best to determine if it was really as negative as it had seemed in his first reading.

Lackluster Performance Dims Celebration

by Kyle Schmidt

It's the July long weekend, and you sit on the edge of your seat expecting to be delighted and entertained.

Not for you the artificial excitement of the cool crepuscular hours, with the momentary bursts from sky rockets, Roman candles, and fountains against a darkling sky. For the baseball fan, what's needed is the sizzling heat of the afternoon, explosions of bat against ball, and headlong rushes of two-hundred-pound men into small rectangular bases.

Let the game begin!

Except—perhaps someone forget to tell the Toronto Matrix what day it was. Because their performance yesterday afternoon was lackluster, dismal, and sporadic; it left the 30,000 fans in attendance desperately seeking something else to celebrate....

Shaking his head, Lawrence folded the paper and set it aside before picking up the sports section of the *Register's* rival newspaper, the *Toronto Daily News*.

He turned to Ginny Lovejoy's column. Lawrence could count on Ginny to write something he could understand.

Matrix Need to Put a Lid on It

by Ginny Lovejoy

It could have been so different yesterday. The Matrix started off with two runs in the first inning. Going to be a great afternoon! Except those two runs were all they got—while giving up five.

Overall, the team turned in a tired performance that made you wonder if perhaps they'd been out celebrating a day early. But then, when do baseball players have time to celebrate? The end of the season, I suppose. And how many teams get to celebrate then?

So there's no point in ragging on them. One dreary loss doesn't negate all the great games we've had this year. They've still got three months to show us what they can do!

But they really need to get it together. Rumors have it that at least one player was so disgusted by the performance of the rest of the team yesterday that he trashed a television set and put a hole in a wall in the clubhouse during the ninth inning. Please, guys, we don't need things like that....

Lawrence cringed. The unnamed player was Rico, he was sure of that. Lawrence shook his head. He never lost his own temper, and he tended to mistrust anyone who did.

A noisy ringing began, and he looked at his clock. Ten to one. Nearly time. The radio was already on, but he turned up its volume and got settled in to listen. As the news ended, trumpets announced the *Stasey Simon Show*, and then she was on, her deep, warm voice caressing the airwaves.

"Stasey Simon here. For the next three hours, we're going to talk about sports in a way no one else can. Because there's only one Stasey Simon. But ya'll know that, don't you? So pull up a chair, or find a place to park so you can give me your full attention, because for the next few hours, you're mine.

"Now, what are we going to talk about today? How about the Matrix? Wasn't that game yesterday pathetic? As if they had no heart. And I'm wondering if they do. We've been fed a line this year about how the Matrix are one big, happy family—'one for all and all for one'—but what I saw yesterday was an edgy, maybe even dysfunctional team. I hear there are a number of different factions, some of which barely speak to the others. And I didn't see a leader out there, either. Makes me really wonder.

"On the other hand, you don't need to be happy to win games. And the Matrix, for the most part, have been winning this year. Should we care about anything else?

"Uh oh, the Beast is giving me the look. We have to take a break. We'll be right back after these messages. Ya'll know the number."

Lawrence Smith knew the number. He prided himself on being one of the most faithful fans of the local sports station, WIN 730. But although he listened regularly to Iain Foley and as much as possible to some of the other hosts, he never missed Stasey Simon.

Lawrence got through and waited for the show's producer—nicknamed "The Beast" by Stasey, who considered herself "The Beauty"—to tell him he was on air.

The ad ended. Lawrence waited patiently during the sports update.

"I'm back," Stasey said. "So what were we saying? Oh, yeah. The Matrix. What I think is that the players are going to bust their jerseys one of these days if they don't let out some of the hostility and dislike. I think everything the management's told us about how united they are and how well they get along is a load of you-know-what."

The producer spoke in Lawrence's ear. "Get ready, Lawrence."

Lawrence turned down the volume on his radio. Otherwise, he knew from experience he'd get confused by both the time delay and the echo of his own voice.

Then Stasey said, "Lawrence, buddy, is that you?"

He remembered it wasn't enough to nod; she couldn't see him. "It's me, Stasey," he said clearly.

"All right, buddy. How's it going? What have you got for me today?"

"It's going good, Stasey. I love listening to you. I really missed you over the weekend. It's bad enough on normal weekends, but I especially hate long weekends where I have to wait from Friday to Tuesday to hear you again."

"Thanks, buddy. So, what do you want to talk about?"

"The team, Stasey. I agree they didn't play very well yesterday. But are you sure they don't like each other? That makes me feel so sad, Stasey. What do you think can be done to turn things around? I'll hang up so you can answer." Lawrence ended the call and quickly turned the radio's volume up to hear Stasey's response.

"Lots of winning teams have had players who weren't speaking to each other. What bugs me most is that the management insists they're one big happy family. Baloney!

"If you really want my opinion, I think the problems the Matrix are having can be traced back to the arrival of Rico Velasquez. Armando Santana is very popular here in Toronto, not only with the fans but with the other players, too. From the moment Rico took Armando's spot on the starting rotation, things haven't been the same.

"They should have traded or released Armando. That would have helped with the loyalty issue—player and fan alike. Secondly, Rico goes way beyond not speaking to teammates. I hear he was so angry about the way the team lost the game yesterday that he had a temper tantrum in the locker room. And the saddest part is the management's unwillingness to admit anything's wrong. The first step toward change is admitting there's a need for it."

Nestled in the rocking chair, Lawrence's body rocked rhythmically in time with Stasey's voice. His face was morose as he thought about what Rico's coming had done to the team.

On the radio, Stasey moved on to the next caller. "Hi, Pete. What do you want to get off your chest today?"

"This is Ms. Garrett, Miss MacPherson. I'm afraid your father is in China on a business trip. He's away for two more weeks, and he's asked me not to disturb him unless it's an extreme emergency. I believe I sent you a memo to that effect."

"Does my eloping with a baseball player from Cuba count?"

"I believe your father would want me to advise you to think about the very generous allowance he gives you before doing anything so foolish."

Eva made a face at the phone. "There's something I want to talk to him about. I need advice."

"Would you like me to make an appointment with someone for you? Your psychiatrist, your personal trainer, your hair stylist, your massage therapist, your—"

"Oh, give it a rest!"

"I'm sure you'll be fine, Miss MacPherson."

"Yeah, sure." Eva clicked the button to turn off the speaker phone and then spit at it.

After a moment's thought, she picked up her half-empty flute of champagne and walked to the bathroom, where she set down the flute and picked up her magnifying mirror. She observed the area surrounding her left eye. Still had a grayish-blue look. She pursed her lips. Stupid to even think of asking her father for help! Unless it involved money and contracts, he wouldn't have a clue anyway.

But who else was there to ask? Last week, after several sleepless nights trying to figure out what to do, she'd actually gone to see her psychiatrist. His solution was a prescription for sleeping pills.

She shrugged her shoulders and began to apply an expensive blemish cream. It wasn't the first time she'd had a black eye, and it likely wouldn't be the last.

She made a face in the mirror. What had somebody said? You can't pick a rose without getting pricked by a thorn?

Speaking of roses—her eyes slid down past her shoulders to the lacy slip she was wearing, and she smiled. After several disappointments, she'd found a seamstress who'd not only taken on the challenge with enthusiasm, but had done a fabulous job of recreating the slip Marilyn Monroe had worn in the movie *Niagara*.

Eva sighed. The only problem was that despite some padding here and there, she just didn't fill it out the way Marilyn had. She'd even hired a personal trainer to improve her shape, but all he'd done for his hundred bucks an hour was yell at her for not exercising regularly and tell her he'd wash his hands of her if she kept eating rich desserts and drinking so much.

What was the use of being old enough to do whatever you wanted if other people still had rules about what you should and shouldn't do? And why pay people to yell at her?

Her hair stylist was just as bad. He'd bleached her hair and cut it to look like Marilyn's, but he'd complained the whole time, saying it didn't suit her. Fat lot he knew! Her new look had snared one of the most eligible bachelors in the country. She was the envy of thousands of women.

As for the black eye, nothing came without a little bit of pain. Her father had told her that often enough. So suck it up and keep your chin up. That was another of his sayings.

She glanced at the clock on her wall. Almost time for the interview. She never listened to sports radio, but Pat Davis, Rico's agent, was being interviewed today on the *Stasey Simon Show*, and although it would be boring, she ought to turn it on. But first, she went to her well-stocked bar to fortify herself with more champagne.

Some miles away, Stasey Simon sat at a table in the largest of WIN 730's three claustrophobic sound rooms. The news was on, so she raised her hands high above her head and thrust her legs forward and out, toes pointing up, heels down, feeling the stretch through her muscular shoulders and down the length of her very healthy five-foot-two inch frame. She stood up as her twenty-two-year-old producer Ted Benedetto came in from the control booth.

"Is Pat here?" she asked.

"He's in the washroom."

"Not being sick, I hope."

"No. He wanted to make sure he wouldn't get the urge to go while on air."

"Okay." Her tone changed, becoming cold and hard. "You put through a call from Lawrence."

"I know."

"I told you Friday—" she made eye contact with Ted, even though it hurt her neck to have to look up nearly a foot to do so "—he calls too much. Frankly, he's starting to give me the creeps. I told you to only let him on once a week now. Or had you forgotten?"

"I remember. It's just he's—he's so earnest. He says he listens to your every word and he loves the show, and—"

Stasey poked Ted in the chest with her long, burgundy fingernails. "He's totally weird. I find myself being nice and agreeing with him because I'm afraid not to. If I ever pick up a stalker, it'll be him."

"I think he's just, you know, slow. Mentally challenged or whatever they call it."

"I don't care if he's the head of MENSA. He gets one call a week!" She turned her back on Ted and sat down.

A heavy-set, middle-aged man wearing a brown tweed sports jacket and tan pants stepped hesitantly into the room. Ted escorted him to a chair and hooked him up with headphones. When Pat was connected, Ted leaned over to whisper a joke in his ear and was rewarded by a tight smile.

On air again, Stasey was going over the highlights from the day before. Baseball was the priority, but there had been a major trade in the Canadian Football League, a death in the golf world, and a hearts-and-flowers story in the world of horse racing. Stasey ran down the page of news items, making a comment off the top of her head for each one.

Then it was time to interview Pat.

"I have with me today a very special guest. It's Pat Davis, the agent for Ricardo Velasquez." She listed a few names of other sports figures who used Pat as an agent, reviewed the well-worn rumor of how Rico had been spirited out of Cuba by an unknown baseball fan, mentioned Rico's stats, and then said, "So tell me what it's like to represent a player who speaks very little English. Do you speak Spanish?"

Pat sighed and relaxed in his chair. Whatever question he'd been dreading, it wasn't this one. "Well, Rico speaks some English, but not a lot. And I don't speak Spanish. I'm well aware there can be misunderstandings when both parties aren't completely clear about important things, so I employ two interpreters whenever I'm working on business details with someone who doesn't speak English well."

"So when you and Rico worked out the contract, you had two people there interpreting?"

"That's right."

"Isn't one enough?"

"I want one there to present Rico's side and one there to present mine. I once—years ago—employed an interpreter who was lying to a player about what I was saying. I didn't know it, and neither did the player, and it caused a lot of confusion and hard feelings. So now I have two. I try to hire people who don't know each other, so there's no collusion, and I tell each of them straight out to let us know if the other one's not on the up and up."

"You do this for your protection?"

"For mine and the player's as well."

"Fascinating." Stasey paused to light a cigarette. "So, tell me, is Rico the same person in real life as he is on the mound?"

As Stasey began her question, Pat's thick, stubby fingers grasped the edges of the table as if he was dangling from a cliff edge. As she completed the question, his fingers dropped into his lap and he coughed once before answering. "Rico is more or less what you see. He knows a lot about baseball—not just the game, but the history of the game. He's determined to win both a World Series and a Cy Young Award."

Stasey inhaled from her cigarette and blew out the smoke. "Really? I'd have thought he'd be happy just to play ball and make money. Not to mention having the opportunity to live in a country where he's free to do pretty well anything he wants to do."

Pat shifted forward in his chair, resting his elbows on the table in front of him and interlacing his fingers, thumbs pressed together in a steeple. "Well, of course, he's thrilled to be living here in Canada, and to be on a Major League team. The other things—they're just dreams he's added on now that he has the ability to dream. In Cuba, his future was simply to keep playing until he was too old to play. Now he has the joy of playing for a great team, making a very good living, and dreaming new dreams."

"Pat, you're waxing poetic on me here. So tell me—" Stasey leaned forward, her eyes gleaming, "—if Rico is so happy to be here, why is it the players on his team would be glad to get rid of him?"

Pat pressed his back against his chair and squared his shoulders as if taking part in a tug of war with an invisible rope. His voice rose slightly. "I think you're generalizing. There may be a few players who don't like Rico—"

"Oh, come now—" Stasey's tone of voice didn't change "—most of the players and everyone else who knows what goes on in the locker room think Rico is a jerk."

Pat cleared his throat. "He's in a strange country where he doesn't speak the language very well, and he's anxious to succeed, so he might have stepped on a few egos. People need to be more tolerant."

Stasey took a fourth puff from her cigarette before stubbing it out in a saucer Ted had found in the station's tiny kitchen and now put out for her use every day. "Pat, I realize you're making a lot of money from the guy, so you have to defend him. But, can you honestly tell me it doesn't bother you to go to all the effort you have—even your two interpreters—and then have to clean up after his messes? You're an intelligent man. Is the money worth it?"

With his right hand, Pat rubbed the front of head, displacing strands of brown hair that had been carefully combed to cover his thinning pate.

Dead air space beckoned.

Stasey grinned. "Pat, tell us the truth. Did you know what he was like when you took him on?"

Pat licked his lips before answering. "I knew he was a great young pitcher," he said doggedly.

"Did you know anything about him as a person?"

Pat glanced toward Ted, busy in the booth. "Not much," he said slowly.

Stasey was lighting another cigarette as she said, "It must have been an unpleasant surprise to discover what he's like."

"He's not as bad as you're making out. He's—"

"A jerk."

"—just getting accustomed to living here and being famous. It'll take a while. Lots of players find it hard to make the adjustment to a new lifestyle. And being in the public eye all the time is hard for anyone."

"And meanwhile, he has that very nice signing bonus and that very nice contract, and you're getting your share, right?"

"I—I—"

"We have to take a break for a sports update. I'll be back in a jiffy to take your calls."

When he was sure they were off the air, Pat said, "I thought you wanted to interview me. All you did was attack Rico."

"I said what I thought my listeners wanted me to say," Stasey said. "Those are the questions they wanted asked."

Pat's eyes went past her. "So there's nothing personal in your making me look like a money-hungry fool?"

"Nothing."

Pat sighed. "You know, I really wish you'd give Rico a chance. With your influence, you could change the way people think."

From the control room, Ted's voice interrupted. "Back on the air in five … four … three … two … one."

"This is the *Stasey Simon Show* and my guest today is Pat Davis, agent for Ricardo Velasquez, fondly or perhaps not-so-fondly known by his fans and teammates as Rico. Why don't you give us a call with your question for Pat?" She took a long drag from her cigarette. "So, Pat, you think Rico has been treated unfairly? You think we're expecting too much of him?"

Pat cleared his throat before responding. "He's a bit like a kid visiting a candy store for the first time. He'll settle down. People need to give him the benefit of the doubt."

"Translated, I guess that means as long as he pitches well, he should get away with behaving like a spoiled brat?"

"That's not what—"

"Okay, here's our first caller. Joe, how are you doing?"

"I'm doing great, Stasey. You know, I don't think we need players from Cuba coming in and taking jobs from our North American players. Look what's happened in hockey with all the European players coming in! I don't like it. I think Rico should go back to Cuba and play there. Leave the job for one of our own people."

"Okay, Joe. Always on your toes, aren't you? Who's our next caller? Brian, what have you got to say?"

"Hi, Stasey? How are you today?"

She rolled her eyes. "Just fine, Brian. What's on your mind?"

"Hi, Pat. Stasey, I like Rico. Sure, he gets a little upset with the other players if they make a mistake, but I like that. I'd rather have someone with his emotions on his sleeve than someone with no emotions at all. And the last caller was crazy. If we didn't have players from outside the U.S. and Canada, we wouldn't have had Fernando

Valenzuela, Roberto Clemente, George Bell, Alfredo Griffin, Tony Fernandez, El Duke, Hideki Matsui, and many other fine players. I want to see the best, Stasey. And I don't care where they come from."

"All right, Brian. Thanks. And you're so right. We've had lots of fine players from outside North America—many of whom were also fine people." She paused for a second. "Anyone else out there have a question for Pat? Annie, you're on the *Stasey Simon Show*."

"Thanks, Stasey. Mr. Davis, the report in the paper says he trashed the locker room. I teach high school, and I shudder to think my kids might copy him. And saying he'll settle down eventually is ludicrous. No one 'settles down' without discipline. He has to learn what's right and wrong, what's appropriate behavior and what isn't. You have to give him rules to follow and hold him accountable. As his agent, it's your responsibility to be a mentor to him."

Pat rubbed his hands together. "Well—Annie, is it?"

"Yes."

"Annie, I hear what you're saying. And I agree. When I say we need to give Rico time to adjust, I don't mean just wait. We're working with him—I am, his manager Blake Harrison is, and some others are. I know Ferdinand Ortes has taken him under his wing. But I still say the adjustment will take time. And let's face it, Toronto is a bit of a fish bowl."

Stasey interrupted. "Meaning?"

"Meaning professional athletes here get more than usual coverage from the media. And their personal lives go under more scrutiny."

"What does all that have to do with our expecting him to show some team spirit and self-control?" Before Pat could respond, Stasey switched gears and asked, "Who's our next caller? Wayne? What would you like to say to Pat?"

"Just this. I want a team that wins! So make sure this guy doesn't mess it up. He should be grateful to us for giving him the chance to play here, and he'd better behave! And you'd better see that he does!"

"Okay, Wayne!" Stasey was grinning. She waited for a beat before saying, "Well, somebody has to pay the bills. We'll be back after a sports update and a commercial."

Stasey leaned toward Pat. "Looks like you've got some work to do."

His nervousness seemed to have dissipated. "Do I get a rebuttal time?"

"We've got a few minutes," Stasey said. "What the heck? Sure. You can say your piece."

"Thank you."

The update ended. Stasey read a commercial for suntan lotion. Then she said, "So, Pat, going along with your idea of giving people a lot of rope—if you could say anything you wanted, right here and right now, what would you say?"

"I'd say we often expect more from other people than we do from ourselves. I'm not perfect, and I don't think you are either, Stasey. Sure, Rico makes mistakes, but most of our listeners do, too. It might be good to think about that old saying about not judging someone unless you've walked a mile or so in his moccasins."

"Is that a tear in my eye? No, no, I'm okay. Nice recovery, Pat. And thanks for being on the show today."

"Thank you, Stasey. Any time."

Ted helped Pat remove the headset. After a weak smile at Stasey, he walked out of the booth, limping very slightly.

On-air, Stasey said, "Ever wondered why people have agents? Now you know. If you pay them well enough, your agent will do his or her best to make you look like a poor misguided young lad struggling to survive instead of the selfish jerk you are."

Stasey made a throat-slashing movement to Ted. "I'll be back in one minute."

A commercial went on.

Ted's voice came through her earphone, "You were a bit hard on him."

"He's a slimeball."

"He's just doing his job."

"So am I."

"When you treat guests like that, you make my job harder."

"They always come back. They know any publicity is better than none."

"You're on air in three ... two ... one."

"Let's switch topics now from baseball to football for the next half hour. ..."

In his suite in the Diamond Hotel, which was situated next to the Diamond Dome, Rico Velasquez had listened to the *Stasey Simon Show* with the team's shortstop, Ferdinand Ortes. Since Ferdinand spoke fluent English as well as Spanish, he was able to translate anything Rico didn't understand. But Rico didn't need Ferdinand's help when Stasey called him a jerk.

Using his native Spanish, Rico called Stasey quite a few things.

Ferdinand laughed. "You did go overboard yesterday. I mean, breaking the TV was a bit much! And the wall—not exactly the brightest thing you've ever done."

"Yeah," Rico said. "I wasted my energy on that stupid wall. Next time I'll choose a better target." He smiled. "You know what I'd really like? One of these days, I'd like to take a bat to Stasey Simon's head!"

Ginny Lovejoy, the sports columnist for the *Toronto Daily News*, was waiting in the small foyer when Pat Davis came out of the elevator after leaving the WIN offices.

"You look like a man who could use a drink," she said.

"I sure wouldn't say no to one."

Together, they walked the ninety feet to Dana's Place, a popular hangout for the staff and guests of WIN. Ginny led the way to a booth near the back and sat, as always, with her back to the wall.

"Did you hear her?" Pat asked.

"Mmm hmm."

"Why I put myself into her clutches, I'll never know."

"You did it because it's your job to make Rico look good."

"I wasn't very successful."

She looked thoughtful. "A lot of Stasey's listeners are delighted when she looks bad, and she looked bad today—as if she has it in for Rico. I think, overall, you did him a big favor. What you said had a lot of truth to it."

"I feel I just got tackled by an entire offensive line."

A waitress came and took their order. When she was gone, Pat said, "I have to confess, I prefer the print media people."

Ginny grinned. "That's because we have a different agenda. And we're nicer."

Pat smiled. "Well, some of you are."

"But she's right, you know. Rico is a bit of a pain."

He sighed. "Off the record?"

"Of course."

"He's the biggest pain in the butt I've ever had for a client. And I'm stuck with him." He leaned forward. "You know I took him on as a favor to Tony Kanberra?"

Ginny shook her head. "I didn't know that."

"Before Rico even left Cuba, Tony called me and asked me to take Rico on as a client. So I said sure. How many times does the team's GM hand you a gift like that? Some gift."

"Maybe they didn't know what to expect."

"Could be. I dunno."

"So what are you going to do next?"

"The team is just as concerned as I am. They're trying to project a family image, and Rico is really stretching it."

"The saving factor is that so far he's been going ballistic in the locker room, and not in public—as I may have mentioned in my column this morning, and Stasey definitely mentioned this afternoon."

Pat groaned. "At least you didn't give his name."

"What can the Matrix do? Trade him?"

"The guy has a golden arm. No way they're going to trade him. No way I can let him go, either. He could make me rich."

"Tough."

He nodded.

"But, Pat, can you really sit back and do nothing? I mean, if someone doesn't try to check him, he'll think he can get away with murder. Somebody needs to talk to him, or fine him, or set down some basic rules."

"Yeah, yeah, but—" He glanced around as if to make sure no one was eavesdropping, then leaned forward. "You won't let any of this out, right? At least not connected with me?"

She put her arms on the table and leaned in so her face was only a few inches from his. "Not unless you tell me I can."

"Well, between you and me and the lamp post, we've got a plan in motion. You know we got Rico out of Cuba." He shook his head slightly. "I don't mean literally 'we.' I have no idea how it was done."

"Right. So—?"

"So we're getting his wife out. We figure if anyone can settle Rico down, she can."

Ginny's eyes widened. "Rico is married?"

"Yep."

"From what I've heard, he hasn't been acting very married."

"Exactly. We figure she'll have a calming influence."

"Who is she?"

"An elementary school teacher. She's from a good family, she's well-educated, and she speaks English. They were married less than a year ago. All in all, she sounds like the one person who might have some influence on Rico."

"Wow! Can I use this Pat? You know what a great story it would make."

He sat back and shook his head. "I don't want to be the one to spill the beans."

She thought for a moment. "What if I find out some other way? Is she coming by plane? Will the ticket be in her name?"

"Likely."

"When is she coming?"

"Tomorrow."

"What if I happened to be at the airport and saw her name on a list?"

"You can do that?"

"If I find a way, can I use it? I promise I won't mention you anywhere."

"I like you, Ginny. And I'd like to see you have the story before Stasey gets hold of it. So, I guess so. But make sure there's nothing that would lead anyone to me, okay?"

TWO

At one of the Air Canada ticket counters at the Lester B. Pearson airport, Ginny Lovejoy was pulling in every favor she'd ever done for her mother's next-door neighbor as she addressed that neighbor's daughter Beth, a dewy-eyed innocent in her first real job.

"I'm not supposed to give names of passengers to anyone."

"I'm not just anyone," Ginny explained for the fourth time. "I'm the press. We get special treatment, you know? That's how we get our stories out on time. Trust me, it's fair. We all have people we go to for information, just like the police do."

"Well, if my mom told you to come, I guess maybe—"

"The name is Velasquez—V-E-L-A-S-Q-U-E-Z—and she's likely coming from Florida."

Beth typed the name into her computer and waited.

Ginny held her breath.

After a minute that seemed tenfold in Ginny's mind, Beth said, "There's a Velasquez on a flight from Tampa tomorrow morning."

"Do you have a first name?"

"A-L-I-T-A. I don't know how you pronounce that."

"Me neither, but I'll sure find out." Anxious to dash to the car and speed away to write her story, Ginny forced herself to look the younger woman directly in the eyes and say, "Thanks, Beth. You've been a lifesaver. I won't forget it. Any time you or your mom need something, just let me know."

As soon as she was out of Beth's view, she raced for her car, excitement tingling up and down her spine. It was so hard to get a scoop these days, but she'd done it! Now all she had to do was drive to the ballpark, write her story, and keep her fellow scribes from suspecting anything was up.

As her show ended a few minutes before four, Stasey Simon allowed a deep sigh to escape. Another day, another bunch of dollars. She laughed. There were harder ways to make your living than being the only female talk-show host on an all-sports radio station.

Ted came over. "Good show, I think. You'll need to be careful with Pat, though. Smooth the ruffled feathers."

"He'll be fine once he's had a chance to sulk for a while," Stasey replied. "Never be afraid to stretch the envelope, but always keep 'em wanting more." That was her motto for life as well as her talk show. "Always keep ahead of the boys" was the unwritten corollary.

"I suppose you've been spitting all over the mic again. You know, I really don't need your germs." Iain Foley's voice was the kind that sent heat waves reverberating through a room. There was no word for it other than beautiful. Deep and rich, it had the ability to gather people in and soothe them. Not that Stasey found his voice anything but grating.

Unfortunately, forty-five-year-old Iain's appearance didn't quite match his voice. He wasn't bad-looking: just not what people envisioned. A solid, compact five-foot-nine, he had a sallow complexion, undistinguished brown hair, hazel eyes, and a droopy mustache patterned after that of his all-time favorite hockey player, Lanny MacDonald. A producer once commented that he was perfect to play the cab driver, but never the hero. So he stayed in radio when he would have preferred to try his hand at television.

A star athlete in high school and college despite his size disadvantage, Iain hadn't had quite enough skills to get him to the NHL. Coaching had never interested him, but an astute college coach had suggested he change his major to broadcasting, and he'd never looked back.

Now he held the station's top position as host of the *Prime Time Show*.

At Iain's entrance, Ted had eased quietly out of the room.

"I wish you'd stop smoking in here," Iain continued. "Not only is it against the city bylaws, but you aren't the only person who uses this room. I hate the smell after you've been in."

Stasey laughed. "Heard the interview with Pat, did you?"

"You know I never listen to your show if I can help it."

"No, you just make your producer listen, and then you holler at him for not getting you the people first."

Iain shrugged. "So you've got a sharp producer."

"And I know you've tried more than once to steal him."

"Why he takes your abuse is beyond me."

"You'd never understand."

Stasey glanced toward the glass-enclosed sound booth where Iain's producer, Greg Mintress, a tired-looking man in a stained T-shirt with a rip on one sleeve, sat in the chair Ted had occupied. Greg had his headphones on, so Stasey assumed he'd heard the entire conversation; but his face gave nothing away.

"You treat your producer so nicely."

"Greg's got nothing to worry about," Iain said. "He'll be doing this till he's an old man."

"And he's ready to go." Stasey smiled at Iain. "So I'd better get a move on." She walked out, swinging her hips from side to side, and knowing Iain would correctly interpret the invitation to kiss her in places he wouldn't care to.

Iain dumped Stasey's used butts into the wastebasket in the producer's cubicle before sitting in the chair and putting on the headphones he'd brought with him. Taking a handkerchief from his pocket, he wiped the microphone. When he was satisfied Stasey's germs were gone, he pulled his notes from their compartment in his briefcase and set them out, then cleared his throat.

His music began, followed by the announcer's voice on tape. "Ladies and Gentlemen, are you ready? Are you ready? Because this is the Main Event! And in our corner, ready to take you out of your day-to-day lives on a journey to the stars, the one and only Champion of the Airwaves—Eeeee-aaaan Fo-oh-le-y!" Cheers, then more music, fading.

Iain began his spiel, his rich tones both soothing and invigorating. "Welcome to everyone on your way home or relaxing with a pint or two before you head out. We'll do our best to keep you alert for the next two and a half hours as you wend your way to wherever you're going. That's right. The show is shortened by half an hour again tonight because of WIN's presentation of the baseball game. And speaking of baseball—" He picked up the first page of his notes and read a prepared statement with his view of yesterday's game. "Some people in our city have been crucifying Ricardo Velasquez for his behavior in the clubhouse yesterday where, annoyed by the lackluster performance of his teammates, Rico threw some equipment around.

"In my opinion, the flurry about Rico is all nonsense. This sort of thing goes on all the time. The real problem is that here in Toronto, the team chose to have an early-season promotional campaign in which they strenuously promoted baseball as a game for the entire family. I said it in the spring, and I'll say it now: baseball isn't wholesome family entertainment. Baseball is a man's game. That's why there's never been a woman on a major league team. Baseball is played by grown men who A. have the skills and B. get paid to display those skills. They are not in this to be role models. And sissies don't play baseball. ..."

Stasey listened to Iain on the hall speakers as she walked to Ted's tiny cubicle, where he was talking to someone on the telephone. "Aren't you finished?" Stasey griped. "Let's get out of here."

Ted held up his hand. "One minute."

Stasey leaned against the door frame, tapping one foot as she extracted her cigarette pack from a pocket in her capris. She lit a cigarette and took a deep drag.

She could still hear Iain's voice from the hall speaker. She shook her head. "He's anchored in the sixties."

"So Thursday is the best time for him?" Ted said into the phone.

"It's no wonder my ratings are climbing while his are dropping."

Still speaking to the phone, Ted said, "I wonder if we can work something out that would help both of us."

Stasey studied her producer. At several inches over six feet, he was thin and gangly looking. His glossy black hair, inherited from his Chinese mother, was worn shoulder length and tied back, adding to his long, lean appearance. Today, as always, he wore torn faded jeans, a wrinkled white T-shirt with a bizarre saying on it, dirty white runners, and two small earrings in each ear. The only discordant note was the pair of gold-rimmed glasses that perched on his nose and gave him an odd, stork-like look.

Stasey took another drag of the cigarette, then strode forward to mash it in an empty Styrofoam cup. "Let's go," she said.

Ted wrinkled his face at her while continuing to concentrate on the person on the other end of the phone. "I was thinking Friday would be best for us. Stasey likes to end the week on an up note. He'd be a hard act to follow this week. What do you think?"

"Who are you talking to?" Stasey asked.

To the phone, Ted said. "Okay. That's great. Consider it done, then. We'll see you both Friday." He hung up.

"Who was that?"

"The agent for Friday's guest," he said.

"Who?"

"It's a surprise. Tell you later."

Stasey was used to Ted's not telling her the guests' names too far in advance. He said it was because so many times people canceled, and there was no point getting prepared until you knew they would actually arrive. Stasey thought it was because he liked to have power over her. Keep her guessing. But as long as he kept reeling in good guests, she didn't care if he never told her.

"Let's go," Stasey said. "We've got a baseball game to cover."

Ginny Lovejoy had gone straight to the Diamond Dome from the airport. The game that night had a seven o'clock start—early enough for downtown workers to head over straight from the office, or families with young children to get the kids into bed at a decent hour. But media people tended to gather several hours prior to game time, looking for chance comments that suggested story ideas, information on who was hurting where, gossip about anyone who had a chip on his shoulder against a member of the other team, or useful philosophical gems from old-timers.

Even after a year, Ginny still felt a shiver of excitement each time she walked through the Diamond Dome's media entrance.

Some of it was due to her love for the spectacular home the Diamond Corporation had built for the Matrix two years earlier. But most of it came from the thrill she felt every time she realized that she, Ginny Lovejoy, had the right to walk freely through hallways the public never saw, and not only talk to the players, but even enter into their locker room. The reality of her day-to-day life was so far beyond any dream she'd had that not a day went by she didn't want to pinch herself to make sure it was real.

A green-eyed redhead with fair skin and a sprinkling of freckles, five-foot-four, 145-pound Ginny had a figure most people called "curvy," Ginny deemed "cuddly," and her mother referred to as "chubby." A stadium potato who loved watching other people run around, it had never entered her mind that she could be a sports reporter.

She fell into her job one Monday morning when she was the only person available after the regular sports columnist showed up too hung over to cover the unexpected trade of a very popular hockey player. Twenty-four-year-old Ginny had been hired a few weeks earlier to write feature articles for the life pages, but the column she turned in on the news conference, coupled with the regular columnist's failure to show even a smidgen of remorse over his hangover, landed her in the locker room and her colleague on unemployment.

In the intervening year, the editor had never regretted his sudden decision. Ginny and sports reporting were a perfect coupling, like fish and chips or tortillas and salsa. In baseball parlance, she was a "natural."

As she did most days, she walked reverently through the red and gold hallways to the elevator that would take her to the lower floor, then along the hall that led to the field. As she stepped onto the field, her eyes went up, past the six levels of red and gold seats to the very top of the glass dome with its multitude of facets that mimicked an enormous diamond. The thousands of glass windows were hooked up to a computer system that allowed each window to be opened, shut, or slanted to allow in the warm summer air but keep out the rain, snow, and wind. The rays of the sun hitting the windows created a prismatic effect, making the entire dome glitter just like a diamond. Ginny stood gazing up in delight for several minutes before sighing in satisfaction and walking over to stand behind the batting cage, where Jonas Newland was swinging his bat and joking with the hitting coach.

She watched Jonas lay down two perfect bunts, one to either side of the field, and then take a few swings. He caught one of the pitches and sent the ball soaring toward the center-field stands just as Blake Harrison, the manager of the Matrix, walked by.

A stocky man with a pronounced paunch, Blake had played professional baseball for twenty years before becoming a minor-league coach. At fifty-eight, he was in his fourth year as manager of the Matrix. Seeing the ball land in the third deck of straightaway center field, Blake called out, "How about repeating that one in the game?"

"I wish!" Jonas readied himself for the next pitch.

The team's shortstop, Ferdinand Ortes, was waiting to bat next. "Jonas will be lucky if he catches a foul tip off Willow," he said, a merry twinkle in his eyes.

"Huh!" Jonas replied in kind, "You'll be lucky if you get within a foot of the ball."

Ferdinand slowly shook his head. "Willow was lucky the last time. This time, I'll be ready for him."

Jonas took a few half-swings as the hitting coach said, "Willow's last game against us was a two-hitter. And one of those hits was because Barry connected for a line drive with his eyes shut. Not to mention that if the shortstop had been one more foot to his right on Ferdinand's hit, he'd have had an easy out instead of a dive that injured his shoulder and let the ball get by."

Ferdinand grinned at Ginny, and she grinned back. Only twenty-four, and a smallish player (five-ten, 174 pounds), Ferdinand was a third-year starter with the Matrix. Well-liked by both players and management, an even bet to make the all-star team this year, maybe even get a Gold Glove, Ferdinand was a dream of a shortstop. He'd already earned the nickname Spiderman because, like Spidey, he was able to do amazing things. Lithe as a long-distance runner, agile as a circus tumbler, and quick as a hare, he had an uncanny ability to not only grab balls that should have gone by him, but to then turn in mid-air and throw bullets that caught unsuspecting runners.

Ferdinand was from New York City, born of immigrant parents from Argentina who knew nothing about baseball until their son's junior high coach told them they had a potential star on their hands.

From that day, nothing was too good for the precocious young man who chose to accept a college scholarship, which led him to a degree in commerce along with a trip to the big leagues with only a wave at triple A.

Now he grew serious. With clear, concise diction, just a hint of an accent showing, he said, "Ah, but I've been watching video of the last game and studying how he pitches, and now I'm ready. I kid you not: I'll take him out of the park today."

"Never mind trying to hit one out of the park," the hitting coach growled. "Just get the ball in play. That's all I ask. Get the ball in play."

"So how do *you* think we can hit him, Coach?" Jonas asked as he swung though a nonexistent pitch.

"Any pitcher can be hit. Take your time, wait for a good pitch, and meet the ball. That's it. No fancy stuff."

"But, Coach—" the third baseman had come up "—what if the ball's moving so fast you can't even see it?"

Ginny laughed and moved on.

She caught a glimpse of Kyle Schmidt, a columnist for the other major Toronto newspaper, the *Toronto Register*, sitting in the dugout beside the rookie left-fielder, Arthur Kling. They were no doubt discussing the role-playing video game that had been giving Arthur trouble for the last month. The video game seemed to be the only problem Arthur had in his life, and Ginny knew from experience he was more than willing to explain it in great detail to any sympathetic ear. Every now and then you tossed in a baseball-related question and got a vague response. Then he went back to the video game as if nothing in his life was more important. And it probably wasn't. Ginny grinned. *Rookies,* she thought. *Gotta love 'em.*

Ginny turned toward the field, where some players were stretching and others playing catch or sprinting. Pitcher Armando Santana, an imposing man with milk chocolate skin, dark brown hair, and piercing brown eyes, was walking off the field, a towel around his neck, sweat gleaming on his forehead. Assuming he was headed for the dugout, Ginny moved to intercept.

"Warm day," she said by way of greeting.

He nodded.

"Want to talk?"

"Not right now." Armando hesitated and in a gentler voice said, "Sorry, Ginny. This isn't a good time."

"Sure. No problem."

Armando continued walking toward Blake Harrison, who was in conversation with the first base coach.

Ginny saw the two men stop talking at Armando's approach. Then the coach moved away and Armando said something to Blake.

Ginny started to move closer in hope of picking up a few words of the conversation.

"Hey, beautiful. Looking for me?"

Ginny turned toward the speaker and grinned. "Hi, Muddy. How's it going?"

"Never better." He beamed. Seventy-year-old pitching coach, Muddy Ames, was a short, chestnut-skinned man with a bit of a paunch and a lined face that wore a perpetual smile. Things had to be near disaster level to induce a negative response from Muddy. "And you look prettier every time I see you."

She made a mock curtsy. "I need you to have a talk with my mother."

"Now what could she be telling you?"

"That if I don't lose some weight and get busy, I'm never going to find a husband."

Muddy laughed. "What you want with a husband? He'd just want you to stop hanging out with us. Tell your mama you're doing fine the way you are."

"I'll try, but she doesn't listen to me much."

Muddy nodded. "I do know 'bout that. My mama—God rest her soul—she never heard much either. Thought she always knew best." He chuckled. "Trouble is, usually she was right!"

"About the game yesterday," Ginny said, "you've had time to think it over. Anything you should have done differently? Would you have put in a different relief pitcher?'"

"I don't think so. Course, I wish I'd told Armando to leave off throwing the outside pitch, but since our stats show us that Billy-Joe has trouble with outside pitches, I never would have said that. Just our luck Billy-Joe decides yesterday is the day to prove all the statisticians wrong. Three-run double. Should never have happened, but it did."

"What about Rico's reaction to the loss? Don't you think it was a little excessive?"

"Tell you something, beautiful. You give me a player who stomps around and gets upset any day rather than one who shrugs and says, 'So what? I got my money.'"

"So Rico's little tantrum didn't bother you."

"Heck, no. Didn't bother me one little bitty bit."

"What about Armando? Would you tell Blake to put him in today if you need him?"

"Sure I would. First off, he didn't put the three runners on the bases. Brett did that. Maybe Armando didn't make a great pitch to Billy Joe, but it wasn't a bad pitch. Just apparently the one Billy Joe had been preparing himself for."

Ginny decided to try a harder question. "I've heard rumors of Armando maybe being traded. What do you think?"

"You know me, beautiful, I don't listen to rumors. I just work with the pitchers they decide to give me. You'll have to ask Mr. Kanberra about the trades and business plans."

"Thanks, Muddy. Take care."

"You too, beautiful."

Ginny watched the older man move across the infield to the visiting team's dugout, where he would embrace his many friends on the other team, as he always did. And no one would mind.

Ginny turned to where Blake and Armando had been talking, but they were gone. Scanning the area, she couldn't see either one, so she started toward the dugout. Before she reached it, the starting pitcher for yesterday's game, Brett Moore, stepped out of the shadows and walked toward her.

As happy as she always was to talk to Muddy Ames, Ginny would have been even happier if she never had to talk to Brett Moore. The good-looking twenty-seven-year-old pitcher represented everything Ginny didn't like about baseball.

"Well, if it isn't the carrot-topped reporter. Seen any big, strong ballplayers that interest you today, babe?"

Swallowing what she really wanted to say, she smiled and said, "By the way, great pitching yesterday."

He shrugged and said, "Be sure to write down how many touchdowns we score in each inning, eh?"

Still smiling, she said, "I'll do my best," and walked by him to the dugout where Kyle Schmidt still sat next to Arthur Kling. Several other players had gathered around them, all focused on the video game.

Seeing Ginny, Kyle extricated himself from the group and strolled over. Raising his eyebrows, he said, "You look glum."

"Just had a momentary attack of sanity and wondered why we do this day after day. If I wasn't a reporter, I'd think Brett Moore is a wonderful pitcher and a wonderful person. Instead, every time I see him out there, I remember the dumb things he says to me and the way he has of looking out for only himself, and I don't know whether to cheer for him or not. Makes me very ambivalent."

"You can always copy me."

"But I don't want to be like you, all businesslike and cold. I want to cheer for the team. It's way more fun."

"Well, enjoy. I have to go file a story."

"Latest tips for video-game addicts?"

"Cute. As a matter of fact, I do have a story in there someplace. I just need a magnifying glass to find it."

Eyes narrowed, Ginny watched Kyle head up to the press box. The first thing she'd done when she reached the ballpark was write and send in her column, but of course she had no intention of letting anyone know that.

She'd go through the motions, even writing another column. Whatever it took to protect her scoop.

Half an hour later, Kyle Schmidt sat in the press box at his computer. His pre-game story in, he was writing out his resignation.

Thin and fine-boned, with delicate features, blond curls, and pale blue eyes, twenty-nine-year-old Kyle was as much of an anomaly in the world of sports reporting as Ginny Lovejoy. But while she reveled in it, he bore it as a cross.

Fresh out of high school and certain he was destined to be the next William Faulkner, he'd earned a degree in creative writing, finishing at the top of his class. He immediately began work on his first literary masterpiece, but after starving for over a year, one dreary winter day he'd read his book and burned the pages one by one with the aid of a candle and a steel garbage can.

Dejected and hungry, the only writing job he could find was that of copy editor for the *Register's* sports pages. Eventually, he was given writing assignments. Then one day, in a fit of anger at his lot in life, he'd written an editorial on the futility of being a sports fan. The editor thought it was tongue-in-cheek and loved it. The readers also loved it. And Kyle became a sports columnist, where he'd remained for five long years.

He wrote a resignation letter at least once a week. Sometimes two or three in one evening if he was really frustrated. Only one letter had actually been sent. It was followed by a hasty e-mail saying, "Sorry. I was just messing around. Didn't mean to send it." The editor, like most of Kyle's peers, knew of his resignation-letter writing habit and ignored it.

"I quit," he typed now. "Not only do I quit, but I never want to see another press box as long as I live. Not only do I never want to see another press box, but I also never want to see another overpaid athlete. Not only do I never want to see another athlete, but I never want to see another sports reporter or broadcaster for either radio or television, another talk show host, or another fan of the aforementioned athletes or—"

"What a busy bee!" Stasey Simon had wandered into the press box and was standing behind him.

Kyle grimaced and closed his file. "Nothing important," he said as he turned to face her.

"I won't keep you." Stasey plopped into the adjacent chair. "Somebody told me you might have some information about Rico and how he spends his off hours."

"Me?"

"That's what I was told."

"By a little bird, no doubt."

"A small one."

"Not a very smart one. Having to watch Rico in a game is enough for me."

"The way I hear it, you hired somebody to follow him."

His eyes widened in amazement. "Why would I do that?"

"Gee, I don't know. Why would you?"

Kyle tilted his head and narrowed his eyes. "And you want to know because?"

"I want in on it. I'll pay part of his salary."

Kyle raised his hands, palms up. "Sorry, your informant was wrong. I'm not paying anyone to follow Rico."

Stasey pulled out a cigarette and put it in her mouth without lighting it. "You're up to something."

Kyle frowned. "Stasey, you're very suspicious. Paranoia setting in?"

"What annoys me is people who think they can bluff me and get away with it." She found her lighter and lit the cigarette. "So," she said after a moment, "do you want to come on my show tomorrow? Blake's a guest. You can tell him whatever you've dug up. Should be interesting."

"Assuming, of course, that I actually have 'dug up' something."

She tapped the fingers of her right hand on her knee. "Do you want to come on or not? Be great exposure for you."

"Thanks, but no thanks. I'm not looking for great exposure just now."

Since game time was approaching, other members of the Toronto media had begun trickling into the press box, along with reporters from the visiting team's city and a few other out-of-town spots. The room took up a hum of noise as people chatted and computer keyboards began to click away.

Ginny came up. "Have you two solved the world's problems?" she asked.

"Just the Third World's," Kyle said. "We'll tackle our problems tomorrow."

"Slumming, Stasey?" asked Craig Wilcox, who covered the Matrix for the *Hamilton Express*. Stasey rarely watched a game from the press box, preferring to sit in the restaurant behind center field or in her seat on the first base line.

Privately, Kyle believed part of it was that she didn't want to associate herself with the lowly scum who wrote for print papers. On the other hand, she also looked down on the play-by-play broadcasters, calling them the team's parrots.

Ignoring Craig's question, Stasey stood up, then leaned toward Kyle, allowing him a better view of the low-cut ice-green velour top she was wearing. "If you change your mind, let me know," she said softly. "I can do a lot of good for people I like." She picked up her purse and sauntered out of the area.

"What on earth was that all about?" Ginny asked as she seated herself where Stasey had been. "Yuck! She left most of her cigarette here. Why she lights the stupid things and takes about two puffs before butting them out I don't know."

"It's her method of stopping smoking," Kyle said.

"An expensive method, if you ask me."

"I don't believe anyone did."

"I guess not." Ginny shrugged and leaned toward Kyle. "Okay, give. What did she want?"

Kyle shrugged. "Beats me. She wanted me to go on her show tomorrow and share any inside information I have."

"She did?"

"Like I would give my scoop to her instead of using it in my paper."

Ginny gave him an intent look. "What scoop?"

"Supposing I had one, of course."

Ginny continued to observe him thoughtfully, but with a small shrug, Kyle turned to watch the players being introduced.

All eyes that night were on the starting pitcher, Miles Patterson, who was having the season of his life and, along with Rico and Ferdinand, was the focus of the team's pennant hopes. Since the opposing pitcher was Oakland's ace, the media, along with the fans, settled in to watch what everyone hoped would be a terrific game.

By the fifth inning, it was clear that things were going the way the home fans wanted. Patterson was firing the ball into Jonas's mitt as if they were playing catch, and the opposition batters seemed stymied, with many going out on called strikes.

In the press box, Ginny yawned and stretched. The humidity that was permeating the press box in spite of the air conditioning was making her sinuses gripe. She could always tell when a low pressure area was coming. "We're in for a thunderstorm," she remarked to anyone within hearing. A few people nodded.

On the field, Ferdinand Ortes ended the sixth inning with a double play that took Oakland out of a threatening situation.

Ginny got up and wandered toward the back of the room. Her mind was crawling with thoughts about the story she'd written and the possible repercussions of Rico's wife's appearance. Wouldn't it be neat if she could talk to Rico alone? But her Spanish was virtually non-existent. Still …. She studied the dugout and the bullpen. Rico didn't seem to be in either one.

Deciding it was worth a try, Ginny grabbed her purse, which contained among other things her steno notebook, asked Kyle to keep track of the next inning for her, and left, knowing everyone would assume she'd gone to the ladies' room.

She took the elevator down and used her press pass to get into the hallway outside the home team's clubhouse.

"Is Rico inside?" she asked the security guard.

The guard barely looked at her. "No idea."

"I'd really like to talk to him."

The guard didn't move.

"Can you just ask someone?" Ginny pleaded.

After a long look, in which he took in a lot more than her press pass, he opened the door a few inches and addressed someone inside.

A roar from the stands made Ginny glance at one of the screens that dotted the hallways. The Matrix right fielder had hit a ball into the left field corner. At least a double.

The guard shut the door. "He'll talk to you in press room C."

She thanked him and walked down the hall to the area reserved for press conferences and private post-game interviews, opened the door to a small room, and went in. After deciding on a seat at the large table that took up most of the room, she pulled her notebook and its attached pen from her purse, opened the notebook to a blank page, and prepared to wait. But it was only a few minutes before Rico entered through a second door.

Tall and well-built, with olive skin, wavy black hair, a new goatee, and flashing black eyes, Rico was attractive enough to make most women take a long look, and enough of a presence for men to take a second glance as well.

The story was that Rico had left Cuba without his birth certificate. He claimed to be twenty-five. That probably meant he was at least twenty-eight, maybe thirty.

He had his uniform on, but was buttoning the shirt as he entered the room. "You want to talk?" He smiled as he groped for words, his accent heavy.

"Yes, I'd love to talk to you." Ginny spoke slowly, carefully enunciating the words, hoping somehow to connect.

He nodded and sat down at the table across from her.

"Rico, you came here from Cuba?"

"Cuba. *Si*." He nodded.

"Do you like it here in Canada?'

"*Si*. I like ver' much."

She smiled.

He leaned closer toward her and smiled back.

He really wasn't a bad-looking guy, she thought. Sort of a Desi Arnez type, only much sexier. "You like baseball here?"

"Baseball here?"

"Playing? You like to play here more than in Cuba? Better here than Cuba?"

"Better here?" Nodding his head up and down, he said, "*Si*. Is better here."

"That's good." She made a few notes. "Do you miss your wife? *Esposa!*"

He rocked back. "*Esposa?*"

"Yes, your wife, Alita."

"Cuba," he said. "She stay there."

"Don't you wish she could join you here in Canada?"

He frowned. "'Lita in Canada?"

She nodded."

He shook his head in alarm. "'Lita in Cuba. Stay there." He lost the frightened look and began to grin. "But, you here."

The glint in his eyes made Ginny decide she'd learned all she needed to know. She grabbed her purse with one hand and her notebook and pen with the other, and stood up to leave. "Thank you," she said. "I'm sure you want to go back and watch the game." She hurried out of the room.

He shouted something at her in Spanish, but she kept going, racing upstairs to the press room, slowing down just before she entered it. She strolled into the room, her heart pounding so hard she was afraid others would hear it, and sank into her chair.

"You were away long enough," Kyle said, his brows raised.

"This humidity is giving me a headache."

"You do look flushed."

"How's the game going?"

He didn't answer—just let her see his notes. She relaxed and updated the game story on her computer. The Matrix had added a run in the sixth on a triple by the right fielder and a long sacrifice fly by Jonas Newland. Patterson had struck out the side in ten pitches in the first half of seventh. She busied herself checking the stats to find out how many times pitchers had struck out the side on nine pitches.

In the clubhouse, Rico Velasquez got his cell phone out of his locker, dialed rapidly, and shouted a mixture of English and Spanish into the phone. The game was showing on two monitors in the lounge, and several players were watching. They began to yell encouragement. Rico walked over to the doorway to stare at one of the monitors. Patterson had thrown two more strikeouts and was on the verge of a third. He threw a called third strike. The crowd cheered. The players in the lounge cheered.

In Spanish, Rico said, "About time!" He picked up a baseball from a box on one of the tables. Wary looks appeared on the faces of the other players. Rico noticed and for one second looked angry enough to throw the ball. Then a smile broke out and he laughed and tossed the ball back into the box.

THREE

Miles Patterson ended getting a one-hitter and tying the American League record for strike-outs in a nine-inning game. The Matrix won 6 to 0 and the hope of seeing another pennant fluttering from the rafters grew stronger.

Ginny and Kyle joined the group of media people following the players into the locker room and surrounding the elated young pitcher. As usual, the press had to wait while the television crews got their brief "Talk to me about the game" video clips. Then the print and radio press asked their thought-proving questions, like "Why did you shake off Jonas's call and throw two fastballs in a row to George in the fifth?" and "Was there a hit and run sign in the third or did you see something that made you decide to go on your own?"

Ginny asked a few questions, jotting down notes in her personal form of shorthand, trying to hear everyone else's questions and get those answers down, too.

When the group had enough copy from the pitcher, they moved almost en masse to catcher Jonas Newland, who was waiting for them at his locker. A tall, muscular man with ebony skin, a shaved head, and numerous scars from catching without proper equipment in his early years, Jonas was as patient with the press as he was with a rookie pitcher. "The game was a breeze to call because every pitch was dead on. Sure, there are some pitchers you could compare him too, and most of them are in the Hall of Fame."

When the crowd had enough copy from Jonas, they broke into smaller groups and looked for players who had scored runs, made good defensive plays, or just seemed to be looking for some company.

Kyle joined a group gathered around short-stop Ferdinand Ortes, who had gone two for three with a walk and a superb catch off a sharp line drive that kept the game from being a two-hitter.

Ginny drifted to the far corner where a single player sat alone. Bare-chested and barefoot, with skin the color of coffee and dark brown chin stubble that matched his medium-length dreadlocked hair, Armando Santana had pulled on jeans and was about to cover his sinewy arms with a denim shirt. At thirty-four, Armando's best days appeared to be behind him. After three bad starts at the beginning of the season, he'd been bumped from the starting lineup into the bullpen to be used in relief. For the first month, he'd been engulfed by a wave of depression. With help from Jonas Newland and a few other players, plus the wisdom of Muddy Ames, his pitching coach, he had gradually seemed to accept what he clearly saw as a demotion, but Ginny knew his self-confidence teetered on the edge.

"How's it going?" she said.

"On or off the record?" Armando replied quietly as he put one arm through a sleeve.

"Pretty good game today, huh?"

A smile touched his lips. "Amazing game. It was a pleasure to watch."

"How are you feeling?" she asked.

He made a face. "I'll survive."

"I'd hoped to talk to you yesterday, but I didn't see you. And you didn't answer your phone."

"Took it off the hook."

"Hmm. What did you and Blake talk about just before the game today?"

He shrugged.

"On the record," she said, "any thought of retiring?"

"No." His voice turned cold.

"I didn't imply that you should. Just wondered if it had crossed your mind?"

"If I didn't think I could help the team, maybe. But I think I can. And I think I'm realistic." He finished doing up the buttons on his shirt and held his large hands palm up. "Maybe they'll have to drag me off the field one day, or ship me to triple A to get it through to me that my career is over. I don't know. I hope not."

Ginny was about to respond when a flurry of angry Spanish behind her made her turn. Pat Davis had walked into the room, and Rico was all over him, shouting in Spanish.

Ginny quickly turned back to Armando. "What did Rico just say?"

Armando looked at her. "He wants to know why some crazy female reporter was asking if he had a wife."

"Weird," Ginny said, carefully keeping her back to the room. "Has Rico ever mentioned having a wife?"

"Not in my hearing, but I'd be surprised if he didn't have one. Common-law, at least."

"Yeah?"

"Yes."

"If he does, I wonder what Eva will think of it."

"Or what the wife will think of Eva," Armando said slowly. He raised his eyebrows. "I wonder which female reporter he was talking to. Not many around here."

Pat Davis was careful not to look at Ginny when he came into the locker room. Stupid of him to have told her about Alita, but he'd been tired after Stasey's grilling, and Ginny was such a sweet girl—at least compared to Stasey. Add to that the drinks he'd had— A mark, that's what he'd been. Like the good cop, bad cop, Stasey had unwittingly set him up for Ginny, who had clearly taken advantage of him.

Pat only caught one or two in ten of Rico's words, but he caught enough. "Can we go someplace quiet to talk?" he asked. When Rico ignored him, he called out, "Spidey?"

Ferdinand glanced over from where he was still talking to a couple of reporters.

"Can you help me for a minute? Tell him what I'm saying?"

"I expect he knows," Ferdinand said. He told the other reporters he was finished taking questions for the day and walked lazily over to Pat and Rico. "Understands more English than you think," he said.

"I need to talk to him. Tell him to get dressed and we'll go somewhere quiet. Ask him if he wants it all over the papers?"

Ferdinand translated, then asked Pat, "What's up?"

"I'm sure he'll tell you later," Pat said.

"Don't you need me to come along and translate?"

Pat looked at Rico, then back at Ferdinand. He sighed. "Meet me at The Fifth Base. I'll get us a table at the back. And Spidey, try to keep the reporters out of this. Please."

Ferdinand looked quizzically at Pat before speaking to Rico in Spanish.

Twenty minutes later, both players walked into The Fifth Base, a popular sports bar across the street from the Diamond Dome. Pat waved from a back table. They ordered drinks from the attentive waiter and waited until the drinks had been delivered.

"How many reporters know what we were talking about?" Pat asked.

"I told them nothing." Ferdinand laced the fingers of his hands together and sat back expectantly. "Couldn't very well tell them what I don't know. I said Rico was annoyed with a question about his personal life." He looked from Pat to Rico. "So, what's up?"

Pat grimaced. "I'm not quite sure how to phrase this. I guess just say it. Rico's wife is on her way here."

Ferdinand turned to Rico and translated. Rico's face became red and he spoke rapidly in Spanish.

"Rico isn't very pleased," Ferdinand said. His eyes were sparkling and the beginning of a grin tugged at the corners of his lips. "Did anybody think to ask Rico if he wanted his wife here?"

Pat squirmed. "I had nothing to do with this, okay? It was the Diamond Corporation's idea. Or rather, their advertising team."

Ferdinand made a face. "What can they do?"

Pat sighed. "It's their idea that we have this big happy family marketing motif for the team, right?"

Ferdinand nodded. "Right."

"And you know ticket sales have been up since the Matrix went on this 'bring your whole family to the game' advertising campaign?"

"Yeah."

"How do you think the team feels when they see Rico throwing temper tantrums like the one he threw after yesterday's loss?"

Ferdinand pursed his lips. "I think they aren't very happy."

"Anything but happy. So somebody came up with the fact that Rico has a wife back in Cuba. And the brain trust decides maybe she can calm him down and see that he behaves. You have to admit it's not that far-fetched."

Ferdinand nodded.

"Can you explain all this without him throwing a tantrum right here?"

Mischievous brown eyes flashing, Ferdinand grinned and turned to Rico. They began a long exchange in Spanish.

Pat finished his drink and signalled to the waiter for another.

Rico gulped down the remains of his drink and also demanded another.

"When does she arrive?" Ferdinand asked Pat suddenly.

"Tomorrow morning at five after ten."

"Who will meet her?"

"I will. Unless Rico …?"

"No. He says it's better if she's brought to him."

Pat relaxed. So far, so good.

"Rico says she speaks fine English."

"Good."

"Yes. She has an education from the University of Havana. She's an elementary school teacher; she teaches English."

Curious, Pat asked, "How did she and Rico meet, do you know?"

Ferdinand asked Rico, who became voluble again. Ferdinand translated. "Her father works for the government and is a baseball fan. When the Cuban team won the World Baseball classic last year, some of the government people went to a celebration party for the players. Her dad took his family, including Alita, she met Rico, one thing led to another, and they were married in late August."

"I see."

"But her father was very upset when they married. He's a fan of baseball, but he didn't want his daughter marrying a player. Rico wants to know if her father knows she's left Cuba?"

Pat shrugged. "No idea."

"The Corporation engineered this?"

"You know how it is—money speaks. And the Diamond Corporation has money. Gobs of it."

"Why they don't tell me?" Rico said in English.

"I don't know." Pat shook his head and shrugged his shoulders. "Maybe they wanted to surprise you. Maybe the fewer people who knew, the less chance something would go wrong."

Rico and Ferdinand conversed again.

"Rico isn't happy," Ferdinand said.

"I can see that." Pat put his elbows on the table and, although he still spoke to Ferdinand, leaned forward to make sure Rico could see his lips. "Rico needs to realize this is his own fault. If he'd acted more wisely, no one would have looked for ways to control him."

Ferdinand relayed the message, but before he was finished, Rico slammed his fist on the table, making the glasses jump.

"That's exactly the kind of thing he can't do!" Pat's voice rose. "You don't think this place has about eighteen reporters in it? You don't think every move he makes isn't being observed?" Pat glared at Ferdinand, their eyes meeting. "And yours, too, you know," Pat added.

Ferdinand said evenly, "I'm okay."

Rico said something to Ferdinand. Pat caught Eva's name.

Pat sighed. "Ask him if he knows the meaning of the word 'discreet.'"

Ferdinand grinned.

Eva MacPherson was sitting in a black convertible parked in a No Parking spot in front of the Diamond Dome entrance, drumming her diamond-laden fingers on the steering wheel, when Rico came out of the Fifth Base.

"Hey, baby." Rico showed most of his teeth in a wide grin.

Eva pouted. "I thought you were never coming."

"I have to talk to people."

"Where's Ferdinand?"

"He will meet us. He has one stop to make."

She smiled up at him. "Well, hop in."

He jumped over the door into the passenger seat and leaned to kiss her. She allowed one kiss before pushing his hands away.

"No messing up the make-up," she said. "Don't forget the seatbelt." She pointed to it.

Rico always forgot the seatbelt, but he no longer argued when reminded. Pat had told him he was insured for a lot of money, but if he had an accident and wasn't wearing a seatbelt, the insurance company might not want to pay up.

Eva gunned the motor and squealed tires as she made a U-turn and headed out of the parking lot into traffic.

"Hey, you have million-dollar man here!"

"Don't worry. I'm a good driver."

He touched her thigh. "You're very good."

"You want to get there in one piece, you better keep your hands to yourself."

In a far corner of the crowded Fifth Base, far from where Pat and the two players had been seated, Ginny Lovejoy was mentally going over her column for the next day and toying with the idea of sending Rico a thank-you card for making her job so easy.

"Good, you found one. I didn't think there'd be any tables left." Kyle Schmidt collapsed into the chair across from Ginny's. "Rico took off with his blond bimbo."

Ginny placed her right elbow on the table and leaned her chin on her hand. "You didn't try to follow them?"

"Tailing Eva is like putting your head under a guillotine and asking somebody to test it to see if it works."

"She's that bad, what's Rico doing in the car with her?"

"Search me. I wish I knew what he and Pat and Ferdinand were talking about." Kyle took a sip of the Irish coffee Ginny had ordered for him and settled into the padded chair.

"Too bad we couldn't get a closer table." Ginny stirred her hot chocolate, then took a sip. She was afraid to look directly at Kyle because he might see the excitement in her eyes.

"Did you hear Stasey's show today?" Kyle asked, a smile playing with the edges of his mouth.

"You know I never listen to her if I have a choice."

Kyle allowed his smile to grow. "She was fairly nasty to poor old Pat Davis."

"I'd be willing to let her be nasty to me if I made the money Pat does." ˙

Kyle laughed. "Sure, you would."

Ginny made a face, then looked down again as she said, "Don't look back."

Kyle immediately turned, then jerked back just as quickly. But the new arrivals had noticed them. A hand closed on Kyle's right shoulder, and Stasey Simon sat down in the seat next to him.

"Order for me," Stasey commanded Ted, who walked over to the bar without a word.

"I need to get something, too," Kyle said. He left.

Stasey turned to Ginny. "You don't mind, do you? The place is packed."

Ginny pasted on a smile she hoped looked as genuine as Stasey's and shook her head.

"Got your story filed already?" Stasey asked.

Ginny immediately bristled, then told herself to relax. She had no idea if Stasey meant to be accusatory, but it seemed as though Stasey was implying she should still be hard at work instead of lounging in a bar. It irritated her that she was always on the defensive around Stasey. "I had a personal piece done earlier, and I put the game story in half an hour after the game."

"The wonders of laptops and the internet," Stasey said.

"Yeah," Ginny replied.

"Oh, come on, girl! Loosen up! In case you haven't noticed, it's you and me against a whole lot of testosterone. We have to stick together."

"Hmm." Ginny took a last sip of her hot chocolate. She wanted to say, *Female or not, I don't particularly like you,* but she held her tongue.

"You ordered anything yet?"

"Food, you mean?"

Stasey looked around. "What's Ted doing with my drink?"

"He's coming," Kyle said as he sat down again. "You have him well-trained."

Stasey raised her eyebrows. "So brave. Is that a challenge?"

"No, I was complimenting you."

Ted came up with a drink in each hand and sat beside Ginny.

"You're usually so careful about what you say," Stasey said to Kyle.

"Well, one always wants to be polite."

She snorted. "Yeah, polite goes a long way with me."

"If I'm not careful, you might say something nasty about me on your show."

"I suppose you couldn't say something nasty about me in your column?"

"I never get personal in my column."

A waiter appeared to take their orders. When the young man was gone, Stasey pulled out a cigarette.

"You can't smoke in here," Ted said quietly.

Eyes on Kyle, Stasey said, "So what did you put in tomorrow's column?"

"I reviewed the game, as usual."

"And …?"

"And what?" Kyle was frowning.

"Well, duh."

"I gave the facts. What was said. I reported the news."

"Totally without bias or prejudice?"

"I try not to judge."

"But you did throw your opinion in somewhere, right? Between the lines, if nowhere else?"

"Perhaps."

Stasey got out a lighter.

"You can't smoke in here," Ted repeated.

She looked at the cigarette. "Oh, right. I wasn't thinking. Keep forgetting we have all these ridiculous laws." She put the lighter away. "What was I saying? Oh, yes, opinions. That's really all I do. I give my opinion. If, in my opinion, somebody is a jerk, I say so. Fair and simple. If somebody disagrees with my opinion, they can always come on my show and disprove it."

"I could name you half a dozen players besides Rico who I think are jerks," Kyle said.

Stasey waved the hand holding the cigarette. "But Rico is the news right now. So—"

The waiter returned with their salads, and after Stasey had ordered a second whiskey and finally put away her cigarette, they bent to the task of eating.

They were finishing their entrees when Iain Foley appeared and, grabbing a chair from another table, pulled it up to one end. "Thought I'd stop by for a drink. If no one minds ...?"

They shook their heads, and Iain got a waiter's attention and ordered scotch and soda.

Stasey ordered her third whiskey.

"Good game today, eh? Should be an interesting home stand," Iain offered.

"Yes." Kyle stirred his coffee. "Makes it a lot easier for you people to do your job when the team's in town, huh?"

"Oh, I don't know," Iain said. "With cell phones, it's not difficult."

Kyle thought for a minute. "Yeah, I guess the days of the person having to be in the station to be interviewed are long gone. Must make it a little tougher, though. There's nothing like getting two people in the same room to get the juices flowing and sparks flying."

Stasey started to pull out a pack of cigarettes, then thrust them back into her pocket. "I think we can still create some excitement. Of course, making nice-nice with the players isn't as necessary in our job as it is in yours."

Kyle looked at her. "Meaning—?"

Stasey shrugged. "Nothing. You have to see them every day, so presumably you need to build some kind of rapport with them. I don't. I can be totally objective."

"And we can't?" There was a note of anger in Kyle's voice.

"I didn't say that. Just that it's harder for you people."

Ted intervened. "Reporters, Stasey. They're called reporters. And they do a great job."

"You know something I've never understood?" Stasey slurred the words a little. "I've never understood how two people who have so little first-hand knowledge about sports—who've probably never been on a decent team in their lives—can write about the athletes who get paid to play the game. One of you want to explain that to me?"

"No," Kyle said. "What I will explain is that I detest trying to have an intelligent conversation with someone who can't hold her alcohol." He stood up. "Coming, Ginny?"

"Yeah, I guess." Ginny gulped down the last of her wine and grabbing her purse from under the seat, threw some money on the table. "See you again, Stasey, Iain. Bye, Ted."

She ran after Kyle, who was talking to the waiter and pulling out his charge card.

Showing no sign of missing the two people who had just left, Iain said, "So now it's just us, Stasey,"

She pointed across the table to her producer. "You forget. Ted is still here."

"I'm sure you could get rid of him with a single word."

She tilted her head back. "But I don't want to get rid of him."

"I think you need to have an early night tonight. Usually your insults are a lot more interesting than that."

Ted spoke. "It's about time we left, Stasey. Unless you want to order some coffee?"

Iain laughed. "You need a nursemaid more than you do a producer, Stasey."

"Know what makes you different from those two?" Stasey took another long drink. "Because they never had dreams about being athletes themselves, they can be objective. You ex-jocks are all alike. You weren't good enough back then, but you've convinced yourself that if you'd just had this break or that, it would have been you making all that money and having all those fans. It still gets you, doesn't it?"

Iain's jaw was clenched as he placed some money on the table and stood. "As Kyle so eloquently implied, 'I have better things to do.' Good night, Stasey. Ted, if you ever want a job where you don't have to moonlight as your boss's keeper, let me know." Head up, he walked away.

When they were alone, Ted crossed his arms in front of his chest. "Stasey, you really shouldn't drink so much."

"I didn't drink much."

"In your case, one drink might be too much."

Some miles from the Diamond Dome, in the Blue Mandrake Club, with its dimly lit crystal candelabra, smoldering floor show, and well-stocked bar, Rico Velasquez had forgotten his frustrations. With the beautiful Eva on one side and his good friend Ferdinand on the other, he felt invincible. Never had he felt this way in Cuba. Never had he known such freedom.

As for the money to spend on what he chose—in Cuba he was lucky to get a decent meal each day: here he could have anything he wanted, any time he wanted. He'd already developed a taste for the finest caviar and tender steak, and since Eva had introduced him to Marilyn Monroe's favorite drink, Dom Perignon champagne, when they were together, they drank it exclusively.

Ferdinand Ortes was laughing, his arm around the waist of a dark-haired beauty in a creamy gauze gown that showed off a sizable amount of well-tanned flesh. The girl, a bank clerk named Taffy, had voiced her availability as he was leaving the Diamond Dome after a game a few weeks earlier. Now, she was running her fingers up and down his chest and kissing his hand.

Eva was clinging to Rico and giggling about something—he had no idea what. He laughed aloud. Cuba seemed like a dream—no, a nightmare—from a distant past. His family, the baseball team he'd played on, even Alita. He shook his head. He'd been reborn when he arrived in Canada. Nothing and no one would ever make him go back to Cuba.

"I think it's time we moved on," Ferdinand said.

Rico reached for Eva, who melted into his shoulder.

"We'll take a cab," Ferdinand said. "Have someone pick up the cars in the morning."

Rico nodded. Eva was a bad enough driver sober. No way he was driving with her now.

Rico's eyes teared up. Ferdinand took care of him so well. Never before had he had such a friend.

Far away, on a small beach in south-western Florida, a very tired young woman with dark eyes and hair and nutmeg-colored skin removed the heavy gray blanket that had been wrapped around her and clasped the hand of the man who had just lifted her out of the small fishing boat. Oh, to be on land again!

"You're a wonderful person," she said to him in Spanish.

"My pleasure." The man in the black turtleneck sweater, long, black oilskin coat, and broad-brimmed black hat, who she knew only as Zandor, spoke fluent Spanish. He smiled, then kissed her hand. "For the wife of Rico Velasquez—" his hand swept through an arc that seemed to relegate the frightening trip to a mere afternoon outing "—nothing is too much trouble: not ocean waters, not storms, not anything."

She let him kiss her hand, but quickly pulled it back. Her biggest fear was that he would want more than a kiss, and if so, how could she, a defenseless woman in a strange land, stop him?

The fishing boat was pulling away, headed for home.

"How far do they have to go?" she asked.

"Their home is about three hours from here." Zandor motioned for Alita to go first up a worn dirt path. "The cottage is right up this path. Let's get you at least a few hours' rest."

She started up the path, wanting to get away from the water, which she hated, and eager to know, good or bad, what lay before her. When Rico had suddenly left Cuba, she'd been terrified she'd never see him again. Even though he'd written to say he was fine and doing well in Canada—with all the money he could want—she'd never quite believed it. Only when she saw him with her own eyes would she know all was truly well.

So now—if this was a trick to get her in the clutches of white slavers, well, the sooner she knew, the better. It was the apprehension that hurt the most. She went straight to the small, unpainted cottage and tried to open the door. It was locked.

"Maybe we should knock," the man behind her suggested.

She stepped back. *What was I thinking to come with this man?*

Zandor knocked loudly on the wooden door. In a few moments, it opened a crack. Slowly, it opened further.

"It is you!" said a thin, grey-haired woman, who flung the door wide open.

Alita was surprised that, like Zandor, the woman spoke Spanish.

"You were supposed to arrive yesterday! I'd almost given up. What happened?"

Zandor shook his head. "We had wind and waves that nearly swept us over many times. The lady was seasick much of the journey.

I felt a little queasy myself. And we had to stay clear of the coast guard, who seemed to be everywhere."

The lady shivered. "Glad I wasn't with you." She stepped back. "Well, come in. No need for you to hover on the doorstep."

"I have to make a call," Zandor said.

"Go ahead." She nodded to the room on their right, which had a few chairs, a television, and a couple of tables.

A sitting room, thought Alita. *A room that serves no function except to sit in and talk or watch television.* Her home had been far too crowded to have the luxury of a room that was not in constant use.

Zandor punched numbers on his cell phone. Alita wondered if he'd memorized the number so that if they were caught, he wouldn't have it on him. Someone must have answered, because he spoke, this time in English. "The package is here. All is well."

There was a pause while he listened. Then, "Right." Another pause. He said, "Yes," and hung up.

"All right," he said to the grey-haired woman, still speaking English. "I'll retrieve my belongings and be on my way."

The woman nodded, then went over to a small stand in the corner of the room and felt underneath it. When she rose, there was a key in her hand, which she held out to Zandor.

Alita studied him as he took the key. With his dark hair, light skin, piercing, intelligent blue eyes, aristocratic nose and jaw, and the smile that trembled on the edges of his firm lips, he was a man who would no doubt be able to attract all the attention and women he would wish for. Not that she felt any attraction toward him. She was a happily married woman.

"Thanks," he said as he took the key. With a nod of satisfaction, he headed for the door. But once there, he paused, turning back toward Alita. In Spanish, he said, "If you ever need me in the future, I will come." At her look of astonishment, he kissed the tips of his fingers, gestured toward her, and said, "Have a good life, Dear One."

Then Alita was standing alone in the hallway with the grey-haired woman, her last link to Cuba gone. She shivered.

"Don't worry," the woman said in Spanish. "You've nothing to fear. Everything's in order."

Alita pulled herself together, willing her voice to sound friendly and not terrified. In English, she said, "Thank you."

"I bought a few things for you. Wasn't sure what you'd want or how they'll fit, but they'll have to do until you get to Toronto. Now, you need to drink a cup of my chicken broth and then get some sleep. You must be exhausted. I'll wake you up in a few hours and give you the new clothes. Then we'll get you on that airplane." She led Alita to a room at the back of the house. It had a single bed, a dresser, and a night stand with a small lamp. Again, Alita marveled. A room only for sleeping. How extravagant.

After drinking the broth, Alita removed the clothes she'd worn for the past three days and put on the long pink nightgown she found lying on the bed. She went to the small bathroom the woman had pointed out and took great care brushing her hair and washing her face. She looked longingly at the bathtub but was reluctant to put herself in such a vulnerable position in this strange house. Perhaps in the morning.

She slept fitfully, awakening every few hours to the roll of the boat on the waves and the face of the man who had guided them all to safety, only to realize that both boat and man were gone and she was alone in an unknown world.

FOUR

Somewhere in the Muskokas, in a log cabin nestled beside a blue-green lake and sheltered by a grove of evergreens, wonderfully alone, Kyle Schmidt sat at an oak desk working on his masterpiece. No neighbors. No cares. Just his computer, a shelf of favorite books, a thesaurus, and a comforting log fire. Above all, no harsh, demanding phone. Like the one ringing in his ear.

Kyle pulled his pillow over his head.

The phone rang four more times.

Kyle's mind cleared. He was in his bachelor apartment in the middle of downtown Toronto. And someone wanted to talk to him. Someone who wasn't about to give up. Likely Ginny.

Sighing, he reached for his phone. "Yeah?"

"Have you seen Ginny's article? Did you know about this?"

Not Ginny's voice. A woman, though. Angry with Ginny. "Stasey, is that you?"

"The world is moving on, Kyle. Are you still in bed?"

"Everyone knows I'm not a morning person."

"Well, let me be the first to tell you then. Your little friend Ginny Lovejoy just scooped the pants off you."

Kyle sat up on his elbow. "What are you talking about?"

"I quote. 'Ever been all alone in a strange country where you understand only a few of the words, where there are puzzling new customs and traditions to learn, where you have to rely on other people for vital information, and, oh yes, where your struggles to adjust are put on view every single day before millions of people who feel they not only have the right to know every move you make, but to give their opinion of it?

"'I've just described the life of Ricardo Velasquez since he left Cuba a little over four months ago.

"'It's easy for onlookers, secure in their own country and their own opinions, to criticize Rico. But perhaps it would be more logical to get behind this young man—Rico is only twenty-five-years old, remember—and give him the support he needs.

"'That seems to be the decision the Matrix management has come to. This very morning a plane is winging its way to Toronto from Florida. On that airplane is a young woman named Alita Velasquez. We'll likely never know how this young woman, like Rico, was smuggled out of Cuba. But she was. And she's on her way here right now to throw her support behind her husband.

"'Rico and Alita had just over six short months together before Rico took his one chance to follow his dream and left his young bride behind, not knowing when they would be together again.

"'The reunion between these newlyweds is today. I want to be the first to congratulate Rico and Alita on their new life here in Canada, and to applaud whoever made this possible. We know Rico's teammates must be delighted for him.

"'When the Matrix talk about the team being family and baseball being a family game, they aren't just whistling in the dark or trying out a new slogan of the month. Today, they've sent a message the fans simply can't ignore. I for one hope there's a full house tonight to welcome Alita Velasquez to our country, and to show Rico that we're all behind him as he and his bride begin their new life together in our wonderful, free country.'"

There was a long silence. At last, Kyle said, "Ginny never said anything to me."

"Of course not. You assume that because she's young and she always smiles and says nice things, she's harmless. So you jolly her along and let her think how lucky she is to have a real reporter as her mentor. You even thought she was your friend. But what's friendship compared to a genuine scoop?"

"Do you know if it's true?"

"I just called Tony's office. His secretary finally condescended to tell me there was 'some validity to the article.'"

Kyle had long believed that people who sprinkle their speech with swear words are uneducated slobs with limited vocabularies. Right now, however, he was feeling perhaps his own vocabulary was more limited than he'd thought. All he could think of were those swear words.

"Have you tried calling Ginny?" he asked.

"She's supposed to be your friend, not mine."

"I'll give her a call then. Thanks for the heads-up."

Kyle cut the connection and lay on his back staring at the ceiling, his mind actively working on a new resignation letter. After several minutes, he groaned, then hoisted himself to a sitting position on the edge of the bed. When he felt sufficiently awake, he dialed Ginny's number. But all he heard was Ginny's happy voice saying, "I'm so sorry, but I can't get to the phone just now. Please leave a message with your name and number and I'll call back as soon as I can."

It was twelve-thirty when the limo carrying Pat Davis, Alita Velasquez, and Tony Kanberra arrived at the Diamond Hotel, where Rico had a room for the duration of the season.

The meeting at the airport had gone well enough. Because of Ginny's article, Tony paid a limousine driver to hold up a sign saying "Alita Velasquez" at the gate where the crowds congregated. That attracted any press or media people.

Meanwhile, airport staff brought Alita to a private entrance used by government officials and media stars where a second limousine driver was waiting. That driver had Tony's business card, on which was written the word, "Secure," the code word Zandor had given her so she would know which person to trust.

Pat and Tony, waiting nervously in the limo, relaxed when they saw the young woman with light brown skin and black hair walking next to their driver. "Good morning," she said with only a small accent as the driver helped her inside. She settled on the seat across from Pat and arranged the folds of her long cotton skirt and her light shawl.

"I'm Pat Davis, Rico's agent. This is Tony Kanberra, the general manager of the Matrix."

They shook hands.

"I hope your flight went well," Tony said. A tall, rather stout older man with grizzled salt-and-pepper hair, Tony had a permanent tan from frequent visits to the family home in Florida where his wife lived year-round.

"Very well. It was not frightening at all. I much prefer air to water."

Tony nodded and said, "Yes, me too."

"You are taking me to Rico?"

Both men nodded.

"Where does he live?"

Pat answered, "The Diamond Hotel."

Alita's eyes widened. "He lives in a hotel? Is that not very expensive?"

"There are always players who prefer to live in a hotel," Tony said. "They have a home someplace else, usually, and just want a place to hang up their hat when they're in Toronto."

"But it must cost a lot of money. And I don't think I should like to live in a hotel."

"It's a guy thing," Tony said.

Clearly puzzled, she repeated, "A 'guy thing'?"

Pat said, "Something a man would do, but a woman usually wouldn't."

She continued to look confused. "Then where will I go?"

"You can stay with Rico for now," Pat said. "We'll look for an apartment you can sublet." He spent the next few minutes explaining how one would sublet an apartment, assuring her that what she wanted (a kitchen with a stove and a refrigerator, a bathroom, a room to sleep with a place to hang up your clothing, and at least one window that gave good light) was easy to get.

"I'm afraid I'll have to get some other clothing, too," she said. "I have only what I am wearing and the clothes I had on when we left Cuba. I believe I'll freeze in Canada, no?"

Pat smiled. "Not in July. It gets pretty hot here in July." Then he realized he hadn't answered her real concern. "I'm sure one of the players' wives will take you shopping."

Alita hesitated before asking, "Would—do you not have a wife, Mr. Davis?"

"Yes. Yes, I do. But she's—well, the truth is she's expecting a baby in a few weeks, so she isn't up to doing too much running around."

"Oh, that is so nice." Alita smiled. "You will forgive me? I had not thought you to have such a young family."

"This is my second wife—second family. My other family—my kids—are in their twenties. My current wife is only thirty-one, so in a way it's like starting all over again. I just hope I can keep up with this new kid as he gets older."

Alita smiled. "I too would like to have a family," she said, her cheeks reddening slightly.

Tony, who had been happy to let his wife raise their children and rarely saw them now that they were grown, said, "Yeah, it's good to have kids. Be a family."

Pat tried to picture Rico with a baby on his knee. It wasn't an easy image to capture. Easier to see Rico with a bat in his hand, swinging it at the water cooler as he had done a few days ago after one of his teammate made a costly error. Pat felt his stomach sink. They'd brought Alita here in the hope that, as his wife, she might be able to control Rico. But what if she couldn't? What if they were just opening her up for a lot of heartache?

They reached the hotel before Pat was able to convince himself everything would be okay.

"This is where Rico lives?" Alita stood on the sidewalk staring up at the Diamond Hotel. Like the Diamond Dome next door, the hotel was ablaze in the summer sunshine. "I've never seen such a thing. To live here, it must cost a great deal of money."

"Quite a bit," Tony said. "But he's got a lot."

She shook her head. "He must not spend it all! He must send some home to his family. He must save some. He must—"

"Why don't we go in and you can tell him all that?" Tony took her arm and propelled her inside.

Alita's eyes grew huge as she took in the high gold ceilings, thick burgundy carpets, gold papered walls, black leather sofas, and mahogany tables with fresh bouquets of red and yellow flowers in gold vases. "*Magnifico!* I cannot believe Rico lives here."

Tony smiled again. "You'll be able to talk it over with him in a few minutes."

She smoothed her hair and squared her shoulders.

Carrying the small bag that held all of Alita's possessions, Pat led the way to the elevator and down the hallway that led to Rico's door. He knocked on the door. No response. He checked his watch, then knocked again, louder this time. No answer.

Alita looked at each of the two men. "He is not here?"

"It kind of looks that way," Tony admitted.

"He knows I'm coming?"

Pat bit his lower lip. "He told me to bring you here."

Tony and Pat looked at each other. After a moment, Pat said, "You know, it's lunch time. Maybe Rico went for lunch."

Tony quickly picked up on the thought. "We can check the restaurant. Maybe get something ourselves." He turned to Alita. "You must be hungry, too."

She nodded slowly. "Yes, I'm perhaps a little hungry. But I don't understand. Did Rico not know when I was coming?"

Pat said, "He may have just stepped out for a minute. I'm sure he'll be right back. We can wait in the restaurant."

She held back. "I have no money to eat in such a place."

"Not to worry," Tony stepped in. "It's on the team."

"If you think it's wise—"

"Absolutely!" Tony led the way back to the elevator.

Once they were seated in the hotel restaurant, Alita insisted that all she wanted was a glass of water, but Pat and Tony assured her she could have anything she wanted, and at last she ordered a chicken sandwich.

"I'll be right back." Pat threw a meaningful look at Tony before he strolled out of the room. Once around the corner, he pulled out his cell phone and dialed Rico's room. No answer. He dialed Ferdinand's number. When Ferdinand answered, he said, "Where's Rico? ... What do you mean, he's there? I'm at the hotel with his wife! ... Well, get him over here fast. Is that Eva's voice I hear? ... Why would you let him do something that stupid? ... Never mind, just get him here in a hurry. And lose Eva!"

Forty minutes later, as Alita, Pat, and Tony were finishing the strawberry shortcake Tony had ordered for dessert, Rico walked in.

"Rico!" Alita shouted. She jumped up from her chair to run to him, saying in Spanish, "I was so afraid. I've come so far, and it was so frightening! We almost drowned! I can't believe it's really you at last!" Throwing herself into his arms, she burst into tears.

He held her for a moment, then gave her a quick kiss. "You have no worries now. I'm a very important man here."

Pulling back, she looked up at him. "They say you live in this building—in this hotel?"

"Soon I'll buy a house—a gigantic house."

Pat Davis stood and prepared to leave. "You'll be fine now." He smiled at Alita. "Rico will take care of you."

"Yes," she replied in English as she wiped away her tears with her hands. "Thank you for helping me, and for the lunch. It was so beautiful." She gave him a quick hug.

Tony, who had been busy paying the bill, shook her hand, and the two men left.

Rico told Alita to follow him up to his room. As she picked up her bag, he said, "You'll have a lot to learn. It's very different here. I'm a very big man. You'll have to get used to that."

Stasey Simon's sultry voice said, "Blake, it's so nice to have you on the show today."

Lawrence Smith grinned. He could feel the tension right over the air waves. Stasey was setting Blake Harrison up. Would the manager of the Matrix be able to handle it, or would he lose his temper? Stasey's show was like a chess game, and most of the time Stasey won. But there was always a risk. Lawrence loved that risk.

The Matrix manager sounded composed and ready for combat. "Thanks, Stasey. Great to be here."

"Fantastic game yesterday—just one hit and a few walks from perfection. That has to make you feel good."

"Very good." Blake sounded cheerful. "But in baseball, we don't get much chance to rest on our laurels. We have another game tonight, so we have to be thinking ahead, figuring out how to win that one, too."

"You never get a break, huh?"

"A lot like you guys. We always have to have something left over for the next day."

"Good point, Blake."

"I think this year has been a particularly good one, Stasey. Both offensively and defensively, there are a lot of positives."

"Yet the story too often seems to focus on the negatives, doesn't it, Blake?"

"Depends on who's doing the talking. I prefer to look at the positives myself."

Stasey's voice was smooth as silk. "So you don't consider the problems you've been having with Rico as important?"

"What problems?" Before she had a chance to enumerate them, Blake went on, "We have no serious problems. Nothing I would really even call a problem. Rico likes to vent his feelings, but that's all it is. Once he gets the steam out of his system, he's fine."

"So the story in the paper this morning is wrong? You guys aren't bringing over Rico's wife?" Stasey sounded eager and interested.

Blake coughed. "No, that's true. His wife is here. But they're newlyweds, for crying out loud. It's not as if he planned to leave her in Cuba forever."

"So her coming here has nothing to do with Rico's behavior?"

"Rico's a great pitcher. He's intense. He hates losing. If you did a study of the really great pitchers, you'd discover many of them were very much like Rico."

"So when he throws a hissy fit, you all just grin and say, 'There goes Rico being intense again?'"

Blake laughed nervously. "Well, I doubt if I'd say those exact words. I know for sure I wouldn't say anyone had a hissy fit."

"What would you call it then?" Stasey continued. "A temper tantrum? An out-of-control episode? A man gone berserk? A—"

"I'd call it a frustrated player."

"His threatening some of his teammates doesn't bother you?"

"Threatening, as in… ?"

"Little things like, 'I'll get you for that' and 'I'll kill you'."

"Rico's English isn't very good yet. I'm sure he didn't mean—"

"Doesn't exactly go with the one big happy family line you guys have been spewing since spring training, now does it?"

"I—"

"Sorry folks, we have to go to commercial. Back in a jiff with your calls."

Lawrence had been sitting transfixed by the conversation. Now he hurried to the phone and dialed the station number.

"Lawrence, is that you?"

"It's me, Ted."

"I'm sorry, Lawrence. We have a new rule on the show. So as to get more callers—more new callers, that is—we have to limit people to one call-in per week."

"I can't talk to Stasey?"

"Not today, Lawrence."

"When?"

"Next week. You can call in and talk to Stasey any day next week. But you just get to talk to her one time next week. Understand?"

Lawrence repeated the words slowly. "'One time next week.' But how will I—? It's easier to call when I have a question."

"Yeah, buddy, I know. But we need to get more callers—different people, you know?"

"Okay, Ted. Can I call when Iain's there? Or Frankie?"

"Sure, Ted. Those are different shows. They have their own rules. Gotta go now buddy, okay?"

"Okay, Ted." Lawrence hung up the receiver and sat staring at the telephone. It had been so nice to call up Stasey whenever he wanted. Of course, he didn't always get through. But still—that was part of the fun, part of the challenge. Now he couldn't even try. Once a week, and he had already used up his once for this week.

Lawrence sat on his rocking chair glumly resting his chin on his hands. If there was only a way to make the station's program manager change his mind.

Or—what if this was Stasey's idea? What if the new rule was because she didn't want to talk to him?

"Don't waste your breath asking me to come on your show again," Blake said to Stasey as the news came on. "I'm sick of the way you do things, going for the throat every time."

Stasey shrugged as she lit a cigarette. "Just giving my fans what they want."

"One of our pitchers has a one-hitter and ties the American league strike-out record, and what do you focus on? Rumors and innuendo about a different pitcher! That's ridiculous!"

"We talked about the good stuff. But my listeners want to explore everything. They don't want the garbage swept under the rug, and neither do I."

"Well, in the future, you can find some other sucker to manipulate. It won't be me." He threw the headphones onto the table and got to his feet.

"The Diamond Corporation likes the publicity of having their people on my show."

"Then let the members of the Corporation come on."

"Speaking of which, I'd love to have them." She looked at him speculatively. "But no one ever gets back to me except some lawyer's assistant. Do you know who the actual people who own the Diamond Corporation are? Have you met any of them?"

"Haven't you?"

"No." She blew out the smoke, watching it hit his face.

He didn't react. "Good luck getting them on the show."

"You don't know any more about them than I do, do you?"

"They sign my pay check. That's all I need to know." Blake walked out.

Stasey checked her coffee cup. "Beastie, if you're listening, I need more coffee."

Ted walked in a moment later with a fresh cup.

"You heard," she said without looking at him.

"Yeah."

She put her cigarette out in the old cup. "They all come back."

"Not quite all."

"There are always more fish in the sea."

Ted pursed his lips. "But sometimes you have to throw the small ones back."

She took a sip of coffee before answering. "Blake isn't a small one."

"Well, when you catch the big ones, if you mount them up on a wall, you don't get to catch them again."

"You're nuts," she said. "Stark raving—"

"You're back on air."

Stasey was saying her farewell bit when Iain Foley walked into the studio, a sheaf of notes in his right hand. "Heard your interview with

Blake," he said when she was finished. "Though calling it an interview is perhaps giving it a reputation it doesn't deserve."

"You know, Iain—" she took a drag from a new cigarette "—I've heard jealousy's a form of envy, so I don't mind."

"Stasey, trust me, I don't feel envy. I think your program is on a par with the WWF. Not my style at all."

"No, you want everybody who goes on your show to become your friend." She placed her right hand on her heart. "And you can tell the world how important you are because of who your friends are."

Iain spoke patiently, as if to a child. "Maybe I think being a friend to people will get you better results in the long run. They'll be lining up to come on my show when your producer's given up trying to find anyone crazy enough to appear on yours."

"Fat chance!"

"Iain, we have a show starting in three minutes," said the calm voice of Iain's producer.

Stasey rose so Iain could take her place, but she took her time picking up her purse.

"Don't forget your cigarette butts this time," Iain said. "You know, one of these days I'm going to report you. Smoking isn't allowed in offices in Toronto, and you know that as well as I do."

Stasey picked up her saucer. "Have a nice gentle family show," she said as she walked out.

When Kyle Schmidt entered the press box an hour before the game, he sat at the back instead of going up front to his usual spot beside Ginny.

Since the call from Stasey that morning, he'd been thinking about how much he and Ginny did together. Although their newspapers were competitors, and they could easily have become antagonists when Ginny began working the sports beat for the *Daily News*, she was so ingenuous and so bubbling over with enthusiasm that it was hard to think of her as a rival—especially since she seemed to look up to Kyle, who'd been doing his column for a couple of years and knew the ropes well enough to help her clear a few hurdles.

They discussed the teams, shared insights they weren't using in their columns, occasionally took notes for each other, and basically formed a small unit within the context of the larger media group surrounding the Toronto sports teams. They'd even taken to attending some functions together, not with any romantic intentions, but simply because neither was into the dating scene, and it was convenient to have a partner without expectations. If you'd asked Ginny what she thought of Kyle, he assumed she'd have said he was like a big brother. And Kyle, an only child, would have said Ginny was the kid sister he'd never had.

But now Kyle was wondering if perhaps he was the naive one. Maybe Stasey was right, and some of Ginny's open-faced sweetness was too good to be true. It wasn't only her scoop this morning. He'd been reading her columns lately and comparing them to his own, and the feeling had been growing on him that she had a lot more depth than he'd realized.

And now Ginny's scoop on Alita—more importantly, the stealth with which she'd kept it from Kyle—had him wondering if she might have a tiny bit of Stasey's unscrupulousness. His editor had asked him why he didn't know about Rico's wife. He'd had no answer. Had no idea how Ginny had come by the information.

From his seat at the back of the press box, he could see her tapping away on her keyboard. People called out greetings and she answered them all cheerfully. When they complimented her on her big story, she laughed and said she'd had a lucky break. No indication she thought she was anything special; no implication she was better than them. Yet it still seemed to Kyle as if she'd said, "I'll be your friend if it's convenient for me, but I'll show you up if I get the chance."

It occurred to him that perhaps, in a small way, he now understood how Armando Santana must feel about Rico.

He saw Ginny stand up, and the next thing he knew she was beside him.

"What's up?" she asked, concern in her eyes. "Why are you sitting way back here? You aren't getting the bug are you?" A nasty flu had been roaming the city for the past month.

"No, I'm fine." He wished she'd just leave him alone. He didn't want to have to explain his feelings to her. Not now, anyway.

"So what's up?"

When he didn't respond, she sat down. "You're mad, aren't you? About my column."

"I'm not mad."

"I was afraid you'd be ticked off. But I've never had a big scoop like that before, and I wanted to see if I could do it—you know, keep it to myself, actually get it all the way to the paper without spilling the beans. I nearly told you about—oh, about six times. But I knew you'd tell me that was dumb—I mean, we're friends, but we still have to do our jobs the best we can, right? You told me that. I mean, if it had been you, you wouldn't have told me, would you?"

In his heart he knew she was right. He wouldn't have told her. But that was because he was the pro—the experienced journalist. He was expected to get the scoops. She was his apprentice. Oh, what was he saying? She was every bit as good as he was, if not better, and he had no right to be standoffish or make her feel bad. There was nothing personal in it.

It was Stasey's fault. If she hadn't phoned him—if he'd just read the story over breakfast— But Stasey had caught him off-guard and made him feel cheated somehow.

He stood up. "You're right. I'd have laughed all the way to the editor's desk. You done good, kid!"

Together, they moved up front and he sat next to her in his usual spot. He ignored the niggling thought in the back of his mind that said, "So, how are you going to come up with a story to top hers?"

By seven-thirty that evening, Alita Velasquez was sitting behind the Matrix dugout in a section reserved for the families and friends of players. Wedged between two women she didn't know, in the midst of more women and a few men and lots of children, surrounded by an entire stadium filled with strangers, she felt lost and alone. Out on the field in front of her was her husband, the only person in this whole country she did know. But a few hours with him had convinced her he was not the man she had married. Oh, he was Rico, no denying that. But could the shy, hopeful man she'd known in Cuba have become this belligerent, self-centered bully? Her father's words floated through her mind. "He doesn't love you, Alita. He's after what he thinks you can give him. You'll see."

She sat like a stone, seeing nothing of the game being played on the field before her, hearing none of the comments from the people in her section. After a long time, she bit her bottom lip to keep herself from bursting into tears, clenched her hands into fists to keep from screaming, and concentrated on taking one breath, then another. What was she going to do? She'd left her country, her family, her job, everything she knew, for a man she barely recognized. What a fool she'd been! Every breath hurt, as though someone was sitting on her chest forcing all the air out and not allowing more to come in. "*O Dios, !ayudame!*" she whispered. "*Por favor.*"

"What did you say?" the women next to her asked. "Did you have a question?"

Alita shook her head.

"The restroom is right at the top of the stairs, across the foyer. There's a sign."

"Thank you." Alita had no need for a room to rest in, but perhaps getting up and moving would help. She had to pass three players' wives and several children to get out of the row. The woman at the end asked if she needed help. Alita forced her lips into what she hoped looked like a smile and shook her head. Inside she was screaming, *Help me! Please, help me!*

She grabbed the railing and forced herself to move up the stairs, one step, then another, her feet like lead weights. Everything was happening in slow motion. Her breath came in ragged gasps.

As she reached the top of the stairs, a big man in a blue shirt moved toward her, but although she saw his lips move, she heard no words.

He reached out to her, but she pushed him away and staggered through a short hallway and into a large walkway. She looked around. Signs screamed at her, and people walked in every direction. She had no idea where to go. She turned and stumbled forward just as strong arms enveloped her from behind. Terrified, she wondered if the man in blue was a policeman and if he would arrest her. She craned her neck to see if it was him holding her.

"I told you I'd be around if you needed me," Zandor said in Spanish as she fainted into his arms.

FIVE

Lawrence Smith sat high in the rafters, his hands resting on his knees, elbows stuck out to the sides as he leaned forward, mouth open, eyes glued to binoculars that helped him see the game below. The headphones of his well-used Walkman connected him to the official radio voices of the Toronto Matrix, and he listened intently to the play-by-play description of the game.

It was the eighth inning, Rico had a two-hitter going, and the Matrix was leading 3 to 1. But a walk, a stolen base, an infield hit, and an error by the third baseman meant that the bases were loaded with nobody out. And Blake Harrison had just signalled for Armando Santana to come in from the bullpen. But Rico was talking rapidly to Blake, no doubt in Spanish, refusing to give up the ball, and gesturing to the third baseman as if to say this was his fault. Then he pointed to Jonas Newland and shouted at him.

Lawrence jumped to his feet and yelled, "Rico, don't be so stupid!" Then he sat down quickly, hoping no one had heard him.

Ferdinand Ortes came in from his position between second and third bases and put his arm around Rico. Lawrence sighed in relief. Rico gave the ball to Ferdinand, who passed it to Blake. As Rico walked away, Blake handed the ball to Armando Santana, who'd been waiting a few feet behind the pitcher's mound, looking as if he'd rather be anywhere else.

The crowd gasped, and Lawrence swung his binoculars so he could see the dugout, where Rico was kicking the water-cooler. The other players were moving out of his way. Then Rico picked up several things and started throwing them on the field. A jacket, several batting helmets ....

Lawrence saw one of the coaches—he thought Muddy Ames—go over to Rico. After a few minutes, they sat down in the dugout.

With a sigh of relief, Lawrence also sat down and relaxed his body for a moment before resuming his vigilant posture.

Oakland's designated hitter was up to bat with the bases loaded and nobody out.

Armando Santana threw a pitch the radio commentators said was a slider. Strike one. Then a curve ball the ump said was inside. Ball one.

In the dugout, Rico was standing up again, and shouting.

Armando threw another ball.

Rico was still shouting.

Armando threw a fastball and the crack of bat against ball was heard throughout the stadium. No one had any doubt about where that pitch was going.

Lawrence had shut his eyes in pain the moment the ball was hit. Slowly, he opened them and stood up to get a better look at the home team's dugout. Yes, he could just see Rico. But what was he doing? Oh, no! Two of the coaches and several players were restraining him.

Lawrence removed the earphones and sank back in his seat, wishing he had a magic wand so he could make all the bad things go away.

Armando Santana stood on the pitcher's mound, shoulders slumped in defeat, waiting for Blake Harrison to come out.

Jonas walked to the mound. He had his mask off and was rubbing the back of his neck. "Tough break."

Without looking at Jonas, Armando said, "Lousy pitch." He kicked at the dirt. "It got away from me."

Rico's voice called out something in Spanish.

Armando clenched his teeth.

"What's he yelling?" Jonas asked.

"He's insulting me again. Saying I'm no good."

Blake Harrison walked out slowly. A new pitcher was on his way in. Without a word to Armando or Jonas, Blake took the ball from Armando, who walked hesitantly toward the dugout.

His arms were restrained, but Rico continued to yell at Armando in Spanish. "Why do they keep you on the team? You must have a hold on them somehow. You're old and useless. You need a cane to lean on."

Armando gritted his teeth.

The taunts continued as Armando stepped inside the dugout. "Just an old man who doesn't have the heart to argue. An old man who has no stomach for—"

Armando swung around, took three quick strides, and landed a solid right on Rico's chin, sending Rico and several other people sprawling onto the dugout benches and floor.

"That's enough!" Blake Harrison's voice snapped like a whip. "Armando, get into the clubhouse and cool off. We don't need this kind of thing." Turning to Rico, he said, "We need a trainer to look at that bruise."

Rico slowly got to his feet, helped by a couple of teammates who were trying to keep from showing any expression.

Armando, jaw clenched, glared at Rico before nodding toward Blake and walking into the clubhouse.

"Did you see?" Rico asked Blake. "He hit me!"

"I saw it."

"He is—"

"Stow it!"

Rico may not have understood the phrase, but he understood the tone. He backed away and stood at the end of the dugout, leaning on the wall. A trainer rushed over to check him.

On the field, the new relief pitcher cut down the next two batters with six solid strikes.

The team headed toward the dugout.

Jonas Newland walked directly to Blake. "What happened?"

Blake shrugged.

"Did Armando hit him?"

Blake nodded. "He's gone. Soon as I talk to Tony. Could be an outright release if nobody else wants him."

"That's not fair, Blake."

"He's lost it, Jonas."

"But Rico was—"

"Rico wasn't out there on the mound with him."

"He was yelling insults the whole time Armando was trying to pitch. What does that do for your concentration?"

"We're still in a game, Jonas. Maybe you should concentrate on that." Blake walked away.

The game ended without either team managing to score again, and Ginny joined the other reporters scrambling for the elevators and crowding into the home team's locker room.

The group around Rico was huge. Another group focused on Blake Harrison.

Ginny looked for Armando, but there was no sign of him. She wandered over to Jonas, who was sitting on a chair untying his shoes. "Where's Armando?"

Jonas looked up and his frown faded. "No idea."

"He in trouble?"

"I think you could say that." Jonas went back to his shoelaces.

"Interesting game," Ginny said.

"Very."

"How are you feeling?"

"On or off the record?"

"On, first."

He grimaced. "It's important we stay focused on beating the other teams and not on navel-gazing."

"And off?"

"Like a farmhouse doormat."

"Bringing Rico's wife here doesn't seem to have helped yet."

"Speaking of which, nice column today."

"I thought you guys didn't look at the papers."

"I read your column. That's about it, unless someone tells me about something I might be interested in seeing."

"Well, thanks. I'll take that as a compliment."

"That's how it was meant."

A loud voice interrupted their tête-à-tête. "So Jonas, baby, what's the good word today?" A reporter from a small out-of-town rag had come up. Walking away from Jonas, Ginny looked toward Rico. Still a crowd. She sighed. Her editor would expect her to be in the middle of it, getting all the dirt she could. She spotted Ferdinand standing at his locker, naked except for a towel around the middle. She wandered over. Ferdinand was always approachable and affable, and everyone liked him; yet there was something about him—she couldn't put a finger on it—that puzzled her. "Nice play in the third," she said. "I didn't think you'd get to the ball, never mind throw him out."

He chuckled. "Just doing my job."

"Doing a heck of a job."

His grin increased.

"So what do you honestly think of the team's chances this year?" she asked.

He shrugged. "I think we look good. Should be right in there until the end."

"What do you think needs to be done to improve the team?"

"Maybe one or two minor changes. Nothing more."

"Do you think having his wife around will help calm Rico down?"

He grinned as a photographer's camera flashed. "Don't know. I've never been married. Never wanted someone to calm me down, either." Grinning, he added in an undertone, "Unless maybe you'd like to give it a shot?"

"I've never felt the need to be a calming influence."

"Touché." He was still grinning.

"Better luck in tomorrow's game," Ginny said before moving away.

The crowd around Rico had thinned, but there were still a few people asking him questions. Someone asked about his pitching arm.

"My arm is good. *Magnifico.* I will pitch ver' well Monday. Ver' well. The other team, they will have no chance."

"What'll you do if Armando pitches in relief for you again?"

"Monday, I will need no relief. Maybe I'll pitch a no-hitter."

"I'd like to see that," Ginny said aloud.

Rico turned to her. "You will see eet. If not Monday, then soon." He pounded his chest with his fists. "In Cuba, I have no-hitters. Here, I will, too."

"We'll look forward to it, Rico," she said absently, her mind already picturing the headline and first paragraph of her next column. "Thanks for the tip."

Her mind in overdrive, she headed up to the press room. Once at her monitor, she wrote madly for thirty-five minutes, read and edited her work, and sent it in. Another day, another story.

Alita had trailed after the other players' wives when the game ended. She was standing at the back of the group wondering what to do when Rico and Ferdinand came and whisked her away with them.

They were barely seated in The Blue Mandrake at the secluded table Ferdinand kept reserved for home game nights when the waiter arrived to take their order. Ferdinand ordered for all of them, then sat back.

"Well," Ferdinand said in Spanish, looking at Alita. "What did you think of your first major league game?"

"It was—interesting," she said.

"Just 'interesting'?"

She looked at him earnestly. "I find it difficult to sit and watch men playing a game. I have the feeling I should be up and doing something more—productive."

"You think baseball is childish?" Ferdinand said, his smile taking the harshness from the words.

"I know it's a very difficult game and you need a great deal of skill and hard work to play well. What I find difficult is for me to sit and watch. I feel I should be doing something."

"She's a school teacher," Rico said dismissively. "She likes to be with little children, teaching them to speak English." He shook his head in wonder that anyone could find enthusiasm for such a job.

"I like to teach children," Alita said. "I feel useful."

"Maybe you need to look for a job here in Toronto," Ferdinand suggested. "Maybe you could teach English to immigrants who only speak Spanish."

"She doesn't need to work!" Rico said. "With all the money I make, anything she got paid would be meaningless!"

"But you don't want her bored and lonely, do you, Rico?" Ferdinand raised his left eyebrow.

Rico started to say something, then paused to think. After a moment, he said, "You're right. She'd be happier if she had a job."

Their soup arrived and they busied themselves eating.

"It's very good," Alita said after a few minutes.

"You sound surprised." Ferdinand smiled. "You'll have to get used to it. We accept only the best."

"Yes," she said slowly. "I'm beginning to realize that."

"Watch this!" Rico broke in. He snapped his fingers and a waiter immediately appeared. "No good!" Rico said in English. "Make it hot!"

"Spicier?" The waiter asked, his eyes roaming from Rico to Ferdinand. Rico said, "Spice. *Si*! Hot!"

Ferdinand nodded. The waiter left, appearing a few minutes later with a brand new dish.

"What do you think?" Rico said. "Not bad, eh? If we say jump, they jump."

"Very—very impressive," Alita said.

Rico grinned. "You want to see it again? I'll tell him this is too much spice—"

Alita held up her hand. "No. I understand."

"Everywhere we go, it's like this. We're heroes."

"It must feel very good," Alita said.

They continued the meal, a salad course following the soup, then the entree—prime rib for the men, a light filet for Alita. The best of wines. A meringue torte for dessert. Brandy.

"I don't think I've ever eaten this much at one time," Alita said as she finished her dessert. "And I don't think food has ever tasted this good."

Ferdinand grinned. "I found this place the first week I got called up. I've been eating here as often as possible ever since. But I don't tell just anyone. Only those I think will appreciate it."

"It's very nice," Alita said, "but also, I'm certain, very expensive."

"Very!" Ferdinand said. "But we can afford it."

She frowned. "My father told me stories of famous ballplayers who spent all their money while they were playing and later had nothing."

"No fear." Ferdinand grinned. "I have a number of solid investments, and I've let Rico in on some of them. Neither of us will be out begging in the streets ten years from now."

She looked slowly from Ferdinand to Rico before saying, "It's good of you to take such care of Rico."

He shrugged. "Somebody had to."

"Yes, I see that," she said slowly.

"Nobody has to take care of me!" Rico said. He flexed his left arm. "This arm will take care of everything."

Ferdinand looked at Rico, raising his eyebrows slightly.

"Well, aren't the three of you having a good time!" said a woman's voice.

Alita looked up. A young woman with very blond hair stood watching them. The woman wore a white halter dress with diamonds sparkling on her ears and on her arms and fingers, and very high silver sandals. Alita had seen Marilyn Monroe in movies, and her first thought was how much this woman looked like her. But something was wrong. She was like Marilyn, but a poor imitation. And the woman was swaying as if she was dizzy.

"Whassamatter, boys?" the woman said. "Did you forget to invite me?"

Ferdinand got up and put his arm around the blond woman's shoulders. "You've had too much to drink, Eva. Let me take you back to your table."

"*This* is my table, as you well know. Just because this Cuba—Cuban—female has turned up—this wife—doesn't mean I'm going to just disappear, you know? I don't get put in a box and shipped off by anybody. Especially not by him." She glared at Ferdinand. "Not by you, either."

"Who is this person?" Alita asked in Spanish, her voice tight.

"She's nobody," Rico replied. "Nobody important."

"She's drunk," Alita said. She switched to English. "Why are you here? How do you know my husband?"

Eva spat at her. "It's me he wants. Not you!"

Alita covered her mouth with her hands and jumped up. Tears filled her eyes as she ran to the ladies restroom, which Ferdinand had pointed out to her earlier.

Ten minutes later, a young woman who worked in the restaurant persuaded Alita to come out. Ferdinand was waiting for her.

"Where is she?" Alita asked.

"I sent her home in a taxi."

"Rico?"

"He's at the table waiting for us."

"I knew there was someone else. I could tell when I first met him in the hotel. He wasn't happy to see me. But I didn't expect someone like this."

"She's just a groupie. She doesn't mean anything to him."

"I don't know him any more," Alita said slowly, choosing each word. "I don't belong in this world."

Ferdinand leaned against the door frame and looked down at her. "The two of you will be fine. Just takes some adjustments."

She shook her head. "I don't know."

"He was lonely. He's got needs, you know. Every man does."

"But I don't think every man forgets his wife so quickly."

"He didn't know when he would see you again."

"That girl—she means nothing to him?"

Ferdinand formed a zero with his thumb and middle finger. "Nothing."

"Who is she?"

"Just a girl who gets her thrills from being with famous guys. That's all. She'll move on to somebody else."

Alita shivered. "What a terrible life."

"Not your problem. Or mine. Or Rico's. She has a choice."

"Does she? Perhaps she needs the money men pay her."

Ferdinand shook his head. "Nobody pays her. She's not a prostitute. Just a groupie." At the question in her eyes, he added, "Somebody who gets their kicks hanging around famous people."

Alita shook her head. "It's all so sad."

"There's tons of people like that," Ferdinand said.

"And do the—the famous people—ever fall in love with these—groupies?"

"Not usually." He shook his head. "Hardly ever."

She sighed. "Then I feel very sorry for these people. It seems they have no life of their own, but only the scraps they are thrown from others."

Ferdinand put a hand on her shoulder. "Rico needs you. He really does."

She shook her head. "I know better. And right now I'm not sure I need him."

"You'll work it out. He's sorry."

"Perhaps when I've had a chance to get to know him again. But I want my own room. Otherwise, I will not stay."

At her insistence, Ferdinand took her out to the car and then brought Rico out. Rico sat in the front and Alita in the back.

Ferdinand made some conversation, but neither Rico nor Alita spoke. At the hotel, Ferdinand got another room for Alita and she packed her belongings and left without speaking to Rico again.

Afterwards, Rico said to Ferdinand, "I can't be married to this woman. She's just a little country girl. She doesn't know how to behave here. I want her gone."

Ferdinand sighed. "Rico, for now, the team wants you to pretend you're a happily married man, so do it. Otherwise, you'll make enemies."

Rico put his hands on his hips. "What do I care? They need me. I can do what I want."

"Just pretend, that's all. For a while."

"Then she needs to do what I say. After all, she's my wife. I'm the boss."

"You don't want to make a scene. Give her some time to adjust. She'll come around to seeing it your way. For now, no one needs to know she has her own room."

At nine o'clock Thursday morning, Karen Newland walked into the bedroom she shared with her husband and opened the curtains to let bright sunshine in.

Jonas looked at the clock and groaned.

"Nice to see you, too," Karen said.

"What's wrong?"

"How do you know something's wrong?"

"I know."

"What if I was just feeling amorous?"

"With four kids downstairs?"

She laughed. "Six. Two of the neighborhood kids are already over. Anyway, you win. Armando's here. I gave him a cup of coffee and put him on the recliner in the living room. He looks as if he's been up all night. Thought I'd make him some ham and eggs. You want some?"

Jonas shook his head to clear the cobwebs. "I'll have a quick shower and be right down. Did he say where he went last night?" "I didn't ask."

Jonas threw back the covers. "Keep him here until I come."

"The smell of food ought to keep him," Karen said as she left the room.

Jonas groaned again as he rolled into a sitting position on the side of the bed. Every muscle in his body seemed to have a fire burning inside. He'd have to make sure he got to the stadium early enough to get a good massage and spend time in the whirlpool. Not that he didn't always do that, but today he felt his body needed even more attention than usual. Last night's game had been a killer. He'd jarred his left shoulder trying to harness a wild pitch, twisted his left knee covering the plate on a tough put out, caught a foul tip on the instep of his right foot, and—

No point thinking about it now. He'd let the trainers sort out the various bruises and strains later. A quick shower to wake him up, and then Armando.

Jonas had tried to find him last night. Checked several of his favorite hangouts, called his apartment, asked a few people he thought might know. Nothing. But at least Armando was here now, wanting to talk to him. He moved his neck in a slow circle. Why did he have to feel at least a hundred years old?

A few minutes later, Jonas entered the kitchen of the two-story house in the suburbs and found Armando making inroads on a huge plate of ham, eggs, fried potatoes, orange slices, and toast.

"You hungry?" Karen asked.

"When I've had some coffee so I can keep both eyes open."

"Sorry to bother you this early," Armando said, his mouth full.

Jonas took a chair across the table. "I'm just glad you're all right. Where did you go last night, man? I looked everywhere!"

"I walked around the city for a long, long time. It was a beautiful night, warm and sweet-smelling, like newly mown grass. Actually caught a few winks on a bench in a park. When I woke up, it was around six. I walked some more. Then I decided to come here."

"I'm glad you did. But Blake might have been trying to get hold of you."

"That's one reason I came here. Wanted to talk to you first." Armando took another mouthful of ham.

"I think—"

Armando held up his hand. "Wait," he said. He swallowed the ham and washed it down with a mouthful of coffee. "I've decided to retire. I don't have it any more. And it's stopped being fun, Jonas."

"That's only because of Rico."

"I can't stay here with things the way they are. And I don't want to have to start over somewhere else."

"What would you do?"

Armando filled his fork with egg. "Never thought about it before. Thought I had lots of time before I needed to worry about my future. You think you're invincible, and then—bam!"

"I hate it to end this way, Armando."

"I don't see a choice. Do you?"

SIX

Lawrence followed a specific routine each morning: he awoke to the chiming of an ancient, rather battered, grandfather clock, the only thing of any value he'd inherited from his mother; he showered and dressed carefully, making sure his clothes matched—one day black, the next day navy, the third brown; he ate his breakfast—a bowl of bran cereal with one percent milk and an apple; and finally, he put a Toronto Matrix jersey over his shirt. He had several dozen jerseys, each with a different player's name on the back. Every morning he carefully chose the one he felt like wearing. Today, it was Ferdinand Ortes.

His morning routine complete, he sat down to read the sports pages from both newspapers. First, he tossed the other sections aside and set the sports sections together, one on top of the other. Then he read the game stories from the night before. Not until last did he read his two favorite columnists: Kyle Schmidt first one day, Ginny Lovejoy next. This morning, it was Kyle's turn to be first.

Matrix Lose More Than Game

by Kyle Schmidt

This spring, the management of the Matrix carried out a heavy marketing campaign based on the concept of baseball as a family sport. They made grandiose speeches outlining how attending a game was a character-improving outing for the entire family. They offered discounts and promotional items to encourage us to test their claims. They offered a plethora of pre-game hoopla. In short, they almost convinced even the skeptics among us that the Matrix team was one big happy family with every player a viable role model for kids.

Like a Douglas Fir in close single combat with a lumberjack, that myth became cut and bruised. For a while, it teetered back and forth in the wind, close to toppling. Yesterday, thanks largely to the antics of Rico Velasquez, the myth was felled once and for all, never to rise again.

Not only are the Matrix not the big happy family management claimed they were, but underneath the myth lurk naked anger, rampant dislike, and even hatred. The Matrix is, at best, a very dysfunctional family—one that needs the services of a full-time counselor.

Lost in the tantrum by the supposed ace pitcher was the fact that the Matrix ceded a game they should have won. Armando Santana, for whatever reason, showed once more that he's not a relief pitcher. Someone please put him out of his misery.

And someone, please, put Rico on a leash, or in a cage.

Lawrence slowly set down the paper. A tear shone on his cheek. Much as he hated doing so, he had to admit that everything Kyle said was true. Well, as much as he could understand, anyway. Kyle had a habit of throwing in words that didn't make complete sense to Lawrence—like *ceded*.

But Lawrence had seen the game, and he knew what Kyle meant. They should have won.

Taking a deep breath, Lawrence finished reading Kyle's column before turning to Ginny's. Whether he enjoyed it or not, he had to read everything about the Matrix before he could move on to the next item on his daily schedule.

In his bachelor apartment in downtown Toronto, Kyle Schmidt was also reading the sports news. Sitting up in bed, he, too, turned to Ginny's column.

Hard to Dream with Your Eyes Wide Open

by Ginny Lovejoy

Ever wondered what it really means to follow your dreams? I asked myself that last night as I watched the Matrix.

We often think of athletes as if they were charmed individuals who can ignore the harsh realities the rest of us face and live contented lives playing children's games for salaries most of us can never hope to attain.

And for that reason, I think we tend to be a little harsh with them at times. Whenever we see a little smudge on the dream, we quickly try to wipe it off. And whenever the dream becomes a nightmare, we shut our eyes tight.

A stain has gradually been spreading through the Matrix dream. It began when Rico Velasquez began to blame his teammates and lose his temper. It went into nightmare regions as Rico Velasquez showered insults on one of his teammates. And it became a night terror when that teammate, who had apparently taken all he could stand, floored Rico with a very hard right.

There's an unwritten code in baseball—part of the dream—that players are nice guys and role models, and that they play fair. But last night, Rico was not playing fair. He was anything but a nice guy, and he was the antithesis of a role model.

I've heard the excuse that perhaps in Cuba these things are allowed. But I don't think so. I believe Rico knew better, but that for some reason of his own, he chose to ignore what he knew.

Rico says he was frustrated for the team—he didn't want to lose. His agent, Pat Davis, says Rico was trying to get the team fired up so they'd play better. Coach Blake Harrison says there's no problem—boys will be boys. I don't think so. I think they've forgotten what baseball is about. Baseball is a game for dreamers. Some people just happen to make money from it.

Baseball is supposed to be fun. It's supposed to be hot dogs and popcorn and beer; cheering the team on even when they haven't got a prayer; doing the wave; standing up to watch in ecstasy or agony as the ball slips over the center field fence in extra innings; oohing and aahing when a well-hit ball goes into the top deck, the runner steals a base in a cloud of dust, the fielder makes an impossible catch, or the pitcher throws a no-hitter. Baseball is a stadium full of people rejoicing together when the home team wins or consoling each other with "next time" when it loses.

But of course, that's the dream side of baseball. The realists see the strikeouts, the blow-outs, the errors, the returns to the minors, and the many who enjoy a brief bittersweet moment before they quietly fade away into obscurity.

The dark, nightmare side of baseball includes a certain callousness about the whole thing—a survival-of-the fittest mentality. And tough luck to the one who doesn't quite have it. Worst of all is the agony of the one who thought he had the brass ring in his grasp, only to watch it slip away from those eager fingers.

Rico, I wish I could speak Spanish better so I could say this face to face. Maybe someone will do it for me. Rico, the brass ring that looks so shiny is going to slip away from you because you just don't get it. Baseball is a team game, Rico. T.E.A.M. You need those other guys. They might be the very ones who give you a boost up the ladder—or ease the slide for you on your way down.

I feel for you, Rico. I feel for any player who fails to understand that the way you play ball is a mirror image of how you will live your life.

Think about it. Please.

Kyle sat for a moment deep in thought. After a while, he pulled out the *Register* and, ripping out the page his column was on, began to shred the page into narrow strips, which he then tore into small pieces.

When he was finished, he tossed the pieces up in the air: they landed around him in a shower of newsprint.

Stasey Simon walked into her producer's cubicle. "I want Rico on my show today."

Ted looked her straight in the eye. "He won't come. Pat said he'd come in himself tomorrow, but only if you guarantee you won't turn on him the way you did last time."

"I don't want Pat: I want Rico." Stasey pouted. "What about his wife? I hear she speaks English."

"Pat said there's no way on this earth he'd let her come on your show." Pat had used a few other words—like viper and vampire, but Ted thought it prudent not to mention those words to her just now.

Making a fist with her right hand, she punched the open palm of her left hand several times. "Don't they know what I can do? Wouldn't they rather have a chance to say their bit?" She glared at Ted. "What about Armando?"

"I tried calling him, but either he isn't home or he isn't answering his phone. And his agent says he doesn't know where he is."

"Call Jonas. He'll know."

"Okay."

"And you'd better shape up, Ted, or you're out of here on your ear!" Stasey was reaching for her package of cigarettes as she walked out.

Ted stared after her for a long moment before turning to pick up his phone.

Half an hour later, the *Stasey Simon Show* began. As her theme music and intro came on, her face became animated, her voice filled with emotion. "Stasey Simon is on the prowl, folks. She's pumped and primed and ready to roar. So hang on and I'll see that you get a few thrills.

"I suppose I have to talk about baseball first. Truthfully? I'd rather talk about almost anything else.

"But July is the wrong time of year for hockey or basketball. Curling doesn't start for a number of months yet. I don't think there's much speed skating going on. Or figure skating for that matter. No luge or bobsled. Has anybody broken the high jump record lately? Nope? Too bad.

"Okay, we could talk golf, and I will for part of the time, but I have to start with baseball, don't I? Because there was a game last night. And not only did we lose the game, but there was an episode in the home team's dugout that demands an explanation.

"Four words, Rico. GO BACK TO CUBA. You pitched lousy last night. You aren't worth the trouble you cause.

"Armando Santana has been a very good player for quite a few years. Not only that, but he's a decent person too. He certainly didn't deserve to have one of his own teammates shouting insults at him while he stood alone on that mound trying to make a perfect pitch.

"If baseball was a game of decency, it would be Rico who's out of here on his ear. But baseball isn't a game of decency, is it? It isn't all Mom and apple pie. It's a game of winning and losing, and big, big money. That's why, when the dust settles over the latest in a series of incidents involving Rico Velasquez, it will be Armando Santana who packs his bags."

Her voice became businesslike. "Later we'll talk to a few members of the Matrix and see what they have to say. But first, we have to pay the bills." As an ad came on, Stasey grabbed for a cigarette and her lighter. Cigarette dangling from her mouth, she called out. "Ted, did you get hold of him yet?"

In the sound booth, Ted shook his head.

Stasey swore.

The light went on to indicate Stasey was back on air.

Cigarette still dangling, she said, "Okay, I'm back and we're ready to rock and roll. Just remember not to yell at me: I didn't do it." She removed the cigarette and pressed a button. "Who's on first? Or is he on second? I don't know. Third base. Okay, no more joking. Who's our first caller? Jerry? What have you got to say, buddy?"

"Stasey, I think you're a—bleep—bleep—and you should go—bleep—yourself."

Stasey chuckled. "Thanks Jer, that was helpful. Eddy, you got anything better to say than Jerry?"

"Hello?"

"Yeah, Eddy, baby, you're on the air. Hello-oo."

"Hi, Stasey. How are you?"

Stasey rolled her eyes. If she had a dime for every caller who thought he had to be polite and ask her how she was, she'd be a millionaire. Did they even think about what they were saying? Did they expect an answer? "I'm doing fine, buddy. What have you got to say today?"

"Stasey, things are getting out of hand. The coach needs to take control of the team."

"Eddy, you make a good point. But these people are over twenty-one. Why should they need a babysitter? Stan, my man, what do you think? You're on the air with Stasey Simon."

"Hi, Stasey. If I was the GM, I'd keep Armando and get rid of Rico. Armando's a good guy. Maybe he's not pitching so well right now, but he could get it back. Rico is too—too much like one of those things you never know when it's going to erupt, you know?"

"You mean like a volcano, Stan?"

"Yeah, a volcano. Sure, he can pitch, but you don't know if he'll explode out on the field."

"So you'd trade him?"

"In a heartbeat."

"What do you think you could get for him?"

"Well, maybe another pitcher, or a couple of youngsters."

Stasey adroitly moved the conversation into a discussion of which players other teams might part with to get Rico Velasquez, and kept it going for the next three callers. Then it was time for a sports update and the traffic and weather, plus three commercials.

"Beastie, you get hold of Armando yet?"

"He's at Jonas's. But he doesn't want to go on air."

"Get him on the line for me."

"I'll try."

Stasey drummed her fingertips on the desk surface.

"He's on line one."

"How long do I have?"

"Thirty seconds."

"Manny, I need you to go on the air with me," Stasey said into the phone.

Armando's voice was cold and withdrawn. "I told Ted no."

"Yeah, I know, but it's a good idea. Trust me on this one."

"Stasey, I don't think—"

"I'm putting you on, Manny. Stay there. Don't let me down."

She pushed a button, waited for the signal, and began her spiel, "You're listening to Stasey Simon, and I've got a treat for you. Armando Santana has agreed to come on the air with me to talk about last night. Armando, it's good to have you here."

His voice was low and hesitant. "Thank you, Stasey."

"Armando, we saw the game, either live, on TV, or in our minds as we listened to the radio broadcast. Most of us have read the newspapers. We've seen the blogs. We've heard what's been said on the shows today. Armando, what we don't know is how you feel about what happened last night."

"I—I don't know what to say. I've never done anything like that before."

"You've never given up some runs?"

"No. I meant what happened afterwards."

"You mean when you decked Rico. Frankly, Armando, I think they should pin a medal on you for that. And a lot of people agree with me."

"It was wrong of me."

"From what I hear, Rico was on you from the moment you started pitching."

"I've heard insults before."

"From one of your own teammates?"

His voice was patient. "I've been on teams before where not everyone agreed—where one player might not even speak to another. I shouldn't have let it bother me."

"So why did you let it bother you this time?"

"I think maybe because I was afraid it could be true."

"He said things like you were over the hill, right?"

There was a long pause.

"Armando, you still there?"

"Yes, Stasey." Armando's voice was weary.

"According to Kyle Schmidt's column today, you're going to be traded or released. Have you talked to Tony yet?"

"I haven't talked to anyone."

"How do you feel? Is it unfair of the team if they trade you?"

"I would like to not talk about it any more, Stasey."

"Will you take a few callers' questions?"

"No, Stasey, not this time. I'm sorry." There was a click.

"Manny?"

No response.

"Armando is obviously all choked up over what happened. I want to thank you, Armando, for making the effort to come on with me at such an emotional time. I know you did it for the fans out there. How about it folks, what do you want to say to Armando?" She gave the number to call and looked toward Ted as a short commercial came on.

"Beastie, I don't want any negative callers. Screen 'em out."

"What about Lawrence? He's called twice."

"No way! He's had his call this week. Only if he's pro-Armando and you're short on callers." She turned her microphone back on. "Okay, let's take some calls here. It's no secret what I think. I've been saying it all week. No matter how well Rico Velasquez can pitch, we don't need him here. And if the management can't figure that out, maybe it's up to us to see that they get the idea.

"Armando got it started with that nice uppercut, but apparently that wasn't enough. Maybe somebody should see if a thirty-three-ounce bat applied to the skull would get the message across."

"Blake, you've got to do something about Rico." Jonas Newland plunked himself down on a chair in his manager's office. "The guy's a walking time bomb."

Most people found Jonas Newland imposing, if not fearsome. Blake Harrison, who, after playing third base for several pro teams, had found a home in Toronto first as an infield coach and then as the manager, wasn't one of them. He picked up a baseball and tossed it lightly from one hand to the other. After a moment, he said, "I don't think he's all that bad."

As usual, the morning after a game, Blake's voice was harsh and gravelly—the result of not only yelling at umps and shouting to players for most of his life, but also thirty-five years of chain smoking. He'd quit a year ago, but his voice hadn't improved. "He's just getting his feet under him. He'll settle down eventually. And he can pitch."

Jonas sat forward, elbows on the arms of his chair, hands together as if in supplication. "Nobody's denying he can pitch," he said. "But he sets everyone on edge. And he doesn't take the blame for anything." He shifted in the chair. "Blake, it's not just Armando. You heard him when Larry dropped that grounder. Rico could have made a better pitch, but no, he doesn't mention that. Just yells at Larry. I don't know how many times I've had to get between him and another player, and frankly I don't want to have to do that too often. I get enough grief behind the plate."

Blake said, "Rico also indicated he wasn't too thrilled with your selection of pitches."

"Rico complains at least twice every inning." Jonas shook his head. "He always blames somebody else. As far as I know, he's never yet admitted to having a single fault or apologized for making a mistake."

"And Armando is a good friend of yours."

"You know we room together on the road."

Blake put his elbows on the desk, just touching the tips of his well-tanned fingers. "Rico's here to stay. The management went to a lot of effort, not to mention expense, to get him out of Cuba. He's going to stick like glue."

Jonas brought his fist down on the desk. "Look, I'm not asking you to trade him—just find a way to get it through to him that he needs to stop blowing up at his teammates."

Blake smiled. "Get real, Jonas. You want everyone to be happy. Well, I could give you ten examples of teams that won big while carrying players who hated each other's guts. And you could probably give me ten more."

Jonas sank back in his chair as if someone had pulled a plug. "Yeah, I know." He ran his hand over his smooth head. "It's just— aw, Blake—before Rico came, we had such a good team. A lot of camaraderie, players taking time to help each other improve, picking each another up, enjoying the game. ... Since Rico came, it's been a nightmare—sniping, backstabbing, fights. It's mind-boggling what a difference it's made having him here."

"You're the team leader, Jonas. Maybe you need to figure out a way to pull the team together to help Rico adjust."

"You're the manager, Blake. Give me some help."

"I'm concerned with two things: how well he pitches and him staying healthy. Anybody throws a punch or does anything physical, there'll be a big fine. If it's only words, who cares?"

"Words lead to punches."

"That will lead to fines and suspensions."

"And Armando?"

"I'll be talking to him later today."

"He wants to retire. I think I talked him out of it for now. He needs more time to adjust to the bullpen."

Blake shuffled a few of the papers on his desk. "Maybe. Maybe not."

"Rico loaded the bases, not Armando."

"But Armando let them score. All of them."

"Anybody could have given up that home run last night."

"*Anybody* wasn't pitching. Armando was. And if he can't handle a tight situation, what use is he to us?" Blake looked at his watch. "I have an appointment soon," he said in clipped tones. "Tell the rest of the team to give Rico more slack."

As Jonas got up, he added, "By the way, we're having a reception for the media tonight to welcome Rico's wife. Seven o'clock in the conference room. Just talked to Pat about it. You need to be there. Get some of the other players there, too. It wouldn't look good for them to be absent."

Jonas nodded and left the room, but he was seething inside. Even though what he'd said was exactly what most of the players were thinking, he'd known before he went in there was little chance Blake would do anything. Still, he had to try. As Blake had said, Jonas was the unofficial team leader, the one the other players looked up to, the one who had no fear of talking to Blake and laying things on the line. For all the good it did!

Jonas sighed. He'd have preferred to be home right now, playing with his kids. Thinking of them made him grin. He was one lucky man. The grin faded. He had so little time with them. But in a few years he'd retire, and then his family would get one hundred per cent of his attention.

Right now, though, his world was that of the baseball team, and Armando was waiting in the locker room to hear what Blake had said.

Even before he reached the locker room, Jonas heard loud, angry voices. Hurrying, he found Armando and Rico standing in the middle of the room shouting at each other.

Despite genuine effort on his part, Jonas's Spanish vocabulary remained in the vicinity of "throw another fastball" or "pass the ketchup." Whatever Rico was shouting at Armando was too much for him.

Armando was yelling back, his brown face even darker than usual. Both men gestured wildly with their hands.

Something touched his shoulder and Jonas jumped. Ferdinand Ortes smiled at him.

A spontaneous grin touched one side of Jonas's mouth. You couldn't help liking Ferdinand. Right now, he was the picture of a contented athlete: gleaming, dark brown skin framed by curly black hair; deceptively casual tan sports jacket with jeans and an open-necked red shirt; a gold chain and earrings with a Rolex diamond watch and a matching diamond ring; topped by an ever-ready grin and a large helping of charm that spread out from him like icing on a warm cake.

Ferdinand smiled at Jonas. "These two hombres have been going at it for a while now. I warned them if they fight, Blake will be very angry, so they've stuck to yelling so far. But …?" He held out his hands, palms up, and Jonas nodded.

"I'm not getting in the middle," Jonas said.

Ferdinand nodded. "I was thinking more of throwing a net over them."

"Ice water might work."

Ferdinand grinned. "Now there are two of us, perhaps we can each corral one." He began speaking in fluent Spanish. Jonas heard his own name once or twice.

"What deed Blake say?" Armando Santana called out to Jonas, his English tinged with a stronger accent than usual, but easily understandable.

Jonas shook his head. "Nada."

Armando swore in English and then apparently translated it into Spanish.

Rico responded with another long rant, fists raised and chest thrust forward.

Jonas shook his head. Young and strong, and for the first time in his life free to do what he pleased, Rico should have been on top of the world. Instead, here he stood with nostrils flared, distaste on his face, and anger in every motion, shouting at a man who should have been his mentor. Such a waste of emotion and energy.

With a sigh, Jonas stepped forward. "Rico, you're not a wild animal. You're a man. And a baseball player. But if you keep acting like this, you won't have many friends on the team."

Rico glared at Jonas.

"Tell him what I said," Jonas said over his shoulder to Ferdinand, who quickly translated.

Rico said something to Ferdinand and then spat at Armando, his spittle landing on Armando's orange sports shirt.

Armando moved forward, fists raised.

Jonas grabbed him by the shoulders. "No, you don't. You'll be fined."

"Eet would be worth eet!"

"No, it wouldn't. You know it wouldn't."

Armando clenched his lips.

Ferdinand had grabbed Rico from behind and seemed to be holding his arms back in a way that made it impossible for Rico to do anything. *Neat move*, thought Jonas. *The boy wonder strikes again.*

"Enough!" Jonas said out loud. "Both of you stop acting like children! Tell him that, Spidey."

Ferdinand said much more than Jonas thought necessary to translate his few words, but it seemed to work. Ferdinand let go and Rico, with one last angry glance, sat down at the far end of the room.

"He's waiting for Pat," Ferdinand said. "I suggest you clear out."

"We're gone." Jonas propelled Armando toward the door. Over his shoulder, he called to Ferdinand, "Thanks for the help."

As they headed down the hall, Armando swore, then said, "Thanks for nothing."

Jonas handed him a small towel he'd picked up on the way out and Armando used it to wipe off his shirt. "He's a—a—" A string of swear words followed, English and Spanish tossed together like a garden salad.

"You've got to learn to ignore him," Jonas said patiently. "He doesn't know what he's talking about half the time."

After a few more angry words, mostly in Spanish, Armando said, "The things he said to me—you can't ignore those kinds of things." He led the way to the exit where Jonas's van was parked.

"You know I haven't a clue what he said." Jonas moistened his lips. "But aside from that—" Jonas glanced sideways at his teammate. "Armando, let's face it, you really haven't pitched well this year."

Armando stopped and glared at Jonas. "And how am I supposed to pitch well with him taking my job right at the start of spring training? I've never before been a relief pitcher in all my life! I hate it!"

"Well, the truth is you didn't pitch all that well in the homestretch last fall, either."

After a long, tense silence, Armando said, "It was a long season. I was tired."

Jonas said softly. "Same number of games as usual."

Armando sighed. "Okay, so I'm getting older."

Jonas knew he was pressing his luck, but he couldn't seem to stop. "You've gained weight, you know. You could stand to work out more than you do."

"You think the trainers let me forget?"

"It's their job to keep everybody healthy."

"I know, but—well, the more they tell me I need to lose weight, the more I resent it. I'm not a little kid. I know what I have to do."

"So why don't you do it?"

There was another long silence until they reached Jonas's van. Finally, Armando said, "Did Blake say anything to you about a trade?"

"No."

"It's likely no one wants me."

"Manny—"

"Yes, I know. I have a job. I'm still getting paid."

Jonas unlocked the doors of his van and got in.

As he got into the passenger seat, Armando said, "You don't know what it's like in the bullpen." His voice was heavy with emotion. "I don't know how to warm up quickly in case I have to go in. And it's even worse when I do warm up and then I don't get in. And going out to pitch when I'm only allowed to face one batter, or when the bases are loaded and no one is out—I hate it, Jonas. I can't get into a rhythm. And there's so much pressure." He paused for a moment before saying, "I'd rather leave baseball than have to be a reliever for the rest of my career."

"Manny—"

Armando's voice became almost a whisper. "Jonas, am I really so bad no one wants me?"

"Manny, you know it isn't that simple. A trade has to work both ways. Could be Tony's asking too much for you. Or the player he wants isn't available. You're the one who told me making trades is a lot like playing poker. Give it some time."

"Time? While my days of playing at this level are ticking away? And meanwhile I have to put up with that—" Armando switched into Spanish, as he usually did when talking about his innermost feelings.

Jonas waited until he was through. "Manny, it'll work out."

There was a long pause. Finally, Armando said, "I'd hate to leave you and some of my other teammates. You're my best friends. I wanted to finish my career here. I like the city and the people. But since Rico came, everything has changed. It's no longer a happy place."

Jonas sighed. "The mood of the whole team is different. Playing ball isn't nearly as much fun."

"How can we tell the management it would be doing everyone a favor if they would get rid of him?"

"I've told Blake. Tony would never listen to me. And as for the owners—"

"Yes, I know. When they say 'run,' we ask, 'how far?'"

SEVEN

Pat Davis had come into the clubhouse earlier, while Rico and Armando were shouting at each other. Feeling like a coward, he'd retreated to the restroom. When the angry voices quieted, he decided it was safe to appear.

Ferdinand saw him first. "Good, you're here." He and Rico both looked at Pat expectantly.

"Okay, here's the deal," Pat said. "I talked to Tony earlier, and we came up with a plan. All the reporters want to talk to you and Alita, so the team's giving a reception tonight. You and Alita have to be here at seven tonight." Pat turned to Ferdinand. "Can you explain to him?"

Ferdinand grinned and a flurry of Spanish words came from his mouth. In a few moments Rico was nodding and smiling. To Pat, Ferdinand said, "I told him it's a party for him. He likes that idea."

Pat sat down on a chair. "Also, Rico, so you know, I'm going on the *Stasey Simon Show* again tomorrow."

"Stasey Simon? Radio? You talk to her more?"

"That's right."

Rico leaped to his feet. "No!"

"I have to, Rico. If I don't, she'll just say more rotten stuff."

"She hates me. Do you not listen?"

"Sure, I listen to her. As do half the people who live in this city. She's a phenom—a woman who knows tons about sports, and who doesn't come across as either a jock-envier or a feminist with an ax to grind. Tell him, Ferdinand."

Ferdinand translated.

"She hates me!" Rico glared at Pat.

Pat chose his words carefully. "She isn't crazy about some of the things you do. Like knocking your teammates."

"Knocking?" Rico looked perplexed. He broke into a flurry of Spanish.

Grinning, Ferdinand said to Pat, "He says he's very careful not to injure himself. If he doesn't pitch every game, he doesn't get all his money, so he can't afford to get hurt. He should knock you for making the contract."

"Yeah? Well, tell him this. This team helped get you out of Cuba, didn't it? And gave you a very nice signing bonus. And you're very happy to be here. So just be glad for the contract you've got, and don't mess up! As for the *Stasey Simon Show*, I'll give her a song and dance about how your parents used to hit you when you were a kid, and how your manager in Cuba used to do the same thing, so you just figure everybody does that."

A minute later, Ferdinand said, "His parents did hit him when he was a kid."

"Well, then, it'll be true."

"But he says his manger didn't. What he did do was lock him in his room the night before he pitched so he couldn't go out and get drunk or find a woman."

"Boy, was he ever mistreated!"

"He says he's old enough to know what to do."

"Yeah? So if his manager hadn't locked him in, what would he have done?"

Ferdinand repeated the question and Rico grinned.

Ferdinand smiled at Pat. "He would have gone out and got drunk and found a woman."

Pat sighed. "Speaking of women, where's Alita?"

Ferdinand nodded. "We took her shopping this morning, so I assume she's unpacking her new clothes."

"I'd better come with you so I can tell her about tonight."

"Um, we might have to tell you a few things about last night, too." Ferdinand led the way into the hallway and Rico followed.

Pat ambled after them, muttering to himself. "I'm no better than a babysitter."

After a late breakfast and missed lunch, Iain Foley felt a bit peck-ish. He decided to go across the street to Dana's Place and grab a snack before his four o'clock *Prime Time Show*. He also had reason to believe Kyle Schmidt was there.

Sure enough, Kyle was alone in a corner at a table for two. Lined up neatly in front of him stood five empty shot glasses.

"You waiting for someone?" Iain asked as he touched the back of the empty chair.

Kyle shook his head.

"Mind if I join you?"

"If you aren't too fussy."

Iain smiled. "Not feeling so good?"

"Feeling just fine. Thinking about my column for tomorrow. No game today, so I can write on whatever I choose."

"No shortage of material these days."

"True." Kyle mused on this for a moment as he studied his empty glass. Then he looked at Iain. "You read my column?"

"I always read your column, along with the rest of the sports pages."

"You read Ginny's column today?"

"Yes."

"What did you think?"

Iain tilted his head. "It was interesting. A bit hearts and flowers. Not really my style."

"But she cares. It stands out a mile. She cares about the stupid game."

"I guess. Considering."

"Considering what?"

Iain looked down at the table for a moment before answering. "I guess I can say this to you. Considering she's a woman. I mean, she can never truly understand the game. She's never played it."

"She's played it as much as I have."

"You sound angry."

"Not angry." Kyle held up his hand as the waiter appeared. "Another one," he said. "Just one more."

"Ham on rye and a Coke with a twist of lime," Iain said. As the waiter left, he said to Kyle. "I have to work in a few minutes."

"Does it drive you crazy having Stasey on before you every day?" Kyle asked.

"Does it drive you crazy competing with Ginny every day?" Iain countered.

Kyle nodded. "I didn't think so, but now I'm not so sure."

Iain fingered the lapel of his sports coat. "I see." He cleared his throat, not looking at Kyle. "Yeah, I suppose it bothers me to follow Stasey. Mostly because she's a slob." A smile touched one corner of his mouth. "But it would bother me even more if she followed me."

"If she—?" Kyle's face was blank. Then he laughed. "Oh, I get it. You've got the best spot, right?"

"That's why they call it prime time."

Kyle nodded and smiled.

The waiter brought Iain's sandwich and their drinks. Kyle gulped his down.

"Don't you think you'd better go easy on that?" Iain suggested.

"Sure I should."

"But you're not going to, right?"

"Everybody can mess up once in a while. And with no game to cover today, what does it matter?"

"Sounds like you have a plan."

"I do."

"You know there's a reception tonight?"

"Yeah." Kyle tapped the cell phone in his breast pocket. "They called me."

"Fine." Iain sipped his Coke. "So, how do you feel about the team's chances?"

"My thinking changes every hour. How about you?"

"Off the record?"

"Just two guys talking in a bar."

"Okay, I think they're two or three players away from a contender."

Kyle's face registered surprise. "That's not what most people would say."

Iain grimaced. "I'm not most people." He looked thoughtful. "I find that Torontonians for the most part tend to be overly optimistic about their teams' chances. Most of the time their teams are clear underdogs, but for some reason the fans see that as a positive—as if they expect the underdog to win. And then they're surprised and disappointed when the team fails to achieve everything they'd hoped for. But by next season, the fans act like they didn't see that one coming, and cheerfully go on expecting their team to win this year, even though there's been little change." Iain shook his head. "Maybe it has something to do with the cold winters."

Staring at his empty glass, Kyle said, "Once in a long while the underdog does win."

Ian frowned. "If it were up to me, I'd get rid of Rico tomorrow. I don't trust him to get the team through a tough pennant drive this fall. As for Armando, I have to say I agree with you. He's washed up."

Ignoring what he'd written in his morning column, Kyle said, "Armando was okay last year, eleven and nine. He had a few tough losses, and a couple he had in control but the closer couldn't close. And he did have that knee injury that took him out of a few games."

Iain leaned forward, his voice earnest. "Eleven and nine isn't going to win you a World Series ring. They were right to go after another pitcher. But Rico isn't it. I don't have any confidence in him. He's all over the place. Jekyll and Hyde."

"Yeah." Kyle signalled a passing waiter to bring a new drink.

"But it's not my concern," Iain said, "any more than your getting drunk at three in the afternoon is my concern."

"What I do is nobody's concern," Kyle said. Then, remembering the topic of conversation, he added, "Might be the team's concern if Rico doesn't know how to handle himself."

"Rico is an adult. As is his guardian angel."

Kyle's forehead wrinkled as he turned the comment over in his mind. Then he smiled as he arrived at the answer. "You mean Ferdinand?"

"Yes."

Kyle leaned toward Iain, his voice lowered as if confiding a great secret. "You know, I may have a few things I haven't mentioned to anyone. Maybe I could have had a scoop if I'd used them."

"What sort of things?"

Kyle shook his head. "Just some things."

"About Rico?"

Kyle finished his drink before responding. "Maybe." Kyle swirled the tiny bit of liquid left in the bottom of his glass. "Maybe not." There was a long silence while Iain finished his sandwich and gulped down the last of his Coke. "Well, I have a show to do. Nice talking to you. Go easy on those chasers. Whatever's on your mind, it'll be easier to solve if you can think straight."

Iain entered the station and went straight to his producer's cubbyhole. "How's the show looking?" he asked after the usual greetings.

In his normal monotone, Greg said, "Not too bad. Nobody wants to talk about last night, though."

"Did you get Ginny to come on?"

"She says she can write, not talk."

"How's Stasey doing?"

"She had Armando on, but not for long, and he sounded as though he hated every minute."

Iain compressed his lips. "How did she get him on?"

Greg was making notes. "Stasey has her methods."

"Doesn't she, though?" Iain absently tapped his fingers on his thigh. "Kyle Schmidt's a no-go. He's at Dana's Place all right, but he's getting plastered. I gathered it's got something to do with Ginny's column."

Greg looked up. "Why don't *you* talk to Ginny? Convince her you'll make sure she does okay."

"Sure, why not?"

A few seconds later, Iain was using all his persuasive abilities to convince Ginny Lovejoy that being a guest on his show was exactly what she needed to do to reinforce her newspaper column and get in touch with her readers.

A short time later, Ginny was on live via her phone saying, "It's true that lots of people have escaped from ghettos or other difficult situations because of sports like baseball, football, boxing, and basketball. There wouldn't be a dream if it wasn't anchored in reality. But we tend to ignore the dark side.

"I grew up assuming certain players were wonderful people just because they were such marvellous athletes. But later, I learned about their lives away from sports, and I realized they're just like the rest of us—human beings, with all the faults that human beings have.

"Maybe it comes from ancient Greece or something, this desire to put our heroes on a pedestal. But so often, when we find out the truth, it's as if they fall off that pedestal and get kicked into the gutter. Sometimes it's because they fail to do what we want them to do—like the pitcher who gives up the game-winning home run in the bottom of the ninth. Sometimes it's because we discover their victory was tainted because they were using steroids or illegal pitches or some such thing. Or it might be drugs, alcohol, wife abuse, paternity suits—so many things go on in the world of sports, just as they do in real life.

"Sure, there are some people who can bear the scrutiny—the Roberto Clementes and Walter Paytons, the Paul Hendersons and David Robinsons and Michael Clemons—people who are genuinely warm and caring and whose lives are open books—"

Iain cut in, "So what you're saying is that we need to understand that athletes are people with the same problems and distractions as the rest of us?"

"Exactly. We get upset because a player didn't have a good game, and we're ready to run that player out of town. Well, maybe that player was thinking about the jerk his daughter is dating, or the argument he and his wife had that morning, or what the tests on his mother will show. We expect athletes to rise above their personal concerns, or at least put them aside, so that we can enjoy the game and forget about our own struggles."

"This has been fascinating, Ginny. If you don't mind, after the next commercial we'll take a few calls and see what our listeners have to say about this whole angle of sports."

Stasey was listening in her office. "Give me a break," she muttered. "Ginny Lovejoy? What kind of guest is she? Bleeding heart."

Ted stepped in.

"Did you hear?" she asked. "He's got Ginny Lovejoy on!"

Ted shrugged. "Maybe Iain's decided there's something to the female angle."

"If you can't beat 'em, join 'em?"

"He's got Tony Kanberra on after her."

"And Tony turned you down?" Stasey's voice was indignant.

"Wouldn't even discuss it."

Stasey slammed her fist on the desk. For a few moments, a steady stream of four- and five-letter words flowed from her mouth. Then she reached for a new cigarette and said softly, "I seem to need a new producer."

At ten to seven that evening, Ginny Lovejoy entered the Diamond Dome through the media doors and walked along the hallways leading to the reception room. As she walked, she was thinking about the changes baseball had seen over the years.

One of the biggest changes was the playing field itself. While some stadiums still had real grass, many, including the Diamond Dome, now used artificial turf. Used to be they watered and mowed and raked it: nowadays they sewed and scissored and pressed it. *Nothing stays the same*, Ginny thought. *The only constant is change.*

Which reminded her, she'd have to do something spectacular to make up for tonight. Months ago, her mom had planned a family meal around the team's off-day, and now Ginny was at the Diamond Dome once more while her entire family gathered at her mom's for a potluck.

As she passed a small lounge area containing soft drink and snack dispensers along with a few couches and some pub-style tables where you could sit and talk, she heard a laugh that sounded like Kyle's.

She'd tried to call Kyle to see if he wanted to grab some dinner after the reception, but he hadn't answered his cell phone. She knew he was here, however, because she'd asked the security guard at the door. Now, she stopped and peeked around the corner. Kyle was sitting alone on a couch, nursing a cup of coffee.

She walked in, her black loafers making no sound on the tile floor. "The security guard told me you were feeling pretty good."

He started slightly, but recovered and gave her a lazy smile. "That so?"

"Said you tipped him a twenty dollar bill."

"Did I?"

"He'd hardly lie about a thing like that."

"'Fraid I don't remember."

"That's not like you."

"To give away money?"

"To forget giving it away."

"S'pose not."

"How come?"

"Dunno."

"Kyle?"

He shut his eyes.

"Are you okay?" she asked.

Eyes still shut, he said, "Fine."

"Yeah, right." She was silent for a moment. "If you don't want to talk about it, that's okay. I won't push you."

When he didn't respond, she said, "The reception will be starting soon" and left.

It's that dumb column, she thought, remembering his attitude the night before. *He's still miffed that I scooped him!* For a second, she considered going back to apologize. Then she set her jaw. *I didn't do anything wrong. He'll just have to get over it!*

Ginny entered the largest of the rooms the Matrix used for press conferences and receptions. There were drinks on a sideboard, both pop and beer. Even a few bottles of harder stuff. Trays of tiny sandwiches and vegetables and assorted cakes. A silver tray of good chocolates.

"Sure trying hard, huh?" Stasey Simon had a drink in one hand and an unlit cigarette in the other. "Is this bribery or what?"

As Ginny took a sandwich, she said, "They should do this more often."

"I heard you on *Prime Time* today," Stasey said. "Very sweet. Felt a tear forming in my eye at one point."

"Thank you," Ginny said. She was perfectly aware that "sweet" to Stasey meant banal, trite, and overly sentimental.

"So what do you think of all this?" The hand holding Stasey's glass moved in a circle, indicating the rest of the room. "What do you think the Matrix wants from us?"

Ginny pursed her lips. "I feel a little nervous talking to you. I'm afraid if I do or say something you don't like, you'll ask somebody to hit me over the head."

Stasey took a sip from her glass of wine before smiling. "Heard the show today, did you?"

"Enough."

From just behind Stasey, Ted said, "I told her it was a bit over the top today."

Stasey lit her cigarette and took a drag, then waved her left hand as if changing the air. "Sissies," she said. "You have to walk on the edge to keep the listeners happy. Besides—" another long drag "—it might be a good idea if someone did knock some sense into him."

"Yeah, but what if they did?" Ginny said, genuinely intrigued by the idea. "Couldn't you get charged with inciting an assault?"

Stasey laughed. "Let them try. Be great publicity for the show."

Ted shook his head. "We don't need that kind of publicity."

"If it was me, I'd be checking my insurance," Ginny said. "Oh, and watch out the smoke detectors don't go off. They're very sensitive," she added before wandering away.

Looking around, she saw probably twenty other press and radio or TV people in the room, including photographers and videographers.

Rico and Alita were standing at the front, with General Manager Tony Kanberra flanking Rico and Pat Davis next to Alita. Both men were wearing suits, but while Pat Davis looked as if he'd slept in his, Tony gave the impression that his pin-striped gray suit and white shirt with burgundy tie had been painted onto his frame.

Alita, who was wearing a simple red wrap dress with low heels and a diamond earring and necklace set, was standing as still as a store mannequin, only her eyes giving off any expression. To Ginny, the expression looked like terror.

A number of other players were in the room: catcher Jonas Newland and his wife Karen; the first and second basemen; most of the pitching staff; the right fielder; several utility players; various wives and girlfriends; the coaches; and some of the office staff.

Ginny exchanged a few words with Muddy Ames. Out of the corner of her eye, she saw Blake Harrison wander in with Armando Santana. Right behind them, Ferdinand came in with—Ginny's eyes bulged—Eva MacPherson! What was up with that? She saw Stasey move toward Armando, but he somehow slipped from her path and appeared beside Jonas.

Iain Foley came into the room. He must have rushed over the second his show finished. She saw him pause for a moment to let his eyes go over the occupants before moving toward Blake Harrison and patting him on the back.

Eva and Ferdinand were still together, now talking to Armando and Jonas. Weird.

Ginny suddenly realized Kyle wasn't in the room. His paper would be expecting a story. She wondered if she should go and get him. She started toward the door, then stopped and shuddered. She hated the way her mother was always telling her what she should do. And here she was, about to do it to Kyle.

From the front of the room, Rico also saw Armando come in and then turn away from Stasey, and he smiled. He saw Ferdinand enter with Eva and clenched his teeth.

Blake Harrison and Iain Foley came up and Tony began to talk to them.

In Spanish, Rico said to Alita, "Smile. Look happy."

"I don't feel happy," she said.

"You should. This is a great country. And you have a very important husband now. I'm much more important in this country than your father is in Cuba."

The man from the radio—Iain something—came over and asked Alita about her first impression of Canada. Satisfied with her answer, Rico wandered over to Ferdinand. "I see you're not alone tonight," he said in Spanish.

"Hi, Rico." Eva peeked out from behind Ferdinand's arm. "Remember me?"

"She wanted to come." Ferdinand raised an eyebrow. "I thought you'd want me to take care of her."

"Miss me, Rico?" Eva teased. "Ferdinand is taking very good care of me."

Rico scowled. "I thought you were my friend."

"Would you rather I left her to make a big scene?"

"Keep her away from my wife," Rico said. "You, I speak with later." He turned to walk away, but Armando was standing in his path, talking to Karen Newland.

Rico stopped dead.

Armando turned slowly, and the two men stared at each other for a moment before Rico grinned and spoke softly in Spanish.

As Armando's hands clenched into fists, Karen Newland put a hand on his shoulder. Slowly, Armando moved to one side so Rico could pass.

After a long moment, he did.

At the front of the room, Tony Kanberra took a pair of reading glasses from his jacket pocket and adjusted the microphone. He read a prepared speech, telling everyone how delighted he was to have the opportunity to get together like this, how the Matrix team really was one big happy family, and how great it was that Rico now had his wife with him.

Tony Kanberra presented Alita with a bouquet of roses, which she blushingly accepted.

Blake Harrison took the podium. "As the manager, I have a lot of personal contact with my players and I really like to see them happy. I'm sure Alita's arrival will help Rico feel more comfortable here in Canada. It's been very difficult for him trying to focus on the business of baseball without knowing when he'd see his bride again."

Rico repeated a few lines they'd given him about how happy he was to have Alita here. His stomach churned. Did they think he was a puppet? But he knew he had no choice. Ferdinand had explained it all to him. For now, he belonged to this team, to these people. Later, he would be able to call the shots.

When Rico moved away from the microphone, it was Alita's turn to speak. Slowly, but in precise English, she repeated the words they had written for her that afternoon, after Mr. Kanberra and Mr. Davis explained to her why she and Rico needed to make everyone think they were a happy couple. "I'm very glad to be in Canada," she said. "I'm sure I'll be happy here. I've missed Rico very much. I want to thank the Matrix for helping me be with my husband once more."

Tony Kanberra came back. "Now, we'll take a few questions from the media."

Stasey's hand went up first. "Alita, I want to know," she asked when Tony reluctantly acknowledged her, "what you think of the way your husband's been acting toward other members of his own team?"

Rico took several quick steps toward Stasey, but the tall young man who was always with her stepped between them even as other hands grabbed Rico from behind.

"Not here, and not now," Jonas Newland said urgently in Rico's ear. "Unless you want your picture plastered all over every newspaper and television in both Canada and the United States."

"Touch her and you'll be arrested for assault." Pat Davis said quietly from Rico's other side. "Nothing I can do."

Rico wanted to shake them off, but he understood enough to know they were right. "She hates me," he said. "She's my enemy."

Ted shook his head. "She's just doing her job, man. Nothing personal."

Pat pulled on his arm. "Come on Rico. Back off."

Rico allowed Pat and Jonas to lead him away from Stasey and back to the front of the room.

At the mic, Tony Kanberra said, "I think we should restrict this to questions Mrs. Velasquez is able to answer."

Kyle Schmidt walked into the room just in time to hear Kanberrra's comment. He began to laugh.

Ginny hurried toward him. "Be quiet," she urged. "You're drunk and loud."

"Not drunk. Just feel better than I have for ages. Feel great."

"Then stop shouting."

"I'm not—"

"Yes, you are!"

"I never shout!"

By now, most of the people in the room had turned to check out the source of the commotion at the back of the room. There was a second door near the front of the room. As the others turned to look at Kyle, Alita Velasquez quickly slipped through that door. By the time people began to looked at the front of the room again, she was gone.

When he realized she wasn't in the room, Rico swore.

Tony Kanberra immediately censured his assistant, Cecily Jones, for not watching Alita.

After a huddled discussion between Tony, Rico, Pat Davis, and Blake Harrison, Cecily left the room with a security guard, and Tony came to the microphone. "I'm afraid this has all been too much for Mrs. Velasquez. She feels overwhelmed by all the adjustments to a new country and all the attention she's received. I'm sure you understand. Perhaps we can do this again at a later date. No rush to leave—finish up the food and drinks."

Stasey started to say something, but a well-aimed elbow to her stomach from Ted altered her words to a low "Oof."

"Not now, Stasey," he said.

She swore at him. "I was only going to say—"

"Let it go."

She raised her voice. "You just crossed the line, my friend. As of this minute, you're fired. I don't ever want to see your face again."

Ted grimaced. "Stasey, don't—"

"Get away from me. Now."

Without another word, Ted left the room.

"Problem, Stasey?" Iain Foley was beside her, looking down at her quizzically.

"Nothing I can't handle without your help."

"Okay. Sorry for intruding." Iain backed off, a smile tugging on his lips.

As most of the press and other guests left, Stasey poured herself another drink and gulped it down.

"Where is she?" Rico asked Cecily Jones and the security guard, who'd returned to the room alone.

Both of them looked puzzled. "We didn't see her," Cecily said. "I don't understand—"

"Don't worry," Pat said. "She can't have gone far."

"That's ridiculous," Tony said. "You must not have looked properly. There's no way out of there." He looked around. "Well, don't just stand here gawking. Go and find her!"

A few minutes later, Rico walked through the trainers' room. Seeing no sign of Alita, he tried the door that led directly to the bullpen. It was usually locked, but today it opened.

He sighed. In all honesty, he'd be very happy if Alita had found a way out of the building to a taxi stand and was on her way to the airport and back to Cuba. There was no place for her in this life. He'd thought so before she came; now he was sure.

As Rico walked toward the end of the bullpen and surveyed the majestic interior of the Diamond Dome, a deep satisfaction engulfed him. This was his rightful place, his destiny. Each time he stepped on the pitcher's mound, he felt a thrill such as no woman could ever give. It was as if he had been expressly made for those moments when he faced a batter. Like a skilled matador, he stood alone against muscular creatures who wielded their bats with such force they could take his head off with one swing.

He chuckled. First they had to hit the ball. Not an easy task when he was pitching. With his cunning and skill, he could defeat a batter as deftly as a champion matador armed only with cape and sword could lay waste a massive bull.

Like a matador acknowledging the applause of the crowd, he bowed.

He heard a movement behind him. Someone else looking for Alita? Or maybe she actually had come this way. He began to rise and turn. "Ali—?"

The word became a sigh as he crumpled to the ground.

The matador was down.

PART II

*"No, Virginia, there is no Auntie Mame,
she is a distillation and a moonbeam
and nothing more."*

—PATRICK DENNIS, on the eve of the
Broadway première of *Auntie Mame.*
NY Times, 28 Oct, 1956

EIGHT

After arriving at police headquarters at 8:00 AM, Paul Manziuk called the number he'd put in his address book. "Detective Inspector Paul Manziuk here. I was told the doctor would be seeing Woodward Craig this morning at seven. What can you tell me?"

The voice at the other end was female and inquisitive. Why exactly did he want to know?

"If you'll look at his chart, you'll see that Craig's wife signed a form saying you can release information to me."

And just who was he, again?

"Detective Inspector Paul Manziuk."

Oh, yes. It seemed the release was there after all. And the doctor had been in. Should she read what he'd written?

"Please."

Paul listened as the nurse relayed the doctor's information. His face relaxed. At one point he grinned. Then he became serious again. "Okay, thanks very much."

After hanging up, he moved a few feet to stare out the window and took a deep breath, then exhaled. They'd cleared Woody for bypass surgery. Once that was out of the way, he should be able to lead a completely normal life.

But, of course, police work wasn't normal. Woody would be given the golden handshake and he'd have to start a new life as a retired police officer. His place as Manziuk's partner would be filled by someone else.

After a long moment, Paul called home.

Loretta answered on the first ring. "Did you call the hospital?"

"Yes."

"And?"

"They've booked him for surgery on Monday. Then it'll be a month or two for recuperation. They advise against further field work."

"That's what you expected."

She was right, but her saying it irritated him. "Yes."

"But?"

"It seems so final."

"It nearly was final."

"I know. And I'm very glad he's going to be okay. But—"

"You hate having to break in a new partner."

"More than that."

"Of course it is." Her voice was measured, practical. "But you have to look at it in two ways. Woody is still here, and he's still your friend. That's separate from his being your partner."

"But I liked having a partner who was also a good friend." Paul knew he was whining like a little kid.

"You'll have to make a friend of your new partner."

"It isn't that easy."

"Nothing worthwhile is. Or so I heard a rather intelligent man tell his son this morning."

Paul grinned. "Is he still mad at me?"

"No. He blames himself for bothering you, especially with Woody in the hospital. Thinks he was selfish and inconsiderate."

A smile touched Paul's lips. "We'll have to look at the budget and see what we can do."

"Maybe you can find time to explain everything so he understands the situation."

"I wonder—maybe he and I could make it to a Matrix game. Maybe next weekend."

Her voice was doubtful. "You could try. Have to make sure he doesn't have a tournament scheduled."

"And hope nobody schedules a murder."

"That would be a blessing any time. Oh, don't forget we said we'd be at the hospital tonight at seven."

"Do my best."

A few minutes later, Paul reluctantly left his office to apprise Superintendent Cliff Seldon of the doctor's report. They had to fill Woody's position immediately. There was never a surplus of people on homicide.

When Paul Manziuk left Seldon's office, he headed straight for the small cubicle where Detective Constable Jacqueline Ryan was busy at her computer. Coming up behind her, he said quietly, "Can you come to my office?"

At the sound of his voice, Ryan jumped just a fraction of an inch, then turned. He was already halfway to his office.

When she reached it, he was sitting behind his desk. She stopped just inside the doorway.

"You looked busy," he said. "Your report not done yet?"

She rolled her eyes. "You must be joking. I'll be at it until midnight."

"Let's hope no one decides to bump someone off today."

"Do you have yours done?" she countered.

"You must be joking." His face was still, like a mask.

A smile touching her lips, she moved into the room. "You know, I used to be terrified of you."

"You should be," he said, still without expression.

She sat sideways on the corner of his desk, her eyes on him.

He winced.

She quickly jumped off. "Sorry," she said. "That's a bad habit of mine."

"I yelled at you for doing that once before, didn't I?"

"Yes, you did. I'm sorry. I guess you don't like informality."

He shook his head. "It's not that. Woody sits—he sat—there a lot."

"Oh," she said in a small voice. "How is Detective Sergeant Craig?"

"He seems to be doing okay, except he'll have to take early retirement. But as soon as he's recovered from the bypass, he should be able to go fishing and take a world cruise and do a few other things he's talked about."

"You'll miss him."

"Yes."

Neither spoke for a long moment.

"He was a good cop," Manziuk said, giving what sounded to his ears too much like an impromptu eulogy.

After another strained moment of silence, Ryan asked a question about the case they'd recently solved. For several minutes, they moved into a brief discussion of a few technicalities. Any tension had evaporated by the time the phone rang.

Manziuk picked it up. "Yeah? …. Oh, that's just great! I don't have the report done for the last one. You know, I think I'm overdue for a few days R & R. … I'm going on a cruise with Woody when the doctor says he's fit enough to travel, and you won't be able to call me in the middle of the ocean. … Who's available for secondary?"

Ryan took a couple of steps so she could stare at the picture on Manziuk's wall. It showed a serene valley with a tiny mouse just visible in the grass, and in the sky an eagle searching for prey. Ryan bit her bottom lip.

"Yeah, I guess." There was a long pause. "Okay, I'll take care of it." Manziuk hung up. "They've got a body."

Ryan continued to stare at the picture as if fascinated. "Oh?" she asked, her voice implying it was no concern of hers.

"I guess nobody told whoever did it that I was tired and needed a rest."

"I guess." She moved toward the door. "Well, good luck."

"I'll need a secondary."

She turned to look at him.

"You doing anything?" He was looking directly at her, his eyes measuring.

She put one hand on the doorknob. "You want to take along a female who can't keep quiet?"

He shrugged. "At least it doesn't get boring with you around."

She put her free hand on her hip. "I'm not sure my blood pressure can stand working with you."

He kept his eyes on her. "If you do your own job instead of trying to do mine as well, I won't have to yell at you more than once a day."

"Thanks a lot." She shifted her weight to the balls of her feet. "You just need to pay more attention to what I say. You aren't the only one who can think, you know."

He stood up. "Are you planning to talk all day, or are you going to back me up here?"

Her jaw set, she faced him. "Just tell me one thing. Do you want a partner or a secretary?"

"Why would I need a secretary?"

She released the door and took a step toward him. "You *don't* need a secretary."

"I didn't think so." He stepped from behind his desk, grabbed his hat, and pushed past her to lead the way out of the office. "You a baseball fan?" he asked over his shoulder.

"What's that got to do with anything?"

"Some baseball player's been found dead at the stadium. In the bullpen."

She had to run to keep up. "Murdered?"

"Looks like it."

As they hurried through the silent outer office, she made a quick detour to grab her purse. Lunging into the elevator as the door was closing, she asked, "Did you say they found the body in a bullpen? Why on earth would they have cattle at a baseball game?"

The elevator started its downward journey.

"Exactly how much do you know about baseball?" Manziuk asked.

She looked at the pocket on his suit jacket. "Well, nothing."

He sighed. "The bullpen is where relief pitchers warm up."

"Relief pitchers?"

"The game starts with a pitcher who can work a number of innings—ideally throw the ball a hundred or more times. If he gets tired, or if he's getting hit a lot, they bring in another pitcher. That one's called a relief pitcher. When there's any chance that the starting pitcher might need to be replaced, the relief pitcher gets up to throw in the bullpen. If they don't warm up properly before they pitch, they get arm problems."

"Why on earth do they call it a bullpen?"

"I have no idea."

Since the police station and the ball park were both downtown, it was a relatively short drive. Manziuk pulled into a space near the main entrance to the Diamond Dome. "By the way," he said as he began to open his door. "I'm in charge of the investigation, so until I give you the go ahead, I ask the questions."

"So you *do* want a secretary?"

"No," he said patiently, "I want someone who will observe and listen. See how I ask the questions. Study my style. When you have it figured out, we'll talk about how you can help."

"Don't I even get a chance to show you what I can do?"

He sighed. "How about if I let you take a few on your own?" Before she could respond, he added, "I'll decide which ones."

A red-faced security guard with sweat dripping from his face stood in front of the main doors to the Diamond Dome, holding a crowd of people and cameras at bay.

Motioning toward Manziuk, the guard shouted, "You can't park there!"

"Police," Manziuk countered.

"I'll need to see your badge."

Manziuk pushed through the crowd and held it out.

"Thank you, sir." The guard took a key ring from his pocket. "I'll let you inside."

"I'll call for more police," Manziuk said. "They'll cordon it off."

The man bobbed his head up and down. "Thank you, sir. I'd sure appreciate some help. These people are—"

During their brief conversation, Manziuk had been aware of questions being flung at him from the crowd of eight or nine people, both male and female, all of whom were holding something: a camera, a digital recorder, a cell phone, or pen and paper.

Their voices had melded together into a somewhat discordant chorus.

"What's happened?"

"We need some sort of statement."

"Please. Nobody's talking to us!"

"We have deadlines to meet."

"We have a right to know what's going on!"

"Can you tell us the nature of the injury?"

"Can you verify that it's a member of the Matrix?"

From the doorway, Manziuk held up his hand for silence. When he had it, he said, "Right now, I know little more than you do. Please address your questions to Special Constable Benson when he arrives. He's on his way."

The guard had unlocked the door and was holding it open. The crowd of press people pushed forward, and as Manziuk and Ryan went through the door, a woman darted in after them.

"Please, I just need to get inside for a few minutes!" she exclaimed as the guard, sweat dripping from his flushed forehead, grabbed her arm and hung on.

"Officers, can you help?" The guard called out.

Manziuk and Ryan turned. A young woman with a blond pony-tail, a blue velour top and matching capris, and reflecting sunglasses was tussling with the guard. Behind her was a tall young man holding a microphone, and behind him surged the rest of the group.

"I have to get inside!" the woman said.

"And why is that?" Manziuk asked.

She stopped struggling. "My show goes on at one o'clock, and I need up-to-date information. I need to know what's happening now!"

Manziuk revised his estimation of her age. Young, but not as young as he'd first thought. "Your show?"

"I'm Stasey Simon."

The guard released her and stepped back as if burned, his eyes fixed on Manziuk.

Manziuk, who'd listened to her show more than a few times, said, "Well, Ms. Simon, I don't think your need to know is half as important as mine, and right now I don't know anything."

"I have a source inside. We need to verify what he told me."

"Well, perhaps that source will update you if you go back to your office and wait for a phone call."

"We were across the street at The Fifth Base."

"Well, go there then. Because if you stay here, you're going to be arrested for impeding a police investigation. Understand?"

"Do *you* understand what it means for a reporter to scoop everyone else?"

"I do."

"And?"

"And the only scoop you're going to get if you stay here is about your own arrest."

She made a face.

"Out!" he said.

Stasey scowled and stamped her foot, but she and the young man left, pushing through the rest of the press people, who backed away.

The guard threw a tired grin at Manziuk before going back to his post. A moment later, they heard him turn the key.

"The *Stasey Simon Show*?" Ryan said as she and Manziuk started down the hallway.

"Sports radio talk show."

"She talks about sports?"

"Right?"

"You mean guy sports? Like baseball?"

"You think only men should talk about sports?"

Ryan had no chance to reply because a tall, somewhat overweight, and rather imposing older man with graying dark hair was coming toward them. "Are you Manziuk?"

"Yes, and this is Detective Constable Ryan."

"It's about time. We have to get the body out of here and get ready for the game tonight. The teams need to get on the field to practice right after lunch. And there are police all over the place saying nothing can be done until you give the okay."

"And you are?"

"Sorry," the man said. "I assumed you'd know. Tony Kanberra."

Manziuk looked toward Ryan. "Mr. Kanberra is the general manager of the Matrix."

To Kanberra, he said, "Why don't you take us to the body?"

"That's exactly what I'm here to do. Follow me."

Five minutes later, the three of them were standing in an enclosed area staring at a male body lying face down on the ground. The body was clothed in a bright blue sports shirt, black pants, and shiny, black loafers.

Tony Kanberra, his face drawn, said, "I'll just—you—you're okay now? You don't need me any more, do you?"

"We're fine for now."

He was gone before Manziuk finished the sentence.

Manziuk knelt down, looking but not touching. The body reminded him of a child's rag doll, the limp kind that splayed out when dropped. But this rag doll wasn't only limp, it was broken. Surprisingly little blood, but the back of the neck and base of the skull were crushed. A pool of what might be blood lay under his right ear.

Manziuk stood and spoke to the uniformed police officer who'd been guarding the area. "Is Ident on the way?"

The officer took a step forward. "They should be here any minute. The pathologist should be here soon, too."

"I'll wait to turn him until they're here." Manziuk looked closely at the officers. "And you are?"

"Constable Strathroy, sir," said the woman.

"When did you arrive?"

"I was just down the street when the call came in. I got here within a couple of minutes."

"Who found the body?"

"The groundskeepers found it when they came in to get ready for today's game. One of them came close enough to touch his hand and make sure he was dead, but otherwise, they didn't touch anything. Two of them stayed here and the other two went to tell Mr. Kanberra. His assistant, a Miss Cecily Jones, called 911. That's it."

"Has anyone else been here?"

"Mr. Kanberra and his assistant came to the doorway, but no further."

Manziuk nodded. "Anything on the most likely time of death?"

"Apparently there was some kind of reception here last night, but everyone was out of the building by nine-thirty."

"Have you asked for a list of people who have ongoing access to the Diamond Dome or who were here last night?"

"Mr. Kanberra said he'd have his assistant put one together."

"Do we have a tentative ID on the body?"

"They seem to think it was a member of the baseball team called Rico Velasquez," she said.

Manziuk whistled.

"I take it that means something to you," Ryan said.

"I'll say it does." To the constable, he said, "Good. You've done well."

Constable Strathroy quickly stepped back, resuming her former position.

Ryan asked, "So, who is he?"

"A pitcher from Cuba who's been making a lot of noise in more ways than one."

"You really follow this, don't you?"

"I try. But nothing like my son, Michael. He's an avid fan."

"Nice to have a source."

"This is going to upset him."

"This Rico guy have a family?"

"I would imagine."

"They'll be pretty upset, too."

Nodding, Manziuk got out a tape measure and began to take measurements, recording them on a small sketch pad. Watching him, Ryan wrote a few comments in her own notebook.

When Manziuk was finished sketching the scene, he took out a small digital recorder and read his notes into it.

As he was doing this, two other men came into the enclosure, waiting until Manziuk noticed them before coming forward. The taller, younger man was Special Constable Ford, a seasoned veteran of the police force and the head of the Ident team that would comb the area for any little detail that might be relevant. Although a couple of inches under six feet, Ford's husky build, combined with the long scar that ran across his left cheek, made him very intimidating. In a trench coat and fedora, he could have melded perfectly into the role of the brusque, no-nonsense cop in any Raymond Chandler movie. In reality, he was a hard-working, methodical man who spent hours checking facts and allocated his spare time to caring for his tropical fish. "Ready for us?"

Manziuk said, "Yes. Full team. Highest priority."

Ford nodded and turned back to give instructions to his team, who were waiting in a tight group out on the field.

Manziuk looked to the older man and said, "Well, Munsen, we have another one for you."

The pathologist nodded. "If I'd known you were going to be so busy, I'd have told Weaver to take his holidays some other time."

"Tough."

"Not exactly a picnic for you, either."

"Let's get it over with. I'd like to see what the front looks like."

Dr. Munsen knelt beside the body and did a quick check of body temperature, pinched the cheek that was lying toward the ground, moved several body parts, took a few samples from the mouth, nose, and ear tissues, and then did a cursory examination of the back of the head.

"Any thoughts?" Manziuk asked.

"Looks like it might have been only one blow. But one was enough. There's leakage of cerebrospinal fluid through the right ear and brain stem damage as well as spinal cord. Likely went into a coma and died within an hour, maybe even less. Of course, that's purely a guess. I'll know more when I've done the autopsy." He stood.

Two of the Ident team members moved in, one snapping pictures and the other using a video camera.

Manziuk and Dr. Munsen walked a short distance away. Ryan followed them.

"Weapon?" Manziuk said.

"Offhand, I'd say it was two to four inches wide, and fairly heavy."

"A baseball bat fit?"

He nodded. "Yes, I expect it could have been a bat. I'll check when I do the measurements."

Ryan said, "There's a whole rack of bats against that wall."

"Could be one of them." Dr. Munsen said. "Ident will need to check them all." He sighed. "I can maybe fit him in Monday morning."

Manziuk looked at him. "You wish! I'm afraid yesterday won't be soon enough for this one. This is a player, and that means this case is going to be very high profile."

Munsen sighed once more. "I knew you were going to say that." He thought for a moment. "Okay, I'll try to fit him in tonight or tomorrow morning. Can't do any better than that."

"It'll have to be good enough, then."

"I don't think there's going to be anything earthshaking."

"What about time of death?"

"From the body temperature, the fixed lividity, and the fact that rigor mortis is pronounced, I'd say from ten to fourteen hours. I can maybe be a little more definite later on."

The photographers finished and a couple of members of the Ident team brought in a gurney and a body bag. With Dr. Munsen fussing to make sure the back of the head received no further damage or displacement of bone or skin, they lifted the body and turned it over onto the waiting body bag. Now they could see the front. The shirt was open part way down, exposing a gathering of curly black hair. Around his neck was a heavy gold chain. He had a gold Rolex watch on his right wrist, a heavy gold ID bracelet on the left. Each hand had a ring on the fourth finger, both gold, with a large ruby-like stone in one and what looked like a diamond in the other.

His face had a darkened, bruised appearance, especially on the right side where his cheek had rested on the ground. His open eyes were cloudy in their darkened sockets.

Ryan swallowed and looked away for a moment, then forced herself to look at him. This wasn't her first body, and by now, she'd have thought she'd be used to seeing death. But it was as if each body brought its own unique aura of tragedy. Try as she might, she didn't see just a body—she saw a good-looking young man in the prime of life. It was such a waste. Anger rose up in her. It was the anger that kept her here; the sense that somebody had to do something to make the killing stop.

More photos were taken. The video camera rolled.

"Not robbery," she heard Manziuk say. "The rings, the watch, the chain …."

When the photographers were finished, Manziuk put on a plastic glove he'd pulled from his pocket, and gingerly extracted the contents of Rico's pants' pockets. A wallet. He flipped it open. Cards and bills looked out. "Definitely not robbery," he repeated. He pulled a few more things out of the pockets and deposited them into a plastic bag Ford held out. Keys, toothpicks, several tissues, a business card, a small address book, and a few other odds and ends. He stepped back. "Okay, take him."

Ryan stood beside Manziuk watching as the body bag was closed and the straps pulled tight. It was lifted to the gurney. In a small funereal procession, Rico Velasquez left the stadium for the last time.

NINE

To Manziuk's request for an office he could use to interview people, Tony Kanberra said, "Yeah, use this office. Or—no, better yet, maybe Cecily can find you a tidier spot.

Pretty well anything would have been tidier than Tony Kanberra's office. The walls were almost hidden by signed pictures of baseball players, alone or with Tony, as well as a plethora of plaques, mounted baseballs, the odd glove, and four or five signed bats. A multitude of file folders and loose papers littered the desk and the top of the filing cabinet. More files, papers, videos, and books covered the credenza and the visitors' chairs and spilled onto the floor.

"The room seems to breed," Ryan whispered to Manziuk while Kanberra punched a button on his intercom.

A woman with a light brown cherubic face entered the office, and Kanberra introduced her as his executive assistant, Cecily Jones.

A well-proportioned, bespectacled woman who looked to be in her mid-forties, Cecily's upswept hairdo reminded Manziuk of Audrey Hepburn in a movie whose title he forgot. Her two-piece, short-sleeved suit in ice blue with white three-inch-heeled sandals and long dangly earrings seemed to him a bit over the top for someone working for a baseball team, yet they suited her.

Her alto voice was clear and precise, with strong pronunciation of each syllable. "Very glad to meet you, Inspector. And Constable. I'll give you all the help I can."

They followed Cecily and Tony to a room down the hall. There was a blotter on the large oak desk, on which rested a pen and a small notepad. Every other surface in the room was barren. Along with the executive swivel chair behind the desk, there were two high-end barrel chairs in front.

"This will do," Manziuk said.

Tony said, "Wonderful. So you can do your thing here, and we'll concentrate on the game tonight."

"There won't be a game tonight," Manziuk said quietly.

Kanberra's jaw clenched. "There *is* a game tonight. You do what you need to do and then get out of our way."

"The Ident team won't be through for some time, and no one can come into the area until they're completely finished."

"But—"

"No. Game. Today." Manziuk repeated, emphasizing each word. "And if you want to get this cleared up, you could speed up the list of people who have access to the stadium and who were here last night."

"We'll see about that," Kanberra said. He walked out of the room.

"I have the list almost ready, Inspector," Cecily Jones said softly. "I'll go and finish it. Is there anything else I can get you? Coffee?"

"No, thanks. Just the list."

"Right away." She left.

Ryan threw her purse on the desk and took off her jacket. "This room doesn't seem to be used."

"Warm in here." Manziuk set his hat on the corner of the credenza and laid his suit jacket beside it. "They used to have four assistants to the general manager. They got rid of one last winter and haven't replaced him. Probably his office."

There was a muffled rapping on the door.

"Come in," Manziuk said.

Special Constable Sam Benson walked in. Blond and good-looking, with an instinctive charm and a quick wit, Benson had been ear-marked as a natural for public affairs the day he joined the police force. Now in his late thirties, he gave seminars to police groups around the country on how to deal with the public.

"I thought we'd see you shortly," Manziuk said.

Benson sighed. "This is a nightmare."

Manziuk nodded.

"Media people are swarming outside. Phones are ringing non-stop." Benson shook his head. "Not at all what I needed." He noticed an empty chair and collapsed into it. "I planned to take this weekend off and glue myself to the hammock in my backyard to catch up on all the sleep I've missed the last few months."

"What do you need?"

"Anything you can give me. Has it been verified who the body is?"

"It was either Rico Velasquez or his clone."

Benson groaned. "Just what I needed! We're going to have the whole country of Cuba on our backs as well as every baseball fan in North America."

"They have a game scheduled for tonight."

"I feel a severe headache coming on."

"I've told them it's no go. I'm not sure they believe me."

"Do you have any leads?"

"I don't even have a list of people to talk to yet!"

"You're going to have to push this one. Do what you need to do, come down hard. We need this solved fast."

"Do you know of any other way?" Ryan asked, her tone curious.

"Huh?"

"This is only the third time I've met you, but both other times you wanted things done instantly, too."

With a straight face, Benson said, "This time I need it solved double fast."

Ryan rolled her eyes.

Manziuk spoke brusquely. "Ryan, why don't you ask Mr. Kanberra if he'll come in for a few minutes? You might want to mention again that there'll be no game tonight."

As soon as the door was closed, Benson leaned forward. "Paul, this is probably the highest profile case we've ever had. Do you have any idea what kind of press relations nightmare this is? We're going to have everyone upset. All the people who don't like Cuba. All the people who do like Cuba. All the people who hate pro sports. All the people who love pro sports. They'll all be taking sides and point-ing fingers.

"Please solve this before it turns into some kind of international incident!"

Tony Kanberra slouched through the doorway ahead of Ryan and stood behind the chair Benson had vacated a few minutes before. "I just talked to the police commissioner," he said in a hushed voice. "Nothing I said could budge her. We have to postpone the game tonight."

Having won his point, Manziuk decided sympathy was in order. "I know it means a lot of work for you," he said.

Kanberra sighed and came closer so he could sit in the chair. "Oh, not so much, I suppose. Treat it like a rainout. It happens all the time. Only it doesn't happen here anymore."

"Not in this stadium." Manziuk smiled.

"Still, it might be a good thing not to have a game. No need to have people speculating about where the body was found. Give everyone a day to cool off. Give the coaches and players some time to deal with the impact of this blow to the team, too."

Manziuk could hear the echo of the police commissioner's voice in every word Kanberra uttered, but he simply nodded agreement.

"The best thing we can do is cooperate with your investigation. The sooner you finish with us, the sooner this will be over."

"We'll do our best to stay out of everyone's way," Manziuk responded, "and to complete our investigation as quickly as possible. Of course, the more help you and your staff give us, the better we can do our job."

"Yes, yes, I see that." He stared into a corner of the room. "It all seems so—so unbelievable. I can't imagine why anyone would want to kill him." He paused and then said, "It had to be someone from Cuba."

"Maybe. But we can't rule out anyone just yet."

"Yes, I see that, but—"

"Mr. Kanberra—"

"Everybody calls me Tony."

"All right, Tony. Can you tell us more about Rico Velasquez? How did he come to be on this team?"

Tony leaned back and closed his eyes for a moment as though focusing his thoughts. "We first heard about him when he played on the Cuban National Team that lost to Japan in the finals of the World Baseball Classic last year. Some great Cubans have managed to slip out and play for teams in the U.S. Everyone's heard of Livan and Orlando Hernandez. So of course we were interested in any Cuban players who might want to come to us. When we heard Rico was looking for a team that would take him if he was able to get out of Cuba, we jumped at the opportunity. We wanted to get him out through proper channels, but there's a ton of red tape, and Rico didn't want anyone getting wind of what he was trying to do, so it was all hush hush. I have no idea how he managed to leave Cuba, or who helped him. But he arrived in Florida at the beginning of spring training, and made the team, and that's that."

"Did Rico speak much English?"

"I think he understands—understood—more than he let on. He certainly wasn't fluent. But we have several players on the team who speak Spanish, so we could always get them to help translate."

"Did he mention being afraid of retaliation from Cuba?"

"If he did, I wasn't aware of it. He seemed like one happy camper. Like a rooster in a henhouse, if you know what I mean. Didn't seem to be looking over his shoulder at all."

"Who would have talked to him the most?"

Tony thought for a moment. "Blake Harrison would know a lot more than me, but the person he spent the most time with was our shortstop, Ferdinand Ortes."

"Are all of Rico's family back in Cuba?"

"I suppose so. Except his wife, of course."

"His wife?"

He looked at Manziuk in surprise. "Don't you people read the papers? It's been all over them. Rico's wife just arrived in Canada two days ago."

Ignoring the implied insult, Manziuk said, "All right. We'll want to talk to her. Does she speak English?"

"She has an accent, of course, but she speaks it way better than he did."

"Has someone told her about his death?"

"Er … well … I don't really know."

"I'll need to talk to her immediately."

"She'll likely be over at the Diamond Hotel. Rico's been living in a suite there."

"What's the fastest way to get there?"

Tony Kanberra led Manziuk and Ryan through a series of locked doors, and within minutes, they were inside the Diamond Hotel. Manziuk knocked on the door of Rico's room.

There was no response.

He knocked again.

Ryan spotted a maid pushing a cart of clean towels. Pulling out her badge, she approached the woman and convinced her to use her passkey to open the door.

As she unlocked it, the woman said, "I was here earlier, Miss. No one slept here last night."

"Thanks. Please go back to your towels now. We're investigating a crime."

The woman was gone in an instant.

The door opened into a long hallway. With Tony trailing behind, Ryan and Manziuk followed it to two rooms: one a combined kitchen and living room, the other a bedroom with an attached bathroom. The rooms were clean and empty, though somewhat messy. There were stacks of magazines and newspapers on the floor, a tangle of toiletries and men's jewelry on top of the dresser; piles of CDs and DVDs everywhere.

"I don't see much sign of a woman's presence," Manziuk said as he opened the doors to a walk-in closet with latex-gloved hands.

Pulling on her gloves, Ryan opened a drawer in the bureau and began a quick search through socks, T-shirts, and briefs.

Manziuk shut the closet door. "Lots of clothes, but all men's."

"Could this be hers?" Ryan held up a filmy black teddy.

"Somehow I doubt it."

"You know, this is a lot more information than I need," Tony said. "Can I wait for you downstairs in the bar?"

Manziuk quickly agreed.

As soon as Tony was out of the room, Ryan continued, "Several boxes of condoms and some stuff they sell at adult sex stores. I'd guess Rico wasn't too inconvenienced by the fact that his wife was in Cuba." She straightened up. "The wife seems to have taken herself off."

"We need to seal this place until Ident can get up here to do a thorough search."

Ryan used her cell phone to call for a uniformed policeman to take charge of the rooms. While they were waiting for him to arrive, they checked the bathroom and kitchen cupboards. Nothing out of the ordinary, unless you counted the number of bottles of rum, vodka, whiskey, and champagne.

"If the wife comes back, keep her here and call me," Manziuk ordered the guard as he and Ryan left.

Tony was sitting on a stool in the hotel bar sipping what looked like a cola with lime. When Manziuk told him there was no sign of Rico's wife ever having been in the room, he grimaced. "I know she hadn't brought much with her. Just a little bag. Maybe you missed it."

"Possibly, but that doesn't explain where she is."

Tony stared into space for a long moment. "Well, there was a little problem, you see."

"Problem?"

"Yes. She sort of went missing last night. Near the end of the reception. No one saw her leave, and we never found her. We assumed she'd gone back to the hotel with Rico."

"Did anyone try to check with him?"

He looked down. "I don't know."

"Why would Rico have been in the bullpen last night?" Manziuk asked.

Startled by the change in topic, Tony thought a minute and then shrugged. "I don't know. Looking for her, I guess."

"What was their relationship like?"

Tony raised himself up and down in his chair as if trying to find a more comfortable position. "I really couldn't say. She was his wife. They'd been apart for quite a while. I assume they were happy to see each other again." He shrugged. "But she was nervous. You know, over the whole celebrity thing. And being in a new country and all."

"Do you think she could have killed him?" Ryan asked.

Tony's jaw dropped. "Why would she do that?"

"Why would anyone kill him?" Ryan countered.

"It has to be a communist plot or something. Maybe Cuban militants."

Ignoring the comment, Manziuk said, "Can you think of anyone who was here last night who hated Rico enough to kill him?"

"Of course not."

"All right," Manziuk said. "I'd like you to write down when you saw Rico last, and where you were, and who you saw from that time on. Can you do that?"

"We were in the conference room. Then we all went looking for Alita."

"Okay, write down who was in the room when you realized she was missing, and then tell me everything you did, everywhere you went, and everyone you saw after that."

"That's a lot of work—"

"The more information we get, the faster we can solve this."

Tony caved in. "Okay. Okay. I can do that. But I think you're wasting your time."

"Well, it's my time to waste, isn't it?" Manziuk smiled.

Tony looked away. "I suppose so."

"Good." Manziuk smiled. "Now, we need to go through that list of people. Hopefully Ms. Jones has it ready.

Moments after they'd returned to the office they were using, Cecily Jones appeared with a gold folder. "I've printed off three lists for you. The first is the list of everyone who has a key to any area of the building. That includes custodial and security people as well as concession people and people from the various teams.

"The second is a list of everyone who was invited to the press conference last night. Now, not everyone came, so I've put a mark beside the names of those who told me ahead of time they wouldn't be here. The security guard had to check everyone who came in.

"The third list is the team roster."

Manziuk passed the folder to Ryan and said, "Thank you, Ms. Jones. I appreciate your help. Could you just go over some of these names with us so we know who the people are?"

"Of course."

Manziuk moved the two visitor chairs to the desk, and the three of them bent their head over the lists, Manziuk reading out names he didn't recognize and Kanberra's assistant providing rapid-fire answers.

At the end, she said, "I think a few of the players and other team personnel may have already been in the building preparing for the game tonight when we were told no one could leave or come in. Do you want to talk to them first?"

"Absolutely. I'm told that Ferdinand Ortes was Mr. Velasquez's best friend on the team. I'd like to speak with him now, too."

She nodded.

"I'd like to see them one at a time, one right after the other. If you can have someone bring them here, that would be a big help."

She smiled. "I believe the team's manager, Blake Harrison, is in his office, so I'll bring him in first. And I'll see that the rest of the players who were here last night are contacted and asked to come in. Will they be allowed into the building?"

"I'll make sure they are," Manziuk said. "One more question. Who looked after the food and drinks in the press conference room?"

"The hotel. They bring the trays of food over and set them up, and then they come back early in the morning to clear up."

"Would there be servers?"

"Yes, there were two. I'll get their names."

"Was there any other way in last night except through the door with the security guard?"

"No. The stadium is locked. There are security guards around all the time. It's impossible for somebody to get in unless they have a key or are escorted inside."

"Could another security guard have opened a door?"

"I can ask them, but I don't think they would have done so. There were four here last night and they've all been here for some time and have excellent dossiers."

"So you think the murderer had to be somebody who was here for the reception last night?"

"Yes, I do."

"Could someone have been at the game the day before and stayed in the building afterward?"

"It's not completely impossible, but it's highly doubtful. The cleaning crew goes through every part of stadium and all the washrooms and other side rooms after each game."

"What about someone on the cleaning crew staying here?"

"They all have to check in and out. We're very security conscious. We've had a number of bomb threats, so we keep it tight as a drum."

"Can you show us the room used last night?"

"My pleasure."

She took them down several levels and along a hallway to a door at the back of the stadium. "This is the media entrance. It was the only door open last night, and it had a security guard checking off names of the people who came in to make sure they were on the guest list or the team roster."

She led them down a hallway past a number of locked doors, several small lounges, and several washrooms to an elevator. They went down a couple more levels and walked along another hallway to a door guarded by a security guard who checked their ID. Then down another hallway and past more closed doors, more washrooms, and several more lounges. Finally they came to a wider hallway that led to several large rooms, the third of which was the media room used for the reception. Now, it was simply a large room with a few tables and chairs set out and others stacked against the walls.

"The door Mrs. Velasquez used is the one at the front of the room," Cecily Jones said.

They opened it and found themselves in yet another hallway, with a number of closed doors.

"Where do the doors go?"

Cecily walked around touching them. "Hallway to players' club-house; hallway to the offices of the Matrix manager and coaches; hallway to the staff rooms used by the trainers, clubhouse staff, and so forth; hallway to the lounges and restrooms reserved for families and friends; hallway to service elevators for the Diamond Dome staff; hallway to elevators going to the premium level of the Diamond Dome, where the boxes are; and hallway leading to an elevator that takes you to a walkway to the Diamond Hotel."

"So she could have gone to any of those locations from here?"

Cecily shook her head. "No. That's what's so puzzling. You see, the Diamond Dome has a state-of-the art computer system that governs everything. The elevators all have touch pads with codes, so she wouldn't have been able to operate them. She could have gone to the clubhouse, to the manager's and coaches' office area, to the family areas, or to the trainers' room and other staff offices. Some of the individual doors may have been locked, but some would have been open."

"Were there other ways out of those areas?"

"Yes, but all of them lead to elevators that she couldn't have used."

"Would the players know the codes?"

"They'd know some of them. Rico, for example, would have known the code for the elevator that led to the Diamond Hotel because he lived there. And in the end, that's what was assumed to be the case—that she'd learned the code from him and gone to the hotel."

"So players can come and go at any time from the hotel?"

She shook her head again. "That's the other strange thing. The codes only work when they're activated, and that night, none of these elevators were activated. Anyone coming from the hotel had to enter through the media entrance, the same as everyone else. So even if she did know the code, she shouldn't have been able to use the elevator. It's all very puzzling. And now you say there was no sign of her in the hotel room, I really don't know what to think. Where could she be?"

After a quick walk through the various areas used by players and staff, Cecily led them back to their office. As the door closed smoothly behind her, Ryan said, "I wonder who actually runs this place?"

Manziuk grinned.

"Which reminds me," Ryan said. "When do I get a chance to ask the questions?"

"You will. Let's focus on the task at hand for now. We need to concentrate on two areas. One is to identify and meet with every person who was in the stadium last night. The second is to create a list of people who were unaccounted for after the reception. Munsen estimated time of death as earlier than midnight, and we know Rico was alive around eight. So we need to find out who had opportunity, and then hope we find a motive."

Only a few minutes elapsed before Cecily Jones ushered Blake Harrison into the office.

He strode in and examined both the room and its occupants before seating himself in the chair opposite Manziuk and fixing his eyes on the other man's face.

"Mr. Harrison?" Ryan, seated behind the desk, held her pen in the air as she addressed him.

Harrison swiveled to look at her. "That's right."

"We only have a few questions to ask at this time."

"All right, shoot." Harrison turned back to Manziuk.

"Was Rico Velasquez was happy here in Canada?" Ryan asked.

Harrison turned slowly to look at Ryan again. This time he kept his eyes on her. "Seemed to like it here just fine."

"Did he get along well with his teammates?"

Harrison crossed his arms and leaned back. "You throw a bunch of men of various ages and nationalities and personalities together in one room, and you're bound to have some you get along with better than others, and some you have a bit of friction with. But I don't think he had any enemies, if that's what you mean."

"You can't think of anyone who would have had a reason to kill him?"

"That's right." Harrison looked back at Manziuk, who remained silent, his face passive.

"Who would have known Rico best?" Ryan asked. "Who did he hang out with?"

Harrison continued to look at Manziuk. "Ortes mostly. A few others. Rico didn't spend much time with anyone who didn't speak Spanish."

"What about his wife?" Ryan asked. "We understand she arrived this week. Was she happy to be here?"

Harrison shrugged. "I suppose so. I didn't see much of her, so I couldn't honestly say."

"Was everything okay between her and Rico?"

Harrison looked at Ryan. "You'll have to ask her."

"Is there anything else you can tell us that might help our investigation?"

"Yeah, don't waste your time or ours." Harrison's eyes moved back to Manziuk. "It's pretty clear he was murdered by somebody who wasn't happy about his leaving Cuba. That's where you should be looking. Not getting in the way here or distracting my players."

For the first time, Manziuk spoke. "We'll keep that in mind." He stood and opened the door. Harrison, with one last look at Ryan's unsmiling face, walked out.

A moment later, Special Constable Ford walked in without stopping to knock.

"Got anything?" Manziuk asked.

"Not really. No sign of a struggle. Looks like he was just standing there and somebody came up from behind and he went down like a sawn-off tree."

Ryan said, "Could a single blow really have been enough to knock him out and kill him?"

"You'll have to ask Munsen about that. I just know there's no sign of a fight, and our photos show no sign of defensive scratches. We'll know more about that after the autopsy."

"So, nothing we can use?" Manziuk asked.

"Not really. Hard to track anything on the artificial turf. Might be a few threads and so forth, but there were a lot of people here last night, and a lot of players use the bullpen every day. We can hope there's something on him—on his clothes—but that's not terribly likely. If they used a bat, they didn't need to touch him at all. Be at arm's length, so to speak."

"Fingerprints should show up on a bat."

"He could have picked up batting gloves from the locker room and put them back afterward. Or if it wasn't premeditated, he could have used a towel to wipe them off."

"What about blood?" Manziuk looked hopeful.

"Not a terrible lot. Could be a few specks at least got onto the murderer's clothes or skin. Of course, unless it was something distinct, like a uniform, there's not much chance of finding it."

"We can find out what people wore to the party last night and ask to see their clothes. See if anyone has trouble finding them."

"Long shot."

"I know."

There was a moment of silence.

Ryan broke it, speaking for the first time since Ford had entered the room. "So we'll probably have to rely on finding a motive."

The two men turned to look at her.

She shrugged. "It may be harder to find, but it makes solving the case more interesting."

Ford nodded slowly, a grin tugging at the corners of his mouth. Manziuk closed his eyes.

TEN

Ford had just shut the door behind him when Cecily Jones opened it. Clearly and evenly, she announced, "This is Armando Santana, one of our pitchers. Armando was here last night and came in early this morning." She disappeared, leaving in her place an imposing man with skin the color of expensive chocolate and prominent, black dreadlocks.

Armando's eyes moved rapidly to check all corners of the room, and then to study Manziuk and Ryan. After a moment, he stepped inside the room, moving as if afraid the carpeted floor might actually be quicksand. Manziuk was reminded of the time he'd needed a root canal. He was sure he'd entered the dentist's office in exactly the same way.

"Mr. Santana, please take a seat," Manziuk said.

Armando's eyes found the empty chair, and he slowly moved forward and sat down.

"Thank you for coming, Mr. Santana."

The pitcher held up his hand. "Please!" His accent spoke strongly of a Spanish heritage. "When you say Mr. Santana, I think you are talking to my father. My name is Armando."

Manziuk leaned back in his chair and put his fingertips together. "Armando, there's been a death—one of your teammates."

Armando nodded.

"We have to investigate."

Armando nodded again.

"You don't seem surprised?"

"I had heard. We all heard."

"How?"

"My right arm, yesterday, it gave me some trouble. This morning I came in early to work with one of the trainers. I was sitting with my arm in the whirlpool when one of the groundskeepers came bursting into the room, shouting so loudly we didn't know what he was saying. We calmed him down and then he said, 'Rico's body is in the bullpen! Somebody clubbed him to death.' Then he ran out. I think he told everyone in the building."

Manziuk sighed.

Ryan had been tapping her pen on the desk as Armando spoke. "All right, so everybody knows. We need you to tell us anything you can that might help us figure out who might have had a reason to kill him."

Armando turned to look at her. "Why do you ask me this?"

With a pointed look at Ryan, Manziuk took over again. "You're on the same team. You must have had a chance to get to know him, observe him. And you were here last night."

Armando crossed his arms over his chest and stuck out his jaw. "Everyone will tell you that I had reason to kill him."

"And why is that?" Manziuk asked, playing dumb. The truth was he had heard several long diatribes from Mike about the situation between Rico and Armando Santana.

"He took my job."

"Your job?"

"I'm a pitcher—a starting pitcher."

"Yes, I understand."

"When Rico came this year, they sent me to the bullpen."

"So you hated him for taking your job?"

Armando shook his head. "No, no, this happens." He leaned forward and raised his hands, palms up, moving them up and down as if to intensify the impact of his comments. "But he does not let it be. He says many bad things to me."

"You have an accent. Is it Spanish?"

"I'm from the Dominican Republic."

"So you could speak to Rico in his own language?"

"Yes."

"And he was unpleasant?"

"He was a—" Armando glanced at Ryan. "I don't like to use the word in front of a lady. Not a nice person. Anyone who knew him—almost anyone who knew him—will tell you that."

Ryan broke in. "Did you kill him?"

"I did not."

Ignoring Manziuk's frown, Ryan said, "Do you have any suspicions as to who might have hated him enough to kill him?"

Armando looked down and carefully folded his hands in front of his chest. "If I were you, I would first suspect me." He looked directly at Manziuk. "But I didn't do it. And I don't know who did."

"Could it have been retaliation from Cuba?" Manziuk said.

He shook his head. "I don't think so. They will be proud of him, take credit for his skill."

Manziuk said, "Tell me everything you can remember about the reception here last night."

"They ask us to please come out if we can. Just for a little while. Many of us do."

"Why did you come?"

"Because they asked us, and because my friends are coming. Afterwards, my friends and I had planned to go out for dinner together."

"What time did you arrive?"

"It is to begin at seven o'clock. I come a little early to speak to someone."

"You came alone?"

"Yes."

"When you arrived, did you go straight to the room where the reception was being held?"

"No."

"Why?"

"Does it matter?"

"I don't know until I hear the answer."

"I went to Mr. Harrison's office and I spoke to him for a few minutes. Then he saw it was nearly seven, so the two of us walked to the conference room together."

"Did you see anyone else during this time?"

"A couple of security guards and the coaches. They were just ahead of us."

"Did you notice Rico during the reception?"

"When we first came in, I saw him and his wife standing with Mr. Kanberra and some of the other suits. I talked to a few of my friends. Then we got some food and drinks from a table on one side. I saw Alita, Rico's wife. I think she is looking afraid. Rico was beside her for a little while. Then I saw him leave. When his wife was alone for a moment, I went up to her and I said, 'Welcome.' When she realized I spoke Spanish, she told me she was a little nervous. I said she would be fine."

"You waited until Rico left before you spoke to her?"

Armando lifted his head high. "I did not wish to give him another chance to insult me."

"Did he say anything to you during the reception?"

"Later. I was standing with Karen Newland, and he came up and his mouth started to work. Always something rude."

"Why do you think he acted like this toward you?"

Shaking his head, Armando said, "I don't know. He comes here and takes my position, and then he insults me every chance he gets! I don't understand."

The tone of Ryan's voice emphasized her disbelief as she said, "You *really* don't know why?"

Armando shook his head.

Ryan continued to probe. "Wouldn't you have expected him to be friendly, maybe even look up to you? You have a common background."

"It's true we're both from the Caribbean. But we're from very different countries. We have no ties at all." He shifted in his chair so he could see Ryan better. "But yes, I did not understand. And I truly don't know what caused it. It was as if he hated me, but I don't know why."

"Were you the only one he treated this way?"

"He was quick to make fun of other people, or to become angry if someone made an error when he was pitching. But I think maybe I was the only one he was nasty to. And it was getting worse."

"And you *really* have no idea why?" Ryan still sounded unconvinced.

Armando caught her eyes and held them. "No," he said, enunciating each word slowly and distinctly, "I really do not."

"Who were his friends?" Manziuk asked.

Armando kept his eyes on Ryan's for a second longer before turning to face Manziuk. "Ferdinand Ortes was his best friend on the team. Off the team—" He hesitated.

"Off the team?" Ryan echoed.

Armando turned again so he could see her. "Before his wife came, he was with a blonde girl. I do not know much about her. I've seen her at a few games sitting with the wives and girlfriends. And I've seen him get into her car after games a few times."

"Do you know her name?"

"Eve, I think. I don't know more. Ferdinand would know."

Manziuk said, "After you got to the room where the reception was being held, did you stay there until it was over?"

"I did leave one time."

"When was that?"

"While Mr. Kanberra is speaking. It was all words I'd heard many times before. I began to feel a little—how you would say—sick to my stomach. I went out into the hallway for a minute."

"Was he still talking when you came back to the room?"

"No. Rico was talking. Saying how happy he was that his wife was here."

"Then what?"

"Then she said the same things. And after that the press were allowed to ask questions. But Stasey Simon asked a nasty question, and everyone was upset, and then Rico's wife left the room and Mr. Kanberra said it was over."

"And you left?" Manziuk asked.

"I talked to a few people for a minute or two, and then I left."

"Alone?"

"Yes."

"You said you were going for dinner with some other people." Ryan's tone was accusing.

"I found I was not hungry, so I told them to go without me. At first, I wondered if I should help look for her since I spoke her language, so I stayed for a few minutes. I even went out the door she'd gone through, and walked down the hallway to the family area. But then I realized Rico wouldn't like it if I found her, so I turned back."

"Can anyone verify when you left the building?" Manziuk said.

"My friends were already gone. The only one who saw me go was the security guard at the outside door who checked me off his list. I don't know if he'll remember the exact time."

"Where was Rico when you last saw him?"

"Shouting at his agent for letting his wife leave. Some of the others had already gone to look for her."

"All right." Manziuk held out a card. "If you remember anything else, let us know."

Armando's shoulders lowered as he relaxed and took the card. "I will." He stood. With a nod to Manziuk and another to Ryan, he left the room.

"I rather thought this was my turn to ask the questions," Manziuk said casually.

She looked away. "Sorry. I—he really—he was bugging me for some reason."

Manziuk sighed.

"Are all baseball players like that?" Ryan asked.

"Like what?"

"I don't know. I had an impression of pent-up energy, and a lot of annoyance. As though he was allowing us to ask our questions, but what he really wanted to do was blow us away. Was it him, or is that what all baseball players are like?"

"I can't say I felt that from him. But let's interview a few more players and find out."

Cecily Jones ushered in Jonas Newland, who also entered the room slowly, as if his bones were aching. Jonas was a tall man, lean and muscular, with skin as near coal black as skin could be: much darker than Armando's brown skin. The whites of his eyes shone against the blackness of his face and the ebony of his beard. His head was clean and smooth.

His sports shirt, open at the neck, was light yellow. His pants were khaki. On his feet were Birkenstocks.

He glanced quickly at Ryan, gave her a brief smile, and then looked directly into Manziuk's eyes. "You have questions for me, Inspector?"

Manziuk motioned toward the chair, and as soon as Jonas was seated, said, "As the team's catcher, you worked with Rico Velasquez quite a bit. I need to know your impressions of him and anything he may have said that could help us find out who murdered him."

Jonas chose to respond to the latter part of Manziuk's question first. "He never said anything to me about anyone wanting to kill him, or about being in danger. We talked only about batters and strategy and so forth." Jonas's voice was low and flat, each sentence ending on a down note.

"What were your impressions of him?"

"He had a live arm."

"A live arm?"

"He could pitch well. When he was hot, he was almost unhittable."

"Could this have led to jealousy or anger from other players?"

"Enough to kill him? No way!"

"You didn't see that kind of hostility?"

Jonas sat up straight and shook his head. "Jealousy, sure. Envy even. But you admire the skill, even if you don't admire the man."

"So you don't think anyone on the team would have been jealous enough to attack him?"

He shook his head again. "No way."

"Did he have enemies on the team for any other reason?"

Jonas moved in his chair as if trying to find a more comfortable position and failing. "I don't know about enemies. There were a number of people who didn't like him. He could be—well, he could be an arrogant you-know-what. But you don't kill somebody because he's arrogant."

"You think it had to do with something else? Perhaps something personal?"

"You seem to be assuming someone on the team did this."

"I have to explore that option."

"The only way it could have happened with someone on the team—and I don't see this as likely—would have been in a fight, where things got out of hand."

"You admit that's possible?"

He pursed his lips. "I suppose it's possible. But I really doubt it happened."

"Can you think of another option? Does it seem likely to you that one of the press people would have wanted to kill him?"

Jonas shook his head again.

"Someone else associated with the team? Someone other than a player."

"Not likely."

"What about his wife?" Manziuk asked. "Did you help look for her?"

Jonas hesitated a moment before answering. "Briefly. I sent my wife and some of our friends ahead to the restaurant where we had planned to have dinner, and I took a quick look in the family area. I even checked the women's restroom, but no dice. And I could hear others searching, so I left."

"Who do you think killed Rico?"

"I think it must have something to do with Cuba."

When Jonas left, after giving a summary of where he'd been and who he'd talked to during the reception, Cecily came in to give them each a cheerful smile and a cup of steaming freshly brewed coffee in team mugs. "The mugs are yours to keep," she said with a smile.

She left before Manziuk could tell her police rules didn't allow then to accept any presents, even a couple of mugs.

Moment's later, Cecily's now-familiar face peered around the corner of the door. "I have Mr. Ortes. He just came in."

She disappeared and the door opened wide to admit a slim, lithe man of ordinary height, with light brown skin and curly black hair worn to his collar. He had on a bright red shirt with tight-fitting blue jeans. On his feet were gold metallic running shoes.

Like Rico, he was wearing several gold chains. On the middle finger of his left hand was a large emerald ring. On the fourth finger of the right hand was a diamond. Small diamond-studded hoops adorned both ears.

Ferdinand sat easily in the chair, feet planted with knees apart, arms relaxed on the armrests, hands still.

"I understand Ricardo Velasquez was a friend of yours," Manziuk said.

Ferdinand's intense black eyes focused on Manziuk's. "I came in to get ready for the game tonight. They told me what happened. I—I guess I'm a little in shock."

"I understand. I'm very sorry for what's happened."

He bowed slightly to acknowledge the words. "As to your question, to be precise, Rico and I spent a good deal of off-time together since his arrival."

"You seem to be qualifying it. Are you saying you weren't friends?"

Ferdinand glanced down, his long lashes covering his eyes. "Let me put it this way. Rico was a very good pitcher; our team needed his skills. Rico didn't speak a lot of English; I speak Spanish. So I took him under my wing, as you might say, to help the team. His death is very, very sad." Tears welled up in his eyes.

"Did you consider him as a friend?"

"Yes—and no." There was a brief pause while Ferdinand apparently looked for the right words. "I tried to help him out, show him the ropes. But he was rough on the edges, and rather volatile. Not the type of personality I would choose for a close friend."

"Would Rico have considered you his friend?"

A lazy smile touched Ferdinand's lips. "Oh, yes. I never gave him reason to think anything else."

"For the good of the team?"

"Yes." Ferdinand's eyes wandered around the room, settling on Ryan for a long moment. "And for the team, this is very, very sad." Again, tears threatened to overflow his eyes.

Manziuk's voice brought Ferdinand's attention back to him. "I'm told Rico had a girlfriend."

Ferdinand nodded.

When he didn't offer any more information, Manziuk said, "And her name—?"

Ferdinand shifted in his chair. "Her name is Eva MacPherson. She lives in an apartment on the waterfront. Do you want me to write out the address for you?"

"Would you, please?"

He took a small notebook from his back pocket. A few seconds later he handed a slip of paper to Manziuk, who said, "Mr. Ortes, do you have any idea who killed Rico?"

Ferdinand shook his head.

"No suspicions?"

"None."

"He never indicated any fears? Perhaps retaliation from Cuba?"

Ferdinand laughed. "Never. He would have been amused at the idea."

"You think it was someone on the team?"

"I have no idea who it was. I suspect it was an accident. Maybe something got out of hand?"

"An argument?"

"Something like that. Or maybe it was, you know, a psycho. Somebody who doesn't like Latino players. Or somebody who hates Cubans. Or a fan who just didn't like Rico. Somebody who let it go to his head and went kind of crazy. You know."

"You mean a total stranger?"

Ferdinand nodded. "Maybe even a stalker. Nowadays, you never really know, do you?"

"True," Manziuk agreed. He waited a moment. "I understand he's been criticizing some of his teammates."

Ferdinand looked down for a moment, as if gathering his thoughts. "Mostly Armando," he said when he looked up. "Some of the other players now and then. Mostly Armando."

"Do you think Armando could have murdered him?"

Ferdinand shrugged. "I doubt that Armando would be that stupid."

"Do you know why Rico antagonized Armando?"

He grinned. "If Rico didn't get a rise out of Armando, would he have kept doing it? I don't think so."

"So you think it was some kind of black humor?"

"I think so, yes."

"But Armando didn't find it funny?"

"He's too intense, man. Too tight."

"Do you think he could have snapped?"

"I don't think so. But when you get down to it, I guess none of us really knows, do we?"

Manziuk changed tactics. "Did you help with the search for Rico's wife?"

He shook his head. "There were more than enough people to find her. And I was with a friend. We left together."

Manziuk and Ryan continued to talk with the other players and team personnel who'd attended or helped with the reception the night before. Reluctantly, they all admitted that Rico had been riding Armando pretty hard. Or so they thought. Those who didn't speak Spanish really didn't know what was said. The ones who did speak Spanish all said Rico was out of line, and they didn't blame Armando for being upset with him, including taking a swing at him. It was clear that while they were in awe of Rico's pitching ability, to a man they preferred Armando as a person. A couple of them also mentioned that Rico hadn't been getting along with Jonas lately either.

The security guards verified who had been in the building, but not when they had arrived or left. The last people had left the building by nine-thirty that night.

When asked if someone's name could have been checked off even though that person hadn't actually been seen leaving, the guard who'd been watching the door admitted sheepishly that it had happened. When Tony Kanberra, who was in the last group to leave, told him Rico and his wife must have gone back to the Diamond Hotel through the internal passageway, even though the guard couldn't see how that had happened since he hadn't activated the elevator, he took their word for it and checked off the names and locked up. He assumed one of the other guards must have activated the elevator even though they weren't supposed to. But, when questioned, all of them denied doing so.

After talking to Ford, Manziuk set in motion a thorough search of the Diamond Dome to look for any evidence of Alita Velasquez, or any unsecured passages into or out of the building. He also got a team of computer experts doing background checks on every person who had access to the Diamond Dome, from cleaners and food kiosk staff to security guards and head office people.

From talking to the players, the security guards, and the staff of the Fifth Base, they were able to ascertain that most of the media people who'd attended the reception had left the Diamond Dome in a large group at the first sign of Alita Velasquez's absence. All but a few had gone across the street to The Fifth Base together and stayed there until nearly midnight: the rest had gone straight home and had someone there who would vouch for them. The exceptions were Kyle Schmidt, Ginny Lovejoy, Iain Foley, Stasey Simon, and Ted Benedetto.

Manziuk sent the names of those who'd been part of the large group to his team for follow-up. He wanted to talk to the others himself.

Ryan tilted her head. "What about that bunch of media types outside the entrance when we arrived? I wonder if any of them are still hanging around? Maybe the ones we want are there."

Cecily Jones was dispatched to find out. When she returned a few minutes later, she said, "Two of the ones on your list are here. But before you see them, I've just remembered something else. How much do you know about the Diamond Corporation?"

Manziuk frowned. "Only that they own the Matrix and they built the Diamond Dome and the Diamond Hotel."

"Anything else?"

"Not really. The company's been the subject of all kinds of speculation ever since they bought the Matrix five or six years ago, but as far as I know, it's a numbered corporation and no one knows who actually owns it."

"That's all correct."

"But?"

"I don't know if I should be telling you this, but since there's been a murder …."

"Yes?"

"If I were you, I'd get in touch with the lawyers for the Diamond Corporation. Tell them what's happened. Ask them if any of the owners were here that night and might have seen anything. That's all I can say."

"Do you have the name and address for their lawyers?"

"Yes, it's a matter of public record. I can get you that information."

ELEVEN

Manziuk had seen Kyle Schmidt's photo in the newspaper a number of times, so he was expecting a slim blond with short, curly hair, intelligent eyes, and a sardonic smile. However, the man who shuffled in had messy, rather than curly hair, and he had his head down, as if counting each step. When he was a few feet inside the door, he stopped and focused bloodshot eyes first at Ryan and then at Manziuk.

"Won't you sit down, Mr. Schmidt?" Manziuk offered.

Kyle observed the empty chair. After a moment, he walked to it, put his hand on the back, and slowly sat, not settling in but perching on the edge, as if waiting for someone to shout, "Change places."

Manziuk waited a moment before saying, "You're a columnist for the *Toronto Register?*"

Kyle nodded once, slowly.

"I believe I've read some of your work. You're a good writer."

Kyle's eyes widened. "You've read my column?" he asked softly.

"I read the sports pages when I can."

"I—I guess I didn't think the police …." His voice trailed away.

"We do have lives. Beyond our jobs, I mean. Some of us, anyway."

"Yes. I suppose so. Only …." Kyle seemed to lose track of where the sentence was going and stopped.

"Only you hadn't thought much about it?"

"Never." A slightly rueful smile appeared. "Sorry, but I'm just a bit hung over. I was rudely awakened around noon by my editor, who demanded that I get over here immediately. I've been hanging around all day, and it's been a complete waste of time. I'm tired and hot, and I have a massive headache. But I'll try to answer your questions. We all have to help the law."

"How well did you know Rico Velasquez?"

"I watched him play. I tried to talk to him a number of times. That's all."

"Tried to talk to him?"

"He didn't speak much English, and I don't speak Cuban, so we had a hard time understanding each other."

"You wouldn't say you knew him well?"

"I wouldn't say I knew him at all."

"What was your reaction to his death?"

"Stunned. And I have to say that whoever did it could have picked a better day."

"You had no reason to suspect anything like this would happen?"

"Of course not."

"Did you observe Rico last night?"

"Not much, I'm afraid."

"You were here?"

"I came to the reception, or press conference, or whatever it was called. But I'd already had a few drinks, and I saw a nice comfy seat, so I sat in it, and then I fell asleep. When I woke up, the party was nearly over. In fact, they were finishing up the speeches when I went in. Since my head was aching, when they said it was time to go, I left."

"Did anyone see you leave?"

"I don't know." He thought for a moment. "I spoke to my photographer. All we really needed from last night were some photos. He had pictures: I had the gist of the evening: there was no reason for either of us to stay any longer."

"So you both left?"

"He left first. He wanted to get his pictures developed right away."

"You stayed?"

"I had to go the washroom, and I might have talked to a few people. It's all kind of hazy. I think I got lost for a couple of minutes. Took a wrong turn. Ended up at a dead end. Then I found the right hallway and I left."

"Alone?"

A lazy smile touched his eyes and Manziuk caught a momentary glimpse of the man he'd expected to see. "You mean do I have a witness to verify that I didn't hang around to kill Rico?"

Manziuk allowed himself a small smile. "Yes."

"Probably not."

"You didn't walk out with anyone?"

He sighed. "Trust me, I really wish I had. But, as I already told you, my photographer left with a bunch of other people. He wanted to get home."

"Did you see anyone else in the hallways when you left?"

"Not really. Everybody kind of took off in all directions."

"What about the security guard at the entrance?"

Kyle pursed his lips. "I saw him and he saw me. He might remember when it was. I don't."

"Where did you go?"

"To the Fifth Base, where I had a few more drinks."

"Anyone see you there?"

"The bartender. And Ginny Lovejoy. She came in a moment or two after me. I think Iain Foley was there, too. Maybe. I'm kind of hazy on the details."

"There were a number of media people there. Did you join them?"

"I didn't feel like talking to anyone."

"Why were you drinking so much yesterday? Or is that the norm for you?"

Kyle rubbed the palms of his hands together. "Not the norm. It was an off-day, and I just felt like doing it." The boyish smile reappeared. "You know how, every once in a while, you want to do something dumb, even though you know it's dumb? I happened to pick yesterday to get blotto drunk."

"So your memories of the entire evening are rather vague?"

"Actually, from about three o'clock in the afternoon on."

"Did you write a column?"

"It was filed by two-thirty, so my time was presumably my own, except they went and messed it up by scheduling the reception. But like I said, all we really needed from that were some photos of Rico and his wife."

Manziuk switched topics. "Do you have any idea who might have hated Rico enough to kill him?"

Kyle snorted. "Rico was a self-centered, obnoxious jerk."

When he didn't say any more, Manziuk said, "Go on."

Kyle frowned. "Well, he knew he was good, and he liked to rub other people's noses into it. He cared only for Rico, not for the team. And he would have tromped on anybody to get what he wanted. I expect when you're like that, you can't help making enemies."

"One of his teammates?"

At this question, Kyle became almost animated. "Are you kidding? With Rico, the team had a shot at the pennant. Without him, they don't. Besides, don't you have to more than dislike somebody to kill him?"

In direct contrast to Kyle Schmidt, Ginny Lovejoy leaned against the leather chair back with her right knee crossed over the left, looking relaxed and ready for a long chat. Her gray tweed A-line skirt, short-sleeved purple top, gold chain and matching earrings, and charcoal gray low-heeled pumps combined with medium-length reddish hair, freckles, and a warm smile, shouted, "Here is a confident, creative woman."

"I try to read your column whenever I can," Manziuk mentioned before he started the interview. "You're a very perceptive writer."

Her eyebrows shot up and she grinned. "Wow! Thank you."

"I hope you can help us now." He allowed a slight smile. "We could use some of that insight. What was your opinion of Rico Velasquez?"

"Rico," she echoed, her head tilting slightly to the right, her eyes bright and inquisitive. There was a short silence. "Well, I guess I have several different opinions. As a baseball fan, I cheered for him. As a person, I didn't particularly like him. As a journalist, I thought of him as pure gold."

"Good copy?"

"You bet."

"So you aren't happy to see him gone?"

"Hardly. The Matrix needed him. And he made my job much easier." She leaned toward Manziuk. "You could say a lot of things about Rico, but you could never call him dull."

"Who do you think would want him dead?"

She considered the question for a moment. "Nowadays you can't tell, can you? I mean with kids taking sawed-off shotguns to schoolyards, fired employees shooting their employers, angry drivers attacking anyone who cuts them off in traffic—you never really know who's next. I don't just mean who's the next victim; I mean who's the next assailant."

"Do you suspect anyone?"

"No one I know is homicidal. Or, if they are, I'm not aware of it."

"Do you think one of his teammates could have done this? Someone with a grudge against him."

"Like Armando, you mean?" Her eyes looked past Manziuk into some world of her own making. She slowly shook her head. "No. Armando is normally one of those nice, stable guys. Not great copy, but the kind of person you might have as a friend."

"Normally?"

"Well, I'll admit Rico's been riding him pretty hard." Her face took on a puzzled look, eyes squinting, forehead wrinkled. "You know, I really don't get it. Armando did nothing to Rico, yet Rico seemed to always have it in for him. It should have been the other way around. Armando should have been angry because Rico took his starting job. But it was as if Rico was the one with the grudge. It never made any sense to me." She pushed out her lower lip slightly. "Unless Rico was afraid that if he faltered, Armando would get the job back."

"Is there anyone else on the team who had a reason to be angry with Rico?"

"He got on nearly everyone's back a bit. I mean, if someone bobbled a ball when he was pitching, he always gave them a dirty look, and he often said something rude. Not the kind of attitude to make people enjoy your presence." She waved one hand as if brushing aside her words. "But oodles of big league players are like that, and I've never heard of anyone killing a teammate over that kind of stuff."

Manziuk watched Ryan make some notes, then looked back at Ginny. "Anything else you can tell us?"

"Depends on what you want to know. When you hang around the team all the time, and it's not only your job, but you enjoy it, you pick up a lot of stuff. But do I know who murdered Rico? No. And I have no particular suspicions either. Just a lot of questions. Like you."

"Was there anyone in the media who had a bad relationship with Rico?"

She thought for a moment. "Just Stasey, but she has a pretty sour relationship with nearly everyone."

"Stasey Simon?"

"You've heard of her, right?"

"Yes."

"Well, she dissed Rico a lot on her show. But, again, that should have made him angry with her, not the other way around."

Manziuk checked the time after Ginny had gone out. Almost seven. He sighed.

"Long day," Ryan commented.

"And we have no idea why he was murdered or who the most likely suspect is."

"You worried about Benson?"

"Benson, Seldon, the mayor, the whole town …. I don't want this to drag out, but I'm afraid it's going to be hard slogging. And for all we know, it actually *was* the Cubans!" He stood up and stretched. "We still need to talk to his agent, this Eva person, Stasey Simon and her producer, and Iain Foley. Do you want to pick up some food before we do more interviews?'

"Sounds good."

Manziuk started toward the door.

"Oh, no," Ryan yelled.

He turned to face her. "What is it?"

"My mother! I was supposed to meet her for dinner at six!" She closed her eyes as if in pain. "I forgot all about it."

"Can you call her?"

Ryan pulled a cell phone out of her purse. "Turned it off," she said, "when we were doing the interviews. Didn't want any distractions. Must have forgotten to put it on vibrate." She flipped it on. "I've missed six calls." She sighed, then hit some keys. "Mom?" She listened for several minutes. "I'm sorry. We're in the middle of an investigation." She listened again. "No, I won't be able to get there. … Yes, a murder. I'll see you at home."

"Home life," Manziuk said as she put the phone in her purse.

"Cops shouldn't have lives," Ryan commented.

"Be simpler in one way. Harder in another."

"Harder?"

"By having lives of our own, we're more apt to remember to talk to people as people rather than as machines. Which reminds me," he said with a sigh. "I need to call my wife. We were going to go over to see Woody—Sergeant Craig—tonight. She'll have to go without me."

After a quick call to see if Pat Davis was in his office on the twelfth floor of a bank building eight blocks from the stadium, they stopped at a fast-food Mexican place. Ryan had rejected all burger places as unhealthy, but she seemed happy with two soft chicken tacos while Manziuk got his beef in a couple of burritos.

As he went to a seat, he stopped to look in the newspaper bin for the sports pages of both daily newspapers. He had suddenly become curious to see what Ginny Lovejoy and Kyle Schmidt had written the day before the murder. It took a bit of searching, but he was successful. He carried the newspapers to the table and read as he ate. The *Register* was on top.

Who Cares?

by Kyle Schmidt

Why is it we care so much about the people who get paid enormous salaries to play games? Is it in our genes? A prehistoric need we have? A habit? Do we do it because other people expect it of us? Sort of like the story about the Emperor's new clothes—where everyone knows the emperor is naked, but no one will be the first to say so because the others might ostracize us.

Who actually cares if there are two teams facing each other in a game of baseball? Why on earth do we go and sit there and watch them while stuffing ourselves with junk food and downing cup after paper cup of beer? Are we really having a good time, or have we just psyched ourselves up to believe we are?

We get fat and lazy and stuff our money into other people's wallets. We wear their names on our T-shirts and buy cards with their pictures, and stand in line for their autographs. And this is entertainment? How about subjugation?

We watch them day after day, year after year, and when we stop, they plead and cajole and berate us, imploring us to have more team spirit. And guiltily, we do as they want.

Wouldn't we all be a lot better if we just went for a walk? Spent some quality time with our spouses? Played games with our kids? Read a good book?

Baseball isn't a religion: it's entertainment. But we act as if it was sacred. As if we had to try to appease these little tin gods.

For crying out loud, it's a bunch of grown men hitting and throwing a little ball, and running around a small field, and we pay them millions of dollars to do it, just so we can have the privilege of watching them! How screwy can you get?

We could do a thousand other things with our money, from buying food for starving people and houses for homeless people, to giving it to scientists to help them find cures for diseases we can't control, to helping deserving kids to go to college.

But no. Those things would make sense. We'd rather believe the propaganda we're fed and pay our own hard-owned money to give contracts worth millions of dollars to these boy-children from Neverland, who haven't grown up, who may never grow up, and who demand our obeisance.

And the reality is that few of us even stop to ask questions. It's just the way things are done. So what?

Manziuk turned to Ginny's column in the *Daily News*.

The Promise of Great Things to Come

by Ginny Lovejoy

I've been thinking over something Rico Velasquez said Wednesday night after the game, which the Matrix lost. As you'll recall, Rico started the game, but Armando Santana came in with the bases loaded in the eighth inning and allowed a home run.

Rico became angry when Coach Harrison brought Armando in, even though the three runners on base were Rico's responsibility and it made perfect sense to bring in a relief pitcher in that situation. In fact, it wouldn't have been at all unusual for the Matrix to have brought in a new pitcher to start the eighth. How many starters pitch complete games these days? Not many. If they get through the seventh, everyone is happy.

But Rico was adamant that Blake should have left him in. Apparently, he had no-hitters in Cuba, so he figures it's logical to assume he'll have them here. And maybe he will. But Rico, no-hitters are rare. And last I heard, baseball is still a team game. Maybe you should start thinking about the fact that there are nine people on the field at any given time.

You know what, Rico? No one really cares if you never have a no-hitter. Just pitch a good game and let your teammates do their job. That's how pennants are won. The game is much bigger than the individuals in it.

But more than that. That's how life is lived. Wasn't it John Donne who said, "No man is an island"? We aren't meant to be alone. We're meant to live in community and work with one another. Even the Lone Ranger had Tonto.

Yes, we're all different, and sometimes we don't understand each other. But instead of putting up walls, we need to seek out ways to work together. Life on a baseball diamond can be a microcosm of the lives we all lead.

You want to show me something Rico? Show me how you can finally become part of the Matrix. That would be a real accomplishment.

It felt odd reading the two columns, knowing that the person who was the catalyst for them both was dead long before the papers hit the streets.

"Anything useful in there?" Ryan asked.

"Not really," Manziuk said. "Just ideas."

The door to the sports agent's outer office was open, so they walked in. No one was at the receptionist's desk. Manziuk rapped on the door of the inner office. "Come on in," said a despondent voice. A disheveled, middle-aged man, who presumably was Pat Davis, was sitting at his desk, a glass in hand, and an almost empty bottle in front of him. "Where's Jennifer?" he asked.

Manziuk said, "Your secretary?"

"Yeah. She was here."

"No one out front."

"Maybe she went home." The words were slurred.

"Pat Davis?"

"Who's asking?"

Manziuk held out his ID. "Detective Inspector Manziuk and Detective Constable Ryan."

"Cops. I knew you were coming."

"We called."

"Yeah."

"Rico Velasquez was your client?"

"Rico. Yeah. Ricardo was his name, you know. Like Lucy's TV husband on the show, Ricky Ricardo. Only it was Rico's first name."

"How long was Rico your client?"

"Since he got here from Cuba. En route, I suppose. Tony's idea. Knew he'd need an agent and asked me to take him on."

"Do you know how he got out of Cuba?"

He shook his head. "I don't ask questions." He sighed. "I got no complaints. I got a great client. He made money, I made money. No complaints." He took a long drink from the amber liquid in his glass.

"How well did you know him?"

"He was a lot of trouble, you know." Pat leaned back in his chair and massaged his right shoulder with his left hand. "A lot of trouble." There was a long silence. "He could barely speak English. Had to explain things to him. A mind of his own, though." He made a face. "Wasn't so simple after all. I earned every dime."

"And now he's gone," Manziuk added.

"Gone."

"What can you tell us about Rico's wife?"

Pat stared at the glass in his hand, swirling the remaining inch of liquid around as though, if he could just read it, the liquid would tell him what he needed to know. "Not his type. Not from what I saw. Spoke English. Not perfect, but pretty good. Seemed unnerved. Not sure what to do." He guffawed. "Of course, Eva didn't exactly help."

"Eva was Rico's girlfriend?"

"Yeah."

"Rico's wife found out about her?"

"And how!"

"Can you tell us what happened?"

"First, I take the wife to the hotel and Rico isn't in his room. I call Ferdinand, and Rico is over at his place—with Eva. Of course no one told his wife about that. But then Eva shows up when they're having dinner after the game that night." Tears formed in his eyes as he doubled over with laughter.

"You should have been there the next day. We had a meeting right here in this office. Rico, the wife, and me. And Ferdinand, here to translate for Rico. Like nothing I'd ever seen before." He wiped the moisture from his eyes with the sleeve of his shirt.

"Of course, we had to double-talk like crazy to get her to agree to stay, and to read the speech Tony wrote for the press conference that night. I wanted to wring Rico's neck. But now, thinking about it, it was so crazy. Like something you'd see in a movie, you know? Only this was real life."

Manziuk nodded. "Where is the wife now?"

Pat held his arms wide. "I couldn't tell you. She was supposed to be staying with him, but she refused. So Ferdinand booked her a separate room. Rico wasn't too happy about it, but Ferdinand convinced him to play along."

"Ferdinand was aware that she had her own room?"

"Sure. He was the one who got it."

"All right. Have you talked to her today?"

"I tried to call her this morning as soon as I got the news, but there was no answer. So I went over to the hotel, but she wasn't in her room or in the restaurant."

"So she's still missing?"

"I couldn't find her."

"Did you go inside her room?"

"Knocked on the door. No answer. I looked for her in the restaurant. Didn't know what else to do."

"Okay, we'll check." Manziuk nodded to Ryan, who left the room.

To Pat, he said, "Did Rico tell you about any enemies he may have had?"

"You mean from Cuba?" Pat laughed. "Naw, he never told me anything like that."

"What about in Canada?"

"You mean like a fan becoming a stalker? All I can say is he sure never gave any sign to me. You ask me, I don't think anything was worrying him—except how to handle both his wife and Eva."

"What about his relationship with the other players?"

Pat sighed. "You mean Armando."

"Yes."

Ryan returned. When Manziuk looked over, she said, "Ford's there. He'll check her room himself."

Pat was weaving a pen through his fingers. After a moment, he spoke without taking his eyes from the pen. "He seemed to see himself as this macho star player who could get away with cutting down the other, lesser players. I kept telling him to quit, but …." Pat looked up. "He didn't listen to me much."

"Did he listen to anyone?"

"Ferdinand, maybe. I don't really know, because I couldn't always tell what they were saying. I relied on Ferdinand a lot to translate for me, but it was a weird feeling. I never knew whether he really was translating what I said and what Rico said, or if he was making up the whole thing and telling Rico and me who knows what."

"You don't trust Ferdinand?"

Pat set the pen down and looked up. "Sure I trust him. It just, you know, feels funny not knowing what other people are saying."

"Do you have any suspicions about who might have killed Rico?"

"You sure it wasn't an accident? Or suicide? Or even just a natural death, like heart attack or something?"

"Officially we have to wait for the autopsy results, but we're going on the assumption that foul play was involved."

"Foul play?" He chuckled. "That's a good one." He turned his head to see Manziuk better. "You like baseball?"

"Yes, I do."

"Then you'll appreciate what's happened here. The Matrix just lost one of the aces of their staff. Probably the number two man. Their pennant and World Series hopes just flew out the window. Oh, they'll be in there trying, but without Rico pitching every fourth or fifth day, they just took a giant step down. Instead of all those nearly guaranteed wins, they'll have—what? Armando Santana?" Pat shook his head. "I hate to say it, but whoever took out Rico, took out this whole team."

"Could that have been the intention?"

He crossed his arms and leaned back in his chair. "Maybe it's— you know—the bookies. Maybe it's another team. Maybe it's a reporter who was running out of good stories. I don't know. Seems to me that's your job."

"All right. Thanks for your time." Manziuk started to stand.

Pat reached up to run his fingers through his already-tousled hair. "Oh, don't go away all huffy. I didn't mean anything. Just that it could have been anybody, including a fan who didn't like the way he pitched in his last game."

"You were at the reception last night?"

Pat shrugged. "Of course, I was. He was my client."

"How long were you there?"

"All of it."

"When did you last see Rico?"

"He was around the whole time. Then Alita disappeared and we all started looking for her. When we got back together, Rico was missing too, so we just assumed he'd found her and taken her back to the hotel. So we left."

He stood up and leaned against the back of his chair. "You have to understand, nobody thought it was a big deal. Karen Newland told Jonas that Alita took off for a while the night before, too, during the game. And even if she did get lost for a bit, there was no reason to think she wasn't perfectly safe." He stopped talking, and his face took on a puzzled expression. "What am I saying? Obviously, she wasn't so safe. You don't think something's happened to her, do you?"

Manziuk got to his feet. "Hopefully we'll find her soon. Just one more thing. Why didn't the GM know Rico's wife had a separate room?"

"They're all one big happy family." He laughed mirthlessly. "We didn't tell him because he wouldn't want to know."

"If you think of anything else, give me a call." Manziuk took out a card with his phone number on it and set it carefully on Pat's desk.

On their way out of the office, they still didn't see the elusive Jennifer. Presumably, she'd gone home long ago.

"Think we should put him in a cab?" Ryan asked. "If he tries to drive home, he could have a problem."

"I don't think he's going anywhere for a good long time."

"Is he a suspect?"

"With Rico, he was going to make a lot of money. I expect he's drinking to dull the pain of thinking about all the money he's lost."

As they were leaving, Ford called to say the room Alita Velasquez had supposedly been using had nothing in it to indicate she'd ever walked through the door. They were dusting for prints.

Manziuk and Ryan drove to the address Ferdinand Ortes had given them for Eva MacPherson. It turned out to be a very nice condo on the waterfront. There was an intercom with TV, plus an attendant at a desk inside the front door. It took a few moments to convince the attendant to let them inside without contacting Eva first.

"Nice place," Ryan said as they walked along the plush mauve carpeting on the eight floor. The hallways were wide, the ceiling very high. "This used to be a warehouse, right?"

"Right. They convert them into apartments, call them condos, and sell them for big bucks."

"So what's this Eva person doing here?"

"Who knows? Maybe Rico was paying. I assume he had lots to spare."

The white enameled door before them was at least nine feet high and four wide, with a brass knocker in the middle. To one side was a doorbell. Manziuk pushed the button.

A few minutes passed before the door was opened a couple of inches. They had a vague impression of someone watching them through the slit.

A soft, hesitant voice said, "Who are you? How did you …? How did you get in?"

Manziuk held up his badge. "Police. We need to talk to you."

"Police?" she repeated.

"Please open the door so we can come in."

"Why do you want … to see me?"

"We're investigating a possible homicide."

"Homi—Somebody … I know?" The door vibrated slightly.

"A baseball player named Ricardo Velasquez."

"Rico?" she said in a hollow voice.

"The chain. Could you please open the door?"

"You really are … police?"

Ryan held her badge out where the woman could see it.

"I—I see." The woman shut the door and then opened it without the chain.

Manziuk and Ryan walked into an enormous room with walls at least eighteen feet high. Gauzy off-white hangings separated the large room into several smaller spaces and framed the row of windows that marched along the entire far end.

The woman before them was blonde, blue-eyed, and red-faced, as if she'd been crying. She was wearing a lacy cream-colored slip, with apparently nothing underneath. Her feet were bare.

"I was just going to have a drink," she said softly as she led them toward the far end of the room.

As they walked past a wall of the gauzy hangings, a gigantic black and white close-up of Marilyn Monroe's face rose up before them on the side wall to their left. The picture was at least ten feet high and equally wide. Around it were a number of smaller black and white pictures, also of Marilyn.

Eva MacPherson stood at a bar in the corner of the room next to the photos. "Do you … want something?" she asked in a soft, breathless voice after making herself a drink.

"No, thanks," Manziuk replied.

"If you do … it's here," she said. Holding up a champagne flute, she added, "Dom Perignon. The best." She carried her drink to an overstuffed white sofa and sank into it. She fluttered her dark eyelashes. "What do you … want … from me?"

Soto voice, Ryan said to Manziuk, "Does she think she's Marilyn Monroe reincarnated or something?"

Ignoring Ryan, Manziuk said to Eva, "We need to ask you a few questions."

"What kind of … questions?"

"Not dumb," Ryan whispered.

Manziuk sat carefully on a flimsy-looking white chair. Fortunately, it held his bulk. "Ricardo Velasquez was found this morning by groundskeepers at the Diamond Dome. He was dead. We're investigating his death."

"What does that … have to do … with me?"

"Were you aware he was dead?"

She seemed to debate with herself. "Yes." After a moment's silence, she added, "Ferdinand called me."

"Then let's talk about what we need to know. When did you see him last?"

She played with the hem of her slip. "At the reception last night."

"You were invited?"

She looked up at him, her eyes wide and ingenuous. "Why shouldn't I be?"

"Did you speak to him?"

"He was with … his wife."

"And you were with—?"

She continued to look at Manziuk, her eyes wide and her voice breathless, pausing slightly between each phrase. "I went with … Ferdinand. That doesn't mean I was … *with* … him. Not every second. I talked to … other people … too."

"Did you talk to Rico?"

"I told you. He was with … his wife. I didn't want … to bother him. He was … busy."

"So you didn't talk to him?"

"Not to have a … you know … a conversation."

"What, specifically, did you say to each other?"

"We've been friends."

"So I gather."

"We were friends. That's all. I showed him around, gave him tips on how to behave, you know, in society."

She looked down again and touched the silk of her slip. "Things like that."

"I see."

Her head came up. "Do you?" When he didn't respond, she said, "And then she arrived and all of a sudden, he had no time for me. And the ironic thing is he doesn't—didn't—even care about her. He only married her because he thought her connections might help him." She seemed to have forgotten to slow the pace of her words, and her voice now sounded more like a petulant young woman than a breathless Marilyn.

"But despite this, when she arrived in Canada, he thought he had to spend his time with her?"

"The team made him. And those stupid reporters with their sob stuff! None of it was true. Rico laughed when I read the stories to him. But the team thought the whole thing was good publicity. And I was a—what did they say? Oh, yeah. A 'liability.' So he had to ditch me for little Miss Speaks-Some-English-and-Looks-Like-a-Lady."

"That must have been difficult for you."

She took a long drink. "It was the pits."

"So Ferdinand stepped in to look after you?" Ryan asked.

Under her dark lashes, Eva flashed Ryan an angry look. "He knew what was going on, and he was trying to help me. There was no reason for Rico to get mad."

Ryan looked over at Manziuk. When he didn't say anything, she continued. "Rico was angry that Ferdinand took you to the reception?"

"There was no reason I shouldn't be there. I didn't make a scene." Her voice had become sulky.

"What did you say to Rico?"

"I didn't bother him, if that's what you mean. All I said was a quick 'Hello' to both of them."

"And what did they say to you?"

"Miss I've-Got-My-Nose-in-the-Air didn't say a word. Rico just looked at me, and then he looked at Spidey. Everyone calls Ferdinand 'Spidey.' After Spiderman, you know? Rico said something to Spidey in Spanish. I don't know what it was. Spidey laughed. Then he and I went over to the buffet table to get something to eat."

"Was that the only time you spoke to Rico."

"Yes."

"When was the last time you saw him?"

"I think he came near us afterwards, but he didn't stop to talk to me."

"And you left with Ferdinand?"

"Yes."

"Were you with him the entire time?"

"Yes." She paused. "Well, not when I went to—you know—the powder room."

"When was that?"

"I don't know. Not too long before we left." As if getting back into character, Eva leaned forward and batted her eyes at Manziuk. "If I'd known … you'd need all this information … I'd have written it down … but not realizing … Rico was going to get himself killed … I didn't see any need … to keep track of every move … I made."

Ryan rolled her eyes. "Did Rico ever tell you he was afraid of anyone?"

Eva uttered a peal of surprised laughter. "Rico? Tell me he was afraid? Oh, that's rich. You really didn't know him, did you?"

She paused, and, returning to her role, crossed her knees demurely and picked at the silk covering her upper thighs.

Finally she spoke again. "Rico wasn't afraid of anything. Rico was—he was on top of the world. No cares. No fears. Not until the team brought his so-called wife over. Then he was angry. But I never saw him afraid. Except maybe …." Her eyes grew thoughtful. "He would have been afraid of going back to Cuba. Not afraid, exactly. I mean, he wasn't afraid he would be hurt or imprisoned or anything. He just never wanted to go back. He was happy here. Until the team brought his wife and told him he had to behave right. Then he was angry. But he was never afraid of them. He knew if this team decided they didn't want him, lots of other teams would."

"So," Ryan said, "who do you think might have killed him?"

Eva looked at Ryan, her eyes wide under the dark lashes. "Was he really killed? You're sure?"

"Could you see him committing suicide?" Ryan asked skeptically.

Eva thought for a second before shaking her head. "No. I can see him getting angry and just blowing up. Not killing himself. Killing the other person, maybe."

"Did he ever indicate he had health problems?"

"No." She sat up straighter. "But you never know do you? What about that figure skater? The one from Russia. He was in great shape, and then one day he just died. An aneurysm or something. That could have happened."

"It could have," Ryan agreed. "But it didn't."

Eva touched her lower lip with one finger and said tragically, "Ferdinand wouldn't tell me how he died."

"Someone bashed his head in," Ryan said bluntly, "probably with a baseball bat."

Eva stared at her, eyes rounding in horror. "Oh—oh, no!" She turned to grab a zebra-striped fuzzy pillow from beside her and, holding it over her face, collapsed in tears. "No! No! No!"

"Great tact," Manziuk whispered to Ryan.

She whispered back. "I wanted to see if there was a real person in there somewhere."

"Satisfied?"

"I suppose."

"See if you can find her doctor's name."

Ryan found Eva's phone and checked its directory. "No doctor, but there's a listing for 'Daddy.'"

"All right. Try the number."

"No!" Eva scrambled off the couch. "Don't you dare call him. I'm fine. You just get out, that's all. Both of you get out of here!"

TWELVE

Stasey Simon lived in a narrow, three-story, brick house in an older neighborhood filled with blocks of narrow brick houses. Some were detached; some semis. Stasey's was detached. Some of the houses looked tired or cluttered, but Stasey's was bright and cheerful, probably because the white trim looked freshly painted and the windows were large and clear, obviously of later date than the rest of the house. Ryan went up the four steps and rang the doorbell.

"Nice," Manziuk said as he took in the well-kept flower garden and green grass. The grass was a bit sparse in places, perhaps, but only because of the spreading roots of the huge maple trees that commanded the main front yard.

They waited.

"No lights on that I can see," Manziuk commented.

Ryan knocked.

An older man, probably in his seventies, was passing by. He called out, "If you're looking for Stasey, go to Carnaby's Pub. Third floor at the back, in the booth on the left. When she's not doing her show or watching a game, she's usually there."

"Thank you," Manziuk said. "Are you a neighbor?"

The man pointed to a house a few doors down. "Lived in that there house for forty-three years. First place I owned, and it'll be the last place, too."

"Do you know Stasey Simon well?"

"Nope. We speak now and then. Pleasant enough. Keeps her house nice. Hires a landscape company to do the outside, a maid company to do the inside. Doesn't have loud parties or pets. Buys you a drink now and then at Carnaby's when she's in the mood. What I call a decent neighbor."

"Thank you Mr.—?"

"Donaldson. Frank Donaldson."

"We appreciate your help, Mr. Donaldson."

"You'll find her there." He pointed toward the south end of the street. "Only a block and a half." He moved on.

"We may as well walk," Manziuk said. "It's a nice evening."

Carnaby's Pub and Grill was on the corner of the residential street and one of Toronto's numerous outlying small business streets. It was actually two three-story century houses that had been gutted and turned into a multi-level grouping of individually decorated rooms with assorted pool tables, large screen TVs, and variegated seating areas, including a second-story terrace out back. They found Stasey Simon in a small third-floor room filled with dark walnut booths with burgundy leather benches. Gold patterned hanging lights created a warm glow; fresh yellow daisies added a homey touch to each table; and the aging bartender, who wore a nametag that said "Joe," seemed content to live out his life in the confines of the secluded bar.

As Mr. Donaldson had told them, Stasey Simon was seated in the booth at the very end of the room. She had a platter of onion rings, fries, and seafood on the table in front of her, and a half-finished drink in her hand.

"Slumming?" she asked as the two police officers came up. "Or were you looking for me? We never did finish our conversation from this afternoon at the Diamond Dome."

"We have a few questions we need to ask you," Manziuk said formally.

She swept her hand toward the empty seat across from her. "Won't you join me?"

"Are you sure you wouldn't rather go back to your house?"

"This is just as much my house as that place is. Anyway, I'm eating."

"We're investigating the death of Rico Velasquez," Manziuk said as he slid into the booth after Ryan.

"Good for you."

"What can you tell us about Rico?"

For a second, Manziuk thought Stasey's smile bordered on being a smirk. She picked up a large onion ring and took a bite. "Rico," she said as she chewed. "What can I say that others haven't? Is that what you want?"

"Something like that. Of course, you have no way of knowing what others have said."

"True."

"So why don't you simply tell us your opinion of him?"

"He was a jerk," she said, still chewing. She swallowed and then took up her fork to place a fried shrimp in her mouth.

"A jerk?"

"You know. A not very bright male who doesn't see two feet beyond his own wants and needs."

"How well did you know Rico?"

"Not very well, I suppose." She took a sip from her glass. "Joe, I need a refill!" she called out.

"If you didn't know him very well, why did you dislike him?"

She finished her drink before answering. "I didn't dislike him. I just thought he was a jerk." She shrugged. "He can be as big a jerk as he wants as long as he gives me material for my show."

"You were at the reception last night?"

She tipped her head slightly. "Naturally."

"Did you talk to Rico?"

Stasey waited while the waiter set down her fresh drink, removed her empty glass, and took orders for coffee from Manziuk and milk from Ryan. "Milk?" She laughed. "How strange! I'd have thought— Oh well, where were we? Oh, yes, you wanted to know if I talked to Rico last night. Well, Inspector, the truth is I've never enjoyed trying to carry on a conversation with somebody who doesn't speak my language."

"So you went to the reception and didn't speak to the person it was for?"

She frowned at him. "Don't be silly. It wasn't for Rico. It was for his wife."

"Did you speak to her?"

"Briefly."

"What did you say?"

"I asked her what she thought of the city, and if she missed Cuba."

"And …?"

"She said, 'This is a very nice city. I am so happy to be here.' Then she said, "I miss my family back in Cuba, but I am so happy to be here with her husband.' It was all a very carefully rehearsed speech."

"Did she say anything else?"

"When I said, 'Now, what do you really think?' the ever-watchful Pat Davis stepped between us and offered to get me a drink. And since I don't take advantage of children and simple-minded females, I went with him."

"Did you have any other conversation with her or Rico last night?"

"Other than the question-and-answer period they had, no. And that lasted only as long as my first question."

"And your question was …?"

She laughed. "You expect me to remember every word I say?" She got out a cigarette and lit it. "I don't know. Something to do with Rico's attitude."

Manziuk looked at her but didn't speak.

She glanced up at him through her eyelashes. Then she laughed. "Okay, I asked what she thought of the rotten way her husband treated his teammates. That got Rico upset, and he made like he was going to deck me, but a couple of people pulled him off. Then Tony said the questions had to be mushy stuff, and Kyle—I think it was Kyle—started to laugh. He was drunk, so his laugh was both loud and annoying. And while everybody was looking at Kyle, dear Alita disappeared. There was some confusion, and then Tony announced that the fun was over. I heard later they went looking for her."

"Did you look for her?"

She speared several fries with her fork, dipped them in ketchup, and shoved them in her mouth. After chewing and swallowing them, she said, "Nuh-uh. The party was dead. I wasn't getting anything interesting. So I left."

"Did you leave with anyone else?"

"The Beast."

At their inquiring glances, she added, "My producer."

"You left together?"

"Well, if you want to get technical, he left first. We hadn't come together. He had his kiddie car and I use the subway."

"Did you actually see him leave?"

"I saw him go out of the reception room."

"You didn't leave together?"

"Not exactly."

"Any particular reason?"

She sighed. "We had a bit of an argument, okay?"

"What about?"

"Nothing to do with Rico's being rubbed out."

"What time was it when you left?"

"How should I know?"

"You didn't look at the time when you were leaving?"

"I had no appointments."

"Did you leave with anyone else?"

"After Ted left, I finished my drink and then I left too. Most of the people had gone by then."

"Where did you go?"

"Here. I was hungry. I didn't get much to eat there."

"Do you have any suspicions as to who might have wanted to kill Rico Velasquez?"

"You mean aside from his wife and Eva, right?"

"Eva?"

"Don't tell me you haven't got the scoop on that. Someone must have given you an earful about the beautiful Eva."

"We're aware that Rico had a friendship with someone else before his wife arrived."

"And did you know that Eva isn't the kind of girl to take getting dumped lightly?"

"I'm not sure—"

"Eva's last boyfriend was the victim of a hit and run driver three days after they split up. He's alive, but it was a close thing."

When they rang the doorbell for his brick two-story townhouse a few miles from where Stasey lived, Iain Foley answered immediately. Despite the late hour, he was impeccably dressed in a short-sleeved navy sports shirt, cream pants, and brown loafers. At his side was a golden retriever who watched and wagged his tail, but neither barked at the visitors nor approached them.

"Mind if we come in?" Ryan asked as she held out her ID.

"Do I have a choice?" Iain asked. Then he smiled. "You must get tired of that response. And of having to introduce yourself. So I'll save you the trouble. Detective Constable Jacqueline Ryan and Detective Inspector Paul Manziuk. Correct?"

Behind Ryan, Manziuk nodded, feeling somewhat at a loss for words. He'd heard Iain on air many times, and recognized his voice immediately, but this was the first time he'd ever seen the man behind the voice, and he felt unsettled. He'd expected someone much bigger and much more impressive.

Iain motioned them to follow him. "Please, come and have a seat. I've actually been expecting you."

As they entered his living room, Manziuk suddenly felt tired. The muted green walls, dark green leather sofa and chairs, off-white accessories and drapes seemed to envelope him and urge him to sit quietly. The large palm in one corner and smaller green plants in pale yellow pots set on a scattering of tables evoked visions of restful afternoons in a warm climate. The paintings of tranquil pastoral scenes in shades of green, yellow, and off-white urged him to lie down and shut his eyes.

Iain's deep, melodic voice added to the mood. "Please, sit anywhere."

Manziuk found one of the oversized green leather chairs near him and sank into it. Ryan perched on the edge of a matching chair.

Iain sat last, right in the middle of the sofa. "Go ahead," Iain nodded to Manziuk.

Manziuk tried to shrug of the lethargic feeling that had come over him. Yes, it was late, but they needed this interview. He looked over at Ryan and tried to send her a signal with his eyes.

She raised her brows slightly before settling back into her chair and clearing her throat. When Iain looked toward her, she said, "Mr. Foley, how well did you know Ricardo Velasquez?"

"Not well at all." Iain waved his hand in the air. "Probably as well as anyone in the media." He leaned forward. "But as a person, I didn't know him at all."

"How did you get along with him?"

"Fine," he answered automatically. Then he shrugged. "I mean, he answered my questions reasonably well. He never threatened me. I had no problem with him."

"Do you have any idea who might have wanted to kill him?"

"None whatsoever. Unless it was someone who wanted the team to miss out on the pennant. Maybe a big gambler who bet against them. That's all I can figure."

"Interesting theory," Ryan said. "So you didn't have any contact with him on your show?"

"Barely any," Iain said. "Rico's agent handled everything to do with the media. The couple of times Rico came on my show, it was always with his agent and an interpreter."

"Last night, you attended the reception for Rico's wife."

"I did," Iain said.

"Did you go with anyone?"

"No. My show didn't finish until seven, so I was a little late."

"Did you speak with Rico or his wife?"

"They were together at the front of the room when I came in. I hadn't missed much. I got a chance to talk to them briefly prior to the press conference. I thought she spoke much better English than he did."

"What was your impression of them during the evening?"

He smiled. "Well, it seems a bit melodramatic to say now, but she seemed scared to death."

"What about?'

"I assumed she wasn't used to having to talk to a bunch of hungry reporters."

"What about Rico?"

"He was on top of the world, bragging about how well he was pitching and how well they were going to do."

"When did you last see Rico on Thursday night?"

"Shortly after he tried to attack Stasey Simon. I assume you've heard about that." Iain changed position slightly, relaxing his shoulders and thrusting out his legs so he could cross his ankles. The dog, who had been curled up on the carpet against his legs, adjusted his position so as to retain the most body contact. "You know," said Iain. "It's really a shame. Stasey has so much ability, but she consistently shoots herself in the foot by going for the jugular. She'd be at home in pro wrestling." He shook his head. "Anyway, after her question that upset everyone, the press conference broke up. I had a bit of a headache, and I had all the information I needed, so I left. Let's face it, the whole thing was redundant. Most of us had pieced together the story long before then."

"Did anyone leave at the same time as you?"

"A large group left just before I did. I waited until they were gone. I hadn't had dinner and there's no sense letting good food go to waste. I don't recall if anyone else left when I did."

"Where did you go?"

"Here. And no, no one saw me. I'm divorced. The only witness I have is Charlie, here." He motioned toward the dog and smiled as he said, "You can ask him if you want, but I doubt he'll do much talking."

"You didn't go anywhere else after you left the Diamond Dome and before you arrived here? To a bar, perhaps?"

"Oh, now that you mention it, I did stop in at the Fifth Base, just briefly. But I was only there a few minutes. I'd already had a drink at the reception, and I was driving, so I decided it was better to head home instead of having another drink."

They left a few minutes later. Manziuk motioned to Ryan to drive. She raised her brows, but only said, "The station?"

"Yes." Manziuk fastened his seat belt and shut his eyes.

Ryan glanced over. "That it for tonight?"

"Yeah." There was a long silence before Manziuk added, "Only one more person we need to talk to right away. Stasey Simon's producer. He'll keep until morning."

"You okay?" she said after a few minutes.

"Yeah." There was a long silence. "Mostly tired." He looked over at her. "Thanks for taking over. You did fine."

"Tried to do some fishing."

"That's all we can do right now."

"Some sleep should help. We haven't had much lately."

"Yeah." Neither spoke for about five minutes. Then Manziuk sat up and opened his eyes to look at her. "It wasn't just tiredness." He paused for a moment. "You're going to think I'm crazy, but I had the strangest experience back there, as if my brain disconnected. I thought at first it was because I was tired, and I'm sure that played a part. But it was more than that.

"You see, I've listened to Iain Foley on the radio lots of times, and I guess I had a picture in my mind of what he'd look like. Only when he came to the door, he looked nothing like I expected. I recognized the voice, but he didn't look right. It gave me a funny feeling, as though something was wrong. Maybe it was because I was so tired, but I couldn't quite get my head around it."

"Not to mention you've been under some stress lately, with all that's been happening with Detective Sergeant Craig. None of us are machines."

"Be easier sometimes if we were." After a moment's silence, he said, "I don't want any mistakes; don't want to miss anything. No excuse, no matter how good, is enough to make up for arresting the wrong person."

"Don't forget," Ryan said as she pulled into the station parking area, "you told me our having lives helps us understand the people we have to interact with. Sometimes the innocents must feel sort of lost, the way you did tonight. Maybe we need to be aware of that."

It was after eleven when Jacquie opened the front door of the townhouse she shared with her mother, grandmother, aunt, and cousin. Seemed like days since she'd left. Seemed like another world.

Her housemates were in the living room watching a Fred Astaire and Ginger Rogers movie.

Her mother put down her crocheting and greeted Jacquie with a cool, "So you finally decided to honor us with your presence, did you?"

Jacquie's face tightened. "Hi, Mom. Sorry I'm so late."

"I suppose from now on we'll have to take every appointment with a grain of salt, knowing you won't make it."

"I'm very sorry, Mom. But we have a high-profile case we have to solve as soon as possible. That means overtime."

"Why can't you take turns? Work an eight-hour shift and then let someone else take over?"

Jacquie sat in an overstuffed chair. This was going to take a few minutes. "Other key people are working on it, Mom. A lot of other people. But it's our case. We have to interview the main people involved—the ones who might be suspects, or who might know something really important. We have to hear everything and try to put it together and look for discrepancies, and decide who might be lying or who isn't telling us everything they know. You can't have a bunch of different people doing that because you'd be all over the place."

"What do you mean, a high profile case? What case is it?"

"Yeah, who is it? An actor? A singer?" Jacquie's cousin, Precious, two years younger than Jacquie and an avid celebrity watcher, leaned forward in anticipation. "Not the mayor, is it?"

"Hello, Precious." Jacquie always dreaded these moments when her family wanted to know details about her job that she didn't feel comfortable giving them. Aside from the fact that there were a lot of things she couldn't tell anyone, talking about what she did at work crossed an invisible line she wanted to keep in place—a line that allowed her to be one person at home and another on the job. She was just as protective about discussing her family or home life with her co-workers.

"Tell us all about it." Her Aunt Vida was always even more inquisitive than her mother or cousin. "Who is it this time?"

"Nobody you'd know," Jacquie said. "And I really can't talk about it."

Precious gave her signature pout.

Jacquie had never understood why Precious thought the pout made her look cute and appealing. It certainly didn't work on Jacquie.

"The least you can do," Precious said, "is to tell us who the victim is."

"Do any of you know where the sports channel is?" Jacquie asked.

Aunt Vida's eyes grew large. "You've never been interested in sports."

Precious jumped off the couch and grabbed the remote, which had been sitting on a table in front of Jacquie's mother. "What channel?"

"Just keep going until you hear somebody talking sports," Aunt Vida said.

"Jacquie, what is this all about?" Her mother sounded annoyed. Jacquie shrugged. "I just wondered what's on the news."

Precious was busy flipping channels. It took a while, but finally she found a channel that was giving the sports news.

"Early this morning, groundskeepers in Toronto discovered the battered body of baseball's rising star, Ricardo Velasquez. The body was found in the bullpen of the Diamond Dome. It appears that Velasquez may have been beaten to death with a baseball bat."

As the news item was being read, they showed a large picture of Rico Velasquez, followed by shots of him pitching, and finally a shot of him and his wife at the reception Thursday night. He was laughing, apparently without a care in the world.

As they switched to another topic, Jacquie walked over to shut the television off.

"You're working on that?" Cousin Precious's eyes were bulging out.

Aunt Vida waved a newspaper in front of her face, using it as a fan. "Ooowheee, girl! You telling me you get to interview all those gorgeous baseball players?"

As usual, her mother's words were like a pail of cold water. "Jacqueline, do you really think you can handle something like this? You know nothing about sports, or how to deal with celebrities. What if you fail?"

Gram had been sitting quietly in her favorite rocking chair. Now she said, "She won't fail. You ought to know that by now, Noelle. This child is good!"

Jacquie's eyes teared up at her grandmother's words. No matter how bad things might get, she always knew—had always known—that, despite the odd grumble, her grandmother was always in her corner ready to towel her off and send her back out.

"Can you get me an autographed picture of Ferdinand Ortes?" Precious asked, her eyes wide. "He's gorgeous."

Gram stood up. "Child, I made my green gungo pea soup today. I'm going to get you a bowl of it right now. It's got yams and sweet potatoes in it, and dumplings. It'll stick to your ribs, and that's what you need after a long, hard day." She headed to the kitchen.

Her mother also stood. "Jacquie, you need to get to bed. You don't want to be late in the morning."

Aunt Vida, still sprawling on the couch, held up her hands, index fingers pointing at Jacquie. "Yes, my dear, you get your beauty sleep so you'll be fresh in the morning. And don't forget to put on some make-up and a real nice outfit. And earrings! I tell you, Jacqueline Ryan, if you can't find one man you like from all those baseball players, I wash my hands of you!"

Paul Manziuk found his son Michael waiting for him when he got home. "Rico Velasquez," Mike said. "That's not your case, is it?" His voice trembled with emotion.

Paul sighed. "Yes, as a matter of fact, it is."

"Wow! Did you—like, were you—you know—in the clubhouse? Did you talk to any of the players?"

"I interviewed quite a few."

"Not—not Ferdinand Ortes? Or Jonas Newland? Or Brett Moore? Or—?"

"Only the ones that were in the stadium last night. As well as some other people."

"Other people? You mean the press, don't you? They would have been there for the reception." Mike's eyes threatened to pop from their sockets. "Like maybe somebody like—like Iain Foley?"

"Just came from his place."

Mike's eyes grew wide. "Oh, wow! This has to be the best case you've ever had, right, Dad?"

"That's one way of putting it."

Loretta, who at five-foot-four was dwarfed by both her husband and son, wrapped an arm around Mike's waist and pushed him gently down the hall. At the same time, she said, "Paul, come into the kitchen and sit down. Are you hungry?"

Taking the hint, Mike left them alone.

Paul smiled. Usually Mike didn't want people to know his dad was a cop, but this would be different. Why were people so hung up on celebrities? When you got to know them, they really weren't so different from anyone else.

Paul collapsed onto the gingham cushion that softened the seat of the oak kitchen chair and leaned his elbows on the table. Loretta handed him a cup of tea, made him some toast with apple butter, and then sat in silence across from him while he ate.

"How's Woody doing?" Paul asked at last.

"He seems to be adjusting. So's Arlie. I think they'll be fine."

"I'll try to get over tomorrow."

"Will you have to work all day?"

"I need to interview a few more people. So far we don't have much to go on."

"You need to get to bed."

Mike burst into the room. "Dad, I totally forgot to tell you. I found a great car!"

Paul shut his eyes.

"They said we can go see it tomorrow morning. You won't have to go into work tomorrow, will you?'

Loretta came over. "Michael, what did I say?"

He hung his head. "Not to' bother dad about it tonight."

"And what did you just do?"

"I was just telling him about the car. I wasn't bothering him. Was I, Dad?"

Paul rubbed his hands through his hair, avoiding the balding patch at the top. "No, you weren't bothering me," he lied. "But I'm afraid I will have to work tomorrow."

Mike's face fell, then became animated again. "Yeah, of course you do. Forget the car. You need to find out who killed Rico before he kills another player, right? Dad, was Rico really killed with a baseball bat?"

Loretta put her hand gently on her son's arm. "Mike, you know your dad can't talk about the details of his cases."

"Maybe we can look at the car on Sunday, if it isn't gone by then," Paul said.

Mike left the room.

Paul sighed.

"Don't worry about him," Loretta said. "He's fine."

"Yeah." Paul fingered the cup. "But what about this car he's found? Do you think I should try to have a look at it? Or maybe send someone over who knows cars?"

Manziuk's cell phone rang. He sighed, but answered. It was Special Constable Benson. "Where are you?"

"Home."

"Already? Have you found out who did it yet?"

"No."

"My phone's ringing off the hook. Are you sure you should be knocking off so early?"

"It's close to midnight and I've done all I can do today. I won't be much good if I don't get some sleep."

"You got anything I can use?"

"Unless we discover another way into the Diamond Dome, we seem to have a locked-room puzzle on our hands."

"You've got to be kidding."

"No. It looks as if it had to be one of a small group of people who were at a press conference held inside the Diamond Dome Thursday night. A few players, a few media people, and so forth."

"What does Ford say?"

"Ford's people are doing an inch-by-inch search of the stadium. The thing is, although the building is huge, the actual space people had access to on Thursday night was limited to the area around a single entranceway that led to the reception room, the team clubhouse, and the Matrix staff offices. The one slip-up is that the door to the bullpen was open, so presumably if Rico could get out to the bullpen, someone else might have come in that way. But if they did, they'd have to have had a key to another entrance to get in and out of the Dome, and that doesn't seem possible.

"We've got another team doing background checks on everyone who works there to make sure we don't have anyone with a Cuban connection, gambling or drug problems, or anything else that might make them vulnerable if someone wanted to use them to get in. But frankly, that whole area seems pretty far-fetched to me. If it had been a bomb, yeah. But trying to knock somebody's head off with a baseball bat isn't your typical terrorist crime."

"Can you make a guess as to who it was?"

"As far as motive is concerned, there are several possibilities. I want to identify the people who had opportunity as soon as possible, and then go deeper into motives."

"Could anyone else be in danger?"

"There's always the risk that someone knows something, and lets on to the killer, either intentionally or inadvertently."

"Could the killer have been a woman?"

"Possibly. She'd have to be strong, though."

"Do we know if Alita Velasquez was strong enough?"

"Until I know better, I'm assuming she was."

"How did she get out of the stadium?"

"That's the sixty-four thousand dollar question. Ford's taking it as a personal challenge to find out."

"There's no sign of her?"

"We've got a city-wide search going on. We'll find her."

From GinnyLovejoy@the torontonews.com
To: GLoveday@express.on.ca
12:15 AM

Hi Graham,

Mom left six phone messages today. Can you tell her just because I wasn't home when she called doesn't mean I was out doing despicable things? And just because I attended the press conference last night to meet the pitcher's wife doesn't mean there was ever any danger of my being murdered. After the reception, I had a few drinks with friends. Then I went home—alone. I didn't even know about the murder until late morning. I spent the rest of the day hanging around the doors of the stadium hoping the police would tell us something. They did call me in for a nice chat, but they wanted to ask all the questions, and they barely gave out any information. Anyway, the main thing is that I am not in any danger, and I am not a suspect as far as I know. Read my column in tomorrow's paper.

Yes, it was kind of fun being questioned by the police. But don't tell Mom I said that. Oh, you *can* tell her my editor loved my column in yesterday's paper even if she didn't. Maybe she should cancel the *Daily News* and stick to the *Register* since she apparently prefers Kyle's columns. No, don't tell her I said that. She'll be hurt.

Do you think Mom has too much time on her hands now that she's only got you at home? What's she going to do in two years when you graduate from college? Maybe we need to find her a job or something. Anything to get her mind off me.

Ginny

PART III

*"Fortune is like glass—
the brighter the glitter,
the more easily broken."*

—PUBLIUS SYRUS (42 B.C.)

THIRTEEN

By eight o'clock Saturday morning, Manziuk and Ryan were in a meeting at the police station with the Ident team. The meeting was memorable only for the things that had been ruled out. There was no trace of Alita Velasquez anywhere in the Diamond Dome, and no unsecured entrance to the stadium had been found. The doorknobs of the door between the bullpen and the trainers' room had been wiped of prints, as had the knobs of the door between the locker room and the trainers' room. Other doorknobs in the area had any number of prints on them, and it would be a while before they could be identified, assuming they ever could. Also, one of the bats on the rack in the bullpen had been wiped clear of prints, and Ident thought they had found traces of blood.

By nine, Manziuk and Ryan were in Manziuk's office going over what they had learned thus far. "What I want to know," said Ryan, "is what's happened to Alita Velasquez? Apparently, no one's seen her since she walked out of the reception. Her possessions have been removed from the hotel. No one of her description has been found in the morgue or in any of the hospitals." Ryan bit her lip. "Could she have gone back to Cuba?"

"She might have had time to catch a plane before we sent out the alert to airport security, so I suppose she could have gone back to Cuba under an assumed name. But I think it's highly unlikely," Manziuk said.

"You think whoever killed Rico kidnapped her? Maybe Rico found her, and they were in the bullpen talking when the killer came up behind them. Or could he have been threatening her? I can see someone like Armando or Jonas acting to protect her. Maybe whoever did it was just trying to stop him, not kill him. And then she might have gone into hiding because she's afraid."

"We've been told Rico was self-centered and somewhat arrogant," Manziuk said, "but do we have any evidence that he was abusive? If he was, why would she have come here in the first place?"

"Maybe he'd changed. Or maybe he was trying to convince her to go back to Cuba because he didn't want her here. Don't forget Eva."

"So where did she go afterward?"

"The killer hid her to keep her from talking to anyone, either against her wishes or with her complicity."

"The only problem with that is that she isn't anywhere in the building. You heard Ford say his team spent the night searching every inch of the place."

"Could the killer have gone out and then returned to get her later, after everyone was gone?"

"Ford says none of the people who were here has a key to the building. They all have to get security to let them in, even Tony Kanberra."

"Okay, what if one of the security guards was involved?" Ryan tapped her pen. "Maybe Alita came here to kill him, and she bribed the security guard to get her out afterward? Maybe the woman wasn't even Alita, but a paid killer disguised as her."

Manziuk stared at her. After a moment, he said slowly, "I think Rico might have said something when she arrived. If he thought she wasn't his wife, I mean."

"Maybe she was a good impersonator."

"Maybe you've seen too many James Bond movies?"

Ryan's eyes fell, and there was a moment's silence. Then she lifted her chin. "I thought we were supposed to solve this. Doesn't that mean looking at all the possibilities? A man is dead and his wife is missing. Why?"

"Don't forget, she's from Cuba. She may be afraid to come to the police. Or maybe she has a friend in Canada no one knows about. A Cuban immigrant." He paused. "See, I can speculate along with the best of them."

Ryan tilted her head and waited.

He continued, "Right now, we need facts. So let's stick to them until we reach a dead end."

"Okay. What are we doing to find her?"

"Benson put out a bulletin yesterday afternoon saying she's wanted for questioning, but is in no way a threat or a suspect. A media picture from the reception is circulating on TV, and it's in both the *Register* and the *Daily News* this morning."

"Okay, what do we do next?"

"Let's go over everything we've learned and look for what's missing, or who left out what. Hopefully, we'll have the autopsy results before long, but I don't think there's much question what killed him. I'd really like to know how they got him to stand still while they attacked."

"They? You think there was more than one?"

"If I said, 'he,' you'd accuse me of being sexist. And it could have been 'she.' So for now, I'll use 'they.'"

An hour later, Ryan and Manziuk had sifted through their notes, amassed a number of questions and observations, and made a list of everyone involved in the reception who had no apparent alibi for at least part of the time between when Alita left the press conference room and the last people left the stadium that night. They had spoken personally to all but one of the people who'd been on Cecily Jones's list, and other officers were speaking to all the staff who had access to the building.

The list of people who might have had an opportunity to kill Rico wasn't that long. Tony Kanberra, Blake Harrison, and the other members of the Matrix head office had never been completely alone, and Pat Davis had been with them. There had also been two security guards with them. They'd moved as either a single large group or several smaller groups from the reception room to the accessible areas—the clubhouse, offices, trainers' room, and family area, and from there back to the reception room and then to the exit. They agreed that none of them had been with fewer than two other people for more than a couple of seconds. And no one had tried the door to the bullpen because they assumed it was locked as usual.

They were left with eight to ten viable suspects:

- **Alita Velasquez.** If she was wandering in the stadium, she could have met Rico, killed him, then fled. But where did she go afterward?

- **Jonas Newland.** He sent his wife and others ahead and joined them maybe five minutes later in the hotel restaurant. He says he looked for Alita briefly, then changed his mind and left.

- **Armando Santana.** He says he left alone shortly after the press conference broke up, but no one noticed him leave.

- **Kyle Schmidt.** He says he got lost on his way out. He arrived at the Fifth Base about ten minutes after the larger group of media people.

- **Ginny Lovejoy.** She claims to have gone to the rest room. She arrived at the Fifth Base after Kyle.

- **Iain Foley.** According to Kyle, he arrived at the Fifth Base just after Ginny. Iain says he stepped inside for a moment and then went home.

- **Stasey Simon.** Claims she left alone, shortly after Ted Benedetto, her producer. She has no idea about the time. The security guard thought it was not too long after the main group.

- **Ted Benedetto.** Not yet questioned. Stasey says he left before she did. No one else seems to have noticed him exit. Security guard vaguely remembers him leaving, but not the time. A couple of people heard Stasey fire Ted Thursday night.

- **Ferdinand Ortes and Eva MacPherson.** Say they were together except for a few minutes while she was in the restroom. On the other hand, they might have done it together—one to distract Rico and one to kill him.

Ryan tapped on the paper. "I find it hard to believe they could have all left separately, using the very same exit route, and not seen each other. Yet none of the reports indicate that they did."

"Keep that in mind. But it's a long, involved, path, so I supposed it's entirely possible that they didn't see each other. For now, let's concentrate on trying to establish an order of who left when. Then we can look into anyone who doesn't have a good alibi. And we need to talk to Ted Benedetto ASAP."

"Wait a minute." Ryan looked up from her notes. "Cecily Jones gave us the name of the legal firm that represents the Diamond Corporation and said we should contact them and ask if any of the owners were in the stadium Thursday night and if so, if they saw anything. Should we do that now?"

An hour and a half later, after a personal call from the police commissioner to Tony Kanberra, a lengthy phone conversation between Manziuk and two of the Diamond Corporation's lawyers, and a call from a Mr. Grant, who was apparently a valet for one of the owners, they were granted what Ryan called an "audience" with a Mr. Brown at two o'clock that afternoon.

They decided to use the intervening time to track down Ted Benedetto, beginning with the radio station where he worked—or had worked, if Stasey really had fired him Thursday night.

"This is a dump," Ryan said as she looked at the 70's architecture and chipped gray walls in the lobby of the building where they'd been told WIN Sports Radio rented a floor. "You sure this is the place?"

"It says so right there." Manziuk pointed to a small homemade sign advertising WIN 730 on the fourth floor.

The elevator was barely big enough for both of them, and the air inside was muggy and stale. The small hallway they found themselves in had three doors, one of which had a white sign taped to it. "WIN 730" had been printed on it with a black marker. They opened the door. The radio station radiated the same look as the elevator—small and stale.

The young, magenta-haired receptionist seemed unimpressed with meeting two homicide detectives. "Ted's here, but he's busy right now working on next week's programs."

"We won't take up much time."

She cracked her gum as she reached for the intercom button, then said, "You better not." To the intercom, she said, "Ted, you got company. Cops."

After a few minutes, a tall, slim, young man with long, black, tied-back hair appeared. Manziuk recognized him as the one who'd followed Stasey Simon inside the Diamond Dome entrance yesterday afternoon. As he had yesterday, he wore black jeans and a white T-shirt with a rather rude saying on the front, and he had a tattoo on each forearm—a long-tailed Asian dragon on the right one, and what looked like a compass on the left. He walked lightly, on the balls of his feet, as if ready to run at a moment's notice.

Manziuk stepped forward. "Ted Benedetto?"

"Look, I'm really busy right now. Can it wait?"

"We won't take long." Manziuk held up his ID.

"You're police?"

"Yes."

"What's this about?"

"You were at a reception Thursday night for Rico Velasquez and his wife?"

"Yes."

"We need to talk to you about it."

"Look, I've got a million things to do this morning. Couldn't this—?" He pursed his lips. "Wait a minute. Let me think." After a moment, he went behind the receptionist's desk and leaned over to speak quietly to the girl. Then he stood up and said, "Okay, come on inside."

He led them through a narrow hallway and into a tiny room containing four cubicles, two of which were occupied. "No," he said. "This is too small. Plus crowded. There must be something better." He looked around as if hoping the mysterious something would jump up and flag him down. His face brightened. "I know. Come this way."

They followed him down another narrow hallway to a closed door. He opened the door and ushered them inside. A rectangular laminate table and two chairs, each with a microphone on a stand in front, occupied most of the small room. The air was warm and smelled stale.

"Let me get another chair. One second." Several minutes passed before Ted returned with a third chair. "Sorry. Had to get the one from my desk." Everyone sat, with Manziuk and Ryan on one side of the table and Ted on the other.

"Sorry it's so hot," the younger man said. "Air conditioning's been acting up. Feel free to take off your jackets."

"We won't be long," Manziuk said. "We're investigating the death of Rico Velasquez. What can you tell us about him?"

Ted lounged in his chair, hands in his pants pockets, feet extended, ankles crossed, and thought for a minute. "Not much. I didn't actually know him. I mean, I've been in the same room a few times, but we weren't bosom buddies."

"Working around the station, you must hear things."

"I hear a lot of things, but I've never heard anyone plotting to murder Rico. Or boasting about it afterwards."

"You were at the reception?"

"Stasey was invited." He took his hands out of his pockets, intertwined his fingers, then tapped his thumbs together. "I'm her producer, so I went with her."

"Did you see Rico there?"

"Sure. He was with the brass and his agent. And his wife, of course. That's what it was all about. Her coming here."

"Did he seem nervous or worried?"

Ted's eyebrows shot up. "Rico? No. He was like a—a peacock." Ted sat up and crossed one knee over the other. "Yeah, that's what he reminded me of. Strutting around. You never really knew what he was saying because he didn't speak very good English, but his body language was easy to read. He was strutting, like it was his right to be the center of attention and everybody had better know it."

Manziuk continued his questions. "Did he leave the room while you were there?"

"You think I had nothing better to do than watch him?"

"So he could have left the room?"

"He could have stood on his head or done a tap dance for all I know. I wasn't that interested in him."

"Who were you watching?"

He shrugged. "Nobody in particular. Stasey, I guess. We were talking about the show, feeling around for ideas."

"Did you see Rico's wife?"

"Yeah, sure." He thought for a moment, then dropped his hands and leaned forward. "Actually, that's what made me think of him being like a peacock. She was so much like a peahen." When

Manziuk didn't respond, Ted continued. "As if she wasn't really there, just her shadow. Although in reality, she had the makings of a very good-looking woman."

"Did you see her leave the room?"

He shrugged again. "I wasn't paying that much attention."

Manziuk smiled. "You seem to have been paying quite a bit of attention."

Ted bit his bottom lip. "What I said, it was only a fleeting impression, nothing more. I just remembered it now when you asked if I saw her."

Ryan leaned forward. "We heard from several people that Stasey Simon fired you during the press conference."

Ted smiled. "Yeah, she did."

"Yet you're still here."

"Stasey fires me at least once a month." The smile grew. "One week, she actually fired me twice."

"So you ignored what she said?"

"I came to work yesterday as usual. No big deal."

With a quick look at Ryan, Manziuk took over the questions again. "Do you have any idea who might have killed Rico?"

Ted shook his head. "Any person in that room could have killed him, for all I know. Or anyone in the country."

Manziuk shifted in the chair and began to rise. "All right. If you think of anything, let—"

The door opened and Stasey Simon walked in.

"Inspector Manziuk? And Constable Ryan. How nice to meet you again."

Manziuk stood and nodded. "Ms. Simon."

Stasey was smiling. "I've had some time to think since last night, and I have a few questions myself, if you don't mind."

"I'm afraid not," Manziuk said. "I only ask them."

She raised her eyebrows. "But I might have some information for you—some things that occurred to me this morning."

"I don't make deals, Ms. Simon."

"A statement. Nothing more."

"Ms. Simon, tell me what you remembered."

Stasey perched on the edge of the table. "I remembered that Rico said something to Eva as he went past her on Thursday night.

He said one word. *Prostituta*. I thought you might find that interesting."

"You heard it clearly? You're sure that's what he said?'

"I did. Perhaps," Stasey offered with a smile, "it's a word that transcends languages?" Catlike, she stretched her hand out toward Manziuk. "I merely want to help. What do you think was the cause of Rico's death? Jealousy? Robbery? Being in the wrong place at the wrong time?"

"We can't say anything about that."

"When will you be able to say?"

"We expect the autopsy results early next week. Then we'll know how he died. It won't tell us why."

"Speaking of motive, is it true that a family member or friend is involved in most murders?"

"The majority of cases. Not all."

"What people are you presently talking with?"

"Everyone who was at the reception Thursday night. Everyone who might have had access to the building. Everyone who might have had a motive."

"Sounds like a lot of people."

"Yes."

Ryan leaned forward. "That's why we don't—"

Manziuk broke in. "Perhaps your listeners have ideas. I'll give a phone number to your producer if that's all right. If any of your listeners know something we might find useful, they should come forward. Call the police station, or call Crimestoppers if you prefer to be anonymous."

Stasey put her hands on her hips and tilted her head as she looked at Manziuk. "You knew all along we were taping this."

"Of course."

She pursed her lips. "Maybe the police aren't so dumb."

"Be careful how you edit it and how you use it; we'll be listening. And make sure my message gets out." He turned to Ted. "By the way, how much of what you told us was accurate, and how much was designed to keep us here until Stasey arrived?"

"It was all accurate," he said quietly.

Ryan glared at Stasey. "Is it true you fire your producer about once a month?"

Stasey glared back. "It might be."

Manziuk said, "So the fact that you were heard firing him Thursday night at the reception means very little?"

"It means I have so much difficulty getting competent help I have to stick with what I've got or take a chance on somebody even worse." Stasey pointed to the door. "Are you through?"

Manziuk took his time walking over to the door. Once there, he paused before saying, "For now."

As Ryan shut the door behind them, she whispered, "You knew we were being taped?"

He threw her a quick glance. "You didn't?"

Manziuk pulled into a Tim Hortons, where they ordered soup and sandwiches. As they were starting to eat, Dr. Munsen called with the preliminary autopsy results. As expected, Rico's death was the result of a single blow to the base of his skull and upper spine. He had not regained consciousness and had likely expired within thirty minutes of the blow.

Other than that, he was in excellent condition, though Munsen would put his age closer to 30 than the 25 it said in his bio. There was a slight amount of alcohol in his blood, but nothing close to the legal limit—certainly nothing that would make him incapable of reacting to a threat. His reaction time might have been a bit slower than normal, but normal for him was probably well above average anyway.

A couple of other things Munsen had noticed. There were signs Rico had had several broken bones that had healed, likely ten or more years before. And he was in the very early stages of osteoporosis.

There were no indications that Rico had defended himself. His hands were without scratches or abrasions of any kind. Nothing under the fingernails, either. The condition of the body was consistent with someone who had been hit from behind. From the angle of the wound, it was possible Rico had been slightly bent over. Although it wasn't his place to speculate, Munsen suggested the most likely scenario was that one person had kept him occupied while the other came up behind him.

Alone in his room, his heart heavy, Lawrence Smith dressed for the Saturday afternoon Matrix game. He'd tried to pump himself up by reading Ginny's and Kyle's special Saturday columns. But, of course, they'd both focused on Rico's murder. He'd also read the front page reports on the murder. How could he not read everything about his beloved Matrix?

His eyes filled with tears and he reached for a tissue.

When Stasey said on her Thursday show that it might be a good idea if someone took a thirty-three-ounce bat to Rico's skull, Lawrence had been appalled. He'd even dreamed about it Thursday night, and awakened in a sweat, only to spend the rest of the night worrying about what would happen if some crazy listener decided to carry out her suggestion.

When he turned on the radio at noon Friday and discovered that Rico was dead and the police were investigating, his heart began thumping so hard he'd thought he might be having a heart attack. It had settled down before too long, but the day had been terrible. Sure, Rico had been annoying. But for someone to kill him! It was too horrible for words.

Stasey's show on Friday had been horrible, too. Naturally, they'd scrapped the planned program and focused on the murder. Pat Davis, Rico's agent, had done a short phone-in interview during which he'd told them how happy Rico had been to be living in Canada and how much he'd looked forward to his future here. Stasey had asked Pat what would happen to Rico's money, and Pat said Rico's wife would likely inherit. And then Stasey asked what would happen if his wife was dead, because no one knew where she was.

It was all so sad.

But it was even worse later in the show, when a few callers blamed Stasey for Rico's death. She assured them she had only been trying to make a point and that never in a million years had she expected anything like this to happen. She sounded so calm that Lawrence felt a bit better.

Iain's show had been quieter. He'd talked to Tony Kanberra and Blake Harrison, both of whom focused on how much Rico had done for the team and how much he'd be missed. Then Iain asked callers to share a memory of Rico or of another sports star whose career had been cut short by tragedy. For a while, Lawrence had felt almost normal. Things were going to be okay.

But then, because the game had been canceled, he'd listened throughout the evening and a good part of the early morning as the station continued its coverage of the investigation, and a number of people phoned in to share their sadness or vent their anger. Quite a few of those callers thought Stasey was to blame for her thoughtless comments.

And, as he listened, in tears, Lawrence, too, felt that if Stasey hadn't said what she had, maybe none of this would have happened. It was almost more than he could stand. He loved Iain and Ginny and Kyle, but Stasey was his favorite. And he knew he wasn't alone. Her show was gaining in the ratings all the time. What would happen now? Would the station fire her? Worse, would the police arrest her?

As for the Matrix, they were so close to winning their division. But how could they stay competitive without Rico?

The sun was coming up as he finally fell asleep, only to dream that Stasey was being executed for inciting someone to murder.

Now, as he pulled on his red and gold Rico Velasquez jersey, his heart was heavy. Did the police know what Stasey had said? What would happen when they found out?

The radio was on in the background. As he mused about the recent upheaval to his world, Stasey's voice suddenly came on. He ran to turn up the volume.

"That's right, people," Stasey said. "Tune in for a special one-and-a-half-hour *Stasey Simon Show* tomorrow—Sunday—at eleven AM. We'll have an in-depth report on the murder of Rico Velasquez, and then I'll be giving you some new information I've discovered. That's the *Stasey Simon Show Special Report*, Sunday morning at eleven, followed by the usual pre-game show at twelve-thirty. You don't want to miss this one."

"Oh, Stasey," Lawrence whispered. "What are you doing now?"

FOURTEEN

At five minutes to two, Manziuk and Ryan walked into the impressive lakefront building where they were to meet one of the elusive owners behind the Diamond Corporation. A burly security guard took his time checking their IDs and calling the condo before reluctantly allowing them to enter the large foyer, with its elegant, subdued gray walls and snow-white baseboards and ceiling. Thick gray carpets muffled their footsteps. The only color was in the random flashes of red in several abstract gray-toned paintings on the walls. The security guard used a card to open one of the elevators and program it to go to the penthouse level. Then he stepped out and they went up alone.

Upon leaving the elevator, they found themselves in a smaller gray foyer facing two doors, one an emergency exit to a stairway; the other a single, massive white door with a large brass knocker. Manziuk lifted the knocker and let it fall. The door swung open, apparently of its own accord, and they moved inside, sinking into a snow white carpet twice as thick as the one in the hallways.

A tall, well-built man in khaki pants and a forest green golf shirt moved toward them. His reddish-blond hair was well cut, though somewhat long, and curling at the ends. Green eyes shone in contrast to his golden-toned skin. His face was void of expression; his eyes, under gold-rimmed glasses, were cool.

"Detective Inspector Manziuk, please come inside. I'm Mr. Brown's valet, Cary Grant." He smiled ruefully. "Before you say anything, yes, I have an unusual name. My parents were big fans." There was a short moment of silence. Then he turned to Ryan. "Detective Constable Ryan? Welcome. Mr. Brown is in his study. If you will follow me, please?"

As they walked down a long, wide hallway, they went past a number of arches leading into other rooms. Everywhere, color was celebrated: snow white carpets; mahogany woodwork; forest green walls and ceilings; cherry red sofas and chairs; bright yellow squat lamps; dark mahogany tables covered with a riot of red, yellow, and blue vases and ornaments; strategically placed pictures of fantastic red, yellow, and blue flowers, with coordinating frames.

Ryan whispered to Manziuk, "This place is like a museum for primary colors."

They turned at last into the study. It, too, was bright, but here the dominant colors were red and gold, the colors of the Toronto Matrix. Pennants, jerseys, and an assortment of balls, bats, and gloves hung on one wall. Two large glass cases on a second wall held what to Manziuk looked like every Matrix item ever created for a giveaway or sale. The third wall held two more cases with trophies and photos arranged on gold and red satin cloths.

Manziuk had asked Ford to find out more about the Diamond Corporation, but he'd apparently hit a brick wall. The Corporation had come out of the blue six years earlier when the Matrix was put up for sale. Their bid had been successful, but although there had been all kinds of speculation in the media about who owned the corporation, the baseball commissioner had only said his lawyers were satisfied with the ownership and so was he. Every trail led back to the Diamond Corporation's lawyers, who simply weren't talking.

Manziuk had envisioned the owner as either a businessman who wasn't a baseball fan but saw the team as a tax shelter or an elderly man or woman who was passionate about baseball but lived a reclusive life.

Instead, seated on a plush red velvet chair, sneaker-clad feet resting on a matching footstool, stubby hands holding a baseball bat, was a man Manziuk guessed to be about thirty. He looked about average height and weight. Short, black hair seemed sculpted to his head. Dark brown eyes gleamed from the middle of his pale face over his rather prominent nose. He wore black pants and a red golf shirt with "Matrix" embroidered in gold.

As Manziuk and Ryan paused inside the door, Mr. Brown looked up at them with eyes swimming in unshed tears. "I can't seem to believe it," he said in a shaky voice. "None of it seems real to me yet."

"Please, sit," the valet said to Manziuk. As he did, the valet asked, "Would you care for some tea, coffee, a soft drink, iced tea, or lemonade?"

"Nothing, thank you," Manziuk said.

Mr. Brown said, "Oh, but you must. It's no trouble. And it's so hot outside." His face grew quizzical. "Not even iced tea with lemon?"

Manziuk took in Mr. Brown's pallid complexion and shaking hands. "Well, perhaps a small glass."

Cary Grant nodded and looked at Ryan. "And you, Miss?"

Ryan had been watching Manziuk. "Cold water, please."

"Certainly. I'll just be a moment." The man disappeared and Manziuk and Ryan perched on chairs in front of Mr. Brown.

Mr. Brown looked at the bat in his hands. "I just—this is all so—I feel numb."

"You were close to Mr. Velasquez?"

Mr. Brown's voice rose. "We were responsible for his leaving Cuba. We brought him here!" One of his unshed tears spilled onto his left cheek. "Does that make us responsible for his death? I suppose so, don't you think? If we hadn't wanted him for our team, he'd still be alive. In Cuba, yes, but alive."

"I don't think you can lay the blame at your door, Mr. Brown. For all we know, the killer might have come here from Cuba."

"I'll never believe she had anything to do with this."

Taken off guard, Manziuk simply stared.

"She?" Ryan asked.

Mr. Brown stared at her. "His wife." He looked back at Manziuk. "Isn't that who you meant?"

Manziuk said, "You think his wife did this?"

"She followed him here from Cuba. But that's our fault, too. We brought her here."

"Iced tea for the Inspector." The valet had slipped into the room and was setting tall glasses in front of Manziuk and Ryan. "Ice water for the Constable." The glasses were based on the primary colors, with the heavy base edged in one of the primary colors and stripes of red, blue, and yellow around the top of each.

He placed a third glass in front of Mr. Brown. "Orange soda for you, sir."

He then took the fourth glass, containing what looked like beer to Manziuk, and sat down.

Mr. Brown was looking at his valet. "We're talking about Rico's wife, Cary. She must be terribly distressed."

The valet shook his head. "Poor woman. Arrives in a new country and first thing she knows her husband is killed. Tragic."

Manziuk said, "Mrs. Velasquez hasn't been seen since she left the press conference last night."

"What?" Mr. Brown leaned forward, his hands on the arms of his chair, his eyes bulging out. "Why, that's—that's just terrible! Maybe whoever killed her husband has—" He raised his hands. "You need to find her!"

"We have people looking for her. Our job—Detective Constable Ryan's and mine—is to piece together the events of last night so we can discover who murdered her husband. If we knew that, it might help us find her."

At Manziuk's words, Mr. Brown visibly relaxed. "If there's anything we can do to help, just tell us."

"When I spoke to your valet this morning, he said you were in the Diamond Dome last night?"

"Yes, certainly."

"You watched the press conference?"

"Yes."

"Where were you while you watched?"

"We were in our private area."

"How did you watch?"

At a look from Mr. Brown, his valet took over the explanation. "Mr. Brown has a closed circuit television system built in so that he can watch a number of venues from his private enclosure, which is connected to his personal box. When he wants to watch something like this press conference, I just have to turn on the system and tell it which camera to pick up."

"And you did this Thursday night? Both of you watched?"

Cary nodded.

"Was anyone else there with you?" Manziuk addressed Mr. Brown again.

"No. Our chauffeur had a funeral to attend this weekend, so my—my valet drove."

"But you didn't come in the media entrance, did you? You weren't on their list."

"When we planned the Diamond Dome, we included an entranceway that looks like a loading dock. It's really a garage. We park in it and then enter by our own private door. We have our own unique security code that allows us to get into our area. So no one sees us come and go. Mr. Kanberra and the head of security are aware of all this, but no one else."

"I don't understand," Ryan said. "Why all the secrecy? It's only a baseball team!"

Mr. Brown looked over at his valet.

Cary said, "Mr. Brown prefers to be out of the spotlight. He loves baseball, but he'd hate the constant attention he'd get if the media knew he was the owner of the Matrix. The Diamond Corporation was formed to protect him from that attention. He's counting on both of you to keep what you've learned today confidential."

"Agreed," Manziuk said, "unless we discover something we feel is crucial to our investigation."

Cary nodded.

Manziuk went back to his questions, "Were you watching when Alita Velasquez left the room? Did you by any chance see her go out?"

Cary nodded. "Yes, we did."

"We were worried about her," Mr. Brown said. "She seemed afraid. She looked around quite desperately, as if seeking a way to escape. Then she just walked out."

"That's right," Cary agreed. "She left the room by herself."

"After a few minutes, they realized she was gone," continued Mr. Brown. "Mr. Kanberra sent a few people to find her. When they came back alone, Mr. Kanberra sent the media people away and everyone else went to look for her. We assumed they found her. I mean, how far could she have gone?"

"What did you do then?"

"We shut off the camera when they left the main room," Mr. Brown said, "and we left shortly after."

"What time?"

Mr. Brown looked at Cary, who answered. "Around nine."

"Do you have all this on tape?"

"No, I'm sorry," Cary said. "We didn't set it to tape."

"And you were together the entire time?"

"Yes," Cary said. "And since Mr. Brown has the most to lose if the Matrix doesn't win this year, he'd hardly murder one of his best players."

Mr. Brown's words were low, as if talking to himself. "It's all that sports lady's fault. She gave somebody the idea."

"The sports lady?" Manziuk said.

Mr. Brown looked at him in surprise. "You know her, don't you? The sports lady. On the radio."

"He means Stasey Simon," Cary said.

Mr. Brown nodded. "She said it would be a good idea for someone to take a bat to Rico Velasquez to knock some sense into him. Looks like somebody followed her advice." He sighed. "Whoever it was swung the bat too hard."

A couple of hours before the four-thirty Saturday game time, Armando Santana was standing at the side of the field, hands on hips, watching the rest of the team warm up when Jonas Newland, in catching gear but holding his mask, came over.

"You look as if you're someplace else," Jonas said. "What are you contemplating?"

"Life." Armando gave him a wry smile. "And death. How easy it is to go from one to the other." He moved his hands from his hips and gestured toward the air above them. "I mean, one minute you're alive, and the next, you're dead. One bullet. One knife. One wrong turn of the steering wheel. And whiff!" He snapped his fingers. "No matter who you are or how fit you are, life is gone." He smiled again. "The human body is very fragile for something so important."

Jonas gave him a quizzical look. "Getting philosophical in your old age?"

"Do you not know what I mean?"

"Yeah, I guess." Jonas played with the mask he was holding. "One minute we're absorbed by life, and then it just ends, and nothing matters any more."

"I can understand why a dictator feels so powerful, or why a soldier can get used to killing. Why put up with someone who annoys you when you can get rid of him so easily?"

Jonas nodded. "I read someplace that if you kill once, it's easier to do it again."

"I'm sure that's true. Unless you discover you've killed someone you care for. Then, I think maybe you go a little crazy." Armando turned and walked toward the bullpen.

Jonas watched him go, a puzzled expression on his face.

Ryan stood in the middle of the locker room wondering what she should be doing. Around her, some of the ballplayers and a few of their contingent of attendants and hangers-on were shuffling cards, talking, stretching, looking after equipment, or otherwise going through their pre-game rituals. Beside her, Manziuk was gazing into Rico's empty locker as if something in it would give him an idea. Ryan shifted her weight to her left foot and sighed. Who knew she should have followed baseball in order to solve murder cases?

Manziuk turned to her. "Let's go through the trainers' room and out to the bullpen."

As they walked, she said, "Did you know there are at least six explanations for calling it that, but no one knows if any of them is the right one?" She glanced at players who were getting treatments or having bandages wrapped around various limbs, but kept talking to Manziuk. "The one that makes the most sense to me is that the relief pitchers were once considered to be like bulls waiting to be slaughtered—going in when the starting pitchers didn't do very well."

Manziuk turned to stare at her. "I thought you didn't know anything about baseball?"

She shrugged. "There's a ton of information on the internet. I thought I should get up to speed about the terms they use. I know now why they call it the Diamond Dome."

"Oh? Why?"

"Because baseball is played on a diamond. The area between home plate and the three bases, all of which are 90 feet apart, is in the shape of a diamond."

"I think there was another reason. The dome is built to resemble the facets of a diamond."

"I assumed that was the only reason. But it isn't."

"Right. Well, let's go and see if we can learn anything else."

Manziuk led the way through the bullpen, where the starting pitcher for today's game was tossing a ball back and forth with another player, like a couple of kids might play catch in a park. Armando Santana stood alone in one corner. As she walked by him, Ryan found herself meeting his eyes. His icy stare made her look away, but, annoyed with herself, she looked right back. Their eyes locked, and this time he looked away.

Ryan followed Manziuk through the bullpen and onto the playing field. After a few steps, she made a face. The artificial turf felt weird. Not soft, like grass. Spongy. Sort of like a carpet, yet not like a carpet. She was glad she was wearing sensible loafers with her navy pants and taupe blazer. A narrow heel might sink right into the turf, or worse, put a hole in it.

They walked along the edge of the field, stopping now and then to survey the scene. Players from the visiting team were stretching, playing catch, and standing talking, watched by a growing number of people who were taking their seats in the stands.

Because of last night's Internet research, Ryan knew they were walking along the first base side of the field toward the dugout. And she knew the dugout had been called that because it had originally been a hole dug in the ground with benches for the players and coaches to sit on. She assumed the rationale was to try to prevent errant balls from hitting the players as easily as they might have if the benches were at field level.

Ryan watched Manziuk, trying to ascertain what he was looking for, but when he stopped and stood staring at the players on the field, apparently deep in thought, she looked around.

Kyle Schmidt was standing about five feet from them. Like Manziuk, he was watching the playing field.

Ryan walked over to him and said, "How's it going?"

Kyle turned and stared at her. "Oh! It's you. The lady cop." He frowned. "Do you want something?"

"Just wondering if you've remembered anything you forgot to tell us. Anything that might help us figure out who murdered Rico."

"Nothing I can think of."

"That's funny."

"What is?"

She smiled. "I thought you people prided yourself on having inside information on everything."

"You must be thinking of some other reporter." He turned back to watch the field.

"Apparently." She paused. "Still feeling sorry for yourself?"

He turned back. "What?"

"Thursday night you were drunk. I think it's because you were feeling sorry for yourself."

"Possibly."

"Are you one of those artistic types you read about? All nerves and insecurities?"

"Does that have anything to do with your investigation?"

"It could. Maybe Rico was threatening you in some way."

He drew his brows together. "Rico barely knew I existed."

"And did that bother you?"

He laughed. "You've got it! I killed Rico because he refused to give me an exclusive interview! Players, beware!"

"This amuses you?"

A wry smile touched his lips. "Lady, if you only knew how much I hate this bloody job."

Her eyes widened. "You hate your job?"

"I'd resign tomorrow if I could win a small amount in the lottery. Enough to take care of me for a year, so I could do some real writing."

"What would you write?"

"Not telling."

"Is it that bad?"

"You'd laugh. Everyone does."

"I might not be everyone."

"You might not. But it would go in your report."

She tilted her head to one side. "I'll find out, you know."

"Not from me." He took a few steps away. "And now, like it or not, I have a job to do here. I have this bourgeois need to eat three square meals a day. Blame my parents."

Ryan watched him go into the Matrix dugout, then turned to look for Manziuk. He was talking to the manager, Blake Harrison.

She took a step in their direction, but stopped abruptly when Ginny Lovejoy materialized in front of her.

"You're the police officer!" Ginny put her hand over her mouth. "Oops, sorry. You aren't here undercover, are you?"

Ryan forced a smile. "I think most of the people around the team know who we are by now."

"Yeah, I guess."

Ginny's smile was so guileless and innocent, Ryan immediately made a mental note not to trust anything she said.

"So," Ginny went on, "do you have any leads? Or clues? Or whatever you call it when you're following a trail? Any idea who did it?"

"We're still in the information-gathering stage."

Ginny nodded sagely. "Right. I do that on a story too. Get every last bit of information I can, and then see how it all fits together. Only you're using it to send somebody to prison for the rest of his life."

"Or her's."

Ginny tilted her head to one side. "Do you really think it could have been a woman?"

"It's not impossible."

"Have you found Alita yet?" Ginny stared at the ground and sighed. "I feel so bad." She looked over at Ryan. "I keep thinking it's my fault she's missing."

"How is it your fault?"

Ginny made a face. "If I hadn't broken the story about her coming and all, they might not have had the reception. And then Rico would still be alive and Alita wouldn't be missing,"

"You don't know that. Anyway, we heard recently that Stasey Simon may have given the murderer the idea."

"I'd say she definitely had a share."

"You heard her?"

"Yeah."

"And she really suggested someone take a bat to his head?"

Ginny shivered. "Yes. You haven't heard it yet?"

"No one thought to mention it to us until a little while ago. We've asked for the tape."

A new thought visibly crossed Ginny's mind. "If you catch the guy and he says he got the idea from Stasey, could she be charged with being an accessory of some kind?"

"That's an interesting question, isn't it?"

"I feel bad just knowing my story about Alita's arrival might have played a part. I don't think I'd sleep if I thought a careless remark of mine had inspired someone to commit murder."

Ryan couldn't stop herself from asking, "Do you think there's a chance Stasey isn't sleeping?"

Ginny considered the question for a moment. "I doubt it. But maybe I'm wrong. You could ask her." Ginny pointed toward the seats behind first base. "She'll be here later. She has season's tickets in the front row."

Ryan decided to change the subject. "I take it you know all the players quite well?"

"Huh?" Ginny looked puzzled for a moment. "Oh, I see what you mean. It's our job to know them, just as it's your job to know who the most likely criminals are."

"Does it ever go beyond business?"

"What do you mean?"

"Well, for instance, could Stasey have a relationship with one of the team members?"

Ginny looked around somewhat guiltily before responding. "I guess someone will tell you—likely Stasey herself." She moved a bit closer. "She and Armando had something going for a while, but I'm pretty sure it ended some months ago."

"Do you know why it ended?"

"Neither of them tells me about their personal stuff."

"Could she have been involved with Rico?"

Ginny thought for a moment. "I don't think so. He had Eva."

"Maybe he thought he could handle several women."

"I never got the impression Stasey could even tolerate Rico." Ginny drew her brows together in thought. "But now that you mention it, I guess there's a remote possibility her antagonism might have been because she made him an offer he refused. I'd have to think about that."

Ryan bit her lip before saying guilelessly, "What about you? Have you had any friendships with players?"

Ginny laughed. "Moi? Well, I adore Muddy Ames, and I'd marry him in a minute if he wasn't old enough to be my dad—and if he didn't already have a wonderful wife."

Ryan allowed a small smile. "Cute," she said.

"And entirely true." Ginny grinned, her eyes crinkling. "And if you have no more real questions, I just saw someone I need to talk to." She vanished as quickly as she'd appeared.

FIFTEEN

As Ryan looked around for Manziuk, her eyes met those of Ferdinand Ortes, who was leaning against the near wall of the dugout. He began walking slowly toward her. "We have a game to play today," he commented, his smile taking away the coldness of the words.

"Yes, I know," Ryan said. "We're just looking for, you know, clues." She gestured toward the field as she spoke.

He raised one eyebrow. "And exactly what kind of clues do you hope to find here?"

"I'm not sure," she said.

"Are you aware that they had a very difficult time finding bats for the game today? Your people took away every one in the stadium."

"They'll bring them back."

"Eventually, perhaps. But we needed bats today."

"There was a murder."

His face took on a very serious look. "True, but today, right now, there is a game."

"I know there's a game—" Ryan's tone was impatient. Then she stopped to consider. "Oh, you mean right now the game is more important than the murder."

He gestured above his head. "The stands are filling with people. The TV cameras will soon be running. While the death of Rico Velasquez is a tragedy of enormous proportions, the game must go on."

She nodded. "I see."

"Therefore, finding bats was very important."

"Let's go," Manziuk spoke in Ryan's ear. She hadn't heard him approach, and only her quick wits kept her from jumping in surprise. "Can't keep the big boss waiting," he added.

"I hope your new bats work okay," Ryan said to Ferdinand as she followed Manziuk, who was himself following a security guard.

After a trip through several long hallways, up several floors in two elevators, and past three entrances guarded by security guards, Manziuk and Ryan arrived at a door with a number on it. The security guard keyed in a code and they waited a moment before there was a buzz. The guard opened the door and held it for them to go through. Once inside, they knocked on the only door in the hallway.

Cary Grant opened it and led them down a hall with several closed doors and into a large room decorated in red and gold, with mirrored walls, several Matrix posters, a fully-stocked bar, and assorted groupings of chairs and tables. At the end of the room, seated in a large red recliner that overlooked the field, Mr. Brown sat wearing a team jersey and eating a hot dog.

Mr. Brown's valet showed Manziuk and Ryan to recliners on one side of Mr. Brown, and gave them each a hot dog from a covered pan.

"I don't—" Ryan was about to protest that she didn't touch hot dogs, which she considered lethal weapons the food industry unleashed on unsuspecting children and their overly trusting parents, but she saw Manziuk's eyes on her and realized he didn't want a fuss.

"Yes, Miss?" Cary asked politely.

"I don't think I've ever had a better seat at a baseball game," she improvised, hoping he didn't ask her how many games she'd seen.

Fortunately, he only smiled.

"Yes, it is a good seat," Mr. Brown said placidly. "I like it."

"And if you want to have a closer look at anything, we have a telescope you can adjust to focus on a particular player or part of the field." Cary pointed to a large telescope set on a tripod at the side of the booth.

Aware that Mr. Brown was watching her, Ryan took a bite of the hot dog. She chewed it slowly, half of her ready to gag at the thought of which parts of an animal she was eating; the other half admitting, if only briefly, that it tasted pretty good. Could use a touch more mustard. Manziuk finished his hot dog before Ryan downed three bites of hers.

Cary appeared with an array of drinks, which he offered. As he had earlier that day, after everyone else had a drink, Cary sat with them. Mr. Brown apparently did nothing without his valet.

Out of the blue, it occurred to Ryan that Mr. Brown was very close to her age. She struggled to control a giggle. If her family knew she was sitting with a man her age who appeared to be unmarried and was very rich, she'd never hear the end of it! Hopefully, they'd never find out.

"They're starting!" Mr. Brown announced. He leaned forward, his face flushed.

Ryan looked out but didn't see anything at first. Then she noticed several people walking onto the field.

Tony Kanberra stood behind a microphone. "I'm sure I speak for every member of the Matrix team, from players and management to all the Diamond Dome staff, when I say we're all feeling the tragic loss of Ricardo Velasquez. Rico will be very much missed by this team and this city. As a memorial gesture for Rico and his family, we ask everyone to rise for two minutes of silence."

The people in the stands rose to their feet. Mr. Brown and his small group stood as well. For two minutes, there was an uneasy silence, broken now and then by a cough or a rustle of movement. Then the anthem music began: first "The Star Spangled Banner," followed immediately by "O, Canada."

Across the field in the press room, Ginny Lovejoy also stood during the two-minute silence and the anthems, her mind busy wondering what the police had learned so far, who they suspected, and who, in fact, had murdered Rico. Would the police be able to track the killer down? And could there, as Detective Ryan had intimated, have been something personal between Stasey and Rico?

Kyle's voice broke into her thoughts. "You can sit down."

She started. "Hmm?"

"Songs are over."

"Oh, yeah." She looked around at the others in the press room, all of whom were seated, and promptly sat.

"Where were you?" Kyle asked in a low voice.

"Thinking."

"About Rico?"

"What else?"

"Kind of takes the fun out of it, eh?" He sat back and crossed his arms.

"I guess there's nothing to say it had to be about baseball."

"No, but it likely was."

Ginny rested her chin on her hand. "Do you think the police have any idea who did it?"

"I haven't noticed them giving me any information."

"Me neither."

Kyle opened a new file on his computer. "Who do you think did it?"

Ginny sighed. "Not a clue. That's the weird thing." She screwed up her face. "You know, if you'd told me ahead of time that Rico would be killed, I'd have been sure I'd know who did it. Or at least have strong suspicions. But I don't."

Kyle shrugged. "Maybe it really is a Cuban thing."

"Maybe he was into gambling and had reneged on what he owed."

"Could be anything."

"Yeah." She sighed. "Anything."

"Are you planning on covering the game?"

"Sure." She shook herself. "Oh, you mean today's game?"

"Yeah. We just made a triple play."

Her lip curled. "You're kidding, right? The last triple play we made was—"

"Okay, it was a joke. But you were in another world."

"Just thinking how nice it would be to get a scoop. You know, figure out who did it and get an exclusive with the killer." She grinned.

As Ginny's cell phone rang, Kyle shut his eyes. "Ginny, don't even think of doing something like that or I know whose body we'll be finding next!"

Stasey and Ted were late arriving for the game. As they walked toward the Diamond Dome's entrance, Ted spotted a disheveled woman standing off to one side of the gates. Her head was hanging down, and she appeared to be crying.

Ted nudged Stasey.

After throwing him an annoyed glance, Stasey looked in the direction he was indicating and stopped to observe the woman for a moment before sauntering over.

"Hi, there," she said.

A distraught Eva MacPherson raised her head.

Stasey took in the bloodshot eyes, streaky mascara, smeared lip-stick, and bruised cheek. "Well, aren't you a mess?" she said.

"Do I know you?"

"I know you."

"I can't find my purse." Eva looked around as if expecting it to suddenly appear.

Stasey shifted her weight to her right foot. "Maybe you left it in your car?"

Eva shook her head.

Ted had followed Stasey over. "Where were you before you came here?"

Eva stared at him.

Stasey laughed. "It's not five o'clock, so happy hour hasn't even started yet. But you've already had quite a few drinks, haven't you, Eva?"

"Whassitoya?"

"Could your purse be in a bar someplace?"

"No." Eva sounded offended.

"Just a thought." Stasey tilted her head to one side. "So, how's it going? You in mourning over Rico?"

Eva crossed her arms in front of her chest. "Don't talk to me about Rico!"

"I guess his death was a big blow to your plans."

Eva stuck out her tongue. "None of your business."

"Maybe I can help."

"Why would you want to help me?" Eva said. "Maybe I had a few drinks, but that doesn't make me stupid."

"But you—"

"Hi, girls. How's it going?" Ginny Lovejoy had come out through the turnstile and hurried toward them. "The game's already started."

"No purse!" Eva said, holding her hands out, palms up. She giggled. "Can't watch the game with no purse—no money, no ticket—nada."

"How about a cup of coffee—on me?" Ginny offered. "It might help you remember where you left your purse."

"Well, aren't you little Miss Sunshine?" Stasey said. "And how do you happen to be here instead of up in the press box?"

"I forgot something in my car."

"Something really important?"

"Important enough."

"Sure you did." Stasey looked around. "Which one of your spies told you?"

Eva shouted suddenly, causing both Stasey and Ginny to look at her. "I need to talk to Spidey," Eva said. "To explain something."

Ted said, "You can't talk to him while the game's on."

Ginny said, "How about we go over to The Fifth Base and get that coffee?"

Stasey put her hands on her hips. "Not without me, you don't."

Ginny shrugged. "So come with us."

"All right, I will. You go to the game, Ted. I'll come later."

"Are you sure?"

"Yes."

Ted obediently went into the stadium. Ginny took one of Eva's arms and Stasey the other, and together they maneuvered her across the busy street to The Fifth Base.

"Coffee all round," Ginny said to the waitress. "Strong."

"Speak for yourself," Stasey said. "Give me a lager."

"Yeah," Eva said. "Dom Perignon all round. The very best you've got.'"

"Coffee," Ginny said to the waiter. "Bring her strong coffee."

"Bring her her purse," Eva said. Then she put her right arm on the table and leaned her forehead on it, giggling. "Not 'her'. 'I' need 'my' purse."

Ginny kept her voice even. "Coffee will help you remember where it is."

"So, who hit you, Eva?" Stasey asked.

Ginny looked first at Stasey, then at Eva.

Eva's right hand moved to her cheek. "Whaddya mean?"

"You have a bruise on your face. Bruises to the face are usually caused by fists."

"Dunno what you're talkin''bout."

"Did Rico do it?" Stasey leaned close to Eva. "Or was it Ferdinand? You were with him Thursday night."

Tears formed in Eva's eyes.

"Drink your coffee, Eva," Ginny said. "It'll help you think."

"How many times did he hit you, Eva?" Stasey asked.

"Stasey, shut up." Ginny gave her a kick under the table. "Leave her alone."

"I want to know which jerk hit her!"

"Why? So you can tell everybody on your show?"

"So they know the truth about what he's like, of course. You want him to get away with this?"

"She's in no shape to talk to you right now. Especially if you're going to come on like a cop."

Eva looked around the room. "Cop?"

"No cop," Stasey said. "Just us girls."

In a soothing voice, Ginny said, "You're safe here."

"I'm not worried." Eva smirked. "Cops don't scare me."

"That's good," Ginny said.

"What does scare you?" Stasey asked.

"Not you." Eva grinned suddenly. "You're all bark."

"Thanks. I've always wanted to be compared to a dog."

Eve continued grinning. "That's what Rico said. 'All bark, no bite.' Just a wannabe man."

"As if Rico knew anything!"

Eva's face distorted and tears appeared. "I won't ever see him again. And I don't care, either. I'm glad he's dead!"

"You don't care?" Stasey lifted her eyebrows.

Breathing heavily, Eva spat out her words. "I was gonna dump the jerk. Only before I could, his wife showed up. Wife! Didn't even tell him she was coming. That's what he said. But I don't care. I was gonna dump him anyway. Marilyn did the same to Joe DiMaggio, you know. Dumped him. Left him heart-broken for years."

As she began sniffling, Ginny handed her several tissues.

Stasey stared at her. "After all this, you still think you're the reincarnation of Marilyn Monroe?"

Eva stood up.

"Where are you going?" Stasey rose as well.

"I feel—I feel—"

Jumping up, Ginny grabbed Eva's arm and propelled her toward the ladies' restroom.

When they returned a few minutes later, Stasey was gone.

"I still don't feel very good," Eva said.

"Do you want something to eat?"

Eva shook her head.

"Have you remembered where you left your purse?"

She shook her head again.

Ginny looked around. "I really should be at the game. It's what I get paid for. How about if I give you some money and put you in a cab? Think you can get home okay?"

Eva pouted. "Came to see Ferdinand."

"Yeah, I know. But you don't have a ticket or any money, and honestly, I don't think you should be here—not like this. Besides, he can't talk to you."

"But I have to see him."

"Why?"

"To tell him about—" She stopped and looked around the room as if checking to make sure no one was eavesdropping.

"About what?"

"Just something I know that he doesn't."

Ginny tilted her head to look at Eva. "Just what do you know?"

Eva drew a circle in the air. "Stuff."

"What kind of stuff?"

She drew another circle. "Just stuff."

"Right, Eva."

Eva locked her hands together and brought her shoulders up, imitating Monroe's look in the famous blast of air scene. "I know all kinds of things you don't."

"Yeah, I'll bet you've got lots of good stories, don't you?"

Eva began to giggle.

"Look," Ginny made a decision, "why don't we move to a table where we can see the game on the big screen? Then we can talk while we watch. Okay?"

Eva brightened. "Okay. And as soon as the game's over, I'll find him and he'll talk to me."

The two sat quietly watching the game, but when Ferdinand hit a triple in the bottom of the fifth inning, Eva jumped up.

"Where do you think you're going?" Ginny said.

"Have to talk to him."

"You can't get inside."

"Have to."

"Even if you had a ticket, you still couldn't talk to him until after the game."

Eva stamped her foot. "I have to see him!"

"Well, do you know where he goes after the game?"

"Of course."

"Maybe you could see him there."

Eva sat down as suddenly as she had jumped up, and they watched the rest of the inning. Then, out of the blue, she said, "You know, he didn't tell me."

Ginny stared at her. "Huh?"

"That he was married."

"Oh, you mean Rico." Ginny covered one of Eva's hands with her own. "I guess some men are like that."

"I hate men."

"Had some rough moments with them?"

Eva pulled her hand away and threw Ginny a scornful look. "I give them the rough moments!"

"Except maybe this time?"

"Rico Velasquez didn't do this—" Eva tried to snap her fingers, but failed. "And neither did Ferdinand Ortes."

"So why do you want to see Ferdinand?"

"I have to tell him something. That's all."

"Okay, how about this? After the game, I always go down to the locker room, so I can give him a message for you. And then I'll drive you to meet him."

Eva's eyes widened. "You'd help me?"

"Sure. But first I have to go write a story about the game and send it in. You stay here. As soon as I see Ferdinand and get my story done, I'll come and get you. Fair enough?"

"And take me to him?"

"Right."

"Okay. But I need a drink."

Ginny took a twenty from her purse. "You'd be better to get some food."

"Maybe."

With a last look back at Eva, Ginny left The Fifth Base and hurried across the street to the stadium. She waited anxiously for the elevator to the press room, pacing and going over in her mind both what she'd learned from Eva and the progress of the game.

"Where on earth have you been?" Kyle said as sat down beside him. "Who phoned you? Why did you race out of here?"

"Pat Davis. He saw Eva out front when he came in and thought she needed help. She's drunk and miserable. I left her at the Fifth Base getting something to eat. Said I'd come back." She opened her computer file. "Now, don't ask me any more questions. I've got a story to write."

"You going for another scoop?" His voice was cold.

She shook her head. "I was just trying to help her out. Honest!"

"All right." His voice was a little warmer, but still cool.

"So, what's the main storyline today?" she asked with a grin.

The game ended with a subdued 3 to 2 Toronto win. Ginny and Kyle wandered down to the locker room with the rest of the media. Ginny waited until the crowds had cleared before singling out Ferdinand.

He raised an eyebrow. "Did you have another question? Or have you finally come to your senses and decided to go out with me?"

Ginny smiled, but she was measuring him with her eyes. "Actually, Eva asked me to give you a message."

He frowned. "Eva?"

"Yeah. She's kind of—well, kind of a mess. She showed up out front drunk and without her purse. I took her across the street to The Fifth Base and got her sobered up. She says she has to talk to you about something."

"Me?"

Ginny nodded. "She said something about meeting you at the place you go after a game."

Ferdinand nodded.

"I told her I'd drive her there if she wanted."

He shrugged. "I didn't think you approved of Eva. Why are you helping her?"

"I've been known to take in stray cats now and then."

He observed her quizzically. "And later, perhaps, write an article about them?"

"Sometimes. Not always."

Ginny went upstairs to the press box and quickly finished up her game story and sent it in. She'd already sent her column. Muttering a quick good-night to Kyle, who was still working on his computer, she grabbed her purse and headed back to The Fifth Base.

But there was no sign of Eva.

After checking the restroom, she found the waiter who'd served them.

"She left not long after you did."

"Was she with anyone?"

The waiter shrugged. "I didn't see her leave. I just know when I looked over at that table about ten minutes after you paid the bill, she was gone."

Fuming, Ginny stomped out to her car and got in.

A hand knocked on the window and she jumped. But it was only Kyle.

She rolled down the window.

"What's up?" he asked. "You look annoyed."

"I told Eva to wait for me. She didn't."

Kyle crossed his arms on the open window. "Do you know where she is?"

She shook her head.

"*I* might."

"Really?"

"Yeah." He turned and started walking away.

She jumped out of the car and ran after him. "Kyle! Aren't you going to tell me?"

He shrugged and kept walking. "Why should I?"

She grabbed his arm. "Why did you imply you knew?"

"So you'd wonder if I had a scoop."

"You're still mad about that, aren't you?"

"Not mad." But he threw the words over his shoulder.

"You're sulking."

"No, I'm not." He kept going.

"Kyle, look at me. You're mad, but I was only doing my job. I get paid to write a column and to come up with fresh ideas. That's all it was. I thought you'd be happy for me. I really did."

He stopped and faced her. "Now you're lying for sure."

She looked at the ground. "Look, we write for rival newspapers. But we've always been friendly rivals, haven't we? What's happened? Is your ego so fragile it can't take my doing something good?"

Kyle turned and hurried away.

Ginny ran after him, but his long strides soon outpaced her much shorter ones. "Kyle," she called to his retreating figure, "I didn't mean that. Kyle!"

Moments after the game ended, a security guard came to guide Manziuk and Ryan from Mr. Brown's private box to the hallway outside the home team's dressing room, where Cecily Jones met them. The small group watched silently while the players came out in their street clothes and left the building. Ryan had no idea what they were looking for. Manziuk had just said he wanted to watch the players as they left the stadium, and Mr. Brown—or rather, his valet—had arranged for Cecily to join them.

A few of the players nodded as they went past. Others, including Ferdinand Ortes and Jonas Newland, greeted them politely. The rest either ignored them or stared curiously. Armando Santana, who was one of the last to leave, looked straight ahead as he passed.

Ryan turned to watch until he was gone. Then she looked at Manziuk. "So?"

He narrowed his eyes as he focused on her. "The more I think about this, the less sense it makes. With the exception of Santana, I can't see any reason why someone connected with this team would want to kill Rico. Assuming they want to win, I mean. And why wouldn't they want to win?" He sighed. "Unless there's something going on that we know absolutely nothing about."

"I know." Ryan sighed. "Gamblers or Cuban spies. So, what about Santana?"

"Pitchers lose their spots in the rotation every day in the major leagues. I've never heard of one killing a rival. Nor does Rico's death assure him of getting his starting job back. They're more likely to trade for another pitcher. I just can't see it."

"Could there have been something else between them? Money? A woman?"

"We've got people doing background checks on every person who was in the building during the time of the murder. I guess they might turn up something."

"What do we do next?"

"Maybe we should turn in early tonight. We've been working eighteen hour days all week, and we still have reports to finish up for the last case. There's not much more we can do on this until we have the rest of the reports from Ident and the other teams tomorrow morning.

"Knocking off is fine with me," Ryan said. "I think I'll head on home. I can work on my reports there."

An easily recognizable voice said, "How's the investigation going?" and they turned to find Iain Foley, dressed in navy pants and a burgundy golf shirt, standing beside them. "Is there any news? Have you found Mrs. Velasquez?"

"I'm afraid not."

"I'm sorry to hear that."

"We're still optimistic that she'll be found," Manziuk said.

"I certainly hope she's okay." He thought for a second. "You know, talking to you today has given me an idea. Maybe a crazy idea, but—nothing ventured, nothing gained. I wonder, Inspector, is there any possibility that one or both of you would be a guest on my program Monday? My listeners would love to get some insight into the way the police solve crimes. And who knows, maybe by talking about the investigation a little bit, somebody will think of something that will help you?"

Ryan said, "No wa—"

"That's an interesting idea," Manziuk said.

Ryan stared at him.

"I'd have to check with my chief, though. So you'll have to let me get back to you."

"That's fine Inspector." Iain gave him a card. "You can call me or my program director." He frowned. "Do you think any of the other players are in danger? Is that why you're here?"

"Until we know who the murderer is, we really don't know what might happen."

Cecily Jones spoke up. "The police have advised Mr. Kanberra and Mr. Harrison to ask the players and staff to take sensible precautions. And we have done that."

"Do you have a suspect in mind?" Iain asked Manziuk.

"We have some ideas. But nothing concrete."

Two men went by wearing red pants with a gold stripe down each leg, and gold T-shirts with "Matrix" in red across the back. "Who are they?" Ryan asked. "They look like members of a marching band without their jackets."

Iain laughed. "That's the clean-up crew. They come in half an hour after every game and clean the whole place from top to bottom."

"So these people are up half the night cleaning the mess the fans make?"

"Pretty well."

"Sounds like a great job."

"But a very important one," Cecily explained. "And that's why the classy uniforms—to help them remember they're critical to the Matrix team.

Manziuk said, "Didn't Ginny Lovejoy write an article about the crew when the Diamond Dome opened?"

Iain looked at him in surprise. "Yes, she did. I'm impressed that you remember."

"So how many cleanup people are there?" Ryan asked.

"Hundreds, at least," Manziuk said.

"The city that never sleeps. I wonder how many people work through the night cleaning up after others?"

"I think the two of you just gave me an idea for another program," Iain said. "Thanks."

On that note, Manziuk and Ryan left the Diamond Dome and drove back to the police station, where they parted.

Ryan picked up some file folders from her desk and copied the report she'd been working on from her computer to her Flash Drive before heading to her red Toyota. She fully intended to go home and work, as she'd told Manziuk, but as she inserted the key into the ignition, she paused.

Something about Armando Santana has been bugging her from the moment he'd walked into the office for the interview. His attitude was—she wanted to call it insolent, but it wasn't quite that. Self-assured, but that wasn't it, either. Bottom line was that her gut instinct said this was a man of whom to be wary. And given that he was still the prime suspect for Rico's murder, she felt the need to determine for herself whether the mysterious aura she sensed was real or a façade, and just what kind of man was hidden beneath it.

She drummed her fingers on the steering wheel. When they'd questioned him, she'd had the impression that if Manziuk hadn't been there, Armando's answers might have been different. How crazy was she to think that? Could there even be a small chance that, because they were both black, he would tell her more if they were alone?

She started her car, but instead of heading home, she drove in the direction of the baseball stadium.

SIXTEEN

Ryan found a parking spot and strode into the Fifth Base.

She had no concrete reason for thinking Armando Santana would be there, but he was, sitting alone at a small table for two near the back. She walked over and paused in front of the table.

After a moment, he looked up.

"Is this seat taken?" she asked.

"I prefer to be alone."

"Your teammates used to that?" She nodded toward the far corner of the room where a number of players were talking and laughing.

"I sometimes like to be alone. They know."

She pulled out the empty chair and sat down across from him, her purse on her knees. "That's good, actually, because I have a few questions I want to ask you—and I think you'd prefer to answer them when you're alone."

He pushed his chair back a little and slouched down in it with the fingers of his hands interlaced on top of the table. "You think I am a suspect?"

She fingered the clasp of her purse. "I don't know any reason why you shouldn't be."

"What happened to innocent until proven guilty?"

Her eyes were fixed on his. "I've always thought 'dead with no chance of recovery' had priority."

He sighed. "Should I call my lawyer to come?"

After a moment, she put her purse on the floor beside her, leaned toward him, and crossed her arms on the table.

"Where's your partner?"

"He had some reports to write."

"And you have some questions to ask?"

"Just one, really."

"Yes?"

"I'm not sure I'm ready to ask it."

A waiter came over and she ordered a glass of milk.

"You will not get any courage from that," commented Armando.

She shook her head. "I've never felt the need to look beyond myself for courage."

He raised his glass in salute. "You are still young."

"Surely courage isn't only the territory of the young."

A smile touched his lips. "The older I get, the less I am sure of anything. And the more I find I need to seek out courage."

She uncrossed her arms and spread her palms wide. "Too many people excuse their lack of action as a lack of courage. I think courage is overrated. Courage comes as the result of doing the right things simply because they are the right things."

"Assuming one knows what those things are. As I get older, that becomes less clear, too."

"I've never considered thirty-four all that old."

He looked down. "In life, perhaps not. But in baseball ...."

"There were players on the field today who looked quite a bit older than you."

"True."

"I've always thought age was more a state of mind than anything else. I have a grandmother who really is old in years, but she's younger than most people I know."

"I would like to meet this grandmother of yours. My own grandmothers—both of them—died when I was quite young."

"I'm sorry." There was a long silence. "Sometime, maybe."

"Assuming I am not a murderer?"

"Assuming I think it would be worth her while to meet you."

His lips again took on the beginnings of a smile. "So, is she proud of her granddaughter the policewoman?"

"I think so."

"It is good for a black woman to be in this position. A homicide detective."

She sat up straighter. "If you think I made it this far just because I'm black—!"

Now he was smiling. "No, no! I don't mean that at all. Just that it is good. I am proud of you."

"I don't see that it has anything to do with you."

He raised an eyebrow.

Ryan looked down. "Okay, maybe I'm a bit prickly. The truth is, I doubt very much that I'd have been promoted this soon if I hadn't been black—and a woman. There's been a lot of hoopla here about having more minorities represented at higher levels, and more women. But I'd like to believe I earned it."

"I'm sure you did. But whatever the reason, you have done well. And it cannot have been easy."

"Aren't you laying it on a little thick?"

He picked up the salt shaker and tossed it lightly from hand to hand. "You know, before you came, I was sitting here thinking about dreams. Do you ever think about dreams?"

Ryan scowled. "The old, 'I have a dream' thing? Martin Luther King did that one."

He laughed. "No, I do not mean that. I mean one's own dream. What each of us wants to accomplish in life. Or did you join the police just for the good salary and the benefits?"

"I joined—" She shook her head. "You don't need to know why."

"You joined because you wanted to do something important. Maybe make a difference. I became a baseball player not merely because I enjoyed the game and had the ability, and not only because I could make good money, but also because I wanted to represent the Dominican Republic well, to make my family and friends proud of me, to do things I couldn't do any other way. Yes, I have been paid a lot more money than most people might think I am worth, but I have also tried to use it responsibly, as if it was only on loan to me.

"But I still feel there is much to do, and when it began to look as if my career might be over, I felt bereft—as if my dream had been cut off before its time, with so much undone. For a while, I felt unable to cope."

"So you decided to get rid of Rico?"

He uttered a short laugh and shook his head. "Rico was a pain: I will be the first to admit that. But Rico did not cause my arm problems or bring himself here. Getting rid of him would have only given me a temporary respite. The real problem would remain. Am I still able to pitch effectively, or is it the end?"

"Rico exacerbated the situation with his taunts."

"True. But I have heard worse."

"Recently?"

He was looking over her head at something in the distance. After a silence, as if he hadn't heard her question, he asked, "Did you ever see him pitch?"

She shook her head.

"Ask for the video footage of the last game against Boston. It was truly one of the great pitching moments of all time."

"What do you mean?"

His eyes met hers. "Do you know much about baseball?"

She pursed her lips. "It's a game played by adult men wearing what look like pajamas for a lot of money."

He grimaced. "You are too hard. To the one who has eyes to see, it is so much more than a game. It can be a work of art. A perfect throw arcing over the field from the distant fence and landing in the catcher's glove in time to catch the speedy runner sliding into home plate, cleats high. A pirouette by an infielder who makes an unbelievable catch, then turns and throws in midair in a movement that defies logic and gravity. A masterful pitcher who controls the ball so well he can send it in and out and up and down, elusively staying away from the swinging bat. These are moments so beautiful you want to cry tears of joy."

She digested his words before saying, "And Rico?"

There was supplication in Armando's eyes as he looked at her, as if he was begging her to understand. "Rico was raw—like the proverbial bull in the china shop. But when he forgot about himself and just threw the ball, he was as good as anyone you will ever see." He leaned toward her. "You are not merely investigating the case of a dead baseball player, but the loss of a great artist. It is a tragedy that he will never throw a ball again. We will never know just how good he might have been. I know it sounds corny, but he was a true diamond in the rough."

Ryan stared at him.

His eyes met hers, and he didn't look away.

A woman's voice broke in. "Well, well. I didn't realize cops let their hair down—figuratively speaking of course—to have drinks with us mortals. Very interesting."

They both looked up.

Stasey Simon pulled a chair from a nearby table and set it down. "Discussing anything important? Should I be concerned? Is there an arrest coming soon?"

The first thing Ginny did when she got back to her apartment after failing to catch Kyle was check for messages. Eight. She once again congratulated herself on having worked up the courage to keep from giving her mother her cell phone number. If there was a true emergency, her brother Regan would contact her. The oldest of her five brothers, Regan was the only member of her family who could lie to her mother and get away with it. The fact that he was a lawyer said it all. Consequently, he was the only one she trusted with her cell number.

She listened to her messages, four of them from her mother, one a wrong number, one from her brother Shannon wondering why she hadn't called her mother today, one from Kyle asking her to call him when she got home, and one from Stasey.

She ignored the others and listened again to the one from Stasey. "Look, you got me thinking about the whole thing with Eva and Rico and all. I don't think you should be trying to solve a murder on your own. If you seriously want to do some crime-solving, maybe we can get together and talk over things like motives and opportunities. What do you think? You've got my number."

Yes, she did have Stasey's number. But did she want to call it? Solve the crime, yes. She'd like to have a go at that. But partnering with Stasey would be like going swimming with piranhas.

As for Kyle, he'd obviously been jealous of her scoop, and he'd called her a liar. On the way home she'd had time to do some thinking. During the past year she'd thought of Kyle first as a mentor who was gracious enough to show her the ropes; more recently as a fellow writer, who shared both the joys and frustrations of coping with power-hungry editors and ever-changing deadlines while coming up with brilliant stories. But tonight, she'd realized for the first time that Kyle was, first and foremost, the competition.

Ginny dialed a number. But it wasn't Kyle's, her mother's, or Stasey's. After a brief conversation, she changed into a burnt-orange skirt and ivory blouse, threw her wallet and a comb into a small gold bag, and went out again.

Armando Santana was happy to find a parking spot right on the street across from the Carnaby Pub. He entered an ordinary-looking side door and mounted the narrow stairway that led to the third floor, which was less populated at all times of day because there was no elevator. He waved to the bartender, who waved back, before sliding onto the seat of the end booth.

On his way in from his car, two people had recognized him. One had asked for an autograph. The other had either been not quite sure or else too shy to bother him. Today it would not have been a bother. His ego needed something, even if just a fan asking for an autograph.

A young man appeared in front of the booth. He was wearing a bright gold T-shirt with cut-off jeans. On his shirt was the pub's logo. "Um, I'm afraid this booth is reserved, sir."

"Yes, I know. I'm meeting her here."

"Oh." There was a brief pause as the waiter, whom Armando didn't remember seeing before, adjusted his thoughts. "Oh, yes. Sorry, sir. I'm new here. Can I get you something?"

"Just a root beer, please."

"Certainly."

He brought it, and a moment later Stasey Simon walked in and sat down across from Armando.

"I just came close to getting kicked out," Armando said. "A new waiter who didn't recognize me."

"I tell them to guard this booth with their lives. The place would likely fold without all the business I give them."

"Do you think you'll ever learn to cook?"

"What for?"

"I don't know. Some people enjoy it."

"Really?"

He sipped his drink while Stasey ordered a beer from the waiter, who had magically reappeared. They ordered entrees without benefit of menus.

Stasey lit a cigarette.

"Thought you were quitting," Armando said.

She blew out the smoke. "Cutting down. I only let myself have a few drags of each one."

"One way to get rid of your money."

She shrugged. "Probably costs less than joining one of those programs or getting the patch thingy. And this way, I can still have one whenever I want. Just not so much of it."

Armando shook his head.

She leaned back against the cool leather and studied his face. "You didn't want to talk at the Fifth Base. How are you now?"

He avoided her eyes. "All right, I guess." There was a moment of silence before he looked at her. "No, that is not true. I'm absolutely miserable."

"Rico?"

He shook his head. "Partly, but not really. It is just—this will sound so selfish, but I simply don't know how to handle any of this!" He brought his hands up, palms open. "Call me a fool, but I never seriously thought this would happen to me. Being demoted to the bullpen. Being told I am not as good as I once was." He screwed up his face to stop the threatening tears. "Part of me wants to tell them they are fools and walk away from them and the game altogether. And the rest of me wants to show them how wrong they are. And now—I do not know what will happen now. Will they put me back into the starting lineup or keep me in the bullpen? Or will they trade me? Or will none of this matter because the police will think I am guilty and arrest me? I feel so stupid."

She shook her head. "No matter what you do, no one will think you're stupid. Proud maybe, but not stupid."

"You think I have been acting too proudly? That I should shut up and accept it?"

She shrugged. "You're getting paid pretty well. If you walk away, no more paychecks."

"Money is not everything."

"Maybe not, but it's something."

"I have to think of my self-respect. I have to look at myself in the mirror each morning."

"You also have a lot of people depending on you."

He looked down. "It is all so difficult."

"Somebody told you it was supposed to be easy?"

"You do not understand." It was a complaint more than an accusation. "You will be able to do your job as long as you please. No one is going to say you are too old. Your voice will not quit on you. Your mind will not stop working."

She snorted. "Nonsense. Everyone grows old. No one ever really knows what'll happen tomorrow. You have to enjoy it while it lasts."

"*Viva para hoy.*" He sighed. "Live for today. It is much easier to say than to do."

The waiter arrived with steak fajitas for Armando and a grilled chicken salad for Stasey. For a while they ate in silence.

Stasey broke it. "What were you doing with the lady cop?"

Armando shrugged. "Nothing. She just appeared and started talking to me. I don't know why."

"Maybe she saw a good-looking man and decided to see what she could do."

He grunted. "I hardly think so. She reminded me of the TV cop, the rumpled one."

"Columbo?"

"Yes. He kept showing up and asking questions of the suspects until they finally confessed just to get rid of him. I think she figures I'm the guilty one."

She shrugged. "Good luck to her."

"As long as she sticks to the truth, I am safe. But you never know. Sometimes they just like to get somebody in jail." He paused, fajita in hand, and looked at her. "Why did you ask me to have dinner with you tonight?"

She shrugged. "Maybe I was bored."

"I have not known you to allow yourself time to get bored."

"There might have been another reason. Maybe I have an answer to that question you asked me a while ago." She took her time lighting another cigarette. "And it's just possible I have a suggestion for how you can get your starting job back."

Ryan had left the Fifth Base when Stasey arrived, but instead of going straight home, she'd picked up a salad at a fast food place and eaten it while mulling over her conversation with Armando Santana. The man was an enigma. She still didn't like him, but her not liking him didn't make him a murderer. She gave up trying to figure him out and returned home to her grandmother's crowded townhouse.

As she walked through the front door, she heard a male voice. She frowned. They didn't have many male visitors. She stopped to listen. Too deep to be the voice of their next door neighbor, who sometimes came over for a cup of coffee with her grandmother. And too young to be that of the pastor of the Baptist church her grandmother attended. She frowned. Had Precious found someone new to invite home to meet the family? Her last boyfriend had been an aspiring rapper who wouldn't say anything without rhyming the words, and he nearly drove them crazy.

Jacquie shook her head and walked into the kitchen. Seated at the table, surrounded by plates holding the remains of a lavish meal of corn bread, beef soup, jerked chicken, soursop juice, and apple pie, was a large black man she didn't recognize. Or did she? Something about him was familiar.

The man looked to be about her age or maybe a few years older. He was wearing a pin-stripe navy suit with a black turtleneck. His hair was longer than the norm and curly, but not tightly curled. He had a gold star earring hanging from his right ear, a heavy gold chain around his neck, a gold watch, and a gold ring with what looked like a diamond. Her mother would consider him a fine figure of a man. Jacquie thought he looked overdone.

"Here's Jacquie now," said her aunt.

Everyone looked at her.

"Jacquie, honey." Her mother's voice had taken on the soft southern drawl she tended to adopt when she was trying to impress somebody. "You remember your second cousin LeRoy? From New York? He was up for Caribana a few years ago. And of course you played with him when you were small, before we left Jamaica. He's come for a visit. Isn't that wonderful?"

His first name brought the memories back. What had Mirella, Jacquie's best friend, called him when he'd been here for Caribana? Oh, yeah. The Cousin of Doom.

Her aunt smiled and said, "So nice to have a man around the house."

Precious was grinning from ear to ear as she poured him a cup of tea.

Her grandmother was seated at the head of the table, her bright eyes watching.

Jacquie forced a smile and held out her hand. She had to control the shudder as he stood up and came around the table to caress her hand between both of his large, beefy ones while bringing his face close enough that she could see the drool. Okay, maybe he wasn't exactly drooling, but he did have something green between his upper front teeth.

"Jacqueline, my dear," he said in his deep voice. "I'm so glad to see you again. It makes the trip worthwhile."

She managed to withdraw her hand, and fought off the desire to run and wash it. "Here on business?"

He smiled. "A little business, a little pleasure. But I couldn't possibly come to Toronto without spending some time visiting my Canadian family."

"I take it you're up for the weekend?"

"I'm not sure yet. It might be longer."

Jacquie labeled his smile a smirk and wondered what he was up to. But she couldn't ask—not in front of everyone. "Well, that's nice. I hope I'll see you again before you leave. But right now I have some work to do. It was a pleasure."

She began to leave the room, but Precious stepped into her path. "Jacquie, you need to know I've moved into your room so LeRoy can have mine. We put the cot up. I hope you don't mind sleeping on it. You know I have trouble sleeping, and after all that police training, I'm sure you could sleep any place." She giggled. "I'm like the girl in that fairy tale—what was it? Oh, yes. The 'Princess and the Pea'." She giggled again. "I expect you wouldn't care if you slept on rocks."

Jacquie counted to five before allowing her mouth to open. "I'll sleep on the cot tonight, but I need to use my desk right now. And I don't want to be interrupted for at least an hour. Okay?"

"Jacquie's working on a very important case," her mother announced to LeRoy. "She's trying to find out who murdered a very important baseball player."

"Not Rico Velasquez?" LeRoy's eyes became huge and his face took on an expression of adulation. "Don't tell me you're working on that case!"

He knew, Jacquie thought. *He came here because of it. Maybe in his crowd, this will make him a hero.* But all she said was, "Yes, and I need to get to work."

"Surely you can spare a few moments of your time for your family, and for me." She had the impression he was waiting to see what effect his words had on her.

Jacquie ached to put a fist through his smiling lips.

"Did you actually see his body?" he asked. "Have you talked to the other players?"

"Yes to both questions, but that's all I can say. Sorry." She started to move away, but his hand caught her forearm.

She went perfectly still, looking first at the hand preventing her from leaving and then at him. He was at least as tall as Manziuk, and much heavier. Very softly, she said, "The last person who grabbed my arm needed sixteen stitches and a couple of pints of blood." She waited until he took his hand away. "Thank you." She moved a few steps away, then looked back. "If I were you, I wouldn't do that again."

He grinned, but there was no amusement in his eyes. "Cousin, you've become some kind of feisty since the last time I saw you."

"If you'll excuse me, I have a lot of work to do." She hurried to her room and shut the door. Then she groaned. Precious had moved in all right. She'd shoved Jacquie's clothes tight to one side of the closet to make room for her own. The dresser was covered with her make-up and jewelry. The floor was covered with piles of her fashion magazines and shoes and who knew what else! As for the desk, along with Jacquie's computer, it now held the stack of books and the other things she'd had on her dresser and her night table.

Jacquie swore. This was too much! She'd been considering finding a place of her own for some time, but she'd been holding off because she knew how upset her family would be if she moved out. But she was twenty-eight years old, and it was high time she had some personal space. She'd start looking for an apartment the first chance she had.

It rarely happened that Ferdinand Ortes ate alone at the Blue Mandrake. But tonight, he'd had some things to think about and didn't want interruptions. Once in a while, he liked quiet.

When he opened the door to his apartment, a light was on in the living room, and the television was showing a 1940s musical he immediately recognized as *Gentlemen Prefer Blondes*.

"Interesting choice of a movie to watch," he said.

"You took so long." Eva was curled up on one of the sofas. Now, she got up and walked somewhat unevenly toward him. "The cab driver was so funny. I made him bring me right here and open the door. It was like he was afraid to take the key. You know, Ferdinand Ortes's door. Like he might croak if he touched anything you touched. Your doorknob … your girl …"

"Sorry. If I'd known you were coming …"

"I tried to talk to you earlier, but I couldn't get into the Diamond Dome. I lost my purse. That funny girl reporter gave me twenty dollars, so I used it to get a ride over here. I didn't know what else to do. You know, you don't have that much food in your kitchen. But the caviar and crackers were good. And the chocolates were divine, darling."

"What did you want to see me about?"

"I don't know. To talk, I guess." She looked back at the screen, where Marilyn Monroe was busy convincing her boyfriend's wealthy father that it made as much sense for a woman to want to marry a rich man as it did for a man to want to marry an attractive woman. Tears came to her eyes. "So many men are jerks."

Ferdinand stepped closer and began to knead the muscles in her shoulders with his long, capable fingers. Looking down at her through his lashes, he said, "All men are jerks. I thought you knew that."

It had been far easier than he expected. Lawrence had called in to his manager and told him he was sick. He'd done that only once before, when he had a terrible flu, so there was no difficulty. Then, as the game was ending, he'd positioned himself so he could follow Stasey Simon as she left the stadium. He stayed far behind her as she crossed the street to The Fifth Base, and watched through a window while she talked to Armando Santana and the black lady who was with him. Then he stayed half a block behind her all the way to the subway.

When she left the subway and went into a small building, Lawrence waited outside. Then he followed her back to the subway. He'd been terrified she'd notice him in the subway that time. The last thing he wanted was for her to think he was a stalker and get upset. He didn't know how he'd explain why he was there. But she didn't seem to notice him. And again, he followed her when she got off.

This time, she walked several blocks and then went into a corner pub. After waiting outside for so long he was afraid he might have missed her, he got up enough nerve to go inside. He didn't see her the first time through, but on his second pass he heard her voice. He thought the man she was with was Armando Santana, but he wasn't sure, and he didn't want to get so close they'd think he was eavesdropping.

He ordered ginger ale and hung around the front of the bar until he saw them paying their bill; then he finished his drink and hurried out ahead of them. But as they walked to a car and Armando opened the passenger door for Stasey, Lawrence's heart stopped. His luck had run out.

With a heavy heart, he watched them drive away. But when he saw the car stopping only a block or so down the street, he ran as fast as he could, and he was just able to see which house they went into.

And now, here he was, at ten o'clock on a Saturday night, spying on a house he hoped with all his heart belonged to Stasey, praying that Armando would soon leave so he, Lawrence, could go up to the door and knock.

All day he'd been picturing what would happen next. Stasey would open the door. She wouldn't recognize his face, but she'd know his voice. She'd heard it countless times when he phoned in to ask a question on her radio program. She'd ask him what he wanted and he'd tell her why he'd come. And he'd know right away whether she hated him or not because her expression would reveal her feelings.

He leaned against a maple tree, his upper body moving rhythmically back and forth as he muttered over and over, "Armando, please leave. Go now. I like you, but you must go so I can talk to Stasey. I need to tell her I forgive her for saying what she did about Rico. I know she didn't mean any harm. And I need to ask her why they won't let me call any more. I need to know if she doesn't like me any more. I need to know what's wrong."

Several miles away, in a large bedroom with pale yellow walls and dark navy couches, Alita Velasquez sat alternately reading her Bible and the newspapers, as she had done for most of the day. She'd gone to bed earlier, but after tossing and turning for more than an hour, she'd finally turned on the light, put her robe over her nightgown, and fixed her pillows so she could sit up to read.

A light tapping sound on her door made her jump.

"Come in," she said in Spanish. As the door opened, she said, "You're still up? Have they discovered the murderer?"

The man she knew only as Zandor said, "Not yet. They're still looking." He entered the room and sat on the arm of one of the chairs. "I thought you were asleep, but your light—"

"Are they still looking for me?"

"Yes."

"They must believe I'm guilty."

"No, I'm sure they don't. Just that you might know something."

She pulled her robe closer around her. "I don't."

"But they're unaware of that."

"Could you not explain to them I don't know anything?"

He smiled slightly. "What do you think?"

A half smile appeared. "Oh, I know. I'm being very foolish. Of course, if you spoke to them, they'd never let you leave until you told them where I am." She wrapped her arms around herself. "But I'm so afraid."

"It's okay. No hurry."

"I'm putting you in danger!"

"I'm not worried about that."

"They'll be very angry with you."

"They'll understand."

She looked away from him, her lower lip trembling. After a few minutes, she said, "I've led such a sheltered life. My father always protected me and told me what to do. By now, he'll know that Rico is dead and I am a—a suspect. He'll be so angry with me for coming here."

"You're a material witness. Not a suspect."

"A witness? But I saw nothing."

"I know."

"The police—they think I'm a terrible person—a criminal." Tears overflowed her eyes and trickled down her cheeks. "I only wanted to do what was right! A wife's place is with her husband. All I wanted was to be here to help him, support him, become a family. And to tell him all I've been learning about God and his love for us." She sighed and closed her eyes. "I was such a fool. It was just as my father said. Rico never loved me. And he wanted nothing to do with God. You should have heard what he said to me, that before he was through, people would treat him as if *he* was God." She shook her head. "And now—" she shook her head sadly "—what am I to do now?"

Zandor left his position on the arm of the chair and came over to sit beside her on the bed. "You could start by telling me about God. I've never thought he existed. What is it you've learned?"

She looked up at him through her tears. "Only that he loves us—so much. I know, that sounds so simple. But it's true. And by accepting his love, even if there is trouble all around us, we can find a wonderful sense of peace and joy." She bowed her head. "Oh, how foolish I've been!" She looked up, her eyes shining. "God will be with me when I go to speak with the police! All this worry is ridiculous. When Paul and Silas were in prison, God was with them. If the police put me into prison, he'll be with me."

Zandor said quietly, "I don't really think they'll put you in prison."

"But I've known people who were put into prison even though they'd done nothing wrong, and it was terrible for them! Maybe that can't happen in Canada: I don't know. But no matter, I'm ready."

SEVENTEEN

Paul Manziuk settled into the faded blue recliner his wife Loretta kept threatening to get rid of, adjusted his feet on the footrest, and shut his eyes.

Loretta entered the room. "You want some tea? Toast?"

"I'd love some toast with strawberry jam."

"Two pieces enough?"

"Perfect."

"Tired?"

"Dog tired. And there's no end in sight."

When she returned with the tea and toast, she said, "It's all over the news. Your case, I mean."

"And because of that, everybody wants it solved yesterday."

"Will you have to go in tomorrow?"

"Yes. I just wish we had something more to go on." He opened his eyes and looked at her. "And then there's Woody. He was awake, so they let me see him for a few minutes. He's in pretty good spirits. Talking about what he's going to do after he gets out—all the things he's wanted to do but never had time for. I sure hope the operation is successful."

"Me too."

"Wish I could spend more time with him."

"He knows."

They were sound asleep when the phone rang at half past one. Loretta woke first and grabbed the receiver.

"What is it?" Paul said. "Woody?"

She handed him the receiver. "For you. Benson."

"Alita Velasquez just walked into the police station with four lawyers," Sam Benson said. "They say she'll only talk to the officers in charge of the case, so get here fast."

Manziuk and Ryan met in the parking lot of the police station just after two.

"Nice night," Ryan said. "Humidity isn't too high. Moon's kind of pretty. Almost full."

Manziuk just looked at her.

Ryan tilted her head. "How on earth did she pick up four lawyers?"

"No idea. They won't talk to Benson. Just us."

"Works for me."

The sergeant at the main desk sent them to the largest of the interview rooms.

Standing in the middle of three men and one woman wearing varied black and charcoal power suits was an attractive young woman in a red floral skirt with a white short-sleeved blouse and a yellow shawl. Her long hair was caught at the back in a loose chignon. She had no jewelry except a plain gold wedding ring and a watch with a white plastic band. Her face was devoid of both makeup and expression.

Benson gestured toward the long table, where chairs had been arranged on both sides. The lawyers positioned themselves on one side with Alita Velasquez in the center and two lawyers on either side of her. Manziuk, Ryan, and Special Constable Benson sat across from them.

"Thank you for coming," said the oldest of the four lawyers, a stocky man with grizzled gray hair and a lined face. "We're very sorry to get you all out of bed, but Mrs. Velasquez felt she needed to talk to you as soon as possible. She was concerned that if you thought she had something to do with her husband's death, and you spent your energy and resources trying to find her, you might not find the actual murderer."

"May I speak directly with her?" Manziuk said. "I understand she speaks English."

The lawyer coughed, then said quietly, "Mrs. Velasquez has prepared a statement."

"Very well." Manziuk nodded. "I'll let you know if I have additional questions."

Everyone looked at Alita, who read from the paper in front of her. "I was very sorry to learn that my husband was dead, and that he was murdered. I'm afraid I don't know anything about this murder. I was in the room for the reception, and then I left. I was a little upset by the questions, but I was more upset because my husband seemed very different from the man I knew in Cuba. He was not happy to see me. The people from the Matrix wanted me to pretend all was well, but I could not. All was not well.

"I was crying and I needed a chance to get away so I could talk to God and ask him what to do. I walked through the door, and then I was in a hallway with many doors leading to other places. I didn't know where to go, so I prayed for help, and immediately, the man who got me out of Cuba opened one of the doors and called to me to come with him. So I did, and he has looked after me ever since. He gave me a television and brought me the newspapers so I would know what has happened, and a little while ago, I realized I had to talk to you."

Manziuk leaned forward. "Who is this man you've been staying with? Is he here?"

She shook her head. "I think he must be an angel. His name is Zandor. I don't know where he is now."

"Where did you get the lawyers?"

The spokesman for the lawyers said, "We've been retained by the Diamond Corporation."

Manziuk sighed. "All right. That isn't important now." He looked at Alita. "What is important is finding out who murdered your husband. Do you really have no idea who could have killed him?"

"None."

Ryan stood up. "What," she asked, "about the fact that your husband had a girlfriend here and you found out?"

The oldest lawyer immediately said, "She doesn't need to answer that question."

As if she could no longer contain herself, Alita lifted both of her hands toward the three police officers. "No, please. I do not want any questions left. The girl was a terrible shock to me. And Rico laughed about it. I knew then I could never be with him as his wife. All I could do was pray for him. But, please, believe me, I would never hurt him."

"Could this Zandor have killed him?"

"After he came to find me, we were together until we left the building. We went in a car to the place where I've been staying. He took me to a room, and then he left, but I know from the stories in the newspapers that Rico was killed during the time Zandor was with me."

"What about the money?" Ryan said slowly. "You could be a very wealthy widow."

The female lawyer sat up straight. "That's not—"

Alita held her hand up toward the lawyer. "It's true." She looked at Ryan. "I'm told Rico was given a lot of money for what's called a signing bonus, and there may be more. But I don't want Rico's money. If it comes to me, I'll use it to help children in my country. It will help some to play baseball with proper equipment, and some to get care and better places to live, and some to get an education. I'm told there's a way to make a—" she looked at the female lawyer, who nodded encouragement "—a thing called a foundation to do this."

"Whose idea was that?" Ryan said.

"It's the right thing to do," Alita said. "Four months ago, I began to attend a small church some Canadians started in my country, and I learned that God loves me. I didn't know this before. I thought God was strict, like my father, and that he must often be displeased with me. I didn't know that it was possible for him to care about me.

"I wanted to come to Canada so I could tell my husband that God loves me—and also him. It was too hard to put it into words on paper or to say by telephone. And now," she wiped away tears, "there's no more I can do for him.

"I've spent the last two days fasting and praying. I know that when there are difficult decisions to make, it's always best to listen to God's voice and follow what he says. In the Bible, there's a place where Jesus told a rich young man to give away all his possessions and follow him. The young man went away sad. His money meant a lot to him. But God has said to me to give the money to those who need it. It was Rico's money, never mine. Now it is God's."

Ryan's tone was skeptical. "Most people dream of having more money, not giving it away."

"I think it is possible that the more you have, the more you need. I have never had much, so my needs are few."

After a moment of silence, Manziuk said, "If we need to talk to you again, how do we get in touch?"

One of the lawyers handed him a card. Then they were gone.

"I never thought it likely she did it," Ryan said as the door shut behind the last lawyer, "but that bit about God telling her to give away the money was pretty weird."

Manziuk shrugged. "You hear all kinds of things in this job."

"You think it's true? That she really won't touch it?"

"I guess we'll see."

Benson sighed. "This doesn't help us much, does it?"

"Presumably, it eliminates one more person from our list," Manziuk said.

"But it may add another," Ryan said. "Who is this guy Zandor?"

Manziuk nodded. "I think tomorrow morning—okay, later this morning—we need to have another conversation with a gentleman we met today," Manziuk said. "I can't say more just now."

Benson looked puzzled, but all he said was, "Time's flying. Are you any closer to making an arrest?"

Manziuk shook his head.

"Do you have a prime suspect?"

"Yes and no. I don't think the motive's strong enough."

"Opportunity?"

"Not more than a dozen people."

"Very funny." Benson yawned, then shook it off. "Seriously, how soon do you think you can wrap it up? We're at a critical point. As everyone in the country now knows from watching TV crime-solving shows, if there isn't an arrest in the first couple of days, the case can drag on forever. And we can't have that here."

"I'd love to say tomorrow," Manziuk said, "but the truth is I have absolutely no idea. Just let us keep working on it, okay?"

Benson made a face. "The Cuban embassy's been calling us. The Consul General has been threatening to send a delegation. They're not at all happy over what's happened. And they're really annoyed that I have nothing to tell them except, 'We're still investigating.'"

"I'm sorry, but I can't help you. Now that we have Alita Velasquez's statement, we have a few more things to follow up on. Then we'll try to fit all the pieces together."

"Are you absolutely sure it was one of the people who were at this reception?"

"Unless there was another way in—and Ford says not—I don't see how it can have been anyone else."

"You're looking at some pretty significant names here."

"Tell me about it."

"So there's nothing more we can do?"

"If I think of anything, I'll call you."

Benson sighed. "You know we have to wrap this up soon. You realize the importance. Everybody—"

"Everybody knows how important it is," Ryan said. "But it's also important that we get some sleep tonight. We have people to see in the morning, and we need to be sharp."

Benson stood up to leave the interview room. "Keep in touch."

Jacquie Ryan got back to bed at a quarter to four Sunday morning and woke up at seven. She tried to calculate how much sleep she'd had in total, but all she knew was it wasn't anywhere close to enough.

Precious had been extremely annoyed when Jacquie's cell phone went off in the middle of the night, but she'd been sound asleep when Jacquie got back, and Jacquie had managed not to awaken her. Jacquie looked over at her now; sound asleep on Jacquie's bed. Jacquie slammed her fist into the cot. *This isn't happening again!*

She dressed as quietly as possible, not because she cared if she woke up Precious, but because she didn't want to have the ensuing conversation, and she left the room with her cousin still in dreamland.

Her grandmother was eating breakfast. Jacquie filled a bowl with bran flakes and added dried cranberries and one percent milk.

As was her custom each Sunday, if Jacquie was up, her grandmother invited her to come to the small Baptist church she attended. As usual, Jacquie smiled and said, "Maybe another time." Jacquie had been eleven when she decided that either there was no God, or, if there was, she wanted nothing to do with him. But she had long ago learned not to argue the point with her grandmother.

Suddenly remembering what Alita had said in the interview, Jacquie said, "Hey, Gram, I've got a question for you. If some long lost relative died and left you a few million dollars, do you think God would tell you to give it all away?"

Her grandmother frowned. "What kind of question is that, child? We don't have any rich relatives."

"No, but I heard about somebody who might inherit a lot of money, and she said God told her to give it all away."

"Well, there's no telling, child. Maybe it's dirty money that was earned through gambling or drugs or something."

"I don't think so."

"Well, maybe she doesn't need it."

"She said something about a rich young man in the Bible."

Her grandmother nodded sagely. "The rich young ruler who loved money more than God."

"So you have to be poor to make God happy?"

"Who's she giving the money to?"

"She said it would go to help kids."

"She'd better make sure it isn't going into somebody else's pockets. There's lots of wolves out there among the sheep, and there's always poor naive souls who are nothing more than prey to people who pretend they're talking for God when they're really just talking for themselves."

"And then," Jacquie said with a mischievous smile, "there are the ones who get religion for purely personal reasons."

"Don't get me into that," her grandmother said. Jacquie's mother and aunt belonged to a large nondenominational church. A couple of months ago, the church had hired a very good-looking, and unmarried, assistant pastor. Since then, Precious had been attending much more regularly than in the past.

"So, Gram, going back to that other lady—do you think there's a possibility she really believes God told her to get rid of the money?"

The older woman thought seriously for a moment before answering. "You're asking me could she believe he did? Of course she could. People believe all kinds of things. But the more important question, which you didn't ask but you really want to know, is could

God have actually said it? Child, of course he could. The problem isn't that God doesn't talk to us—the problem is most people never take the time to listen!"

Cousin LeRoy's voice spoke from the doorway. "You ladies are up early for a Sunday morning. Nothing wrong, I hope."

"We're just fine," Jacquie said as her grandmother rose and carried her dishes to the sink.

LeRoy moved into the room, letting them see the full splendor of his wine and silver satin dressing gown. "Are you ladies working on an extra-special breakfast?" His eyes gleamed.

"Not us," Jacquie said. "We've already had breakfast. I have to be off in a few minutes."

"Some of the members of my church meet early for prayer, so I'll be leaving shortly, too," Gram said. "My ride will be here any minute."

Cousin LeRoy frowned. "Ladies! Ladies! I was hoping to have more time to get to know you. Especially my very interesting cousin."

"I'm sure Precious will be thrilled to be able to spend more time with you," Jacquie said.

He made a face. "You know perfectly well which cousin I meant."

"You're saying Precious isn't interesting?"

"What are you all talking 'bout?" Aunt Vida was tying her robe as she came up behind LeRoy. "You'd think a body could get a little sleep on a Sunday morning. What's that you were saying about my girl? Is she up too?"

"No, Aunt Vida," Jacquie said as she took her empty bowl to the dishwasher. "Precious is still sleeping. LeRoy was just saying how he's going to enjoy spending the day here getting to know the family."

"Well, of course he will." Vida eyed him with obvious approval. "LeRoy, I guess it's up to me to make you some breakfast. What would you like?"

He bowed toward her. "Bacon and eggs are my preference, unless you have a specialty."

"Well, I do have a few little things I like to make. How about some homemade hot chocolate, oatmeal porridge, soft-boiled eggs, bacon, maybe some fried plantains, fried dumplings, and sweet potato pudding?"

"A woman of discernment!" LeRoy laughed. "Bring it on!"

"I am so out of here," Jacquie mumbled to herself as she hurried to the hallway to get her purse and shoes. Then she went back to the kitchen to grab her water bottles and hug her grandmother.

"Are you really going in to work?" her aunt asked. "I was sure you'd have today off. Why, Cousin LeRoy came—"

"Sorry. Nothing I can do about it."

"Will you be back for dinner?"

"Don't plan for me."

"But Cousin Jacquie—" LeRoy started toward her. "I really want to spend some time with you. Maybe I can meet you later? Are you going to be at the baseball game?"

"I honestly don't know. If I can get off, I'll call, but we have to solve this murder as soon as possible."

"Maybe I can help."

Jacquie just looked at him. "If I have time, I'll call. Bye all!" She was gone before he could respond. As she closed the front door, she whispered, "Have a great day with Cousin LeRoy, Precious!"

As soon as he got to his office, Paul Manziuk settled down to drink the coffee he'd picked up and read Ginny's and Kyle's columns in the morning newspapers.

Requiem for a Baseball Player

special by Kyle Schmidt

In last Friday's column, I asked the question, "Who really cares?" I was thinking of the inordinate fuss and bother we make over professional athletes—the people who play sports for salaries well beyond the reach of the ordinary person.

Well, in light of what's happened in the forty-eight hours since that column appeared, all I can say is I was obviously asking the wrong question. I should have been asking, "What's wrong with our heads?"

A professional athlete has been murdered, and it seems that the main suspects are several individuals who are part of the Matrix team and (horrors!) some of the members of the media who make their living (like so many vultures) writing and speaking about the team. (Yes, I know I'm one of them. Sometimes that knowledge makes me want to beat my head against a wall. No, I don't need help.)

In this city, there's been much ado lately about banning guns. Well, let me tell you, if this murder shows us anything, it's that the problem isn't going to be solved by banning guns. Neither is it about checking to be sure we have no sharp objects in our possession. (Yes, a nail file could be used to gouge out someone's eye, so it's very dangerous!)

Rico wasn't killed by a gun—or by a nail file, for that matter. He was killed by what appears to have been the handiest weapon available—a baseball bat! So now what? Do we ban baseball bats? License the owners?

I repeat. The question is: what's wrong with our heads? Who on earth or heaven do we think we are?

I've never chosen to believe in some all-knowing creator. (Although I have to confess that sometimes even I wonder how this amazingly complex world could have occurred by chance.) But now I'm wondering if we need to bring back the idea of a real hell, filled with fire and brimstone. Maybe we need to make people very afraid they'll end up there—so afraid they'll start behaving as we expect human beings to behave, and stop acting like machines that have no hearts and no compassion, that seek only to annihilate whatever—or whoever—gets in their way.

What has gone so wrong with our society that we think a reasonable way to solve our problems is to end another person's life? When did we decide we ourselves are gods, with the power of life and death? Is it the result of the movies and video games that throw bodies around as if they were confetti—and show as much compassion for them as we do for the little dots of paper we toss in the dirt and step on and sweep up and throw away? People have to be worth more than little dots of paper. Don't they?

"Interesting reading?" Ryan walked in with both newspapers under her arm. "I picked them up at the newspaper kiosk on the corner, and skimmed them both. You never know, they might find out something we need to know."

"It's possible." He closed his paper. "Kyle's isn't about baseball, but I have to say I agree with it."

"Yeah." Ryan sat on the chair in front of Manziuk's desk. "So, what do you think? Was it planned or spur of the moment? Somebody who'd thought of it, but never would have done anything, and then—the opportunity is there. But having done it, what happened next? Panic? Or satisfaction?"

"We've seen both," Manziuk said. "Ted Benedetto, Armando Santana, Jonas Newland are all panicky. Stasey Simon, on the other hand, is as smug as a cat with a bowl of cream. So's Ferdinand Ortes, but that may be his normal attitude. Ginny Lovejoy is having the time of her life. Kyle Schmidt—I'm not sure about him. Or Eva MacPherson. I think she's short a spark plug or two."

"This is enlightening. I thought you went by facts instead of intuition. What's your impression of Alita Velasquez?"

"I think she told us exactly what she believes. But she may have been holding something back." He folded the papers and set them on the corner of his desk. "As for using intuition, a police officer is always deciding whether people are telling the truth or not. But it's not just intuition. You have to be watching body language, hesitations, word choices, where their eyes are looking, all kinds of little things."

"And here I was thinking you were getting in touch with your feminine side."

"You want to learn how to be a homicide investigator," Manziuk said. "Well, get ready. From here on in, we're going to be under a great deal of pressure to solve this. And there's no question Armando Santana is the best bet. He's the only one with an acknowledged motive. But as far as I'm concerned, the evidence against him is purely circumstantial.

"That doesn't mean he didn't do it. Just that we need some tangible proof. And if he's innocent, we need to find out who's guilty before the pressure to make an arrest gets so strong that Armando becomes the sacrificial offering to appease the public."

Kyle Schmidt's alarm went off at approximately the same time Manziuk and Ryan walked down to the briefing room to meet with their team. Kyle turned over and slammed his hand on top of the clock radio. The action had no effect on the music, but caused an intense burst of pain in his hand.

"Ouch!" He swore and grabbed his hand.

Reggae music continued to play.

After a few deep breaths, he used his other hand to turn the radio off. He lay there for a moment, realized how close he was to going back to sleep, and made a gargantuan effort to roll out of bed. His head felt as if there were marbles rolling around inside, pounding against his brain. He lay back and shut his eyes.

Idiot! He knew all too well what too much alcohol did to him, and the hangover he'd had Friday had been torture. So why had he gone and done it again?

He rolled to a sitting position and sat for a while with his head in his hands. Eventually, he staggered to the bathroom, where he threw up.

As he looked at his haggard, unshaven face in the mirror, he said to himself, "This has to stop. You hear that? It has to stop."

He shut his eyes and took a deep breath. He knew exactly why he was drinking so much—to get up his nerve to make a decision. But it wasn't exactly helping.

He contemplated calling in sick and going back to bed. He could watch the game on TV.

No, that wouldn't work. He had to go in—had to face Ginny. The fact that she hadn't called him back last night meant she was either mad or hurt, and she had every reason to be both.

He'd have to go to the game and talk to her, maybe help her try to solve the murder. Otherwise she was sure to get in trouble. And he knew things she didn't know. All his holier-than-thou talk about scoops, and he actually knew quite a few things she didn't know.

First things first. Once he made sure Ginny wasn't going to get herself into trouble, he'd be able to think clearly enough to make his decision.

"Where are you, Stasey?" Ted mumbled as looked at his watch for the fifth time. Ten fifty-five. "You've got five lousy minutes. What are you trying to pull off?"

He looked at the control panel and shuffled his notes. Everything was ready for her special ninety-minute Sunday show. Her water with a touch of lemon was there. The ashtray disguised as a saucer was ready. The clips he'd put together were waiting to be played.

It wasn't as if she'd never been late. There was the time she was driving right behind a car that got hit by a school bus filled with nine-year-olds whose frenzied, hyperventilating driver ran a red light. Fortunately, nobody was seriously hurt, but both drivers were hysterical and Stasey ended up talking to the police for more than an hour because she was the only adult witness. There was also the time she couldn't get out her front door after a sudden blizzard dumped four feet of snow in the city. And there was the time she'd been too ill from a severe hangover to come in.

But on each of those occasions, and the few others when she's been sick or delayed, she'd phoned to explain—or more precisely, to complain and blame whatever had caused her to miss the show—including the bartender who had kept serving her at the party. But this time she hadn't phoned.

True, she was known for cutting it close. But not this close.

Ted left the studio and found the program director, Ray Cummings, in his office eating a meatball sub.

Ignoring the fragrant aroma, Ted said bluntly, "Stasey isn't in yet."

"She hasn't called?"

"Nope."

"You tried her cell?"

"I've tried everything."

"But this special show was her idea!"

"I know. I don't understand it."

"So, what do you want to do? Play the clips?"

"Not without Stasey. Better to reschedule. Replay something from earlier in the week."

"Not good."

"I know."

"Better for me to take calls."

"Probably."

"Okay. If I have to, I have to." Ray shoved the rest of his lunch into the small refrigerator he kept next to his filing cabinet and followed Ted down the hall to the studio.

"Come on, Stasey!" Ted muttered under his breath. As he got ready for the show, he kept glancing at the door, expecting her to blow in any minute with a wild story of some sort of mishap.

But a few moments later, the intro was on, and Ray was explaining that something unexpected had come up and Stasey couldn't be here. Her special report would have to wait until Monday. Ray would take her place because he liked to keep his hand in. He joked about the minions forgetting that the old man upstairs had been doing this before half of them were born, and segued into a discussion of rookies vs veterans on baseball teams.

Ginny had WIN 730 streaming through the wireless Internet connection in the press box at the Diamond Dome. When Ray's voice came on, she heard a buzz of conversation and looked around to discover she wasn't the only one surprised to hear Ray Cumming's voice.

"Something's wrong," she said. "Stasey would never miss her special program." She gritted her teeth. "Rats! Why, oh why, didn't I call her back last night?"

"Er—Ginny?"

She took her time looking up. "Good morning, Kyle." She looked more closely. "Kyle, you look crummy. Your eyes are all bloodshot. Were you up all night or did you get drunk again?"

"It doesn't matter."

She turned back to her computer. "I guess not. After all, I'm the competition."

"Ginny, I didn't mean that. I'm sor—"

"Would it interest you to know that Stasey Simon didn't show up for her special show this morning?"

"Wha—? Oh, man! I forgot all about that show." Kyle slumped into the chair next to Ginny's. Then his head shot up. "She didn't make it?" He held up his hand. "Wait. Before you answer, do you have anything for a headache?"

"I might." She started looking through her purse.

"You mean Stasey made a big deal about how she had information about the murder of Rico Velasquez, and got them to give her a special show, and then she didn't show up?"

"Yep." She was still searching in her purse."

"That doesn't make sense. Who's doing the show?"

"Ray Cummings."

He stared at her. "That makes no sense whatsoever."

She found the small tube of tablets she'd been looking for and held it up. As he took it, she looked him straight in the eyes. "So, what's it to be? Are we working on this together or are we doing it separately?"

"Get me some water so I can take this, and then we can talk."

In the clubhouse lounge, several Matrix players, including Jonas Newland and Armando Santana, were also discussing Stasey's absence.

"That's weird," Jonas said as he turned off the radio.

"Yeah." Armando stood up and moved restlessly around the room. "She never misses her regular show. Why would she miss a special?"

Ferdinand Ortes came in. "I just remembered about the Stasey Simon special. I thought you'd have it on."

"Stasey didn't show," Armando said.

"I don't believe it." Ferdinand whistled. "Why not?"

Jonas answered him. "They said she had something unexpected come up and she couldn't be there."

Ferdinand shook his head. "I don't believe it. Something's up."

"I'm going to call her." Armando hurried to the locker room and grabbed his cell phone. Jonas and Ferdinand followed. He tried her home number and then her cell phone, but he got an answering message on both.

The three men looked at each other.

"Something's wrong," Armando said.

Blake Harrison walked into the locker room. "What do you think you're doing in here?" He swore. "Get out on the field with the rest of the team!"

Armando started to say something, but Blake ignored him and walked out of the room. As he went through the door, he barked, "Move it!"

Ferdinand raised his eyebrows in mock surprise, but headed toward the field.

Armando looked at Jonas. "I can't—"

"Ted will take care of it," Jonas said. "We need to get out there."

Armando took a deep breath, thought for a moment, then put his phone back into his locker and followed them onto the field.

While the Matrix players warmed up with stretches and sprints on the field, and Ginny and Kyle sat together in intense discussion, Paul Manziuk and Jacquie Ryan were finishing up the meeting with their team. They'd listened to the tape with Stasey Simon's suggestion that someone needed to apply a bat to Rico's head, gone over the reports from Ident, made a list of a few things that needed further checking, and come up with a plan for what to do next, including more interviews.

Alita Velasquez was who she said she was, and both her father and the Cuban government wanted her returned.

Jonas Newland had an impeccable reputation both as a baseball player and as a husband and father.

Armando Santana had been in minor trouble as a young teen in the Dominican Republic—getting in with the wrong crowd—but had an excellent reputation since then. The only other thing of note was that he'd married at age twenty-three and divorced three years later. There were no children.

Kyle Schmidt had several unpaid parking tickets.

Ginny Lovejoy was squeaky clean, as were all five of her brothers.

Iain Foley had nothing on his record except a car accident three years before on icy roads in January. Neither driver had been charged.

Stasey Simon had several speeding tickets and an arrest for crossing a police line to get an interview. Nothing else.

Ted Benedetto's parents owned a Chinese/Italian restaurant where Ted had worked as a teenager. He'd gone to community college, got a placement as an intern for WIN 730, and quit college to become Stasey Simon's producer. Nothing else.

Ferdinand Ortes had had more than a few speeding tickets, but still had his license.

Eva MacPherson was the daughter of John MacPherson of MacPherson Industries. She had a history of speeding tickets, parking tickets, and a couple of drunk and disorderlies.

Ryan asked someone to check the information that Ginny Lovejoy had offered her the day before—that Stasey Simon and Armando Santana were or had been in a relationship.

As Manziuk and Ryan left for their car, Manziuk checked his watch. "I'd hoped to get out earlier. We've missed the start of the Stasey Simon special."

Ryan got into the passenger seat. "Do you want to go over to the station and find out what she had to say?"

"It's okay. I've got two people taping it and listening for any new information."

As he settled into the driver's seat, Manziuk's cell phone rang. He looked thoughtfully at the number before answering. "Mike? What's wrong? Is Woody okay? ... You know you aren't supposed to call me during work hours. ... What? ... Okay, I'll check it out. ... No, it's good you called. Thanks for letting me know." He ended the call and put the phone away.

"Something up?" Ryan asked hesitantly.

"My son thought I might like to know that Stasey Simon was a no-show for her special this morning."

Ryan thought for a moment. "That doesn't sound good. We should check it out."

When they took the first news break at eleven-thirty, Ray Cummings glanced over at Ted. "You think something's wrong, don't you?"

Ted nodded. "She never misses her show. You know that. Not without calling, anyway. And for sure not this one. She was dying to do it. I spent hours putting it together, and she was here helping me for most of Saturday."

"You think she could be sick? Hurt?"

"I don't know."

Neither one mentioned the recent murder of Rico Velasquez, but that knowledge hung in the air.

Ray said, "Should we call 911?"

Ted nibbled on his lower lip. "She'd kill me if we called the cops and there's nothing wrong."

"What'll we do then? We can't ignore it."

"As soon as the program's over, I'll go over to her place. Try to track her down."

The door opened and Iain Foley walked in. "What is this? Where's Stasey?"

"No idea," Ray said before Ted could get a word in.

"She call in?"

Ted said, "No."

"So where is she?" Iain asked again.

"We don't know."

"The only way she'd miss this show is …." Iain's words trailed off.

"Yeah." Ted nodded.

"Did you call the cops to check her house?"

Ray and Ted shook their heads.

"Don't you think you should?"

"Yeah," Ted said, "but if she's okay, she'd be pretty mad if we called the cops in."

"Still—"

"The second we're done here, I'll go over there," Ted said.

"Yeah," Ray said. "We're just getting spooked because of Rico. I'm sure she's fine."

Iain held up his hands. "It's your call. But if it were me, I'd get the cops involved now."

"What are you doing here?" Ted asked suspiciously.

"Don't get your hackles up," Iain said. "I listened in out of curiosity to hear what Stasey was up to with her 'Special.' When Ray came on instead, I figured something was up, and I decided to come in to see if you needed my help. If you don't need me, I'm out of here."

"Can you take over the show?" Ray said.

"If you want."

"I'd really appreciate it." Ray took off the headphones and moved toward the control room.

"Ted, go find Stasey. And when you find her, tell her she'd better be here on time for her show tomorrow, and she'd better have a good explanation for today."

Ted nodded. On his way down the stairs—he rarely took the elevator—he tried Stasey's numbers again: first the cell, then her home phone. No answer.

"Something's wrong," he said aloud. He ran to his car, a two-month-old lime green smart fortwo cabriolet, and drove the tiny car in and out of traffic as fast as he dared.

He jerked to a stop in front of Stasey's house and looked at the front door. No sign of anything wrong. He raced up the steps and rang the bell. Nothing. No footsteps inside. No sound whatsoever. Now what? He grasped the doorknob, turning it the way you do in movies, where it's never locked. To his shock, the door opened. This wasn't real. Couldn't be real.

Ted slowly opened the door and looked at the lock. It was the kind you had to engage with a key. His mind was spinning. Had Stasey been in such a hurry to leave that she hadn't taken time to lock the door? Or had she forgotten? Neither option sounded like Stasey.

He called her name. No answer. The echo made him shiver.

He walked in slowly, cautiously, expecting her to step out of the next room and ream him out for coming inside uninvited.

But everything remained still and quiet.

She was in the living room, lying on her stomach on top of the antique beige throw rug in the middle of the oak floor. Her hands were flung out, her head turned to one side so he could see only blonde hair, matted and dark with what he knew must be blood.

He knelt beside her, certain she was dead but not willing to accept it—needing to be sure, to verify it for himself before he gave way to the anguish he knew would soon overwhelm him. It was as if he was two people—one of them moving and doing, and the other watching, assessing, deciding.

He touched her hand and started as if he'd received an electric shock. It felt warm. Had he interrupted the murderer? Was he still in the house?

He heard a noise behind him.

PART IV

From Thee all human actions take their springs,
The rise of empires and the fall of kings!
See the vast Theatre of Time display'd,
While o'er the scene succeeding heroes tread!
With pomp the shining images succeed,
What leaders triumph, and what monarchs bleed!
Perform the parts thy providence assign'd,
Their pride, their passions, to thy ends inclin'd:
Awhile they glitter in the face of day,
Then at thy nod the phantoms pass away;
No traces left of all the busy scene,
But that remembrance says—
The things have been!"

—"The Deity." AUTHOR UNKNOWN
Quoted by Henry Fielding in *The History of Tom Jones*

EIGHTEEN

Ted jumped up and looked around wildly for something to use as a weapon.

"Miss Simon, are you here?"

Ted stopped dead and took a deep breath before calling, "Inspector, is that you?" He ran into the front hallway. Manziuk was standing in the open doorway, with Ryan right behind him.

"How did you get in?" Ted said.

"The door was wide open."

"Oh. Yeah. Right. I guess I left it open."

"We have some questions to ask Miss Simon. Is she here?" Manziuk looked more closely at Ted. "What's wrong?"

Ted motioned toward the living room. "She's dead."

They were past him in a flash, Manziuk pulling out his cell phone; Ryan kneeling down next to the body, feeling Stasey's wrist, touching the side of her neck, listening to her chest. "There's a pulse," she said. "Barely."

"She's not dead?" Ted came closer. "But I thought—"

"Not yet," Ryan said. "But it's close. From the appearance of the blood, she's been here for some time."

"What do you mean?"

"The blood on the carpet and in her hair has mostly dried."

Manziuk put his phone away. "How long have you been here?" he asked Ted. "Have you touched anything?"

"I got here just a minute or two before you. I didn't touch anything." He looked down. "Just Stasey's hand."

An ambulance and two police cars arrived in less than five minutes. Both paramedics shook their heads when they checked Stasey's pulse, but after hooking up an IV, and loading her very carefully onto a gurney, they left, siren blaring.

Ted began to follow them, but Manziuk grabbed his shoulder. Ted shook him off. "I should be with her."

"You can go in a few minutes, but first we need to talk."

"I should be near her. Just in case."

"I doubt if she'll regain consciousness any time soon."

Ted stared in the direction of the front door, then nodded. "I was sure she was dead. If you hadn't come …."

"Mr. Benedetto, why don't we go in the kitchen and sit down for a few minutes?"

Ted swallowed hard, then led the way into a spotless kitchen. "Stasey never cooks," he said. "Hardly even comes in here."

Manziuk pulled a chair from the table and held it for Ted to sit down. Then he sat in the chair across the corner.

Ryan put on gloves before opening cupboard doors and the refrigerator. "He's right. Not much to eat. Some beverages. Fast foods. Not much else."

"I told you," Ted said.

"So," Manziuk said, "do you want to tell us what happened? Was there a fight?"

Ted stared at him. "Wait a minute. You think I—you think I hurt Stasey?" He began to stand up, his voice rising to a shout. "You think I hurt Stasey?"

"Please sit." Manziuk didn't move, and his voice remained calm, but Ted immediately dropped back into his chair. "If I thought you'd done it," Manziuk continued, "you'd be in handcuffs now. But I assume you know what happened."

"I don't know anything. I got here a few minutes before you came, and I—"

Ryan interrupted. "How did you get in the house?"

"The door was closed, but when she didn't answer the doorbell or my pounding on the door, I tried it. It wasn't locked."

"Was that unusual?"

"Totally. A few years ago, somebody broke in through an unlocked basement window. She wasn't home and the person didn't take much—just some electronics equipment and some loose cash, but she's been really paranoid since then. Even with service people. She told me she checks their references and watches them the whole time, and she even keeps her phone in her hand, with 911 dialed so she just has to hit the call button at the slightest hint of a threat. She'd never have let anyone in she didn't know."

"If she always locked the door," Ryan said, "why did you bother to try it?"

"I—I don't know. I was worried about her. I thought maybe I could—I don't know—push it in."

Manziuk asked, "Why were you so worried?"

"Because Stasey missed her show." The words were spoken reverently. Ted stared at each of them in turn. "Isn't that why you're here?"

"Is that such a big deal?" Ryan asked. "Can't you just play a rerun?"

"You don't understand. We have a huge audience out there waiting to hear what she's going to say. It has to be current, live, now! Especially the one today. She'd have to be on her deathbed to miss it." Ted's face crumpled. "What am I saying!" His eyes filled and he lowered his head into his hands.

Ryan looked at Manziuk. An unspoken comment—*Is this an act or is it real?*—crossed from each to the other, and, just for an instant, as they realized they'd had the same thought, they stared in disbelief.

After a few minutes, Ted raised his head. Ryan had put a box of tissues on the table next to him. He grabbed a few, which he used to mop his face. "Sorry," he said. "It got to me."

"When did you see Stasey last?"

"At the game yesterday. We sat together. Well, she missed the first few innings because we ran into Eva MacPherson in front of the door. Eva was drunk or high on something. Ginny Lovejoy came out just then, which was odd, so she and Stasey took Eva over to the Fifth Base, ostensibly to sober her up, but you know they were both looking for storylines. Stasey joined me in the middle of the third inning and we stayed to the end. Then we separated. She was going home, but she likely stopped to eat first. There's a pub near her house where she eats a lot."

"Could she have gone back to the Fifth Base?"

Ted shrugged. "Sure. She doesn't tell me where she goes."

"You had no contact with her between when you parted after the game and when you found her today?" Manziuk said.

"None. The special show today was all set up. I'd worked Friday night and Saturday morning and part of the afternoon creating a montage of clips from our shows, beginning with Rico's arrival at spring training camp right up to this week. Stasey was at the station with me from when you were there to talk to me in the morning until we left for the game."

"What was going to happen on this special show?"

"Stasey was going to introduce the show live, and then I would play the clips in order during the first seventy-five minutes, and Stasey would comment on each of them. Then she was going to take the last fifteen minutes to do a live commentary."

"You didn't have any communication with her after you separated following the ball game yesterday?"

"None."

"All right, what happened today?"

"I got in at eight this morning and made sure everything was ready. I expected her in half an hour before the show was going to go on. When she didn't come by ten forty-five, I tried to call her at home and on her cell phone, but there was no answer. I came over here the minute I could get away."

"Why not call us when she didn't arrive on time?"

"Believe me, we thought of it. But then we thought how mad she'd be if she was just off doing something."

"You said it was a special show," Ryan came closer. "How was it special?"

"She doesn't do a Sunday show. Just weekdays. But she talked to the suits and got permission to pre-empt some time to do this."

Ryan gave him a puzzled look. "Suits?"

Ted scrunched up his mouth. "You know, brass, bosses, big shots. The ones who wear suits."

"Why did she feel the need for doing a special show?" Manziuk said.

Ted grimaced. "She said she had an idea how to flush out the killer. Oh my—" His eyes grew round. "Do you think that's what happened? The killer found out and stopped her?"

"That's entirely possible," Manziuk said. "Tell me, in all honesty, do you think Stasey knew who murdered Rico?"

"If she did, she didn't tell me."

There was a long silence.

Finally, looking at a corner of the room, Ted said, "Honestly? I think she just wanted to see if she could stir something up."

"Could she have said or done something to make the murderer think she was on to him?"

"Isn't that obvious?"

A policewoman who'd arrived at the same time as the ambulance came into the kitchen. "No sign of a forced entry anywhere, sir. And nothing out of place that we can tell, except a lamp seems to have been knocked over in the living room near where she was found and the table it was on appears to have been pushed back. The only other thing is that the back door was partly open."

"Thanks, Constable." She left, and Manziuk looked back at Ted. "Could you tell if anything was missing?"

Ted shook his head. "Not really. I've only been here a couple of times, and only on this floor. I don't know much about her personal life." He took a deep breath. "Look, I'd really like to go to the hospital. If by any chance she comes out of it, she'll want me there."

Manziuk said, "Just a few more questions and we'll see that you get driven there."

"I've got my car. I'm okay."

"We'll have someone bring your car to the hospital."

Ted turned that over in his mind. "Okay, thanks." He looked at Manziuk. "So what else do you want to know?"

"Her family. Who needs to be notified?"

"I don't think I've ever heard her mention any family members." He thought for a moment, then snapped his fingers. "If she does have some, their contact info will be at the station, in her personnel file."

"She's never been married?"

"Not that I know of."

"Anyone she's close to?"

"Not really. I mean, not that I know of, anyway." He looked down at his feet. "We just talk about work. Not personal stuff."

Ryan took Ted's car keys and turned him over to a uniformed constable who would drive him to the hospital.

While they waited for the Forensic Identification Team to arrive, Ryan and Manziuk took a quick look around Stasey Simon's house. It was well decorated with all the necessary furnishings, but it was virtually devoid of personal touches

"It's as if she was never actually here," Ryan said. "Did she just sleep here?"

"I wonder if she could have been getting it ready to sell?" Manziuk said as he opened the doors to a media center that held a wide screen TV and a DVD and not much else. No pictures or memorabilia. A few books—all biographies of athletes. Some sports magazines. A few movies—*Field of Dreams*, *Bull Durham*, *Tin Cup*, *The Greatest Game Ever Played*, *League of Their Own*, maybe a dozen more—all sports related. No CDs.

From the bedroom, Ryan called out, "She must be some kind of neat freak. Her clothes are all hung according to color. She even folded her underwear and arranged it in neat rows. Except for the clothes in the closet and drawers, the toiletries in the bathroom cupboard, and several ashtrays with barely touched cigarettes, it's as if this was a model home."

The second bedroom was a workout room with mirrored walls and a home gym, treadmill, stationary bike and stair climber. Again, there was only equipment in the room, nothing personal.

Bedroom three held a desk with a computer, a filing cabinet, and a loveseat. There was no journal, no diary, no personal letters; only business-related files on the computer, business-related folders in the cabinet, and another ashtray half-full of partially smoked cigarettes.

Voices led them downstairs, where they met Ford and his Ident team.

"We have to stop meeting like this," Manziuk said.

"Didn't I just see you a day ago?" Ford said with a grimace. "In fact, I'm getting downright tired of seeing you. Glad I have a few days' vacation coming up."

"We'll try to get by," Manziuk said.

"You think this is related to the ballplayer?"

"It's certainly a possibility."

"I already got word from on top to push it. Seems everyone wants that one solved yesterday."

"Yeah, so I've heard." Manziuk smiled. "Just do what you normally do. That's good enough for me."

"No corpse this time?"

"Not so far. But it's touch and go."

"Where was she?"

Manziuk took him into the living room and they quickly marked off the area where Stasey had been found.

"There's a car out front I want checked as well," Manziuk said. "When you've gone through it, it needs to be driven to the hospital where the victim was taken. The car's owner is there."

"Friend or family?"

"The man who produces her radio program."

"This isn't *the* Stasey Simon, is it?" one of the Ident crew said. "Of the *Stasey Simon Show?*"

Manziuk nodded.

"Holy Smokes, I never realized it was her!"

"We'll get out of here so you can work," Manziuk said, dropping Ted's keys into the hands of the excited Ident team member. "I'll look for a report later today."

Ford sighed. "You'll get it."

"It's as if she was in a witness protection program or something," Ryan said as she and Manziuk left the house. "There's nothing personal."

"She's into sports. That seems to be it."

"But she didn't even have souvenirs from the games she attended. What about all the stuff Mr. Brown had? It's like she was some kind of automaton with no soul or anything. Even the house looks that way—other than the oak woodwork, everything is beige. No personality. Totally bland."

"Curious," Manziuk said, "especially since her public persona is anything but bland. I wonder who, other than Stasey herself, would know if anything's missing?"

At the radio station, program director Ray Cummings expressed his concern and agreed not to mention any details on air until the police gave the okay. Then he found Stasey's personnel file. Next of kin was a George Simonopoulos in Winnipeg, Manitoba.

Within minutes, Manziuk had connected on his cell phone. After identifying himself, he asked Mr. Simonopoulos if he had a daughter named Stasey Simon.

"I—I am sorry. Can you tell me, please, why you are asking me this?"

"A woman by the name of Stasey Simon has been taken to hospital in critical condition. On the personnel form at her job, your name and address were given under next of kin."

"I do have a daughter." The man spoke slowly, in a deep voice with a barely noticeable accent. "Her name is Anastasia Simonopoulos. She liked people to call her Stasey. I do not know about Simon, but it is obviously possible."

"Does your daughter live in Toronto?"

The man hesitated. "I'm afraid I don't know where she lives."

Quickly, Manziuk described Stasey's height, weight, and appearance.

After a long pause, the man said, "Yes, that might be her."

"Do you have a picture we can use for verification?"

"The last picture we have is of her high school graduation. Can you tell me, was it a car accident? How badly hurt is she?"

"It wasn't a car accident. Mr. Simonopoulos, I'm very sorry to have to tell you this, but she's suffered a severe head injury and the doctors don't expect her to survive. It appears to have been attempted murder."

There was a long silence. "I see." Then a shorter silence. "Attempted murder?"

"Yes."

"Do you know who did it?"

"It may be connected with the recent murder of Rico Velasquez, the pitcher for the Matrix. It's possible Stasey discovered who the murderer was."

"I don't understand. What has she to do with a baseball pitcher?"

"She's a talk show host for a sports radio station here in Toronto. She interviews players all the time."

"I see." The icy tone he used for the two little words spoke volumes about his disapproval. "Have you made an arrest?"

"Not yet, but I can assumre you we're doing everything we can to find out who did it."

"I see."

"Are there other family members or friends you'd like us to contact?"

"I'll inform the rest of the family myself. I know nothing of her friends. She hasn't set foot in her home or in this city since she was eighteen years old." There was a pause. "What hospital is she in? Are they treating her or waiting for her to die?"

"They're doing everything they can, but her chances are slim. We'll give you contact information for the hospital."

Manziuk passed the phone to Ryan, who gave Mr. Simonopoulos the address and phone number for the hospital and their contact information in case he wanted to phone them for additional information. She also made arrangements to have his daughter's graduation photo faxed so they could make a better identification.

"Not much help from that direction," Ryan said after she ended the call. "She must have had somebody she confided in. A boyfriend. A neighbor. Somebody from the radio station. What about following up on what Ginny Lovejoy told me yesterday about Stasey and Armando Santana?"

"We'll have to talk to everyone on our suspect list for the Velasquez case. And as soon as the doctors give us a probable time, we'll have to find out where they were when she was attacked. But first, why don't you get a team in here to go through her office and talk to her coworkers? Since Ted Benedetto and Iain Foley are already on our suspect list, we'll talk to them ourselves. Also, let's get a team doing a door-to-door check of Stasey's neighborhood. Start with the neighbor you and I met when we were there Friday night. And someone should check the pub down the street. She may have been there last night."

Ryan called in the orders and then they went back to Ray Cumming's office.

"Just wondering," Manziuk said. "Would you know where we could find Iain Foley right now?"

"Iain left here not that long ago," Ray said. "Shortly before you came. He may have headed home, but if I were you, I'd look first at Dana's Place. Likely grabbing some lunch."

"Does Iain normally work on Sundays?" Manziuk asked.

Ray laughed. "No way. He's our prime time boy."

"What does that mean?" Ryan asked.

"Prime time? Well, it means he has the best time slot—from four to seven on weekdays while people are driving home from work. It means he gets paid the highest salary, gets first choice of the stories, pretty well calls his own shots. So he gets top billing and a few other perks, and he doesn't work weekends."

Ryan had been listening closely. "Where does Stasey's time slot fit?"

"She's afternoon—so she's below him and below the early morning show hosts and of course below the evening show—but that's often a baseball or hockey game so it doesn't really compare. She's on a par with the morning show host. Although, to be fair, the ratings that came out in April showed Stasey's show has climbed to a 5.9 rating, which is stronger than any afternoon show we've had. Nearly as strong as the early morning show. She's picking up new listeners every day—especially women."

"What do you mean by ratings?"

Ray smiled. "Well, how do you know if anyone is listening to your show? One way is they phone in when you have a call-in time. But an even better way is to have someone do a poll. Find out what stations people are listening to and which shows. They do the same thing in TV all the time. American shows live or die when they get the Neilson ratings results. For radio and TV stations in Canada, it's the Bureau of Broadcast Measurement.

"Here in Toronto, you have about 20 stations all wanting a piece of the pie. A sports station is a bit of a niche market, so if you can get four or five percent of the market for any given show, you're doing okay. If you get more than that, and sustain it, you're doing fine. Get nine or ten percent and you're in heaven."

"What does Iain get?"

"He's our strongest show, typically in the low eights. Although, the truth is, he lost a bit of ground in the last two rating checks. He was down to 8.1 from 8.3 last time. You always hope to be growing stronger, so it's a bit of a setback when you lose ground. You try to figure out what happened and how to reverse it."

"But he isn't competing with Stasey's show or the others on your station, right?" Manziuk said.

"No, they're competing with the other shows that are on in their time slots on all the other stations. Not to mention TV and MP3s, and podcasts, and Internet streaming, and all the other things out there nowadays."

"I expect the different hosts do compare themselves to each other, though," Manziuk said.

Ray grinned. "You can bank on it. That's normal. But overall, we're very happy with our market share right now. We're fifteenth out of twenty. Given our specialized programming, that's not bad."

"So," Manziuk said, "getting back to Iain Foley. Why was he here on a Sunday if he wasn't working?"

"Simple. He decided to listen in this morning because he was curious to see what Stasey had up her sleeve—why she wanted this special show. When he heard me come on instead, he realized something was wrong, so he hightailed it down here. He took over the show for me and I took over the controls for Ted so he could go look for Stasey. Iain wanted us to call you guys right away, but Ted was worried Stasey'd be mad if we called you for no reason. And, if the truth be told, so was I. Seems stupid in hindsight—there's no way she'd have missed this show if something wasn't seriously wrong." He paused for a moment. "Do you think it made any difference— the half hour or so lost because we waited until Ted could go over?"

"I'm not a doctor," Manziuk said, "but I think it would have been touch and go even if she'd been found earlier."

"I'd hate to think she could die because we were afraid to make her mad."

Iain Foley was giving the waitress his credit card when Manziuk and Ryan walked up to his table in Dana's Place.

"Do you mind talking to us for a few minutes?" Manziuk asked as he pulled out one of the chairs and sat down.

Iain gave him an ironic smile. "I like the way you make it seem as if I have a choice." His smile disappeared. "This is about Stasey, isn't it? I take it something was wrong?"

"Yes," Ryan said as she pulled out the chair on Iain's other side and sat in it.

Iain nodded. "I knew it. The moment I heard Ray come on, I knew something terrible had happened. I should have just called in, but I felt I needed to come down and help out. So what's happened? How bad is it? Is she—?"

Manziuk said, "She was attacked in her house either last night or this morning."

"Attacked?"

Ryan said, "Hit on the head with something hard."

Iain winced. "She—she's dead?"

"Not quite," Ryan said.

Ian looked from one to the other. "What do you mean?"

"Last we heard, she was still hanging on by a thread."

"So she has a chance of recovering?"

"A very slight chance," Ryan said.

"Where's Ted? Does he know?"

"He found her," Manziuk said.

Iain ran his right hand though his hair. "Of course. We sent him over there. Look, which hospital is she in? I assume Ted's there. I should go over. Do you need something more from me?"

"We have a few questions," Manziuk said. "First of all, we need to know where you were from about nine last night until this morning when you came to the station."

"Oh, of course. I'd forgotten I'm a suspect." He sighed. "Where was I? Last night, I was tired, so I went straight home after the game and I was there all evening watching TV. Again, there's no one to say if I was really there or not. My dog can't speak. I stayed at home until this morning when I came in to the station. I suppose that's a pretty lousy alibi."

"If it's the truth, it's fine," Manziuk said.

"Of course, I didn't know I'd need witnesses." He looked down at the table, then up at Manziuk. "Look officers, someone needs to go and be with Ted. He'll be taking this hard." He gave a short, dry laugh. "I'll never understand why, but he's like the proverbial puppy dog around Stasey. The more she kicks him, the more he comes trotting around. God knows, she doesn't deserve it—she's never appreciated him as she should. But that's how it is, and it's not right for him to be alone now."

Ryan's cell phone rang as they were walking to their car. After a brief, muffled conversation, she took a deep breath and exhaled before climbing into the front seat and looking over at Manziuk. "You were right. Stasey Simon had dinner last night at the Carnaby Pub and Grill." She waited a second before adding, "She wasn't alone."

"Do they know who she was with?"

"The bartender says it was Armando Santana."

There was a short pause before Manziuk said, "Okay. Where would he be right now? What time does the game start?"

"It started at one today."

"It's nearly one-thirty. If he pitches at all, it'll be late in the game. If we go over there now, he should be able to talk to us."

Manziuk pulled out and drove in silence while Ryan stared out the window. They were a few blocks from the Diamond Dome when she looked over at him and said softly, "There's something I need to tell you." She went back to staring out the window while she told him about going to the Fifth Base after the game the day before, her conversation with Armando, and Stasey's appearance.

He listened in silence, then hit the wheel. "I can't believe you'd do something that stupid! What were you thinking?"

Ryan bit her lip. "I thought—I thought he might talk to me if you weren't around because—well, because we're both black."

"So you went to a bar to find him? Didn't it occur to you he might assume you were interested in him?"

"Of course not."

Manziuk shook his head.

"I told you the day we interviewed him that I didn't like him," Ryan said.

"You said you found him annoying. That doesn't necessarily mean you disliked him."

"Okay, maybe it was a really dumb thing to do. But I honestly did think he might talk to me—you know, differently—if you weren't around."

"I'm sure he would."

"Not that way."

"Now I have to decide whether or not I can trust you on this case. If you're involved with a prime suspect—"

"I'm not! I just thought maybe he'd talk to a black sister where he wouldn't talk to a white cop!"

Manziuk turned to glare at her. "So, did he?"

"A little," she said softly. "For what it's worth, I don't think Armando killed Rico. At least, I don't think he killed him because of jealousy or anything to do with his playing baseball."

"And do you have anything to substantiate that belief, or is it your woman's intuition? Or because he's black, when he tells you he didn't do it, you have to believe him?"

It was Ryan's turn to glare at her partner.

Manziuk didn't back down. "I'm waiting. Where's your proof?"

She squirmed in her seat and pushed her hands underneath her thighs. "It was the way he talked about Rico's abilities. Like baseball had lost something. Wait a minute!"

She sat up and reached for her purse. "I wrote some of it down afterward." She pulled out her notebook and flipped the pages. When she found the right one, she read some of Armando's comments aloud.

But when she had finished, Manziuk just said, "Even though he might regret it as a baseball purist, that doesn't mean he wouldn't have killed Rico for his own reasons."

"You didn't hear him."

Emphasizing each word, he said, "No, I didn't, did I?"

She looked down. "Point taken."

"Next time you decide to take a shortcut in a case, talk to me first, please?"

She nodded.

"Pardon?"

"I will. Promise."

Their badges got them into the Diamond Dome, and a security guard took them down to the hallway outside the clubhouse and then went to find Armando Santana and tell him he was needed.

When he finally came out, a perplexed look on his face, Manziuk asked if there was a better place for them to talk. Without a word, Armando led them into the small media room where Ginny had talked to Rico. "What is it?" Armando asked as soon as the door was shut.

Manziuk looked him in the eye. "Have you heard the news?

"News about what? Have you arrested someone?"

"Stasey Simon was attacked some time last night. She's in critical condition."

"Stasey? Attacked?" Armando sank onto a chair. "Not—not with a bat? Like Rico?"

Manziuk took a seat. "We aren't sure, but it's very possible."

"I—I—" He swallowed several times. "Rico died instantly. That's what you said. How is she still alive?"

"According to the pathologist, Rico was struck very hard from behind in a very sensitive area. The blow that struck Stasey hit a different place. But she may still die. And as far as we know, you were the last person to see her alive."

Armando set both elbows on the table and leaned his head on his hands. After a moment, he sat up, looked at Manziuk, and took a couple of deep breaths. "I had dinner with Stasey at the pub down the street from her house. Afterward, I drove her home. I went inside with her so she could give me something, but I left after a few minutes. If I had stayed longer, this might not have happened."

"You don't need to pretend you care," Ryan said from her position against the wall near the door.

Armando jerked his head toward her, his eyes now wide. "But I do care. Very much."

She raised her right eyebrow.

"Please don't misunderstand. Stasey is a friend. More than a friend. A year ago, I asked her to marry me. She said no. A couple of months ago, I asked her again. Neither of us was getting any younger, and we had no illusions about love or romance. We were both lonely. This time she said she would think it over. Last night she invited me to dinner to give me her answer."

"And?" Manziuk prompted.

"With everything that's happened—Rico, the turmoil of going to the bullpen, the murder—I've been doing a lot of thinking. What do I really want? What do I need? And I decided I'm not so old that I should be satisfied with a marriage where there is only friendship, and not love." He shifted in his chair and rubbed the back of his neck. "It was very difficult. You see, Stasey had decided she would marry me after all. And I had to tell her I no longer wanted to marry her. She—at first she was angry, but then she laughed and said she'd been joking and that she had no intention of ever marrying anyone. So in the end, we both pretended it didn't matter, but I'm sure she was very hurt."

"What time did you drop her off?"

"It was after ten o'clock, maybe a quarter past. The waiter might know. Or the bartender. They saw us leave. Or the time might even be on the bill."

"You went inside her house?"

"Only for a moment. She had something to give me."

"What?"

"It has nothing to do with this."

Manziuk said sternly, "Let me decide that."

Armando squirmed in his chair. At last, he said, "When she first arrived, she told me she had something to give me later. And then afterwards, she said I might as well still have it."

Manziuk and Ryan waited for him to continue.

He sighed. "You know I was moved to the bullpen when Rico came?"

"Right," Manziuk said.

"Stasey had something she thought I could use to get my starting job back. Especially with Rico gone."

"What was it?"

"I don't like to say. I—"

Ryan broke in. "For crying out loud, just tell us what it was!"

"I—it's not a good thing. I don't know where she got it." He sighed. "It's a newspaper clipping of Blake Harrison when he was younger and playing Double A ball. He was arrested for drunk driving. Someone was injured. A young girl. And there was also something about soliciting a policewoman." Armando kept his eyes firmly fixed on the table. "Stasey said for me to tell Blake she'd use it on air unless he gave me back my starting job. But I said no, I would not do that." He looked at Manziuk. "It was blackmail. My job isn't that important."

"What happened after she showed you the clipping?"

"I left."

"Did you take the clipping with you?"

"No."

"Did you go straight home afterward?"

Armando's eyes went past Manziuk, and he stared for a moment at the wall behind him. "Unfortunately, no."

"Where did you go?"

Armando's gaze moved to Ryan. He bit his lower lip. "I know you'll find this out sooner or later." He took a deep breath and expelled it. "I went to the police station to see if I could get your number. They offered to call you, but I refused."

Manziuk threw an annoyed glance at Ryan, then focused on Armando. "You wanted to talk to Detective Constable Ryan? Did you have information on Rico's murder?"

"Nothing like that." He looked down. "I wanted to ask her out."

As Armando shut the door on his way back to the clubhouse, Manziuk crossed his arms behind his head, leaned back, and said, "Well, isn't that cozy? The prime suspect in a murder case—sorry, one murder and one attempted murder—wants to date one of the investigating officers." He looked toward Ryan, who was leaning against the wall near the door. "How do you think that'll look if the press gets hold of it?"

She sighed. "It sounds a lot worse than it is."

"It sounds ridiculous—and it would make us look ridiculous if it got out."

"But I'd never go out with him!" She walked along the edge of the room and back. "He doesn't mean any of this. It's all part of a convoluted alibi to distract us while he gets away with murder. I'll bet he killed her! How long would it take to walk into the house with her and bop her over the head, and then run out to his car and drive to the police station and ask for me?"

"Didn't you just tell me he couldn't possibly have killed Rico because he cares so much for the art of baseball?"

She crossed her arms tightly over her chest. "Okay, so the guy's obviously a lot more intelligent than I gave him credit for. He planned it all out and he's playing games with us."

"And if he isn't?"

"He must be."

"But if he isn't?"

"If he isn't, I—I'll simply make him understand that he misunderstood my interest in him; that I was investigating a crime and he got the wrong impression."

"And you won't talk to him—or any of the other suspects—alone in the future?"

"No, of course not. Only—" She bit her lower lip. "I assume the same is true for you? You won't talk to anyone without me?"

"How about we make it the rule that neither of us will talk to a suspect alone without informing the other ahead of time?"

"There still might be a chance something will come up—we'll get separated—and it's expedient to talk to someone."

Between clenched teeth, he said, "If that should happen, though I can't at the moment imagine the circumstances, we'll inform the other person immediately afterward."

"All right." She folded her arms. "I get it."

"I really hope so. You could compromise our case if you allow yourself to become attached to a suspect."

"Right. No allowing yourself to care about anybody who's involved in a case. Not that I do," she said hastily. "I don't even like him."

"Well, don't *start* liking him. At least not until we've solved this case to the best of our ability."

She tilted her head to one side. "And what if it never gets solved?"

"It will."

"So, what do we do next?"

"Well, we have to sort through everything we've learned and all the evidence we have, and decide whether we feel the assault on Stasey Simon was committed by the same person who killed Rico, whether it was a copycat crime, or whether it was entirely unrelated. And if we decide it might have been done by the same person who killed Rico, we have to figure out if there could be another victim, and if so, who that might be. And we need to decide whether or not to put a guard on Stasey Simon—assuming she survives the next few hours."

He stood up. "Come on."

"Where are we going?"

"I want to see how Stasey is, find out if the doctors can tell us any more about the nature of her injury, and check on Ted. And Iain, assuming he really did go there."

"What about that clipping? I didn't see it at Stasey's, did you?"

"If it's there, Ford will find it. If it isn't there—well, Armando had better hope it is."

NINETEEN

Ted was sitting in a small waiting room in the surgery unit holding a magazine and staring into space.

Ryan took the magazine from his limp fingers.

Ted looked up. "They say she's likely going to die. And if she doesn't die, she'll probably be a vegetable." He shook his head. "She'd hate that."

"Is anyone else here?" Manziuk asked. "Or are you alone?"

"Iain's here. He's like a jackrabbit. Can't seem to sit still. He went off to call a few more people he just thought of so they don't hear it on the news. Ray was here for a while. Not much for anyone to do."

"Have you eaten?" Manziuk asked.

Ted shook his head. "Not you, too! I've told Iain eighteen times that I'm not hungry."

"Okay, but you need to keep your energy up."

"One day isn't going to kill me," Ted said in a flat voice. "They're operating. Something about relieving pressure on her brain." He blinked, and his voice took on more animation. "They might tell you more than me." He was getting up as he spoke. "I'll find the nurse."

Ted came back a few minutes later with a serious-looking woman who examined Manziuk's ID before she'd say anything.

"Ms. Simon has a fractured skull and some swelling of her brain. Dr. Kang is operating to relieve the pressure of the swelling. If she makes it through, they'll worry about repairing the fracture. However, even if she does survive, the chances are very high she could stay in a coma or be brain injured."

"If she does recover, what's the likelihood she'll be able to tell us who attacked her?"

"Dr. Kang can answer that question better than me, but from my experience, I'd say that even with a complete recovery she's unlikely to remember the attack."

"Thank you. Is there any way I can talk with the doctor? And I'd like to see the wound, if possible."

The woman frowned. "You'd have to go into the operating room. I don't—"

"Yes, I'd like to do that."

"Well, I suppose it's possible. But you'll have to wash up and get dressed in scrubs."

"That's fine."

Manziuk went to Ryan and said in her ear, "Okay, this is one of those times. I'll tell you what I learn from the doctor. You stay here and observe, but don't ask questions."

Shortly after Manziuk left the waiting room, Iain Foley walked in, saying, "I got most of them. Ray wants to know when he can run the full story."

"Like Stasey cares," Ted said.

Iain noticed Ryan. "Detective Constable, have you learned anything new?"

"We're still investigating," Ryan said. She thought for a moment. "I do have a question. Who knows Stasey best? Who were her friends?"

Iain's eyebrows rose and a quick smile crossed his lips as he shot a glance at Ted, but he didn't speak.

Ted looked down at the floor for a moment, and then looked up at Ryan. "I dunno. Don't think she has friends. Ginny Lovejoy, maybe. But they aren't close. I don't know of anyone else." He shrugged. "But I really don't know much about her personal life."

Ryan looked at Iain, who held up his hands, palms open. "If Ted doesn't know who her friends are, I certainly don't. Though I did hear a rumor about a certain pitcher."

"A pitcher?" Ryan echoed.

"Armando Santana," Ted said disdainfully. "She was seeing him for awhile, but that's old news."

Ryan drummed her fingers on the wall. "How old?"

"Last year. And they were just friends. Not even close friends."

Iain laughed. "Is that the truth or wishful thinking?"

Ted shot him a look, but held his tongue.

"Don't forget the people at WIN 730, Detective," Iain said. "We're her friends."

"Yeah, right," Ted said.

Iain turned to face him. "What's that supposed to mean?"

"I'd hardly call you and Stasey friends."

"She certainly didn't make it easy, but we worked at the same station, and I did my best to get along with her, just as I do with the other people who work there." He looked at Ryan. "The thing with Stasey was, she never let her guard down for a minute. Not with me or Ray or anyone else. Not even with Ted. It was as if she couldn't trust anyone."

Ryan looked at Ted, who nodded. "He's right."

"I often wondered what was inside," Iain said, "and who hurt her so badly she couldn't let anyone else see."

There was a long silence.

"Thanks," Ryan said at last. "Well, we still have a lot of people to talk to. Are you going to stay here?"

"I'm not going anywhere," Ted said.

Iain sat down next to Ted. "It's the least I can do. Indeed, at this point, the only thing. I'll keep vigil with Ted."

Manziuk, now wearing scrubs and a mask, entered the operating theater. A group of green- and blue-clad figures were clustered about a central mound of white that was Stasey Simon.

"Dr. Kang," the nurse said, "I've brought a police inspector with me. He has some questions. I've told him no one can stop work to answer him, and that he has to stay out of the way."

A tall, thin man covered by light blue scrubs, a matching cap, and a white mask looked up, and Manziuk caught a glimpse of two very intense black eyes and a bit of smooth, ivory skin before he looked back down at the area where his hands were occupied. "So you're the one who has to find out who did this?" he said.

"Can you tell me anything that might help?"

"Easier for you with an autopsy, eh?" Dr. Kang didn't wait for an answer; nor did he stop whatever he was doing. "The blow was made by something about three or so inches wide that was heavy and solid and likely rounded. And longish. Not a brick, for instance."

"Something like a baseball bat?" Manziuk said.

"That's possible." Dr. Kang took an instrument from the nurse and continued working on what Manziuk assumed was Stasey's injured head.

A quick glance showed him a patch of something that had a lot of red on it, and he immediately looked away. "How bad is it?" he asked as he focused on a large machine on the far side.

"Severe. There's crushing of the skeletal bone of the head, and that's bad enough by itself, but under that, there are two locations where there's been trauma—some crushing—to the brain itself. The brain is finely balanced inside the skull; not tightly wedged. When someone is hit on the head, the brain can bounce a little. It can even be pushed hard against the skull on the other side. So you often end up with two injuries instead of one. You have the coup injury, which is where the weapon actually struck. And then you have the contre coup injury, caused by the brain bouncing against the skull on the opposite side from where it was struck. Of course, the harder the brain is hit in the first instance, the worse the second injury will be. In fact, the second injury can even be the worse of the two.

"In the case of our patient here, when she fell, she landed on the opposite side to which she was stuck. So the open wound was what was visible, and what appeared to the naked eye as the only real injury. However, the other side of the brain was not only injured by the attack—the contre coup injury—but was further damaged when she hit the ground during her fall."

"Would the one blow have knocked her out immediately?"

"I can't say for sure. But she'd certainly have been disoriented and close to unconscious. The blow hit her at an angle above her ear, and it caused internal bleeding, both at the site and, as I've explained, on the other side of the brain."

"So it was a strong blow?"

"It was very strong. And very likely fatal. Please understand, we're doing all we can, but this is a life-threatening injury."

"Is there any chance you can help her?"

"If you were to bang your thumb with a hammer, what would your thumb do, aside from hurt a lot?"

"Swell up and get red. And maybe bleed."

"Exactly." He continued working while he explained, "This brain also wants to swell up, but while your thumb can swell as big as it wants to, the brain can't. The bony case it's in—the skull—has no give to it, so there's very little space inside for swelling. And the brain also wants to bleed, but there's little room for the blood to go. So pressure builds up inside, and that's very bad.

"We're trying to do two things at the same time: enable the brain to do a little swelling and bleeding while at the same time we keep it from swelling or bleeding too much. So we have her on a ventilator that keeps her breathing steady and easy so there's no stress from that direction. And we've giving her drugs to keep her in an even sleep so she's still. That may seem unnecessary since she's in a coma, but we want to make sure she stays asleep until we're ready for her to wake up. And then, the main thing, we're making room for the brain to swell by removing a small amount of the fluid around the brain and making an opening on the opposite side of the contre coup side of the skull.

"Is there any hope at all that she can survive?"

"There are a few things in her favor. She seems physically very fit. And while the skull was fractured, none of the pieces penetrated the brain. The dura—the membrane that covers the brain—wasn't broken. So there's been no leakage of cerebrospinal fluid. Also, she was hit in a place where the skull is fairly strong. And, finally, she's survived this long."

He called for another instrument. "And now, we're ready for the next step. We'll do a partial close of the skull where it was fractured. Not a complete close because we may need to go back in if the swelling escalates. Then we'll send her to intensive care where we'll watch her blood pressure and her breathing, and hope for the best." He waited while a nurse wiped sweat from his forehead. "But look here, Inspector. Even if she survives, there's very little hope she'll be the same person she was before. Whoever did this may not have killed her outright, but he has, in all likelihood, destroyed her."

"If she does make it through this part and wake up, what are the chances she'll be able to tell us who did it?"

"One chance in a thousand." He bent to his task. "You'll have to find her attacker without her help."

Iain jumped up when Manziuk came back to the waiting room. "I hate to bother you Inspector, but Ray wants to know if we can run the full story yet?"

"Tell him to go ahead."

"How is she?"

"Still alive, but still critical. They'll move her to recovery soon."

"Thanks, Inspector."

Iain left to phone Ray, and Manziuk and Ryan said good-bye to Ted, who was looking tired and somewhat bedraggled.

They were walking to their car when Manziuk's cell phone rang. "What? ... Where? ... We're on our way." He put his phone away. "They say bad things come in threes. Apparently, there's another victim."

The body was hidden behind a bush in the backyard of Stasey's next-door neighbor. It was that of a short, somewhat over-weight, middle-aged man wearing jeans and a Rico Velasquez jersey. There was no question about his condition.

Manziuk and Ryan waited impatiently for Dr. Munsen to finish examining the body.

"Talk about having your brains bashed in," Munsen said at last. "Somebody made sure he was dead, and then some!"

"You think the killer was angry?" Manziuk said.

"I don't think it took ten or twelve blows to kill him."

"Overkill," Ryan said.

Manziuk winced.

"Definitely," Munsen said. "I can see three or four blows to make sure. But not this many."

"Any idea what time he died?"

"He's passed the first stages of rigor mortis. Given the warm weather, that's not surprising. I'd say somewhere between nine last night and two this morning. Of course, I'll know more after the autopsy. If I had to make a guess, I'd say maybe earlier rather than later." Munsen stood up and brushed his pants. "There was a wallet under him," he added. "I gave it to Ford."

Picking up his medical kit, Munsen said, "Well, you don't need me here any more," and left.

A few seconds later, Ford appeared with a plastic bag containing a wallet and a key chain with three keys. "Long time no see. At least four hours. My wife thinks I've forgotten I have a family." He sighed. "We've checked these for prints."

Manziuk flipped the wallet open. There was no driver's license, but there was a debit card, a credit card for Sears, and a subway pass. They all said, "Lawrence Smith." The health card gave his address as Apt. 303, 1835 Spence Avenue.

"We've finished a cursory check of both backyards," Ford said. "There are two sets of footprints, one made by this man's shoes, coming from the back door of the Simon house. It looks as if he climbed the fence between the two houses and the other person followed."

Manziuk looked carefully toward the fence. It was an old one with horizontal slats, and each slat had a few inches between it and the next one, like the type you'd see in an old western movie. Yes, most people could have climbed it.

Ford continued, "My guess would be the victim was present either during the attack on the Simon woman or immediately after. He may even have tried to interfere. The killer chased him outside and over the fence and made sure he didn't get away."

"If that's the case," Ryan said, "Why didn't the killer go back and make sure the Simon woman was dead?"

"Has anyone questioned the people who own this house?" Manziuk asked.

"They aren't home," Ford said. "The neighbors across the street say they went to Hamilton to visit their daughter for the weekend, and they'll be back later tonight. The neighbors can't remember the daughter's married name. I wasn't sure whether to escalate it or not."

"I think it can wait until they get back," Manziuk said with a slight smile. "Maybe they have difficulty finding time to see their family, too."

Ryan stepped forward. "Can you tell where the killer went after?"

"I think so," Ford said. "There are footprints coming partway back to the fence, but stopping and then going along the side of the neighbour's house to the front sidewalk."

"I wonder," Manziuk mused, "if this man might have saved Stasey Simon's life by distracting the killer and getting him out of the house?"

"It's possible."

Ryan looked around the yard, then stopped and stared. "What on earth are they doing here?"

As Manziuk looked to see who Ryan was referring to, Ford said, "Oh yeah," and gestured to the far side of the neighbor's house. "Those two found him. I figured you'd want to talk to them."

Standing together under a tree and looking very sheepish were Ginny Lovejoy and Kyle Schmidt.

Manziuk stared. "You two found him? What on earth were you doing in this backyard?"

Kyle glanced at Ginny before answering. "Iain called to tell us what happened, and Ginny knew where Stasey lived, so—"

"I was here once before," Ginny said.

"—we came to see if we could get more information."

Ginny took up the story. "We didn't think any of the police officers would want to talk to us, so we tried to get close enough to see what was going on without, you know, being in the way. Kyle was trying to get behind that bush when he tripped over the—the body."

Manziuk just looked at them.

"Sir?" One of the uniformed officers had come up. "I think you might want to see this."

Ryan and Ford followed Manziuk and the uniformed officer to a spot about eight feet from where the body was lying.

"There," the police officer pointed to the grass.

Manziuk leaned over, squinting.

"See it?"

"I see it," Ryan said. "To the left, deep in the grass."

"Yes," Manziuk said. "It looks like a sliver of wood."

"Can a bat shatter?" Ryan said.

"Splinter," Manziuk said. "A bat can splinter." He stared at the grass for a moment as if gathering his thoughts. "All right. Cover every inch of ground. And get everybody who isn't with Ident out of here."

Kyle and Ginny started to move away.

Ryan called out, "Where do you two think you're going?"

Kyle shrugged. "He said to leave the area, so …."

"Not you." Ryan said. "We'll go out the front way and then into the house. We can sit in the kitchen."

Ginny gave Kyle a pleased grin.

She wasn't smiling a few minutes later, however, when they were seated at the table in Stasey's kitchen and Manziuk said he ought to arrest them for contaminating a crime scene.

Ginny glanced over at Kyle, who was studying his watch. "Well, we—"

"You've been watching too much television," Manziuk continued. "In real life, reporters don't get in the way of police searching for clues to a murder. In real life, if they do get in the way of the police, they get put in jail. And if they get in the way of a murderer, they die." He looked from Ginny to Kyle. "Do you understand?"

"Yes," Ginny said. "But we did find a body for you."

"Did you take a picture?"

A long hesitation. "Yes."

"Both of you?"

Kyle looked up. "Yeah."

"You can't use it."

"You're telling me!" Ginny said. "If we used it, most of our subscribers would be calling to ask what happened to our nice family newspaper."

"Look," Manziuk said. "I know you want a story. But right now, it's a lot more urgent and more important that we find out who did this." He leaned toward them. "If you have any—and I do mean any—information that might pertain to either of the murders or the attack on Stasey, I want to hear it right now."

"I wish we did have something," Ginny said. "But we don't."

Ryan was a few feet away leaning against the kitchen counter. "How did you know about Stasey?"

"Iain Foley phoned Ginny."

"And the two of you decided to come over here?"

"Yeah." Kyle looked at Ginny. "For a change, Ginny told me instead of rushing off on her own. Oh yeah, in case you care, my car's parked on the next street."

"You do realize this isn't a game, don't you?" Ryan said.

Ginny nodded. In a small voice, she said, "Can you tell us how Stasey is?"

"She's in critical condition," Manziuk said. "Now I have a question for you. Where were you between nine last night and two this morning?"

"Is that when she was hurt?" Ginny exclaimed. "But I thought she wasn't found till this morning?"

"I'm asking the questions," Manziuk said. "Where were you between nine and two?"

"I was in my apartment getting drunk," Kyle said. "Alone. No one saw me."

"What time did you get back to your apartment after last night's game?"

"Some time after nine. I don't really know."

"Did you stop anywhere?"

"No, I already had a full bar."

"And you?" Ryan looked at Ginny.

"Me?" Ginny said. A rosy blush spread over her cheeks. "I was, er … I was …."

Manziuk, Ryan, and Kyle all stared at her, waiting for a response.

"Okay, if you must know, I was with Pat Davis and his wife. At their house."

Kyle stared at her. "You were where—?"

Manziuk glared at him. "I'll ask the questions."

Ginny was still blushing. "I thought maybe Pat knew where Alita was. So I called and told him—I made up this story—" her face was beet red now "—about how Kyle and I had a fight—"

"Ha!" Kyle snorted. "We did have a fight."

She ignored Kyle's interruption "—and how I needed a friend and—well, a bunch of stuff. So they invited me over, and we got talking, and it got late, and then Barbara—Pat's wife—started having contractions, and she thought she was going into labor, so we kept talking, putting in time until the contractions got close enough to go to the hospital. But after a while, they stopped. By then, it was nearly three, so they said to use their guest room instead of going home so late. So I did. I was there until about ten this morning."

"And do they?" Ryan asked.

Ginny stared at her. "Huh?

"Do they know where Alita is?"

"Nope. I'm sure they don't."

"Good thing we do." Ryan smiled.

Lawrence Smith's apartment was on the third floor of a squat, worn-down building in an old part of the city. A convenience store and a dry-cleaner shared the main floor. There was no elevator, only tired stairs. Between the worn patches, the bumps and chips, and the graffiti, the dirty beige walls in the stairwell and hallways were in desperate need of paint. The industrial-strength brown carpet had given up pretending it was anything more than a cover for the cement floors years ago.

The door to Lawrence's apartment matched the hallway. Manziuk knocked, but no one answered. He put on a latex glove before taking out Lawrence's keychain and trying one of the keys in the lock. The door opened immediately.

If the den of the Matrix's owner had been an exhibit for the Matrix, this room was a shrine. The walls of the room were a collage of posters of Matrix players from both past and present. There was a large-screen television on an old brown-painted table in one corner, a smaller blond end table with a boombox and a phone against the near wall, and an open walnut shelf unit filled with bobble-heads and mugs and various other Matrix giveaways and mementos on the other wall.

A rocking chair complete with a patchwork Matrix quilt and matching pillow was drawn up near the radio, in good line for the television. In front of the rocking chair were two white open-sided cubes filled with scrapbooks. More scrapbooks were piled on the floor near the radio.

Manziuk opened the first scrapbook with gloved fingers. Inside were carefully cut-out columns of Ginny Lovejoy. A second scrapbook held the recent columns of Kyle Schmidt.

Ryan had moved past him to the small bedroom, where the single bed was literally surrounded by ceiling-high stacks of boxes. Each box was carefully labeled. Ryan called out, "Tapes of every

Stasey Simon Show for the last year. Tapes of the Iain Foley show. Video and audio tapes of the Matrix games—hundreds of audio and videotapes."

Manziuk came to the doorway.

Ryan was looking under the bed. "There's something here." Together, they pulled out two long, flat plastic storage boxes. Ryan opened the first box. "Cards of some kind."

"Baseball cards," Manziuk said. "Be careful. They could be worth a lot of money."

"Why? They're just cheap cardboard cards."

"Yeah, but to a collector, some cards are worth a lot. In fact, my son told me there's one card out there worth over a million dollars."

She stared at him in disbelief. "You're joking, right? A million dollars for one of these?"

"Yeah. I'll tell you about it some time."

"Well, I don't think these cards can be worth that much. Looks like he only collected Matrix players."

"Even some of their cards could be worth a bit. A rookie card or something."

"I'm sorry," Ryan said, "but this guy was nuts." She closed the box and shoved it back under the bed, then stood and walked into the bathroom. "Okay, this is more normal, if somewhat scary."

Manziuk followed her. The one wall without a shower, mirror, or doorway was covered by a large poster of Stasey Simon, advertising her show. "Looks fairly new," Manziuk said. "I wonder if he got it from the station?"

They moved to the kitchen. Unlike the one in Stasey's house, this kitchen had seen some use. It had basic foods and implements. It also had Matrix posters covering the walls and Matrix mugs and other memorabilia of every sort imaginable filling more than half the cupboards. The doors had been removed from all but the few cupboards that held dishes or food.

"When did Ford say he'd have a team here?"

Ryan looked at her watch. "About five minutes." She looked around. "What about next of kin? Did you see anything?"

They found a phone book in one of the drawers in the kitchen. Beneath it was a small address book, which Manziuk opened. There were only a couple of dozen listings in the entire book. Under S was an Aunt Joan. "She lives in Barrie," he said. "We'll have someone from the Barrie police talk to her and see what they can find out."

"May I see it?" Ryan asked. He handed it to her and she paged through. "Interesting. He has numbers for both the Diamond Dome and WIN 730 in here."

"He does?"

"Yeah."

"So there's a connection. We just have to find it."

The doorbell rang.

"Ident," Manziuk said. "Perfect timing."

They let the team in, gave them the address book with orders to follow up on all the numbers, and headed for their car. As usual, Manziuk made a beeline for the driver's seat.

"I don't think so," Ryan said.

"What?"

"It's got to be my turn to drive and your turn to sit here twiddling your thumbs. Or having a quick nap, maybe?"

"Are you implying I'm getting old?"

"Anybody can get tired."

Remembering how tired he'd felt Friday night when they'd interviewed Iain Foley, he tossed the car keys back and forth from one hand to the other. Finally he said, "All right, you win. You drive." He got in and took his time fastening his seatbelt. "Funny," he said. "I'm used to him now."

"Who?"

"Iain Foley. Now that I've gotten to know him, there's no disconnect the way there was when we first met him. Strange how you get used to things."

"Good. Okay, where to?" Ryan asked.

Manziuk lowered the back of his seat and shut his eyes before answering. "We need to find out where the rest of the people on our short list were last night.

"We have Ginny Lovejoy and Kyle Schmidt's alibis, such as they are. We've talked to Ted and Iain. Who's left?"

Manziuk sat straight up. "Ted and Iain!"

"What about them?"

"The phone number for WIN in Lawrence's address book! We know from the tapes that Lawrence listened to Stasey's and Iain's shows. Maybe he was a regular caller. If so, Ted or Iain would know. We need to go back to the hospital."

As she turned the key, Ryan said, "What do you mean 'regular caller?'"

"Most sports talk shows have a mix of interviews with athletes and coaches and other management people, and times for ordinary people to call in and give their opinions, ask questions, and win prizes. For instance, they may talk about whether a team should have made the trade they did, whether the coach blew the game by not making the right call, why someone isn't playing well this year—all kinds of things."

Ryan made a face. "Don't any of these people have lives? I mean, isn't it enough watching the game without having to spend the rest of your time talking about it or, worse, listening to other people talk about it?"

"I think it feels like you're part of a community. You're in touch with other people with similar interests."

"Have you ever called in?"

"No, but Mike has, lots of times. It's hard to explain the pull. You'll have to listen one of these days."

There was a moment of silence before Ryan said, "I guess they'll have to find somebody to take over her show."

"Yeah."

For a few minutes, neither spoke.

At last, Ryan said, "You're thinking of Inspector Craig, aren't you? Of me taking his place."

Manziuk sighed. "Not that so much." Another long moment of silence. "He has bypass surgery tomorrow morning."

"They do that all the time now."

"Maybe, but it's still major."

"You going in to see him tonight?"

"I hope so."

"You need to do more than hope. You need to do it."

"I also need to get a killer off the streets."

There was another long silence, which Ryan finally broke. "Is he in the same hospital as Stasey?"

"No."

"Too bad."

After a long pause, Ryan said, "So, what do we know about this Lawrence guy anyway? Maybe he tried to murder Stasey, and someone caught him and chased him and they fought."

"In that case, wouldn't the other person have gone for help?"

"Maybe he was injured."

"I guess that's possible."

"Wait! What if Ted killed them last night and then came back this morning. He was shocked that Stasey was still alive. Maybe he's staying at the hospital to be sure she can't identify him."

"I told the doctor earlier that Ted isn't to be left alone with her under any circumstances."

TWENTY

When Manziuk and Ryan arrived at the hospital, Ted was still sitting in the waiting room.

"Lawrence Smith? Sure I know him." He leaned forward on the chair. "I mean, I've never met him, but I've talked to him lots. He's a regular caller on several of the shows: Stasey's and Iain's for sure. I think he calls the noon show sometimes, too."

Manziuk said, "Would you say Lawrence is a bit of a fanatic about the Matrix?"

"Absolutely."

"And Stasey? Would you say he's a bit fanatical about her?"

"Well, he calls in a lot." Ted frowned. "Hey, this week she limited him to one call a week, which got him frustrated." His voice changed. "You don't think Lawrence killed Stasey, do you?"

"I don't think so, but he was involved in some way."

"What way?"

Manziuk ignored the question. "So he'd be on tapes of the shows? You'd recognize his voice? I'd like to hear the kind of things he asked and how he sounded."

"Sure, he's there."

"Could you remember which days he's called in recently?"

"Likely. But what do you mean he might be involved? He's a bit whacko, but he loves Stasey."

"Loves her?"

"He's a big fan. He wouldn't hurt her."

"We'll tell you soon."

"But—"

Ryan looked around. "So where's Iain?"

"He left when Stasey came out of surgery. Said he needed to do a few things and for me to call him if there was any change. Ray and some of the other people from the station are coming down any minute. I told them they won't be able to see her, but they still wanted to come."

"One last question," Manziuk said. "Did Lawrence phone in on Thursday—the day Rico was killed?"

Ted thought for a moment. "Yeah, he did. He was really upset about the whole Rico/Armando storyline. I told him he'd already had his call for that week, but when he called the third time, I let him through. Stasey wanted callers who were pro-Armando, and Lawrence was. He never liked Rico—felt he was bad for the team."

"So he'd have heard Stasey's request for someone to knock some sense into Rico?"

"Sure. But he wasn't at the reception that night. And he never seemed like more than a talker. He was always asking what the hosts thought. I can't see him ever facing up to Rico."

"But," Ryan said. "Rico was struck from behind."

They left Ted in the waiting room and walked to their car. Again, Ryan took the wheel. "Okay, what's the priority?" she asked. "Finding out where the people on our original list were last night?"

"Food. Then we need to make a few calls."

They drove to a Tim Hortons a few blocks from the hospital and ordered some lunch.

"So what about this list?" Ryan asked as they finished eating.

"First things first." Manziuk keyed a number into his phone. "This is Manziuk. Stasey Simon's in recovery now, and she'll be going from there to a private room. There's a chance whoever tried to kill her might try again if he finds out she's alive, so I want a twenty-four-hour guard. No visitors see her without the guard present in the room."

When he'd pocketed the phone, Ryan said, "Okay, we had twelve names on the original list of suspects for Rico's death, including Ferdinand Ortes and Eva MacPherson, who say they were together, and Mr. Brown and his valet.

"As for the rest, Stasey Simon is obviously off the list now. Armando Santana says she was alive when he left her; Ginny Lovejoy was with Pat Davis and his wife; Kyle Schmidt was at home alone getting drunk; Iain Foley and Ted Benedetto were also both home alone. That leaves Jonas Newland, Ferdinand Ortes, Eva MacPherson, Mr. Brown, Cary Grant, Alita Velasquez." She frowned. "Hey, wait a minute! What about this Zandor person that Alita says helped her get out of the stadium? They must have gone out Mr. Brown's door. But neither Mr. Brown nor his valet mentioned him."

"Mr. Brown," they said in unison; then looked at each other suspiciously.

"I'll phone," Manziuk said. "Otherwise we might never get in."

Mr. Brown was unavailable. But when Manziuk explained to the valet why he needed to see them both, Cary first asked for a moment to check the date book and then set up an appointment for two o'clock the next afternoon.

"In the meantime, Inspector," Cary said, "I can assure you I'm appalled by what you've just told me, and Mr. Brown will be too. We'll be happy to meet with you and discuss this tragedy, but neither of us was even in the city last night, as we'll be happy to explain when we see you tomorrow."

No sooner had Manziuk hung up when Ryan's phone rang.

"This is George Simonopoulos, Miss Ryan. My wife and I have been able to look at the pictures of Stasey Simon on the website for the radio station in Toronto. We're certain that she is our daughter, Anastasia."

"Thanks for letting me know."

"Thank you for suggesting we look there. As I told you, my wife and I have no computer, but our neighbor's son was able to find it for us quite easily on his."

"Good."

"Miss Ryan, I thought you would want to know that my wife and I will be coming to Toronto tomorrow morning. In the past, Anastasia wanted to be as far from us as possible, and it is very unlikely, if she gets through this, that she will want our help now." He paused to cough. "But we will come. After all, we are her parents; she is our daughter. If there is anything we can do, we will do it."

The game had been early that afternoon. Since it was after five, Ryan phoned the Newland home. Karen said Jonas had taken his children out to a playground. As for last night, Jonas had come home from the game with his family and spent the night there. He couldn't have gone out without her knowledge. A uniformed officer was dispatched to find Jonas at the playground and verify what his wife had said, but Manziuk expected his story to be the same, if for no other reason than that he had a cell phone.

Ferdinand Ortes and Eva MacPherson were harder to track down, but after following a few rabbit trails, Pat Davis suggested they try a dinner club called The Blue Mandrake. Apparently, Rico had frequently gone there with Ferdinand.

Manziuk frowned. The Blue Mandrake had a reputation for having first-class food at exorbitant prices, and questionable patrons, including some high rollers with suspected links to organized crime. He'd also heard it was a popular haunt of some high-class call girls and a few grunge bands and creative sorts who were trying to live on the edge. The fact that Ferdinand Ortes and Rico Velasquez had been regular customers was unexpected.

When Manziuk and Ryan walked into the restaurant shortly after seven, Ferdinand and Eva were seated in a secluded corner at a table for two, surrounded by palm trees and azaleas. Ferdinand raised his eyebrows when Manziuk and Ryan appeared. "Well, this *is* a surprise. I didn't realize you came here."

"We don't," Manziuk said, with emphasis. "But apparently you do."

Eva laughed. "Do you want to join us? There might be enough room."

"No, thank you. We need to ask a couple of questions, and then we'll leave."

"The beauty of this place," Ferdinand said lazily, "is that they guard my privacy very well. They don't let in the kind of people who would swarm around me if I went out in public."

"Well," Ryan said, "Apparently they didn't know how to keep us out."

He curled his lip into a smile. "Detective Constable, I wasn't referring to you."

"Weren't you?"

"We won't be long," Manziuk said. "We just need to know where you were from nine last night until two this morning."

Ferdinand's smile grew. "That's easy. Eva and I were together at my condo from right after the game until this morning when I drove to the Diamond Dome and she took a cab to her condo."

Manziuk looked at Eva. "Miss MacPherson, where were you last night from about nine until two this morning?"

After a quick look at Ferdinand, Eva shrugged and said, "Like he said. I was at his place. Actually, I got there earlier, about six-thirty or so. A cab driver brought me. And I didn't leave until this morning."

"All right," Manziuk said. "Thanks for your time. We'll let you get back to your dinner."

"Interesting," Ryan said as they walked out. "Neither of them asked why we wanted to know. Plus he was lying. Did you see the look she gave him when he said they were together all evening?"

"Yes. But right now, I can't see any motive for his killing either Rico or Stasey. We'll have to dig some more."

Ford called as they were driving back downtown. "Got a few things."

"Hang on." Manziuk put his phone on speakerphone so they could both listen. "Okay, shoot."

"One. There were three small splinters from a baseball bat. We're going to try to find out if they came from one of the manufacturers who make the ones the Matrix players use.

"Two. We called several numbers from the address book. Are you ready for this? Lawrence Smith was one of the clean-up crew for the Diamond Dome. He's worked there since it was built, and before that he worked at the old stadium. He apparently called in sick Saturday afternoon, but a couple of crew people say they saw him in the Dome during the game.

"Three. There was no press clipping about Blake Harrison in the Simon house, and no other press clippings either.

"Four. A neighbor saw somebody hanging around across the street from the Simon house for a while late last night. The description sounds a lot like Lawrence Smith.

"Five. Another neighbor walking his dog last night saw a man wearing a dark jacket set down a large duffel bag or package of some sort near Stasey Simon's front door before going into her house. It was getting dark, but the front light was on, so he saw a silhouette. He's quite sure it was a man—or a very tall woman."

"Most of the men in this case are tall," Ryan said. "But not the women."

"He also said he had an impression that the man was carrying a stick or rod of some sort. When we asked if it could have been a baseball bat, he said yes."

"Six. Ted Benedetto's statement says nothing about a duffel bag's being at the front door when he arrived this morning. That's verified by another neighbor who was out early and happened to look at Stasey's house, admiring the flowers. She says there was nothing unusual near the door."

"Good work!" Manziuk said.

"Two more things. We contacted the maid service that Stasey Simon used to clean her house. They say nothing's missing. They also thought it was odd how there's so little personal stuff, but they didn't ask her about it. They say there was never much for them to do.

"And last, but not least. There were several dyed blond hairs in Ted Benedetto's car, but they don't belong to Stasey Simon."

"Okay. We'll keep that in mind."

"And now I'm going home to find out if my wife still recognizes me."

"Not a bad idea," Manziuk said. "Talk to you tomorrow."

It was after nine when Jacquie opened the front door, stepped inside, and yawned. Then she took off her shoes and yawned again. What she needed was sleep and lots of it.

The house was quiet except for the hum of the television in the living room. Sounded like a game show. Probably her grandmother was dozing in front of it. Maybe the others had taken Cousin LeRoy out to show him a good time.

She had to pass by the living room on her way to her bedroom.

"Cousin Jacquie," said a deep male voice as she tip-toed past the archway. "I hoped you'd get back before the others."

She'd tensed when she heard his voice. Now, she tried very hard not to show her disappointment. "Cousin LeRoy." She looked around.

He was sitting in a recliner chair, where he'd apparently been watching TV and reading the newspaper.

"Where is everyone?" she asked. "They didn't just leave you here and go out, did they?"

He laughed. "They had a baby shower to attend. I don't think I'd have fit in."

"A baby shower? Oh, no! Not Genevieve's twins! I forgot all about it."

"I believe your mama took a gift from the two of you."

"Not before she complained a lot."

He laughed. "True. But I reminded her you were busy making the streets safe for people to raise their babies."

She had no response to that.

He got up and came toward her. "I hope you'll take pity on me and sit down for a while—maybe even have a nightcap—and let me get to know you a little better."

She was so tired she just wanted to collapse. Did she really have to entertain this unwanted guest?

"Pretty please?" He smiled.

Against her better judgment, she said, "Well, maybe for a few minutes. I am a little hungry."

"Aunt Vida baked a carrot cake, and there's some left."

She led the way to the kitchen, where instead of the cake, she got out some strawberries, cut them up, and put them on top of a cup of plain yogurt and a half-cup of bran.

"I take it you aren't a cake person," he said.

"Not particularly." She sat down at the table. "But feel free to get yourself some."

He smiled, but she could sense his annoyance. *Tough.* If he thought she was going to fawn all over him, he could think again.

He cut a large slice of the carrot cake and found a bottle of ginger beer in the fridge. "What do you want to drink?" he asked, holding the bottle up. "I have some rum if you'd prefer."

She shook her head. "Thanks, but I'll get some water later."

He set his plate and bottle on the table across from her, sat down, and leaned toward her. "So, tell me, how was your day?"

"Good."

"I know you can't give me all the details, but are you close to solving the case?"

"We're making progress."

"Surely you're allowed to say a little more than that. It's not as if I'm going to run around telling everyone what I know." He smiled. "I barely know anybody in Toronto."

All she said was, "I can only say we're making progress. How was your day with the family?"

There was a long silence, which he finally broke. "You, my dear cousin, are an enigma."

"Excuse me?"

"You fascinate me. So beautiful and yet so aloof. You must know that combination drives men crazy."

Jacquie finished her yogurt and strawberries before responding. "Cousin LeRoy," she said at last, "let's just cut to the chase. You came here because you found out I was working on the Velasquez murder. The inevitable family grapevine, no doubt. And you came because you want something from me. So without beating around the bush or making you throw out any more compliments that are going to make me want to gag, tell me straight. What is it you want?"

He started to deny it, but her skeptical look stopped him in mid-sentence. "All right. I heard it from my mother Friday morning just before I left for the airport. Your mother called to tell her."

"You didn't even think about coming here until after my mother's call, did you?"

"So what if I didn't?"

"You might have said that up front. Look, just tell me the truth. What is it you really want?"

He finished off the ginger beer and set the bottle down carefully. "Look, there's something you could do for me if you would. I've always wanted to work in professional sports. And I like it here in Canada. Right now, I'm between jobs, but I've done quite a bit of security work, and there's nothing I'd like better than to work in security for the Matrix, or even for the Diamond Dome. I thought while you're working on this case, you'd meet some people, and then you'd be able to tell me who to contact, maybe even put in a good word for me."

Jacquie stood up slowly and put her bowl and spoon in the dishwasher before turning to face him, her hands on her hips. "Cousin LeRoy, I appreciate your nerve in coming here to try to get a job, but I'm afraid you came to the wrong place. Even if I thought you were the best security guard in the world, I still wouldn't be able to help you. First of all, because I'm busy trying to solve a murder, not looking to see who hires security guards. And second, because I don't like people who go after what they want without regard for other people's feelings. Especially people who pretend to be something they aren't. You lied to my mother and my other family members— you said you were here to see them. I don't appreciate that."

"Cousin Jacquie, don't get mad. I had some time to kill, and I really do want to get to know you and the rest of your family, too. The job was—well, maybe just some wishful thinking. That's all, I swear. I hoped maybe you'd meet somebody—you know—in the course of your work ..."

"Cousin LeRoy, I hope you're telling the truth. If you are, no sweat. If you aren't—well, it's your problem, not mine." She moved toward the doorway. "But I've had a long day, and I really need to get some sleep. I hope you can entertain yourself until the rest of the family gets home."

"You sure you and I can't—"

"Sorry." She went straight to her bedroom, where she discovered that Precious had tossed clothes on the cot Jacquie had used the night before as well as on the bed.

Jacquie ground her teeth as she stared at the cot. Then, feeling a sudden burst of energy, she tossed the clothes on the floor and stripped the sheets from the cot. She grabbed the sheets and clothes from her bed in one big bundle and started to dump them on the cot. She paused.

Better yet... She could hear the television in the living room. Cousin LeRoy was apparently occupied.

She walked down the hallway to her aunt's bedroom, which was quite a bit larger than hers, and dumped the bundle on top of her aunt's pristine bed. Then she went back for the cot and moved it into the room. She stood back and smiled. Both her aunt and cousin would be indignant, but it was worth it.

She made several more trips with the rest of the clothes, magazines, make-up, shoes, and other odds and ends Precious had thought necessary for a few days.

When everything had been moved, Jacquie locked herself in her bedroom and went to bed. She felt good.

Ginny got in at eleven that night and collapsed onto the sofa in her cozy living room. She was so tired she could barely see straight.

Ray Cummings had called her only a few minutes after the police had let her and Kyle leave Stasey's house, wanting to know if she'd take Stasey's Monday afternoon time slot to do a tribute. She'd discussed it with Kyle and decided it was a fair request and she would do it.

But of course, before she could start on that, she'd had to write her game story and her Monday column. She and Kyle had both called in favors to get help with their stories, then written madly for a couple of hours. After a quick stop at a drive-through burger place, Kyle had dropped her off at the station, where Ray was waiting. He would see that she got home okay.

Now, after four hours working with Ray on the script, practising the cues, and learning what buttons to push and what to say and do, she was utterly exhausted.

The phone rang. She almost didn't get up to see who it was, but it occurred to her it might be Ray calling about something he'd forgotten to tell her. Nope. It was her mother. She was about to let her answering service take it when she had a picture of Stasey lying in the hospital room. What was Stasey's mother thinking right now?

"Hi, Mom. ... Yeah, I'm here. Just got in. ... No, not a date. I'm helping out at WIN 730 tomorrow at one o'clock. They needed a host for one of the shows. ... Look, don't worry. I'm fine. ... "Yeah, I know. ... No, nothing dangerous. ... No, Mom, I haven't had much time to watch TV. ... Well, I guess if someone gave me $5,000 to go buy a new wardrobe, I wouldn't say no. ... I haven't seen the show, Mom. Tell you what, write down their tips and I'll try to do better. ... "Oh, yeah, of course. What did Doctor Bailey say? ... A mall-walking group? That could be fun. As long as you don't slip off to shop in the middle of the walk! ... Yeah, Mom, I know it's before the stores open. ... Right. ... See you next Sunday for dinner. ... I promise."

TWENTY-ONE

Paul Manziuk, his wife Loretta, their son Mike, and their twenty-one-year-old daughter Lisa had been visiting with Detective Sergeant Woodward Craig and his wife for half an hour when the nurse and an orderly came in at seven Monday morning to prep Woody for his bypass surgery.

As they left the room, Paul said, "I wish I could stay here with you."

Arlie Craig smiled at him. "So you could pace up and down the whole time?"

Paul smiled. "Am I that bad?"

"Worse," Arlie said.

"We'll phone you the moment we know anything," Loretta said. "Promise."

"It's okay, dad." Lisa gave him a hug. "Nobody understands better than Woody."

"Don't worry, Dad," Mike said. "The doctors know what they're doing."

Paul patted his son on the shoulder. "I know. Okay, I'll go off and do my job. Call me no matter what."

"Are you planning on going to the game today?" Ryan asked as Manziuk came into his office.

"No."

"They won yesterday. Brett Moore pitched a really good game and Ferdinand and Jonas each had three hits. They called up a pitcher from triple A to take Rico's spot. He's got a pretty good ERA. There's still a chance the season isn't lost."

Manziuk stared at her. "Who've you been talking to?"

"I was listening to WIN 730 while I drove here this morning."

He digested that. "Okay. Well, let's get ready for the day. We've got a team meeting at 8:30. Make a note to get someone digging for more information about Ferdinand Ortes and any connection he may have to The Blue Mandrake. And we need to know more about Eva MacPherson, too.

"She's blond."

"Yeah. So?"

"Ford says there were dyed blond hairs in Ted Benedetto's car. Does he have any connection with Eva?"

"Not that I'm aware of. I expect he has a girlfriend somewhere. But make a note."

"Be nice to get a hair from her for comparison."

"Or we could just ask Ted if he knows Eva."

Ryan grinned. "True. But too easy."

"We need to be at the hospital when Stasey Simon's parents arrive. We see Mr. Brown and his valet at two. And someone should find out if there's any possible truth to Santana's story about the press clipping. Shouldn't be difficult to find out where Blake Harrison played in his early years and check the police records there. He'll be listed on the Matrix web site."

Ryan stood up. "We have some time before the team meeting. Let me get on the Internet and see what I can find out."

Blake Harrison was sitting at his desk when Manziuk and Ryan walked in half an hour after their team meeting. He looked up and his eyes narrowed. "What are you doing here?"

"We have a few more questions to ask you," Manziuk said.

"I have a meeting in a couple of minutes."

"Then I'll get right to my questions." Manziuk leaned against the filing cabinet. "When you were twenty-three, playing in double A ball, you were arrested and charged with drunk driving, manslaughter, and trying to bribe a police officer. You got off on a technicality. Tell me, has anyone tried to blackmail you about that lately?"

Harrison's mouth had dropped open. "What right have you to go looking into my background? I had nothing to do with what happened to Rico or Stasey Simon, and you know it. I was never alone in the Diamond Dome that night. And I wasn't alone Saturday night either."

"Just answer the question. Has anyone brought up that arrest recently?"

"No. And I don't know what it has to do with anything."

"What would you be willing to do to keep it quiet?"

"Is that a threat?"

"Just a question."

"Well, the answer to your question is not a thing. If anyone tried to use that story to blackmail me into giving them money or changing how I manage this team, I'd be the first one telling the press about it. I wouldn't stand for that sort of thing."

"He's lying," Ryan said as they left Harrison's office.

"About someone talking to him recently?"

"No, about not paying to keep it quiet."

"Agreed. A lot of bluster, but he was scared stiff. However, he does have an alibi for Saturday night and I believed him when he said no one had talked to him about the arrest recently."

"Which doesn't prove Stasey didn't have the clipping."

"So where is it?"

Manziuk's cell phone rang as they were walking through the halls of the Diamond Dome. He stopped to answer it, then moved a short distance away to talk. A few minutes later, he came back to where Ryan was waiting. "Woody made it through the surgery, but it was worse than expected: they had to do a quintuple bypass. He's okay so far, though."

"That must be a relief."

"Yeah. But it'll be some time until he's out of the woods."

Manziuk and Ryan were in the hospital waiting room with Ted Benedetto late Monday morning when an older couple came in. The woman was wearing an ankle-length blue floral dress and white sandals, and carrying a plain white purse. Her straight, pale yellow hair was pulled tightly back in a bun, accentuating her gaunt, lined face and her sorrowful eyes. The man was of medium height, somewhat overweight, with gray hair and beard. He wore a black shirt, black sweater vest, black pants, and a clerical collar.

"Officer Manziuk?" the man said.

"Yes?"

"Thank you for sending the police officer to bring us here."

"You're welcome."

"I'm George Simonopoulos. My wife, Roxanne."

"You're a priest?"

He bowed slightly. "A Greek Orthodox priest. That is one of the things our Anastasia found unbearable."

"Father Simonopoulos, I didn't realize …."

"Father George. You're familiar with our church?"

"My wife and I attend a Ukrainian Orthodox church."

He smiled. "Then you're familiar with our practices and beliefs."

Manziuk shuffled his feet. "Well, the truth is my wife is the one who attends. I go with her sometimes. This job doesn't give me a lot of free time, even on Sundays."

"I understand. And do you have children?"

"Two sons and a daughter."

"Are they also of the faith?"

"My youngest son attends. My daughter and older son more rarely. I can't say if they'll continue or not."

"My daughter rejected our faith when she was still in her teens. She found it too constricting. She couldn't wait to graduate from school so she could leave. In all these years, she's only had contact with us twice. Two postcards. There has been nothing for five years."

"I'm sorry," Manziuk said.

He shook his head. "We've grown accustomed. We have three sons and seven grandchildren, and until a few years ago we took in foster children. And my wife and I are both very busy in the parish. So the fact that one of our children couldn't live with our faith is a sorrow, but not the overruling factor in our lives."

His wife looked at Manziuk and a smile just touched her lips. "He sounds so cold and hard. But Anastasia—we called her Anna— is our only daughter, and when she was little, she was his favorite. Our hearts broke when she left. And I think perhaps they've been numb ever since."

"That has nothing to do with Officer Manziuk, Roxanne. Officer, are we allowed to see her?"

"I talked with her doctor a few minutes ago. So far, she's responded well to treatment, but she's still in critical condition, and they want to keep her asleep for another day or two. He says you can see her, but she won't be awake."

Father George bowed slightly. "We simply want to see her, perhaps sit with her if we aren't in the way."

"She's on life support, so there'll be a lot of tubes and wires."

"I'm a hospital chaplain, Officer."

"Inspector," Ryan said.

"Pardon?"

"He's an Inspector, not an officer."

"I'm very sorry, Inspector. I should have known."

"Not a problem." Manziuk looked at Ryan. "Not worth mentioning."

Manziuk and Ryan walked Father George and Roxanne Simonopoulos to Stasey's room and nodded to the policewoman guarding the door.

"Is that really necessary?" Father George said. "How can my daughter still be in danger? She's barely alive."

"I don't want to take any chances."

They went inside the room and Father George walked to the near side of the bed; his wife to the far side.

Father George stood looking down at his daughter. "This is what comes from a lifetime of poor choices. It doesn't surprise me. Playing foolish games instead of doing her homework or helping her mother around the house. You reap what you sow."

Roxanne Simonopoulos burst into tears and fell to her knees with her head on the bed next to her daughter, sobbing, "Anna, oh my poor, poor girl."

Ted Benedetto and the police guard had trailed into the room after the others, and stood watching, mouths open. After a long moment where the only sound was that of Roxanne's sobs, Ted spoke up. "I stayed here because I thought somebody should. Now that you're here, I'll get back to the station, where they need me. But first, since Stasey can't, I need to say something. I hate to spoil either of your illusions, but neither of you seems to have known her at all. Stasey Simon enjoyed every minute of her life here in Toronto, she loved this city and she loved her job. Not long ago, she told me that if she died tomorrow, she'd have no regrets, because at least she'd have lived. Which is more than most people can say."

At one o'clock Monday afternoon, Ginny Lovejoy sat in the main recording studio at WIN 730 and gulped. On the other side of the glass, Ray and Ted each gave her a thumbs up. Then Ted's voice said in her ear, "Five ... four ... three ... two ... one ... you're on."

"Good afternoon, everyone. My name is Ginny Lovejoy. As you're no doubt aware, Stasey Simon was attacked in her home late Saturday night by an unknown assailant. At this moment, Stasey is in an intensive care room fighting for her life. In honor of Stasey, WIN 730 asked me to host this program. For the next hour, we'll be playing some of the more memorable of Stasey's on-air moments. Following that, I'll take your calls as you reminisce about Stasey. We'll be making a tape of your calls so we can play it for Stasey when she's up to it. And now, some of the great on-air moments of Stasey Simon."

Two o'clock Monday afternoon found Ryan, Manziuk, and Special Constable Benson at Mr. Brown's penthouse condo.

The same security guard they'd seen when they came the first time let them in, and Cary Grant opened the door to them when they came out of the elevator on the penthouse floor.

"Good evening, Detective Inspector Manziuk and Detective Constable Ryan. And—" Cary looked quizzically at Manziuk. "Inspector Manziuk, I don't believe we've met this gentleman?"

Manziuk introduced Benson and explained his role.

Cary gave him a searching look. "And do you have to make everything you know public, Constable Benson?"

Benson smiled. "No, but if I'm aware of all the details, it's easier for me to choose what to say and what not to say."

The valet smiled. "I see." He thought for a moment. "Yes, that makes sense," he said at last. He turned and led them to a sitting room where Mr. Brown and Alita Velasquez were already seated.

Cary held out chairs for Manziuk and Ryan before taking a chair on the far side of Mr. Brown. Manziuk and Ryan looked expectantly at Mr. Brown, but it was the valet who spoke, "Our lawyers wanted to be here, but we don't feel we need them. We haven't done anything illegal."

"That remains to be seen," Manziuk said. "I think you know what we're here for."

"Yes," Cary said. "In light of the very sad events discovered yesterday, we realize it's high time you knew everything. Not because we've had any involvement in either attack, but so you're better able to focus your attention on finding the real criminal."

"Agreed," Manziuk said. He looked at the Matrix owner. "Mr. Brown?"

"Um, actually," Cary said, "there is no Mr. Brown."

Manziuk's eyes went back to him. "I'm sorry?"

"What I mean is, Mr. Brown is a phony name. The Diamond Corporation is actually owned by two people: my brother and me. But Mr. Brown isn't my brother's name. And, of course, Cary Grant isn't my real name either."

He looked over at Alita. "Neither is Zandor. It's a name I found and used because I liked it. It actually means "protector of people."" He took off his glasses before standing and, using both hands, pulled off his red hair, revealing black hair much like his brother's.

Alita leaped from her chair. "No, it cannot be—"

He spoke to her in Spanish, and she stood still, her eyes wide. She clasped her hands together and brought them tightly to her chest as though in prayer.

Cary continued. "Yes, I was the man Alita knew as Zandor. Right now, I'm wearing false eyebrows and quite a bit of make-up in order to make my skin look more tanned than it is. Alita had never seen Cary before today—only the man she knew as Zandor."

The man who had been called Mr. Brown spoke up. "We also need to apologize about one thing, Inspector. We both hated the necessity of lying to you about not knowing where Alita was. Alastair told me I overdid it a bit. I'm not used to lying. And we felt very bad that the police were looking for Alita when she was right here the whole time. We'll try to make up for it in some way if we can."

"What's your real name?" Ryan asked.

He sighed. "I'm Jeremy. My brother is Alastair."

There was a long silence, which Alastair broke. "Please, let's sit back down and I'll try to explain."

Alita returned to her seat; Cary/Zandor/Alastair did the same.

"You see," he said, "our father died six years ago, just before the Matrix team was put up for sale. My brother and I enjoyed watching baseball, and my brother was very fond of the Matrix. There was a good deal of talk that if a new Canadian owner couldn't be found, the team might be moved out of the country. We didn't want that to happen.

"If our father had been alive, he would never have agreed, but since he'd died a couple of months before, and we inherited every-thing, we could do whatever we wanted. And we—especially my brother—wanted to save the team. So we bought it.

"But no one except our lawyers knew it was us. Everything was done though a corporation we created, called Diamond Corpora-tion. No one, not even Mr. Kanberra, has seen us. They only see our lawyers. And only one of the lawyers actually knows who we are. Of course, we do have a staff: a chauffeur, a cook, a valet, gardeners, and so forth, all of whom have been with us for many years and are more like family than staff."

Manziuk leaned forward. "After Rico's death, you decided to meet with us? Why?"

"Our lawyers thought it would seem very odd if we refused to see the police, so we let you come here. This is our city place, where we spend a good deal of the summer so we can attend all home games. But we didn't want to let out who we were to just anyone, even the police, so we decided that my brother would pretend to be Mr. Brown and I would pretend to be his valet." He looked down. "It must seem very foolish to you, but we had our reasons. And everything else we told you was the truth."

Ryan couldn't keep from asking, "So, who are you exactly?"

Alastair looked over at his brother, who nodded. Alastair said, "You may have heard of a Mr. Timothy Formeister?

Ryan and Manziuk shook their heads, but Benson nodded. "Some rich guy," Benson said, "A bit of a hermit."

"Actually, a very rich guy," Alastair said. "And he preferred to be called 'reclusive'."

"I expect he had a good reason," Manziuk said.

Alastair nodded. "He thought he did. When Timothy was in his late thirties, he married, and he and his wife had a son. When the boy was four, he was kidnapped and held for ransom—a very large ransom. The story has a happy ending—the ransom was paid and the boy was recovered alive. However, he would have died if one of the kidnapper's girlfriends hadn't made a phone call to tell the police where to find him. You see, they'd left the child alone in a forest, where he would eventually have died from exposure.

"After that, my father decided he had to protect his family at any cost. So he built a fortress with heavy security, and we grew up inside it. Everything we needed was brought to us: we never left. Eight years ago, our mother died from cancer. All the security couldn't keep the cancer out. Our father died six years ago, officially from a heart attack, but really from a broken heart. My brother Jeremy and I have been alone since then, trying to figure out what to do with ourselves. Rebuilding the Matrix and giving it a new home filled a very large hole in our lives.

"Jeremy," he motioned toward his brother, "has always loved watching sports—especially baseball, and is very knowledgeable. So he entered into the ownership of the team with all his energy. I took on the challenge of building the Diamond Dome and the Diamond Hotel." He looked around. "But I suppose I needed something more—some kind of adventure. You see, I've watched all the movies, from Douglas Fairbanks to the *Pirates of the Caribbean*.

"When the opportunity arose to help Rico get out of Cuba, we hired someone to look after it. But later, when it came to bringing his wife out, something came over me, and I had to do it myself—to see if I could be as brave and daring as those men in books and on screen. You must understand, I've spent my entire life studying and learning, but never actually doing anything—never putting my knowledge into practice. I'm fluent in eight languages, including Spanish, and I'm trained in the martial arts. Of course, I made all the preparations ahead of time. I had someone contact Alita, hired a boat, rented a cottage, hired a private security agent to look after her when she arrived in Florida and see that she got on the plane, got her a government document to let her come into Canada, and so forth.

"But I wanted to go to Cuba and be there on the boat—to be the one who actually brought her here. I have to confess, the one thing I didn't plan was the unexpected storm, which I'm afraid I found enormously enjoyable, although unfortunately Alita did not." He ventured a look toward her, and was answered by a tight smile.

"After spending the time together and getting to know her a little, I'm afraid I had great difficulty imagining her with the Rico I knew. They seemed to be from two different worlds. I saw her with one of our cameras during the game on Wednesday, and when I realized she was distressed, I went down and spoke to her. She told me she was having trouble accepting that Rico was the same person she'd married, but that she'd give him some time. I told her not to worry, that if she found she simply couldn't stay with him I'd see that she was either returned to Cuba or cared for here. She seemed grateful to know she had an option.

"Then on Thursday night, when we saw her leave the reception room, I ran down and found her and brought her up to our private rooms. She was very upset. So we took her with us through our private entrance, and we had one of our staff pick up her possessions from the hotel. She still thought I was Zandor, a man hired by Mr. Brown to bring her here. Later, when she was ready to talk to the authorities, we had our lawyers go with her."

Manziuk said, "You must have been very angry at Rico. After all the effort and expense to bring first him and then his wife here, he was creating a lot of problems for you."

Alastair nodded. "Yes, there's no question we were disappointed in Rico. But I can assure you our disappointment would never lead us to kill him. First, because whatever his faults, he was an amazing pitcher, and a number of teams had made us very good offers for trades. Second, because neither Jeremy nor I would ever dream of doing such a thing. All life is important to us."

Ryan said, "Where were you Saturday night from about nine until two in the morning?"

Jeremy spoke for the first time. "That's very easy, Constable. We were showing Alita our home. Right after the game Saturday, we drove to our helicopter, which we keep at the Island airport. We flew to our estate, which is about an hour north of Kingston. We have a number of witnesses, including our pilot, our cook, and the rest of our staff. We flew back Sunday morning, and arrived here with just enough time before the game started to eat the picnic lunch our cook had packed for us."

"That's right," Alastair said. "The three of us were nowhere near this city when Stasey Simon was injured."

"One last question," said Ryan. "Which of you is the older?"

Alastair blushed. "Me. I was the boy who was kidnapped and left in the woods to die." He sighed. "It was my fault. I knew perfectly well I shouldn't go near the woman who was offering me candy, but I ignored my better judgment for a single chocolate bar."

TWENTY-TWO

Kyle Schmidt was sitting on one of three battered chairs in WIN's tiny reception area when Ginny came out after finishing the tribute program.

"Great job," he said.

"Thanks. I feel totally drained and yet strangely euphoric."

"That time you were on with Iain, I thought you'd be good. I didn't realize you'd be this good."

"Kyle, you don't need to overdo it."

"I'm not."

Ginny realized the magenta-haired receptionist was watching them with interest. "Let's go," she said.

On the way down in the elevator, she said, "Kyle, they want me to keep doing it. Fill in for Stasey until we know what's going to happen. Not every day; but as much as possible."

"Are you going to do it?"

"I don't know. I kind of liked it. But it's a lot of work."

"Do it for a while at least. Give it a shot. You might like it better than reporting."

"Yeah, I said I'd do it for a few days and then decide. I'm not on tomorrow, but the day after, I am." She gave him a quick sideways glance. "We'll see. Anyway, that's not what I wanted to talk about. Doing this show on Stasey got me fired up. The police are never going to find out who killed Rico and Lawrence and tried to kill Stasey without our help."

"What makes you think that?"

"Because this is our territory. We know the people involved and what makes them tick: they don't. It seems to me that if you and I pool our ideas together, we can solve it. There aren't that many suspects. We know we didn't do it. And we know Armando and Jonas didn't do it. Or Alita."

"We do?"

"Yes, we do."

"How do we know that, Gin?"

"Call it women's intuition if you like."

"Okay, I'll leave that for now. Who's left?"

"Stasey."

"Well, she didn't try to kill herself."

"Ted."

"He'd never hurt Stasey."

"Are you sure?"

"I'm sure."

"And that leaves?"

Ginny was busy writing down names. "That leaves Iain, Ferdinand, and Eva. So, what about Iain? He had no more reason to kill Rico than we did. Unless he's lost his mind."

"Iain doesn't strike me as somebody who's losing his mind."

"He certainly doesn't try to hide the fact he thinks Stasey's too over the top as a host."

"Half of Toronto probably agrees with him," Kyle said. "More to the point, he's a bit of a chauvinist. But he says stuff to me, too. How can I write about a game I haven't played? As if he ever played any sport at the pro level! But it's a bit of a stretch to think he'd kill Stasey just because he doesn't think a woman or a non-athlete should host a show."

"There is one other thing. He'd like Ted to work for him." Ginny grabbed Kyle's arm. "Oh! Maybe he'll get him now!"

"Thin. But, anyway, this started with Rico. Why would Iain want to kill Rico?"

Ginny said, "No reason I can think of."

"That leaves Ferdinand and Eva."

Ginny nodded.

"His best friend and his girlfriend."

"They do say most murders are done by family and friends."

"Can you really see Ferdinand murdering anybody?"

"I don't know." Ginny tilted her head to one side and pursed her lips. "I've always wondered if there wasn't more to Ferdinand than you see. There's always this glint in his eyes, like he's laughing at some joke no one else knows."

"Okay, now you're letting your imagination, or your intuition, or whatever, really get carried away."

"Am I? Kyle, Ferdinand seemed to be Rico's friend, and a totally nice guy, but what if he wasn't? What if he was, you know, putting on an act? Maybe even using him in some way?"

"What way?"

"I don't know. They were always talking in Spanish, so you never really knew what they were saying. Pat told me it got to him sometimes. He'd be having Ferdinand translate for him and find himself wondering what Ferdinand was really saying." She snapped her fingers. "Eva!"

"What about her?"

"She's the key. We have to get Eva to tell us everything she can about Rico's and Ferdinand's relationship. Every little detail. Maybe we'll pick up something—some kind of clue." She looked at Kyle expectantly.

He sighed. "Okay. We have a game to cover now, but afterward I might know a way we can talk to Eva. And we can talk about Jonas and Armando later, too. Just because you like people doesn't necessarily mean they couldn't have done something wrong."

When Ginny and Kyle walked into the Diamond Dome, the Matrix players were just starting their warm-ups. It was obvious that a number of them had been listening to the radio program, because Ginny was soon surrounded by a large group of players, coaches, and staff who thanked her for doing the tribute to Stasey.

The group was broken up by Blake Harrison, who told everyone to get back to work. When Kyle asked him how he felt about everything that had happened in the last few days, Blake said, "My job is to get this team into the playoffs. That's all I care about."

After meeting with Alastair and Jeremy Formeister, Manziuk, Ryan, and Benson spent a good deal of the afternoon going over everything they knew about the two murders and the attempted murder, and trying to come up with a conclusion.

"If we assume Stasey was killed because she knew who killed Rico," Manziuk said at last, "and Lawrence just because he was present, which seems to be the most logical explanation for what happened, then it still comes back to who killed Rico—which, as Ryan said earlier, goes back to the motive. Why would anyone want to kill Rico?"

"Anyone other than Armando," Benson said.

"I know," Manziuk said. "He certainly seems to be the most logical suspect."

"And he doesn't even have a sliver of an alibi for Saturday night," Benson said. "He had opportunity: he himself admits he was right there. Motive: Stasey knew he killed Rico. Weapon: he likely had a bat in his car. Or Stasey had one in her house."

"I'll admit he had the opportunity," Manziuk said, "and I'll even admit he had the best motive for killing Rico that we're aware of, but there's no evidence he had a bat in his car, or that she had one in her house."

Ryan said, "He could have brought one along to use."

"If it was premeditated. But ... can you believe he could kill two people and then walk into a police station to ask for an officer's address? Which he did—we've verified it. And I also don't see why he'd invent the story about the clipping on Blake when he knew we wouldn't find the paper."

Ryan jumped up and paced the floor. "Okay, maybe we need to start thinking illogically. Like for instance ... who do you think will take over Stasey Simon's show? Do you realize Ginny Lovejoy was the host today?"

Benson stared at her. "What? Now you're going way off track."

"No she isn't," Manziuk said. To Ryan, he said, "Go on."

She thought for a moment. "Well, when we look at who gains by the murder of Rico Velasquez, we don't really see anyone, except Alita, who inherits his money, and maybe Armando Santana, but not directly—unless it was for vengeance. But what happens if we look beyond that? For instance, who gains if Stasey Simon dies?"

Benson leaned forward and folded his hands together. "Obviously, the person who killed Rico."

Ryan smiled. "That's what we've been assuming. But what if it was never about Rico? What if—? I know! What if it was about Stasey? What if someone heard Stasey's comments on the show Thursday and saw the chance to get her in trouble? And that person looked for an opportunity to carry out what Stasey had suggested— to knock some sense into Rico's head. And maybe that person went with Rico when they were looking for Alita, or met up with him and convinced him to go into the bullpen—maybe told him Alita was there. And he got Rico to look away, and then grabbed a bat and hit him. And the motive had nothing to do with Rico. It was done just to get Stasey into trouble. Only Stasey figured it out, and she was going to tell all on her special show. So, then, he had to kill her, too."

"Supposing for just one moment that you're right," Benson said. "If Stasey knew who the killer was, why would she let him into her house?"

"Yeah," Ryan said thoughtfully. "Ted Benedetto told us she was paranoid about safety. She'd never knowingly let Rico's killer into the house."

"She didn't know who the killer was," Manziuk said. "I've listened to her show. She bluffed all the time. Either the killer didn't realize she was bluffing or he meant to kill her all along."

"So," Ryan said, "who gains by Stasey Simon's death? Right now, it looks like Ginny Lovejoy."

Manziuk's cell phone rang. After checking the number, he excused himself and left the room.

When he came back, some minutes later, he was drawn and white. "I have to go," he said. "Woody didn't make it after all. He went into respiratory shock and there was nothing more they could do." He took a deep breath. "I'm going to need a couple of hours."

Ryan said, "Oh, no!"

"I'm so sorry to hear that," Benson said. He looked at his watch. "It's seven o'clock. Why don't we all take the rest of the evening off? We'll get together again in the morning and see if this line of thought takes us anywhere."

He started to gather up his papers. "Tell Arlie how sorry we all are. I'll let Seldon know."

Miles Patterson, the Matrix pitcher that night, had a three-hitter but lost 1–0 because of an error by the left fielder, whose sliding attempt to catch a line drive allowed an inside-the-park home run. Feelings after the game were understandingly low. Such amazing pitching let down by an error and no offense! Not that the pitcher complained. And that made it worse. He was such a nice guy, you felt doubly bad about not getting him the win he deserved.

Armando Santana was dressed and preparing to leave the clubhouse when he was told that Blake Harrison wanted to see him. He looked around for Jonas, but he was gone. That was odd. Jonas never went home without saying good-bye.

Armando squared his shoulders. Well, this was probably it. They were going to trade or release him. And he was ready. He'd take it like a man. He'd been doing a lot of thinking the last day or so and had realized he'd allowed himself to become despondent and hopeless, acting as if there was nothing he could do, instead of assessing the situation and taking responsibility for himself and his performance. Jonas was right. He'd been pampering himself; thinking he could relax now. Thinking he'd arrived! He knew perfectly well you couldn't do that. He'd told rookies you could never take anything for granted. No wonder they wanted to get rid of him—he was a bad influence.

Well, no more. Wherever he ended up, even if it was the minor leagues, he'd start working out harder, start eating healthier food, and work on perfecting his pitches. Then they'd see if he was all washed up!

He knocked on the door to Blake's office and heard Blake say, "It's open."

He went inside.

"No need to sit down," Blake barely looked up from his seat behind the desk. "This won't take long." He finished writing something and then looked up at Armando with an unsmiling face. "You're probably expecting to get your old job back now that Rico isn't here any longer. Well, it's not going to happen. Tony just made a trade. Pittsburgh's catcher broke his leg blocking the plate on Friday, and he's out for the season. They need an experienced catcher right away, and they asked for Jonas Newland. Offered us a young pitcher we've had our eyes on. We threw you in for a back-up fielder. Their pitching has been pretty bad, so you'll have your chance to prove you aren't washed up."

Armando stared, his mind blank.

"Jonas is already packing. Good bye." Blake didn't offer to shake hands.

A variety of emotions tumbled through Armando's mind—anger, confusion, fear, relief, and several more he couldn't name.

Blake said, "I believe Jonas has already arranged tickets on a flight tonight."

Armando finally found his voice. "You'll regret this," he said. "Not me—I don't matter. But Jonas is well-liked here. I know you're doing this because he stood up to you about Rico, and now you think you've won. But you'll regret it."

Blake coughed. "Enjoy your new team. They're only twenty or so games out of first place."

Armando stared at him until the older man finally looked down. Then Armando walked out, head high. He found Jonas cleaning out his locker while a group of players and several of the coaches watched.

"I'm real sorry about this, Armando." Muddy Ames came forward to give him a hug, the older man's head coming to the bottom of Armando's chin.

The other players and coaches echoed his words and then moved away as if to give the two who had been traded some space.

"This is all my fault," Armando said. "If you hadn't talked to Blake about Rico and me, he never—"

"Forget it. If not that, it would have been something else. Blake doesn't like having anyone disagree with him, and I was disagreeing more and more all the time."

"Have you called Karen?"

"Yes."

"How is she taking it?"

"Okay. She and the kids are going to stay here until I have a chance to look over the situation in Pittsburgh and see how long term that's likely to be. Then we'll decide about moving. We don't want the kids to have to change schools in mid-year, so we'll need to be settled somewhere by September. Here, Pittsburgh, maybe even Florida! We've talked about that before."

"You were one of the few players who brought his family to Toronto and lived here year round. That should have counted for something."

Jonas smiled. "I don't think so."

Armando put his hands on his hips. "This is all so ridiculous!"

"Maybe, but it's reality." Jonas laughed. "Hey, look at the bright side. You're back in a starting rotation."

"As Blake reminded me, they're at least twenty games out of the playoffs."

"But they've had quite a few close games. And they've got a lot of good young players. A couple of old guys like us could be very helpful to them, give them some stability. I think it's a good trade for them."

Armando sighed. "You might be right. I'll try to be positive."

"We can talk later. Right now, you'd better get packed up. Our flight's at seven tomorrow morning."

Jacqueline Ryan had come home from the meeting with Manziuk and Benson, eaten dinner with her family, and worked on the overdue report for her last case for a couple of hours, all the time pushing more recent events and thoughts to the back of her mind. But when her thoughts finally surfaced and refused to be pushed back down, she'd thrown a quarter of a bottle of bubble bath into the tub, filled it with water as hot as she could stand, and lain there for twenty minutes thinking about how much life can hurt.

She shivered again as she remembered the look on Manziuk's face when he'd told them his partner and best friend was dead. She'd seen that look before, on her grandmother's face when Jacquie was eleven.

Gram had come into her room early one morning and sat down on the side of her bed. The fact that Gram had come to their house so early was warning enough, but Jacquie had also heard unusual sounds from the rest of the house.

"Jacquie, honey," Gram had said. "I'm afraid I have very bad new for you, child."

Icy fingers of fear had climbed Jacquie's spine. "What's wrong?"

"It's your daddy, honey. He—he's had an accident."

"He's dead, isn't he?" Jacquie already knew about death. She'd had goldfish, and they'd all died.

"Yes, child, I'm afraid he is."

"Why?"

"The police think his cab was robbed about four this morning. He—he was shot by the robbers. He died very quickly."

As if his dying quickly should have made her happy. Much better if he'd died slowly, so she could have been there with him and had a chance to say a last few words.

In the distance, Jacquie had heard her mother's howls of anguish, her older sister's sobs, her brother's angry shouting. "I want to be alone now Gram, please," she'd said.

Gram had patted her on the head and left the room.

Jacquie had snuggled under the covers and pulled both pillows over her head so no one would hear her screams.

Now she lay back in the bathtub and let her tears flow into the water. She had no idea who she was crying for—Manziuk, Sergeant Craig, her father, herself, Lawrence Smith, Stasey Simon, Rico Velasquez—all she knew was that she felt limp and empty and very, very sad.

"Jacquie!" Her mother rapped on the door. "You've been in there half an hour. You're going to look like a prune."

"I won't be long."

"Well, there's someone's here to see you."

"Who is it?"

"It's a surprise. Come on out. And put on something pretty."

"God," Jacquie muttered as she pulled the plug on the water and grabbed a towel, "if you really exist (and my grandmother certainly thinks you do), what exactly have I done to you to deserve this?"

She pulled on her housecoat and went to her room to find something to wear. She'd planned to go straight to bed. What time was it anyway? Nearly eleven. Why on earth would anyone, even Cousin LeRoy, who she thought had returned to New York, come by so late?

"Jacquie, you coming?" Her mother was almost singing now.
"Coming, Ma!"

Yeah, sure, she was going to hurry to talk to her big dumb second cousin who thought just because he was a man she ought to swoon over him. She took her time throwing on a pair of pants, a T-shirt, and bedroom slippers before finally leaving her room.

Precious was coming down the hall. "Hurry up!" she said in a loud stage whisper. "If you don't act like you want to see him, he might leave."

"Oh, please, let him leave!" Jacquie whispered back.

Precious stared at her. "What have you got on?"

"Look, I just want to get this over with." Jacquie continued down the hallway, and into the living room. It was empty. Oh, sure, they were back in his favorite place, the kitchen. Every woman in her family believed the only sure way to a man's heart was through his stomach. Well, not her man, assuming she ever found one. As she walked into the kitchen, she said, "Sorry I took so long, but I've had a horrendous day and I'm going to bed. If you—" She stopped dead. The man sitting at the head of the table, with her mother and her aunt on either side, was not Cousin LeRoy.

Armando Santana looked over at her and smiled. "If I had known you had all these wonderful cooks, I would have dropped in to see you a lot sooner."

"How did you get my address?"

"I got your phone number, actually. From one of your co-workers."

"They aren't supposed to give it out."

"Well, I managed to get it. And when I phoned, your aunt invited me over for some of her carrot cake." He grinned. "I cannot remember when I have had carrot cake this good. And these rock buns—amazing!"

"We have several good cooks in my family. But I'm not one of them."

"No one is perfect." He laughed. "Actually, I should have brought along some sweet potato pie. I made way more than I needed yesterday."

Jacquie's mother gasped. "You telling us you make your own sweet potato pie?"

"Cooking is one of my hobbies. And if Aunt Vida here is willing to share her recipe for carrot cake, I would maybe share my recipe for sweet potato pie. It is very good, if I do say so myself."

Aunt Vida, Gram, and Jacquie's mother all made adoring comments.

Armando pushed his chair back and walked toward Jacquie. "I wonder if I could talk you into a short walk? I know you must be tired after everything that has happened, but Jonas and I have been traded, and we leave for Pittsburgh tomorrow morning. I don't know when I will get back to Toronto."

"Traded?"

"It happens frequently in professional sports."

"You mean they can just tell you where you have to live and who you work for? You don't get a say?"

"Right."

"But you're still involved in a police investigation!"

"Yes. That is how I was able to get your number. I called to see if the police would allow me to leave the country, and they passed me on to a Constable Benson, is it? He said I can go, but that I needed to talk to someone from the investigating team, and since Inspector Manziuk was unavailable, I should call you. So he gave me your cell phone number, and your aunt answered it and invited me over."

Jacquie bit her lip. Wait until Manziuk heard about this! She must have left her cell phone in the kitchen when she had dinner, and of course, she'd been in the bath. She'd have to have a long talk with her aunt tomorrow about never, ever touching her things. Meanwhile …. She looked around at the four watching women. She had to deal with this without an audience. "I guess—I guess a short walk would be okay. Let me find a sweater." She hurried back to her room and put on her gun, then grabbed a jacket to cover it. She started for the door, but turned back to check the mirror. Ugh! She quickly dabbed on some blush and powder. Then kicked off her bedroom slippers and grabbed some shoes.

Armando was waiting at the front door. "It is beautiful out tonight. Warm, but not humid. And there's a full moon, so it's quite bright." He held the door for Jacquie, then turned to smile at the other women, who were watching from the hallway. "Thanks for the great food. I will not keep her out long." He shut the door.

"They'll run to the window," Jacquie said.

"Yes," he said. "Let us walk a block or so."

They strode along in silence, Jacquie slightly ahead as if leading the way.

After they'd gone a block and a half, he said, "This should be good. Unless you think they are following us."

She'd been ready to read him the riot act for daring to come to her house, but his comment made her smile. "I don't think they'd do that."

"It must be great to be loved so much," he said.

"What?"

"Your family loves you a great deal."

"Not sure where you're getting that."

He laughed. "It is so obvious. And they are so proud of you!"

She shook her head. "They think I'm nuts and they just barely tolerate me."

"They adore you. And I am beginning to see why."

She was ready to argue, but at his last words, she swallowed hers. "You know you shouldn't be here," she said. "Did Benson say you can leave the country?"

"He said at this point you don't have enough evidence to hold me, so there is no valid reason not to let me go."

"That could change at any time."

"I don't think so. I did not do it." He looked away. "I stopped by to see Stasey tonight. Her parents were there, and a policeman, but they let me see her for a few minutes. It was terrible to see her that way, and to meet her parents under these circumstances."

"So why are you here now?" Ryan said bluntly. "You've got permission to leave. What do you want from me?"

Armando shifted from one foot to the other and cleared his throat. "I would not have come if this trade had not happened. I would have waited until you discovered who is guilty. But after learning about the trade, I didn't want to just leave without saying anything." He looked in her eyes. "I will not be around for the next few months, but when the season is over, hopefully you'll no longer be wondering if I am a murderer, and I would very much like it if we could take some time to get to know each other. Is that possible, do you think?"

"I—I—"

"All I am asking is whether or not you will talk to me if I come to see you. Maybe go for dinner. Nothing more."

She bit her lip and looked at the ground. "I don't know." After a moment, she brought her head up and smiled. "Would I need to become a baseball fan?"

"Not unless you want to." He grinned. "We can always talk about cooking."

She laughed. "Where did you say you're going? Can we get your games on TV up here?"

"This isn't exactly my idea of a fun evening," Ginny Lovejoy whispered across the table to Kyle Schmidt. "These prices are ridiculous. And I never eat this late!"

The two of them had been shown to a small table at The Blue Mandrake, not too far from the table where Eva MacPherson and Ferdinand Ortes were seated.

"You wanted to come," Kyle said.

"I know. I'm sorry. And thank you for inviting me."

"Ferdinand comes here all the time," Kyle said.

"Ferdinand isn't living on a reporter's salary."

"You wanted to see what he and Eva do."

"Yeah. Well, I guess it was a dumb idea." Ginny ate the last bit of her decadent chocolate cheese cake. "On the other hand, the food is the best I've eaten in my entire life. I've probably gained ten pounds."

"And we've learned one thing for sure," Kyle said quietly. "Neither Eva nor Ferdinand seems to be missing Rico much."

"You think they killed him?"

"Why not?"

"So good." She swallowed. "It would fit. The police said there were no signs that Rico had put up a fight. If Eva was keeping him busy, and Ferdinand came up behind him with a baseball bat, that would have worked quite well, don't you think? As for why, Rico was really mad when Ferdinand showed up at the press conference with Eva. Maybe he was giving her a hard time."

"Afraid I'm a bit foggy on what happened at the reception."

"Tell me about it! I've never seen you drunk before." Ginny played with her fork for a second. She was slowly opening her mouth to say something else when Kyle grabbed her arm.

"Ferdinand just slapped Eva!" he said. "She's getting up."

As Eva ran out the front door, Kyle and Ginny waited to see what Ferdinand would do.

He called the waiter over and apparently settled the bill by handing him cash. Then he followed Eva out.

Kyle jerked his head at Ginny and she jumped up to follow while he got out his wallet to pay.

Ginny watched Ferdinand grab Eva's arm as she was about to get into a cab. There was a bit of an argument, and the cabbie got involved. Ferdinand handed him some money and he left. Eva stayed with Ferdinand until a valet brought his Porshe.

Kyle hurried out and he and Ginny ran to where Kyle had parked his car.

"Follow that car!" Ginny grinned as she got in. "I've always wanted to say that."

Kyle and Ginny kept Ferdinand's car in sight, and ended up at Eva's condo. "We'll never get inside," Ginny said as she realized where they were. "They have amazing security."

Kyle smiled. "Oh, ye of little faith." He pulled into a parking space reserved for tenants.

She stared at him. "You know how to get in?"

"As a matter of fact, I do."

She followed him to the door and watched as he tapped some numbers on the pad. The door swung open.

"How did you do that?"

"Shh!"

She watched in amazement as he said, "Hi," to the security guard, a tall young man with the physique of a serious body builder, who nodded and smiled to Kyle as they walked past him to the elevator. Kyle touched a number and they went up.

"What—?"

"Shh!"

She followed him down to a very large black door, and watched as he used a key from his key chain to unlock it.

Ginny followed. "What is this? How did you—?"

"Be patient. I'll tell you."

"Okay."

They went inside. The condo was very large, almost completely open, masculine in tone, and earth-like in green, brown, and beige.

"Okay, I'm listening," Ginny said.

Kyle led the way through areas for sleeping, eating, and working, to a space with a huge TV screen, a stone fireplace, and comfortable seating. "Have a chair," he said.

Ginny perched on the edge of a brown corduroy chair. "All right, give!"

Kyle collapsed in a recliner. "Okay, it's kind of complicated. A month or so ago, I started hanging out in this area, hoping to learn anything I could about Eva and Rico. One night, I stopped in at an upscale bar a block from here, and I overheard this guy complaining about the woman who lived next door to him—how she had a Marilyn Monroe complex. We got talking, and sure enough, it was Eva.

"Turned out this guy and I had a few things in common—he's working in advertising and making a lot more money that I am, but he's had some short stories published, and he's hoping to be able to take an extended, six-month leave soon to complete a novel he's started."

"Yeah, that does sound a lot like you. But I still—you've been staking Eva out?"

"I was originally following Rico, but he spent so much time with her that I started hanging around here, and then when I met this guy, one thing led to another—"

Ginny jumped up and stomped around the room. "I can't believe it!" She threw her hands in the air. "You didn't breathe a single word of this to me, and you had the nerve to get mad when I had my little scoop about Alita!"

"Do you want to hear the rest of it?"

She stopped moving and sat down.

"Ten days ago, he got sent to Spain for a month on this assignment, and he asked me to look after his place. He's got a few plants that need to be watered, and a couple of birds that need to be looked after. Naturally, I agreed."

"So you've been here spying on Eva and Rico?"

"Just a little bit."

She leaned forward. "Cool. So what have you learned?"

"You're not mad any more?"

She made a face. "No. Anyway, you're telling me now. So what have you learned?"

"This whole Marilyn thing is totally obsessive. She's so far into the character, it's as if she doesn't have her own personality. And get this, her father is John MacPherson."

"Not *the* John MacPherson!"

Kyle rolled his eyes. "You have no idea who John MacPherson is, do you?"

"Never heard of him."

"He's an international financier and billionaire who jets around the world all the time."

"Eva's father?"

"Yeah. And get this, Eva's his only daughter, but he's so busy she has to make an appointment to see him."

"Yuck."

"Yeah."

"So you've talked to her?"

"What do you think?"

"Who did you tell her you were?"

"I just told her I was her new neighbor for a few weeks. And she accepted it totally. She invited me over a few times for drinks, including last night. Champagne, no less."

"She really doesn't know who you are?"

"She doesn't read the *Register*. Something about her father having a fight with the owner some years ago. So she's never seen my column or my picture. She thinks my name is Keith Sanders and I'm an unemployed friend of her neighbor's. And she told me about her problems with Rico, and after he died, she told me all about the press conference and—"

"But you were there! Didn't she recognize you from it?"

"Yeah, that was a shock. I never thought she'd be there. But no, she didn't see me. I don't think she saw anybody that night except Alita, Rico, and Ferdinand. She certainly didn't notice any lowly reporters."

"But everybody looked at you when you laughed."

"Not Eva. She was watching Alita."

"Really?"

"Yep. She watched her leave, and then, get this, she followed her. I gather she had a lot she wanted to tell her about Rico. Only it took her a minute or so to get through the people, and by the time she got to the door, there was no sign of Alita. So Eva came back."

"*The Lady Vanishes.*"

"Huh?"

"It's the title of a movie I watched a few weeks ago. Hitchcock." She paused. "So can you hear what's going on next door?"

"Only if they get loud, and then it's better from the balcony." He walked across the room, opened the patio doors, and stepped onto a small balcony. Ginny followed.

There was a murmur of voices from the condo next door, but it was impossible to make out any words.

Kyle said, "I now hate air conditioning. People used to have their windows open so you could hear!"

"I think he's angry."

Something smashed against the glass on the patio doors, but the glass didn't break.

"Ouch!" Kyle looked at Ginny. "I'd bet that was Eva. She has a habit of throwing things."

"Is there any way we can see in?"

"Nope. These balconies are built for privacy."

A man's voice shouted something.

"I think he said she was a stupid cow," Ginny said.

"You do? I didn't hear anything distinct."

"Maybe my ears are better than yours."

"Maybe you have a better imagination," he said. "I should watch the front door in case he leaves. You want to talk to her without him, right?" He hurried back through the condo and opened the front door just a crack.

Sure enough, a few minutes later, the door to Eva's condo opened. Kyle quickly shut his door in case Ferdinand looked that way, counted to ten, and then opened it slightly in time to see the elevator door shut.

Ginny came up behind Kyle. "I heard a door slam. At least I assume that was what I heard. Unless he shot her."

"No, he's gone. And I heard the door slam, too."

"Now what? Should we go and see Eva?"

"Give her a few minutes to cool off," he said.

They waited fifteen minutes and then rang the doorbell. But there was no response either to the doorbell or his knocking.

"Could they have both gone out?"

"I guess so." Kyle shook his head in disgust. "I'd never make it as a private eye."

"Well, it's late. I guess I should head home. Maybe we can try to talk to her tomorrow." Ginny looked at him out of the corner of her eye. "Or you can."

"I'll call you in the morning," Kyle said they went back into his friend's condo so he could lock the patio doors and Ginny could pick up her purse. As they went by Eva's door on their way out, he pushed the bell one more time, but there was only silence.

The security guard was reading a magazine.

"Excuse me," Ginny said.

The young man took his time looking up. "Yeah? What can I do for you?"

"Have you been here for a while?"

"Since nine."

"So you'd have seen anyone who came down in the last half hour or so?"

"Sure."

"Did you see Ferdinand Ortes?"

"The ballplayer? Yeah. He's been here before. I got his autograph for my little cousin."

"Right. So, was Miss MacPherson with him just now?"

"The kooky blonde? Nah, he was alone." The guard looked at her more closely. "Say, what's up. And who are you? I don't recall seeing you here before. And why are you asking all these questions?"

Kyle took over. "Eva MacPherson invited us to have a drink with her tonight, only now she isn't answering the door."

"Yeah?"

"Could she have gone out another way?"

"Nope. This is the only entrance or exit at night. There are fire exits, but if you open them, the alarm goes off."

"What about the parking garage?"

"You have to go through here and take the other elevator. I see everybody."

Ginny turned to Kyle. "Ky—Keith, maybe we should try knocking again?"

"Yeah. Maybe."

They went back up to Eva's door. This time Kyle pounded on it. There was no response.

Ginny shivered. "This is giving me the creeps. Especially after what happened with Rico. Do you think the guy downstairs could open her door?"

It took them ten minutes to convince the security guard to use his passkey. What finally sold him was Kyle's finding a copy of the *Toronto Daily News* in the residents' lounge and getting him to compare Ginny's face to the photo on her column. After she'd autographed the column "for his little cousin," the guard took out his keys.

The lights were on in Eva's condo. The security guard swore. "If I lose my job for this ...."

"You can blame us," Kyle said.

Eva was lying on her back on top of the bed with her blond hair spread over the pillow and her dress crumpled. Her breathing was slow and shallow, and they couldn't awaken her. Ginny found a nearly-empty pill bottle on the night table and an empty champagne flute on the floor near the bed.

"Call 911," Kyle called tersely to the security guard, who was standing in the doorway gaping. "Then go downstairs and let them in."

"Kyle, take her feet," Ginny ordered. "We have to get her off the bed and moving."

TWENTY-THREE

The paramedics hooked Eva up to an IV, put a tube down her throat to keep her airway clear, and gave her oxygen and an injection. The police officers who had answered the call accepted Kyle and Ginny's story of being neighbors who'd been invited over for drinks. After a cursory check, they put the near-empty bottle of sleeping capsules, the champagne flute, and an empty champagne bottle Ginny had found in the living room into plastic bags, and left, taking the bags with them.

When they were alone, Kyle said, "Do you think we should call Ferdinand?"

"Not necessarily," Ginny said. "Give me a minute." Ginny looked around the condo until she spotted Eva's purse on the floor near the sofa. "She must have found it."

"Huh?"

"She didn't have her purse Saturday. She'd lost it. But her wallet and everything's here, so she must have found it." She pulled out a small black book and started flipping through the pages.

"Do you think you should be doing that?"

"Here's a John MacPherson. Do you want to phone him?"

"You're doing well."

"Okay, I'll do it."

Ginny tried the number.

After several rings, a woman answered. "This is Ms. Garrett. How may I help?"

"Is John MacPherson there, please?"

"Who are you? How did you get this number?"

"I'm calling for Eva MacPherson."

The woman sighed. "What is it now?"

"I'm sorry?"

"What kind of trouble is she in now?"

"I got this number from her address book. She's—she's just been taken to the hospital."

"Mr. MacPherson is in China. This is his assistant, Ms. Garrett. Mr. MacPherson doesn't want to be disturbed for anything less than a life-or-death matter."

"Well, this could be one of those."

"Let me judge that. What hospital have they taken her to?"

Ginny gave the name of the hospital and the woman hung up.

Ginny looked at Kyle. "That was so weird."

"Who did you get?"

"Some woman who said she'd look after it. His secretary or something." She shook her head. "Totally weird."

As Kyle drove to the hospital, Ginny said, "We're going to the same hospital Stasey's in, aren't we? When Iain called yesterday, I told him I'd come by, but I really don't want to see her. Ray said he's never seen anything so tragic."

They went to the emergency room desk and found the triage nurse who'd evaluated Eva. Ginny had brought Eva's purse so the admission papers could be filled out.

"If you can't get hold of her next of kin, will it matter?" Ginny asked the nurse. "Will there be any, you know, important decisions? I mean, about treating her or not?"

"I shouldn't think so. It looks like a straightforward suicide attempt, and she seems to have been found in time. She should be all right."

"She'd have died, would she?"

"If she took enough pills, she could have. They'll know more later."

"Right."

It was nearly three by the time the doctor declared Eva out of danger. The nurse told them she was sleeping and they could see her in the morning. They collapsed on chairs in the waiting room.

They woke before seven as people began bustling about and pushing carts. After hitting the restrooms, where they did what they could to erase the evidence that they'd slept in their clothes, they asked to see Eva. The nurse said they'd have to wait until the doctor had made his rounds, so they picked up some breakfast at the hospital's coffee shop. By eight, they were back asking a different nurse if they could see Eva yet. The nurse, who'd just come on duty, asked if they were next of kin.

"We're neighbors," Kyle said. "We found her last night and called the ambulance. My name is Keith Sanders."

"I'll ask if she wants to see you."

The nurse came back in a few minutes and said that Eva would see Mr. and Mrs. Sanders.

Eva was in a large room by herself. Her hair was disheveled, with brown roots showing; her face was pale except for two bright red spots on her cheeks; her eyes had a hollow look.

"Keith? I thought the nurse said it was you. What are you doing here?" Her voice became wary. "Wait a minute. Ginny Lovejoy, is that you?" She raised her head up. "What are you doing with Keith?"

Ginny smiled. "Hi, Eva. Yes, it's me, Ginny."

"Do you two know each other?"

"Um, we've been friends for a while," Kyle said.

"The doctor said neighbors brought me in. Was that you?"

"Yes," Kyle said. "I expect you're angry about that, but—"

"Angry?" Eva stared at him. "Why should I be angry? He said you saved my life."

"But—but you were trying to—"

"I wasn't trying to do anything. I told the doctor, but I don't think he believes me. He tried to kill me."

"He?" Ginny said. "Do you mean the doctor?"

"Of course not." Eva's face took on a sly look. "I'm not saying anything more. Not with a reporter here. I don't want anything getting out."

"I'll leave if you want," Ginny said.

Eva shook her head. "No need. I'm not saying another word to anybody."

"But, Eva," Ginny said, "if you didn't take the pills, you need to tell the police."

"It would just be my word against his, and no one would believe me."

Kyle tried. "Has this anything to do with Rico's death?"

"I don't know," she said slowly. "It might." Her eyes narrowed. "Why do you want to know? What are you doing with her, anyway?"

The nurse walked in and looked suspiciously at Kyle and Ginny. "Perhaps you should leave now. She needs her rest."

"Ginny," Kyle said when they were back in the waiting room. "Do you think we should tell Manziuk? If she really didn't take the pills on purpose, then somebody might have tried to kill her."

"If we tell Manziuk, she may not talk to us again."

"But if she's right, and we don't tell Manziuk, she might end up dead."

"But—"

"Ginny, remember what Manziuk said yesterday. This isn't a movie or a TV show. In real life, people who try to solve murders on their own get killed. Forget the scoop. We need to call this in."

"But, I— Yeah, I guess you're right."

Manziuk was in his office at eight Tuesday morning as usual. It was a habit he'd have great difficulty changing. The night before, he'd gone to the hospital where Loretta and Arlie were waiting for him to help them look after the details, then taken them for a late dinner and mostly listened while Arlie and Loretta talked. It was the least he could do.

They'd picked up Arlie's things and she'd slept at their house, in their oldest son Conrad's rarely used room. Arlie, Loretta and Lisa had talked late into the night, while Paul consoled a distraught Mike until well after two. Then Paul had tossed and turned for another hour.

But when seven o'clock came, he was up, asking Loretta if she thought he should stay home or go to work. "You have a case to solve," she said. "Go."

Ryan followed him into his office when he arrived at the police station, but they'd barely spoken when Manziuk's cell phone rang. Both were secretly glad of the distraction of Kyle's request for them to come to the hospital right away.

They found Ginny and Kyle sitting in the waiting room making notes. "What is it this time?" Manziuk said. "Another body?"

"Well, not quite," Ginny said, "but almost. We're not sure exactly what happened."

"We're listening."

Ginny looked at Kyle, who nodded. "Um, we think—we think maybe somebody tried to kill Eva last night."

"You've got to be kidding," Ryan said.

Manziuk said simply, "Tried?"

"Yeah," Kyle said. "She's alive. They think she'll be okay. But they think she would have died if we hadn't found her and called for help."

"'We' meaning the two of you?"

Ginny nodded.

"Where is she?"

"In the room right over there."

"Thanks," Manziuk said, "we'll take it from here. I'm sure you have other things to do. And please don't put this into your papers until I give you a statement."

Ginny frowned. "Oh, that's just fine. We do all the investigating, and you leave us to twiddle our thumbs!"

Manziuk looked down from his height. "We very much appreciate your calling us. And if you did save her life, we'll see that you get commended for it, but, now, please let us do our job."

Ginny blushed.

Kyle said. "Ginny, don't you have a talk show to do? Why don't we leave this for the professionals and get you ready for your new job."

Reluctance colored her words as Ginny said, "Yeah. Okay. But we'd better stop and see Stasey first—if they'll let us in."

"That shouldn't be a problem," Ryan said.

As Ginny and Kyle left, Manziuk and Ryan went to the nursing desk. A few minutes later, a call went out for Dr. Forrester. A tall, blond young man in a white hospital coat came up the hall, and Manziuk and Ryan moved into a small office with him.

After talking to the doctor, Manziuk and Ryan stepped inside Eva's room. They found her sitting up in bed against a number of pillows, looking unusually small, pale, and tired. An enormous arrangement of colourful flowers in a crystal vase sat on the table next to her bed.

"What the—? What are you doing here? Did they call you?"

"We heard there was a possible attempt on your life. On the other hand, the doctor believes you tried to commit suicide. Do you want to talk about it?"

"Well, I didn't."

"It would fit," Ryan said. "Marilyn died from an overdose."

"She did," Eva said. "But a lot of people think she was murdered."

"Did you take an overdose on purpose?" Manziuk asked gently. "If you did—"

"I did not!"

"Then what happened?"

"Isn't that what you people are for? Shouldn't you be over at my place trying to find out what happened?"

"What did you eat or drink last evening?" Manziuk asked.

"I had dinner at The Blue Mandrake. The food came from the kitchen. I don't think they did anything to it."

"And at home?"

"I didn't eat anything."

"Did you drink something?"

"I finished off a bottle of champagne. That's it."

"Was anyone else in your condo at the time?"

"No."

"Could anyone have put something in your glass?"

"No."

"Are you sure?"

"I'm sure. I've been sitting here trying to figure out what could have happened. The doctor said I overdosed. But I didn't take anything—I'm sure I didn't." She sighed and shut her eyes for a moment before continuing in a tired voice. "The last thing I remember is finishing off the bottle of champagne. But nobody was there then. And I didn't take anything with it."

There was a long silence. Then she sat up straighter. "Wait a minute!" she said. "What if it was in the bottle?"

Manziuk frowned. "Let me get this straight. You poured yourself a glass of champagne from the open bottle and drank it when you were alone? Is that what happened?"

"Two glasses."

"Could someone have taken some of your pills and dissolved them in the champagne bottle without your noticing?"

"I think so. They were gelatin capsules. They could have been opened and the contents poured into the bottle."

"Who was in your condo last night?"

She frowned. "That's the problem. Three people were there."

"At the same time?"

"No." She frowned. "Ted Benedetto was there early on."

"Ted Benedetto?" Manziuk couldn't hide his surprise. "You know him?"

"I only met him last week." She looked at the rings on her hands.

"When last week?" Ryan asked. "Were you in his car?"

"Yeah. Thursday night."

"After the reception?" Manziuk asked.

"Sort of."

"Could you explain, please?"

"I guess it doesn't matter now. And anyway, we didn't do anything wrong. Ferdinand and I were together until we left the building. But I was annoyed with him. I decided he'd only invited me to mess with Rico and Alita." She looked up. "You see, Ferdinand gets bored real fast. He's always looking for ways to make things more interesting. He doesn't mind manipulating people for his own amusement.

"Anyway, afterward, he wanted me to go back to his place, but I said no. So he just left me standing outside the Diamond Dome. And this Ted guy must have been watching, because he came up to me. I saw him at the reception, and he was kind of giving me the once over, you know? I even asked him what was the matter, hadn't he seen a good-looking woman before, and he gave me this snarky answer. He said he'd heard about me, and was just wondering what I look like without the costume. I said what you see is what you get, and he asked me why I thought I need to wear a disguise. I told him I don't *need* to wear anything: I *want* to wear it. And he said he didn't believe me.

"So when Ferdinand left, Ted came up and offered me a ride home. I told him to buzz off. But then he showed me a picture of his car. You should see it! It's this little lime green toy they call a smart car. He says it's the car of the future and it's got a diesel engine and uses hardly any gas. My father—my father would absolutely hate it! He made most of his money selling gas!" She burst into laughter.

"So I let him drive me home because I wanted to see what his car was like. And he was so, like, so weird. Like he was worried about me. Heck, nobody worries about me. So it was kind of different. And he said I have good bones and I'd probably be prettier without all the guck. I told him he was crazy, and he left, and I never expected to see him again.

"But then last night, he buzzed and said he was bringing me some flowers, so I let him come up. He brought daisies! Can you believe that? He said he thought they were prettier than roses. And then he left. Only before he left, I went to the kitchen to put them in water, and it took me a couple of minutes, because, well, to tell you the truth, because I was crying a little and I didn't want him to see. So he could have put something in the champagne bottle. Only I don't think he did. Do you?"

"Where was the bottle of pills?"

"Oh, of course!"

"What?"

"The bottle was in my bedroom, and Ted was never in it! He came with me down the hallway to the great room, and he stayed there the entire time I was in the kitchen. I'd have seen him if he went near the bedroom." A smile lit her face. "It couldn't have been him." She thought a moment longer. "No, of course not. Right after he left, I had a glass of champagne, and I was fine."

"All right. After Ted left," Manziuk said, "what happened next?"

"Well, just after Ted left, Ferdinand phoned to see if I wanted to go for dinner with him after the game. I said okay. I might not have gone, but after Ted left, I was feeling kind of blue.

"But while I was getting ready to go out with Ferdinand, Iain buzzed. I wouldn't have let him up, but he had my purse. He came to give it back."

Ryan said, "Do you mean Iain Foley?"

"Yeah."

"How did Iain Foley get your purse?"

She traced a circle in the cover on her bed. "Well, he sort of spent Friday night with me. I was feeling bad, you know, because of Rico being killed and all, and I needed to talk to somebody, only I was still kind of mad at Ferdinand. So I called Iain, and he came over."

Manziuk said, "You had a relationship with Iain Foley?"

"Not really. I mean, well, I met him at this luncheon thing my daddy had, in, oh, I don't know, the beginning of May, I guess. Iain emceed. And I truly loved his voice. So when he asked me out, I thought, why not? So we went out a few times, but it was never serious. And one night at a party, he introduced me to Ferdinand, and Ferdinand introduced me to Rico, and that was that. I mean, who would pick an ordinary-looking guy with nothing going for him except a great voice over somebody like Rico? And I knew Marilyn went for a baseball player, so there had to be something in it, you know?"

"But how did Iain get your purse?" Ryan asked again.

Eva giggled. "After he came over Friday night, we both had too much to drink." She sat up straight. "I just remembered something else. I took a sleeping pill while Iain was there, because I was having trouble getting to sleep. He asked me if I should be taking it when I'd been drinking, and I said if it was only one, it was okay, but no more than that."

"So he was at your place all night Friday?" Manziuk asked.

"He was there, but not, you know, with me. He slept on the sofa. But then Saturday morning, he got really weird and started into me about dumping him for Rico. I talked him into going out for a late lunch, which we did, and we had a few drinks, too, and he was better, but when we got in the car, he started complaining again about me dating Rico and Ferdinand and not wanting to be seen with him. When I told him I thought of him as a friend, he got kind of funny. Actually, he scared me. Enough that when we stopped at a red light, I opened the door and popped out. Only I forgot my purse, and he drove off with it in his car."

"This was just before the game on Saturday?" Ryan said.

"Yeah. We weren't far from the Diamond Dome, so I walked over there to find Ferdinand and ask him to get my purse back from Iain. Only I had no ticket and no money, and they wouldn't let me

n. And I was kind of, well, kind of drunk." She giggled. "I ended up at the Fifth Base with Stasey Simon and Ginny Lovejoy. And then Ginny gave me twenty dollars, which I used to get a ride over to Ferdinand's house. I watched movies until he came home."

"So," Ryan said, "last night, Iain brought your purse back?"

"Yeah."

"Did he have an opportunity to put your sleeping pills in your champagne bottle?"

She became thoughtful. "Well, Ferdinand was coming soon, so I was busy getting dressed and doing my hair and all that. I was in and out of my bedroom and the bathroom. We were talking the whole time, but of course, I wasn't watching him. He was all apologetic. Said he doesn't drink much and he went over the top. Said he felt real bad about Rico. And he said he felt terrible about Stasey and that poor fan who got killed. It was some guy who used to call in to his show all the time. Iain was real broken up over that. I felt bad, too, even though I never liked Stasey.

"And then Ferdinand buzzed, so we both left. I went down in the elevator first and I told Iain to come down after I'd had time to leave with Ferdinand."

"Wasn't Iain upset that you were going out with Ferdinand?"

"A little, but I told him I was only going with him one last time to say good-bye. And it was true."

"Where was the champagne bottle while Iain was there?"

"You were in my place. I keep the ice bucket on the bar. The bottle was there."

"Could Iain have picked up the bottle of sleeping pills from your bedroom and taken some out without your noticing?"

"I think so. It was right there in plain sight on my night table. And I was in the bathroom." A new thought visibly crossed her mind. "I'm pretty sure he was sitting on my bed at one point while I was trying to decide which shoes to wear."

"All right. So he had the opportunity. Now, what about Ferdinand Ortes? Was he in your bedroom, too?"

"Well, we had a real nice dinner, except for right at the end when I told him I'd realized he only really cares about himself. And it's true. After Saturday night, I started thinking—you know, really thinking—and I realized a few things. Like it was him goading Rico all the time about Armando, and encouraging Rico to act like a big shot. I used to think it was because he was looking out for Rico, but now I think he only did it because he was bored and it was entertaining. So I told him that, and he slapped me, right in the restaurant. And I ran out, but he followed and he apologized. I'm used to that. He's done it before. He slaps all his girls." She looked down again. "But that's all he does. So I said okay, he could take me home.

"So we went to my place, and I told him again that that was the last time. And then—I'd been drinking and I wasn't thinking too smart—I asked him where he'd really been on Saturday night. He told you he was at his place with me, but he wasn't. I was there alone until nearly one. So I asked him where he'd been, and he got mad and said it was none of my business, and then he slapped me again. And I got mad, and I threw a statue at him, and it smashed all over the place. And he looked so angry, I got scared and ran into my bathroom and locked the door and stayed there until he left. He was stomping around and yelling stuff about how I was a stupid cow who didn't know what was good for me. He could have easily taken the capsules and put them in the bottle."

"So you stayed in the bathroom until you were sure he was gone?" Manziuk said.

"Yeah. And then I was feeling blue. What a way to end the evening, eh? So I got the bottle of champagne I'd started earlier. There wasn't much left in it. Just a couple of glasses. And then I started getting dizzy and I could hardly keep my eyes open, so I started for the bedroom. I don't even remember getting into bed because I could hardly keep my eyes open. And I woke up here."

"All right," Manziuk said. "So either Iain Foley or Ferdinand Ortes could have put something in your drink?"

"Yeah."

"Eva, do you know who killed Rico?"

She shook her head. "No."

"You need to tell the truth."

"I don't know. Honest."

"How long were you and Ferdinand apart Thursday night when you went to the restroom?'

"Not long. Really, it was just a couple of minutes."

"Where was he when you came out?"

"Standing there looking bored."

"And you left the building right away?"

"Yeah. We were both bored."

"Did you see anyone on the way out?"

"Just the security guard."

"And do you know who tried to kill Stasey Simon?"

She shook her head.

"Just one more question," Ryan said. "Who gave you the huge bouquet?"

Eva made a face. "Daddy. Or more accurately, his assistant. Apparently somebody called his office last night when they found me, and she was here early this morning. She got me a private room and sent the flowers. Daddy's in China making more money and can't be bothered with unimportant things like me."

Manziuk said, "I understand your father is John MacPherson of MacPherson Industries, the company that just got handed a huge contract by the Chinese government."

Eva laughed. "That's the one all right. Busy, busy man. So busy he prefers it if his only daughter stays out of his hair and doesn't call him in the middle of the night even when someone's trying to kill her." She stuck out her chin. "So it's up to you to find out who it is, because next time he might succeed, and it would really mess up Daddy's schedule to have to come back for a funeral!"

"Which one?" Ryan asked as they left the hospital after posting a guard on Eva MacPherson. "Personally, I can't see Iain Foley having the guts to kill anyone, especially someone like Rico Velasquez. On the other hand, I can't see Ferdinand Ortes getting his hands dirty."

"What were we saying yesterday? Who gains by Eva's death?"

"Where was Ferdinand Saturday night if he wasn't murdering Stasey? If Eva had died, we'd have thought he had an iron-clad alibi."

"Let's have him brought in," Manziuk said.

Kyle and Ginny had paid a quick visit to the still comatose Stasey, met her parents, and then left so that Ginny could get home and change before going to WIN 730.

At one o'clock, Ginny was in the sound booth listening as Ted played the brand new lead-in he and Ray had made for her. Then she began her opening talk.

"If you read my column today in the *Daily News*, you'll know I'm hosting this program to keep the spot warm for Stasey Simon, and not to take advantage of her misfortune. Before I start, I want to address a few of the comments I put into my column to the person who is guilty of the murders of Rico Velasquez and Lawrence Smith, and the attempted murder of Stasey Simon. I'm not a religious person, but as I've thought about what's been happening, I'm reminded of a story in the Bible. I must have heard it when I went to Sunday school while I was growing up. I looked for it yesterday and found it in chapter four of the book of Genesis. It's the story of what may have been the very first murder—where a brother killed his own brother. Cain was the name of the murderer; Abel the victim. But Cain denied doing it at first. Then God said to him, 'Your brother's blood cries out to me from the ground.'

"From what I can gather, the police believe the murderer is someone who attended the reception the Matrix held for Alita Velasquez. Either one of Rico's teammates or one of Stasey Simon's peers in the Toronto media.

"Whoever you are, be assured that you won't get away with it. The blood of Rico Velasquez, the blood of Lawrence Smith, and the blood of Stasey Simon is crying out. Anyone who's watched TV knows that the police have all kinds of new techniques for identifying fingerprints and footprints and DNA. All they need is a trace of your saliva or a hair from your head. A single skin cell. A droplet of blood. They'll have you before long. This is not a game; this is war. And they won't quit—we won't let them quit—until they find you."

Ted went into a commercial, and Ginny took some deep breaths. She looked over and saw Ted and Ray both giving her thumbs up signs from the control room. She nodded. Ted's voice in her ear said, "Five … four … three … two … one … you're on."

"This is Ginny Lovejoy, and I'm back to talk to you about sports. A major trade was announced last night, and I want to know what you think about it. Early this morning, Jonas Newland and Armando Santana flew to Pittsburgh. Never mind what I think. It's time to have your say.

"Andy, hi. What's your opinion of the trade?"

"Ginny, I just don't understand it! We're on a pennant run, for crying out loud! And Jonas Newland is an above-average catcher. It doesn't make any sense to me to bring up a young catcher, no matter how good he is, and put him into this situation. I think this trade means they've given up on this year—which is ridiculous!"

"With the death of Rico Velasquez," Ginny said, thinking aloud, "perhaps they felt they had lost not only one of their best pitchers, but also their momentum."

"If they're going to trade people like Jonas Newland and Armando Santana, they ought to have gone after an experienced, competitive pitcher, not a young pitcher and a back-up fielder."

"You feel they didn't get enough for Jonas and Armando?"

"Not even close to enough!"

"Thanks, Andy. Peter from Richmond Hill, you're on. How are you doing, Peter?"

"I'm doing great, Ginny. I love your column—read it every day. And while I sure hope Stasey recovers, it's a pleasure to have you here. I can't believe you've never done this before. You're a natural."

"You're making me blush. So what do you think of the trade?"

"I think the sooner they get a new GM and a new manager, the better. Why would you trade a man like Jonas Newland, who's been the heart and soul of the club? Makes no sense to me at all. And I think they ought to have gotten a whole lot more for them. Jonas alone was worth more than what they got, and Armando—I hate to say this, but I hope he goes out there and pitches a no-hitter! I think they undermined his confidence, and you know how much of a mind game baseball is."

"I have to say I hope so, too, Peter. Armando and Jonas are both class acts, and I wish them all the best.

While they were waiting for Ferdinand Ortes to be located and brought in, Manziuk's cell phone rang.

"Inspector Manziuk? This is Alastair Formeister. I think I may have some information you need. This morning, we asked the firm of accountants who take care of our holdings to look into Alita's inheritance, including the investments Rico Velasquez had been making prior to his death—investments we believe were made at the advice of Ferdinand Ortes. What they have discovered is rather disturbing."

"The investments were poor ones? They've lost the money?"

"On the contrary, the investments were financially very good ones. They have a very high profit margin."

"Then what's the problem?"

"The problem is what Rico was investing in, Inspector."

Ferdinand Ortes sat at the interview table, demanding that his lawyer be called before he'd say a word.

"We haven't charged you with anything," Manziuk said.

"I've talked to you of my own free will several times, even when I had other things I should have been doing. You had no need to send your officers to get me, as if I was nothing but a common criminal."

Ryan said, "Someone tried to kill Eva MacPherson last night by putting sleeping pills in her bottle of champagne."

Ferdinand raised his eyebrows. "Really?"

"You were there shortly before she drank the champagne."

He sat back in his chair and tapped the fingers of his right hand on the table in front of him. "You said tried. Does that mean the attempt was unsuccessful?"

"Yes," Ryan smiled. "I'm happy to say she's alive and well."

Ferdinand bit his lip for a moment; then nodded and sighed. "Then I assume she's told you I lied about where I was Saturday night."

"She says you got back to your place quite late—close to one."

"True."

Manziuk said, "So let me ask you again. Where were you Saturday night?"

"I wasn't anywhere near Stasey Simon's."

"That's not good enough."

He contemplated his manicure.

"Mr. Ortes, let's skip the small talk," Manziuk said. "You've been investing in some, shall we say, speculative ventures. And the people ou've been dealing with—and getting Rico Velasquez involved with—aren't on our most-solid-citizen list."

Ferdinand sighed. "I suppose you aren't going to let go of this, are you?"

"Not until we know who killed Rico Velasquez and Lawrence Smith."

"And if I can prove I didn't?"

"Then you aren't my problem."

Ferdinand looked at Ryan from under his long eyelashes.

"Or mine," she said.

"Very well. Saturday night I was with a small, very select, group of people who were, er, making some plans for a new company."

"We'll need the names of several of the people who were there and can verify your story."

Ferdinand thought for a moment and then wrote three names on a piece of paper, which he handed to Manziuk. "Will these do?"

Manziuk looked at the names of one of the city's mafia dons, a well-known bookie, and an investment banker he knew was suspected of insider trading and fraud. "They'll do."

"I don't understand," Ryan said. "Don't you make enough money without doing this?"

Ferdinand's lip curled in the beginning of a sneer. "I don't expect you to be able to understand, but having money means nothing to me. It just sits there. It's what you do with the money that matters. The risks you take."

"You could lose it all."

He shrugged. "That's what makes it worth the challenge."

"You're right," she said. "I don't understand."

"As for Rico," Ferdinand said, "while it's a big relief not to have to suffer his presence any longer, it wasn't exactly in my best interests to bring about this investigation into his investments."

"Agreed," Manziuk said.

"So, may I leave?"

"Yes. My officers can drive you home."

"Thank you, but I'd prefer to call a limousine." He looked at his watch, then stood and strode to the door, where he turned and spoke again to Manziuk. "May I suggest you get someone over to WIN 730 fairly soon?"

"How long have you known?" Manziuk asked.

Ferdinand smiled. "Well, when you eliminated the people who couldn't have done it, there weren't many left."

Ryan frowned. "Why didn't you tell us?"

He shrugged. "Why should I? I had no proof."

"It might have saved a life."

"A nobody who got his kicks from phoning sports talk shows? A big-mouth woman who's spent her life trying to top her last rude remark? Why should I care about either of them? Eva MacPherson? If she wasn't John MacPherson's daughter, I'd never have given her a second glance."

"Mr. Ortes," Ryan said through clenched teeth. "Is there anyone you do care about?"

"Just one." He smiled, but his eyes were like steel. "And you're looking at him."

TWENTY-FOUR

At the end of her first official three-hour slot as interim host of the *Stasey Simon Show*, Ginny Lovejoy went into the closing she and Ted had practiced. "Oops! Looks like our time is up for today. I'm sorry we couldn't get to all the callers. Please tune in tomorrow, and we'll continue with this topic so you all get a chance to have your say. We'll also talk to Pat Davis, who was the agent for Rico Velasquez. See you tomorrow. Bye now!" Ginny removed the headphones as Ted started the ads that would lead to the four o'clock news. She sighed. It was over. She'd survived.

Ted stepped in and picked up the headphones. "Good going!" he said. "You're a natural."

"I could never have done it without you. I think you should be doing the program. You're the brains behind it, and you know so much!"

"No way." He smiled. "I like doing the research and negotiating with people to come on, but having to talk on air— Not!"

Iain Foley walked into the room. "Very well done," he said. "Especially for a first time. One thought was that the … er … sermon—or was it a threat?—at the beginning of the show, was a bit over the top. I've never known how blood can cry out, exactly."

"I thought she did well," Ted said.

Iain smiled. "Just trying to be helpful. It's generally better if you don't get into preaching at them."

"You're right, Iain," Ginny said. "But I'm so angry. Eva MacPherson nearly died last night. Whoever's doing this has to be stopped!"

A small muscle in Iain's left cheek jerked. "Eva? Do you mean Rico's girlfriend? Has something happened to her?"

"Somebody tried to make it look as if she'd committed suicide. Fortunately, Kyle and I found her in time, and she's going to be okay. She was at the hospital talking to the police when we left."

"Good," Iain said as he took his headphones out of their case.

"Well," Ginny said, "I'd better get out of here and let you do your show. I'll see you tomorrow."

In the outer room, the receptionist opened her mouth to question Ryan and Manziuk when they burst in, but one look at Manziuk's face stilled her voice. When she saw several police officers in uniform behind them, however, she reached for the intercom. "There's a bunch of cops here."

The intercom was set to go into Ted's earpiece. "Police?" he said aloud.

"What?" Iain asked.

"There are police here. A bunch of them. I don't—"

Ginny had gathered together her papers and was about to leave the room when an arm wrapped around her neck. She dropped the papers.

"I have my Swiss army knife pointed at your heart," Iain's voice said from behind her. "It's open and very sharp. Don't move." He pulled her back with him so they were against a wall.

The door opened and Ryan and Manziuk walked in with guns drawn. "Iain Foley," Ryan said, "you're—"

"Back off please," Iain said evenly. "I don't want to hurt her, but I will if you don't leave."

Ryan stopped. "You can't—"

Ignoring her, Iain said, "Ted, go back to the control booth and have Greg start my music on cue. The rest of you leave." When no one moved, he said, "I won't hurt her if you leave."

"Okay, Iain," Ted said calmly. "I'll get it ready." He stepped between the officers and went into the control booth, where Greg Mintress was watching through the glass with wide eyes.

"Now you," Iain said to Ryan and Manziuk. "Leave. If I hurt her, it will be your fault."

Manziuk touched Ryan's arm. "Come." They backed out of the room and Manziuk shut the door carefully, leaving it open just a crack.

Iain pushed Ginny forward and used his foot to slam the door the rest of the way.

"All right," he said. "If you try to move, I'll stick this knife into you."

"Okay," Ginny whispered.

"You always were the smart one," Iain said. "Much smarter than Stasey."

"Thanks."

"But you realize you've spoiled everything," he said. "If you'd just let Eva die, there'd be no problem."

"I'm afraid I don't understand."

"I'm going to explain." Keeping his left arm around Ginny's neck, he transferred the knife to his left hand and positioned it carefully against Ginny's throat. Then he used his right hand to pick up the headphones from where he'd dropped them on the desk. He put them on and plugged them in, then moved the knife back to his right hand and called out, "Ted!"

"I'm here," Ted said from behind the glass, where he now sat alone.

"All I want is a chance to tell my listeners why I did it," Iain said. "That's only fair. I want them to know I did it all for them."

"Okay," Ted said. "What do you want me to do?"

"Can you still pick up my voice if I stand?"

"Raise the mic so it's as high as possible and I'll turn up the level. Should be fine."

Iain adjusted the microphone and cleared his throat. "All right. Where's Greg?"

"He's not feeling very well. I'll cover for you today."

"Fine. You're better anyway."

"Okay, what now?"

"Play the intro."

"Okay. And five … four … three … two … one …" The taped intro began, first Iain's theme music, and then the announcer, "Ladies and Gentlemen, are you ready? Are you ready? Because this is the Main Event! And in our corner, ready to take you out of your day-to-day lives on a journey to the stars, the One and Only Champion of the Airwaves—Eeeee-aaaan Fo-oh-le-y!" Cheers, then more music, fading.

Iain began to speak, a bit shakily at first, but then with his usual melodic splendor. "Good afternoon, all you wonderful fans of mine. Today's show is going to be a little different. There's so much I need to tell you. Please listen carefully. If you're driving, you might want to stop your car so you can pay attention. What I have to say affects all of you."

"I did what I did, and I'm not sorry. I did it so you wouldn't have to put up with her vulgarity any longer. Day after day, Stasey Simon said things no decent radio personage would ever say. She was rude and insulting. And she was bringing down the level of the station, attracting a younger, rougher crowd—the kind of people who watch wrestling and read those hideous gossip magazines that don't care about accuracy or truth. I felt embarrassed to have to use the same room, the same microphone. It was degrading. Every day, I hated it a little more.

"And then last Thursday at the reception for Alita Velasquez, Stasey did it again. She was rude and obnoxious. I hated being associated with her. And I hated the way she was infecting the Toronto sports community with her coarseness.

"I want you to know what happened so you'll understand that I only did what I was supposed to do—it was fate. When Alita disappeared, I wanted to help, so I went to see if I could find her. I went to the locker room, and then I heard somebody coming, so I—I don't really know why—but I just stepped into the next room, the trainers' room. The steps kept coming, so I instinctively opened the next door, and then I found myself in the bullpen. I'm sure that door is normally locked, but that night it was open. If it hadn't been open, nothing would have happened. But it was fate.

He paused for a while, until Ted's voice said evenly, "You went into the bullpen?"

Iain nodded to him in thanks. "Yes, and then I stepped out of the way, into the corner, just in case, and sure enough, the door opened and Rico came out. I felt stupid being there, so I stayed put. He walked in and had a quick look around, but he didn't turn in my direction. And then he stood still and he was—I think the only word is 'preening.' As if he was saying, 'I'm the man,' you know?"

His arm tightened around Ginny's neck and she whispered, "Iain, that hurts."

"Sorry," he said. He took several deep breaths and then relaxed his arm.

"Thanks," Ginny said, at the same time thinking that the one good thing about being so close to him was that she could hear Ted's voice through the headphones, and maybe she could help Ted keep Iain talking so he didn't have time to think about what the police might be doing.

"Rico," Ted prompted. "He was preening."

Iain nodded to Ted again. "Yes. And I felt this rage inside me—I mean, who was he anyway? Some nobody who couldn't even speak decent English. And I remembered what Stasey said on her show, how somebody needed to knock some sense into his head, and I thought, 'Yes, somebody should.' And then I thought, 'If someone did, who'd get blamed for it? Stasey!'

"At that exact moment, I realized that when Rico turned to leave, he'd see me. So I looked around, and there was a bat lying at my feet, ready. I picked it up, and then—I don't know what he was thinking—but Rico actually took a bow. I was only a few feet behind him. All I had to do was take a few quick steps, and then swing the bat with all my strength."

After a brief silence, Ted said, "And what happened next?"

"I only meant to knock him down and get out before he saw me, and Stasey would be blamed, and they'd fire her. But he lay there not moving. That was a bit scary. Then I realized I needed to get out of there before he came to. So I used my pocket handkerchief—my favorite red one—to wipe my prints off the bat, and I put it in the rack where it belonged, and I left. I remembered to wipe my fingerprints off the door, too. And then I just walked out and kept walking."

Ted said, "You were really thinking, Iain, especially wiping your prints off the door. I don't know if I'd have thought of that. But Iain, no one suspected you! Why did you try to kill Stasey?"

Iain said simply, "Because she knew."

There was another silence.

"She knew?" prompted Ted.

"I overheard her talking to Ray on Friday about doing a special show to 'out the killer.' And when she saw me listening, she winked. And I knew then that she knew. Friday before my show, when I talked to Ray, and to you, Ted, I realized neither of you had any idea what she was going to say on Sunday. That didn't surprise me. She liked to spring things on people. So I knew all I had to do was stop her from doing the show."

"So you went to her house Saturday night?"

"I didn't have a chance to do anything Friday night. I drove down Stasey's street after my show to check the layout, but Eva called me on my cell phone and begged me to go over to her place. I went home to let my dog out first, and I was about to leave for Eva's when the police showed up asking questions. It was clear they didn't suspect me. So I knew I was right, and I just needed a plan to get Stasey out of the way. After the police left my place, I drove over to Eva's. I put my plan together while I was driving.

"On Saturday afternoon, I went to a Salvation Army thrift shop across town and got a coat and a hat to wear, and I found a used bat there, too. I paid cash so no one could trace it. And I disguised my voice so they wouldn't recognize me."

"And then you drove to Stasey's?"

"Later. First I went to the last part of the game. And then I went home and had dinner and got ready. Then I went out. I parked a couple of streets over and walked, and I was just in time to see Armando leaving. If I'd gone to the door while he was there, I don't know what would have happened."

"Did you carry the bat with you?"

"Oh, yes. After Rico, I knew one swing of the bat was all I'd need. I carried it in an old duffel bag, and left the bag and the hat just outside Stasey's house before I rang her doorbell. And I picked them up again later and put the bat back."

"So Stasey let you in?"

"Certainly. She was surprised to see me, but not afraid. She always underestimated me."

"Did you ever consider that you were wrong; that she didn't know it was you who killed Rico?"

"No. She was doing the special show because she knew."

"Okay. So what happened?"

"I said I needed to talk to her about something personal, and we went inside. And she—she mocked me. She asked me if I was there to see if her abilities would rub off on me. Her tongue was always so hateful. The viper! I had the bat behind my back, so I just brought it up and swung. She saw it coming and she tried to duck, but I was too fast. She went right down.

"But I wasn't sure I'd hit her as solidly as I did Rico, so I was going to do it one more time, but before I could, this little middle-aged man, wearing of all things, a Rico Velasquez jersey, came bursting in the front door and grabbed my arm. We struggled, and then I hit him. He fell, but he got up. He was dazed, but when I went after him, he ran out the back door toward the neighbor's house, and I had to chase him." A sob escaped him. "What right did he have to be there?"

Clenching the fist that held the knife, Iain hit the table. "When I caught him," Iain struggled to control his emotions, "I hit him again and again."

The arm around Ginny's throat tightened and she could feel his body trembling. "It was terrible!" He sniffed again. "I hated to do it, but he made me so angry. What right did he have to interfere?"

"Yes, I see. It must have been hard for you."

Iain whispered. "He was one of my own callers."

"I'm sure your listeners understand, Iain. You didn't mean to do it."

"He never should have been there."

"Iain, please!" Ginny whispered. "You're hurting me!"

"Sorry." He relaxed his grip once more.

"Iain," Ted said, "can you explain one more thing to your listeners? What about Eva? Where does she fit in?"

"What about a commercial? We need a commercial."

"Oh, my gosh, you're absolutely right, Iain. I was so interested, I forgot. Okay, go to commercial. Two minutes."

"I expect you're planning to write about this in your column for tomorrow, aren't you?" Iain said in Ginny's ear.

"Only if you don't mind," she whispered.

"I don't mind. I want everyone to know. It was getting so I hated to come to the station because she'd be here fouling the air with her cigarettes and her vulgar language."

"I'm sorry she spoiled it for you, Iain."

"Things are always getting spoiled. I was thinking that earlier today. Did you know my dad only made it to junior hockey? They said he was too small. So, from when I was a little kid, he had me in every kind of hockey program, all winter and all summer. I had the same build as him, but he said if I worked harder than everybody else, I'd make it. That was all he wanted for me, that I'd make the NHL. And I got so close, just one step away, but I was never quite good enough."

"That's rough, Iain," Ginny said. "It must have been difficult for you and for your dad."

"He died last year. And when he was dying, that's what we talked about. How neither of us made it as a hockey player. And he didn't say one word about my being on the radio. I wanted to tell him that what I do is almost as good, but even then Stasey was making it so difficult that I wanted to quit. So I couldn't say a thing."

Ginny felt the warmth of his breath on her neck as he stood behind her, his arm wrapped around her in a deadly embrace. Because they were facing the producer's booth where Ted sat behind the glass, she could also see Ted. Now and then she caught a glimpse of movement near him, but she couldn't tell who it was or what they were doing. She knew notes were being passed back and forth. She thought she'd seen the tip of a rifle barrel raised above the console once. Every so often, she smiled at Ted so he'd assure the police that she was okay.

Her biggest fear wasn't of Iain, but the police. She'd seen too many movies and TV shows where the cops burst into a room guns ablaze. Or they might try to pick off Iain. Either way, she figured they'd likely shoot both her and Iain. She didn't want any guns going off if she could help it.

"Stasey made it really hard for you," Ginny said softly.

"It was a catch twenty-two," he said with a sob. "I couldn't leave. What would I do? I'd be nobody." She felt him shiver. "And if I stayed, there was Stasey always in my face."

Ted's voice broke in. "Okay, Iain, commercial's nearly over. Five…four…three…two…one…you're on. Iain, you were going to tell your listeners what happened with Eva MacPherson?"

"She—she—" Iain's voice quivered. His hand gripped Ginny so tightly she had to force herself to relax and not fight against him.

Ted's voice remained calm and steady. "How well did you know her, Iain?"

"Before she met Rico, Eva was dating me. She—she loved my voice. Said I sounded like a movie star." He took a couple of deep breaths. "But later, she met Rico and got interested in him. I don't understand. What did Rico have that I didn't? He barely even spoke English!"

"So you put sleeping pills in her champagne?"

"Wasn't that clever?" Iain said, relaxing his arm. "She wanted to be like Marilyn Monroe, and of course everyone knows how Marilyn died. I saw the bottle of sleeping pills on Friday night when I was there. It crossed my mind then that it would be so ironic if she took an overdose.

"And on Saturday, she was so unreasonable. Rico was dead and all I wanted was for her to agree to go out with me for a while, just to see if it worked. And she didn't want to. She—I saw it in her face—she was afraid of me. And that worried me."

"And then when I stopped by Sunday night to return her purse and see if she'd changed her mind, she told me she was going out with Ferdinand. What could be more perfect? If she died, the police would blame him and assume he'd killed Rico and Stasey, too. And then she went into the bathroom and shut the door. It was as if she was inviting me to do it. It was fate." He laughed.

During this last speech, Iain continued to hold Ginny close, his left arm still clamped around her neck. But when she glanced down, she could see that his right hand, which still held the knife, had dropped so it was at stomach level.

They were coming to the end of Iain's explanation. Something would have to happen soon. She looked over at Ted, who hadn't once looked upset, though she knew he must be dying to tear down the partition and beat Iain to a pulp. She smiled and gave Ted a slow wink, hoping he'd understand she had a plan, and praying the police would be patient for a bit longer. Manziuk seemed sensible enough, but she wasn't sure about Ryan.

As Iain finished talking, she said, "Fate seems to have been unkind to you, Iain."

He tensed. "What do you mean?"

"Well, first fate tempts you to kill Rico, and everything's okay. But then it seems Stasey knows, so you have to kill her. And that's going well, but then Lawrence comes in and you have to kill him.

One of your fans, Iain. Somebody you've talked to a number of times. Somebody who called you all the time just to hear your opinion of things. Don't you think fate could have seen to it Lawrence wasn't there that night so you didn't have to kill him? I'd say fate has been pretty cruel. And then Eva. Fate led Kyle and me to her place just in time for her to get medical help so she could tell the police everything. You know what? I think fate is a liar and a cheat. Fate led you to think you were going to win, and then cut the ground right out from under you."

"But—"

Iain relaxed his grip on Ginny's throat very slightly.

Shouting, "Now!" Ginny stepped down hard on Iain's left foot. At the same time, she grabbed his right hand tightly with both of hers and pushed back against his chest with her shoulders. As he yelped in pain and surprise, he dropped the knife, and they went down in a heap to the floor, Iain's headphones pulling the microphone off the table on top of them.

As this was happening, Manziuk and Ryan, along with two other officers in uniforms, rushed in with guns drawn. Iain became very still.

As Manziuk helped Ginny to her feet, she looked down at Iain. A moment before, she'd tried to hurt him as much as she possibly could. But now, as she looked at him lying on the floor with so much emptiness in his eyes, the anger evaporated and she had to turn away.

"I'm glad you're okay," Ryan said. "But that move was a little risky."

Ginny tried to grin. "I didn't know what you guys were planning, and I really didn't want an entire SWAT team popping in and blowing us all to bits. I figured this way the worst that could happen was I might get cut a bit. And anyway, I figured his arms were likely close to being numb from holding them in that position so long."

The police constables who'd come with Manziuk and Ryan took Iain out. A moment later, Kyle Schmidt, Ray Cummings, Greg Mintress, and the receptionist piled into the room, all talking wildly.

"Were you here the whole time?" Ginny asked Kyle.

"Yeah, I came to pick you up at four. They made me stay out front. But we heard the whole thing on the internal audio system.

She turned to Ted. "Was it really on air?"

"I played a rerun of the morning show on air while I taped Iain through the internal speakers."

"Ted, you were awesome! I couldn't believe how calm you were. You just kept leading him along."

"Inspector Manziuk was telling me what to do."

Manziuk said, "But you were the one keeping him talking. And your calmness was amazing. Any time you want to get into hostage negotiation, give me a call." He looked at Ginny. "And Miss Lovejoy handled herself like a pro, too. Didn't panic, helped to keep him calm. Although—" he frowned at her "—that last part was more dangerous than you realized."

"It was surreal," Ginny said. "I kept thinking, 'This is just Iain.' Only, of course, it wasn't Iain. Not really."

An hour later, as Kyle and Ginny left the building after Ginny had given her statement to the police, Kyle said, "You and Ted were absolutely amazing. I'm speechless."

"Me too." She giggled. "I need to get some lozenges for my throat. It's so sore. I'm not used to doing that much talking. Iain's arm was right over my windpipe for most of the time, so my neck hurts, too."

"Do you want to pick up something to eat?"

"I probably need to get a story in right away."

"Yeah, of course. I should too, I guess."

"Yeah."

Kyle dropped her off at the *Daily News* building and drove to the *Register*.

Ford phoned while Manziuk and Ryan were driving to the station. "Sometimes we get very lucky," he said. "We found a duffel bag containing a bat with traces of blood and a few missing splinters, a gray canvas jacket with splatters of blood, old jeans with traces of blood, stained gloves, and an old Tilley hat with hairs that are the same color as Iain Foley's. The bag was stuffed in the bottom of a garbage bin behind a Thai restaurant half a dozen blocks from his house. The restaurant owner is fit to be tied. He's a big Stasey Simon fan—used to call in to her show.

"Oh, yeah, if that isn't enough to get a conviction, we found file folder in his desk with a photocopy of a newspaper story con cerning Blake Harrison's conviction for drunk driving and solicitin, a police officer. It has several prints on it, including Stasey Simon' and Armando Santana's.

Over at the Diamond Dome, the pre-game show on WIN 730 wa, playing on the speakers in the Matrix owners' private box.

It was interrupted by a special announcement. "According to : story just picked up off the newswire, Jonas Newland and Armando Santana are going to be on the next flight from Pittsburgh to Seattl to rejoin their Matrix teammates as they start their west coast swing tomorrow. The story off the wire also says that Matrix GM Tom Kanberra and manager Blake Harrison have been fired. Cecily Jones, Kanberra's former executive assistant has been named Gen eral Manager. This is ground-breaking news. Several women have made it as high as Assistant GM, but Ms. Jones is the first female GM in Major League Baseball. As well, pitching coach Muddy Ames replaces Blake Harrison as manager.

"Unconfirmed sources tell us that the Diamond Corporation which owns the Matrix, had not been asked to approve the ori ginal Newland/Santana trade. Their lawyers called the Pirates man agement and worked out a new deal. So ignore the original trade Jonas Newland and Armando Santana aren't going anywhere. A new blockbuster three-way deal between the Matrix, the Pirates and the Seattle Mariners has pitcher Brett Moore and shortstop Ferdinand Ortes going to Seattle. The Matrix gets a new shortstop and a new starting pitcher, and Pittsburgh gets a new catcher and a center fielder.

"Stay tuned. We'll be back with our initial thoughts on the other side of the news."

In the owners' box, the Formeister brothers nodded to each other with satisfaction.

After the game that night, Kyle and Ginny walked over to the Fifth Base to have a late dinner. Kyle had offered to pay. "By the way," Kyle said. "I didn't get much of a chance to say it before, but you did terrific on the program."

"Thanks. Seems like a few days ago."

"Do you really think you can do both this and your column?"

"For a while. We'll see how it goes."

"Yeah. Well, I think you'll do fine."

After they'd ordered and the waiter had gone, Ginny said. "So, what's with you offering to pay? We always go Dutch."

"Well, this is a bit of a—celebration, I guess. I wanted you to be the first to know." He took a deep breath, and exhaled slowly.

"Kyle, what's up?"

"Okay, here goes. I wrote out my resignation this afternoon while I was listening to your show."

"Is that all?" She laughed. "You've written out your resignation a few hundred times."

"But this time, I printed it off and hand-delivered it."

Her smile faded. "You did? And what happened?"

"In two weeks, I'm gone."

"Kyle, I don't understand. Why?"

"Because while I was listening to you on the radio, I was astonished at how good you were. And as I thought about it, I realized no one would have ever known if all this hadn't happened. You'd never have thought to try. And there wouldn't have been an opening.

"And I started to wonder how things happen. Is it all random? Or do we need to make some things happen? We both know I'm only a sports columnist because I couldn't make it as a novelist. But I still want to write novels. And the truth is, as long as I continue to be a sports columnist, I'll have no time or energy to write the novels. I've been struggling with it for quite a while. The last couple of weeks, I even started drinking too much because of the stress of not know what to do. Today, while I was listening to your radio program, I realized that if I wait for the perfect time to write my novels, it'll never happen. There'll always be some good reason to delay."

She nodded.

"And you know my heart isn't in what I'm doing—not like yours. Ginny, even if I end up starving in a garret, I need to do this. I don't know, maybe you have to starve in a garret to do it right. Whatever I have to try."

"I'm so glad," she said.

He stared at her. "You are?"

"Don't get me wrong; you're a very good writer. But you're a lousy sports columnist. You're so cynical. And you don't have any fun. You should do something that's fun."

"Maybe." He smiled. "I'll try."

"I'll miss you," she said. "I've become kind of used to our hanging out together."

"That—well, that's made my decision even harder. I—I'll miss you, too. A lot."

"Where will you go?"

"I'm not sure. I haven't managed to save much money, so I'll have to give up my place. Maybe move to the boonies where it's cheaper to live." He looked down. "Ginny, I tried this before and I failed miserably. There's no guarantee—"

"Kyle, hang on. How old were you then? Twenty-one? And straight out of a fancy creative writing course, of all things! You knew nothing about life and you knew nothing about the kind of writing people want to read. But look at you now! You've written every single day for six years. You've seen life with a capital L. The world of sports holds life up to a magnifying glass—the good, the bad, the beautiful, the ugly …. And you've taken it all in! And you've experienced failure and success and longing and fulfillment. Kyle, you're going to be an awesome novelist!"

"Oh, Ginny, you're so—"

"I mean, it Kyle. You're not the same person you were then. It'll be different."

"You really think so?"

"I know so."

"I just wish—the hardest part of doing this is knowing I won't be seeing you all the time."

She giggled. "Kyle, you're such a numskull."

He looked puzzled. "What?"

"If you think I'm going to let you go off to who knows where, you're crazy. What century are you living in, anyway?"

"I don't know—"

"If we put our enormous brainpower together, maybe we can figure out a way you can do your thing and I can do mine, and we can still spend most of our time together."

"Ginny?" He searched her eyes. "Do you mean that? It's totally the wrong time and everything, but—"

"I don't tend to say things I don't mean."

"I—I do want more than friendship, you know."

"I know." She giggled. "And here I am with all this money from the paper and the radio station burning a hole in my pocket, an apartment that's more than big enough for two, and a mother who's just dying to plan a wedding."

Two days later, after Ricardo Velasquez's ashes had been returned to his family in Cuba and Lawrence Smith's remains had been honored by a horde of Matrix fans and the entire staff of the Diamond Dome in one of the largest funerals ever seen in Barrie, Ontario, Manziuk and Ryan were called to the hospital. They joined Father George and Roxanne Simonopoulos and Ted Benedetto as Doctor Kang awakened Simon Stasey.

"She may not be the same person you knew," Dr. Kang warned them ahead of time. "She's had a very severe brain injury, and we honestly have no idea what to expect. There could be physical or mental disabilities, mood swings, personality changes—a lot of possible outcomes. She may stay as she is right now, or she may slowly improve, or even get worse. We can't predict what will happen."

"Will she know us?" Roxanne asked.

"I honestly don't know."

He went to the bed and talked to the nurse who had been monitoring her. Ten minutes later, he motioned to them to come closer. "She can move her toes," he said. "That's a good sign. She may be able to walk again."

Stasey lay on the bed with her eyes half-open.

Her father moved to one side of the bed; her mother to the other side.

"Daddy?" said a small voice. "Daddy?" Stasey moved an arm to try to push the covers away.

"No, no," Father George said. "Stay there. I'll come." He leaned toward her and put his arms around her. She leaned against him.

Her mother reached over from the other side to touch her.

"Anna?" said her mother.

Stasey turned her head. "Mommy?"

"Oh, Anna, my darling girl."

Stasey leaned toward her, and her mother sobbed.

Stasey tried to look back to her right. "Daddy! Daddy, are you there?"

"Yes, Anastasia, I'm right here."

"I have to get up. I need to go. I'm pitching today."

"You had an accident Anastasia. You're in the hospital."

Ted moved to the foot of the bed. "Hi, Stasey."

"Are you the doctor? Am I hurt? I need to get ready."

"Stasey, I'm Ted. Don't you know me?"

"My name is Anastasia. Mommy? What's wrong? Why am I here? I want to go home."

"Anastasia, we can take you back to Winnipeg in a few weeks."

"I live in Toronto. I have a house. He'll tell you. I need to pitch today."

"I'm here, Stasey. I'm Ted."

"Ted? Daddy, where are you?"

As Father George sat on the edge of Stasey's bed and reassured her that everything would be all right, Manziuk put his hand on Ted's shoulder and jerked his head toward the door.

As they stepped into the hallway, Ted shook his head. "I don't get it. It's as if everything's all jumbled up."

There was a long silence.

"She's never going to be Stasey again, is she?"

"I don't think anyone knows."

"Do you know what's really funny? If God were to come down to talk to her before, she'd have told him to get lost because we'd be better off without him. She's the most irreverent person I know. And her dad is a priest! Go figure."

"We're all learning a lot these days."

"What I want to know is, if there actually is a God, why doesn't he do something to stop people like Iain from hurting other people? What good is it if he knows everything, but he doesn't do anything?"